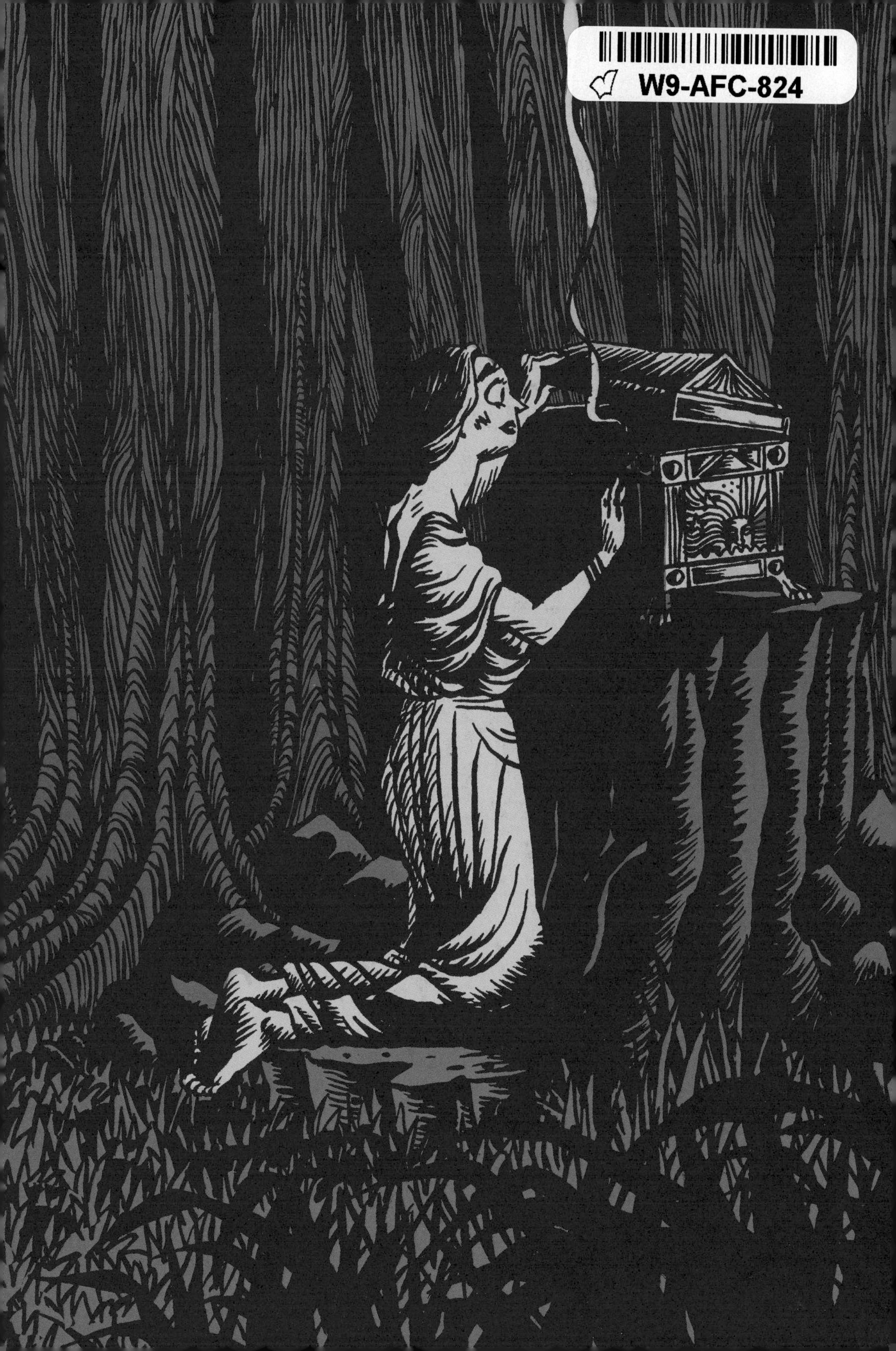

CLASSICS Illustrated® Deluxe

FRANKENSTEIN

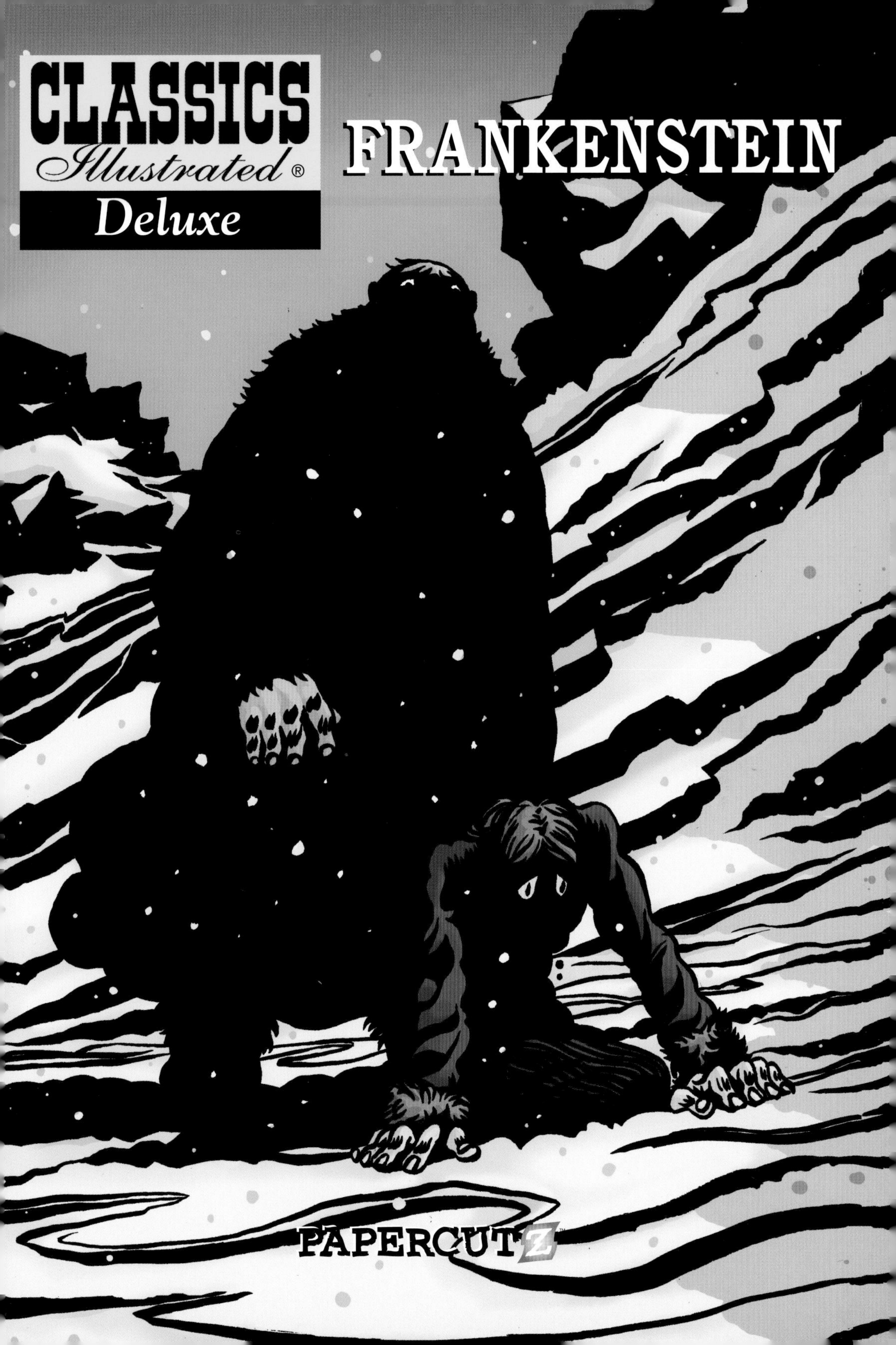

PAPERCUTZ™

CLASSICS ILLUSTRATED GRAPHIC NOVELS AVAILABLE FROM PAPERCUTZ

CLASSICS ILLUSTRATED DELUXE:

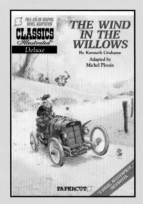

Graphic Novel #1
"The Wind In
The Willows"

Graphic Novel #2
"Tales From The
Brothers Grimm"

Graphic Novel #3
"Frankenstein"

CLASSICS ILLUSTRATED:

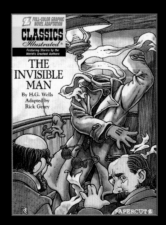

Graphic Novel #1
"Great Expectations"

Graphic Novel #2
"The Invisible Man"

Graphic Novel #3
"Through the Looking-Glass

CLASSICS Illustrated®

Deluxe

#3

FRANKENSTEIN

By Mary Shelly
Adapted by Marion Mousse

PAPERCUTZ™
New York

To JDM and the Gaultier family.

Prometheus, the son of the titan Iapetus, was punished by the Gods for having given to mankind the fire of the Immortals. His punishment for eternity is to be chained to a rock in the Caucasus and condemned to have his liver devoured by an eagle. There is another story about Prometheus told by Ovid, where the son of Iapetus, having mixed clay and water, gives birth to a creature in the image of the Gods, the masters of the universe. Prometheus is punished in this version, too, but the story does not say what became of the creature.

A modern Prometheus, Victor Frankenstein creates life by drinking from the sources of a burgeoning science. But "...supremely frightful would be the effect of any human endeavor to mock the stupendous mechanism of the Creator of the world" (Mary Shelley, quoted from her preface to the 1831 edition).

Frankenstein or, The Modern Prometheus
By Mary Shelly
Adapted by Marion Mousse
Color by Marie Galopin
Translation by Joe Johnson
Lettering by Ortho
Production by Chris Nelson
John Haufe -- Classics Illustrated Historian
Michael Petranek -- Editorial Assistant
Jim Salicrup
Editor-in-Chief

ISBN 13: 978-1-59707-131-4 paperback edition
ISBN 10: 1-59707-131-5 paperback edition
ISBN 13: 978-1-59707-130-7 hardcover edition
ISBN 10: 1-59707-130-7 hardcover edition

Printed in China.
Distributed by Macmillan.
10 9 8 7 6 5 4 3 2 1

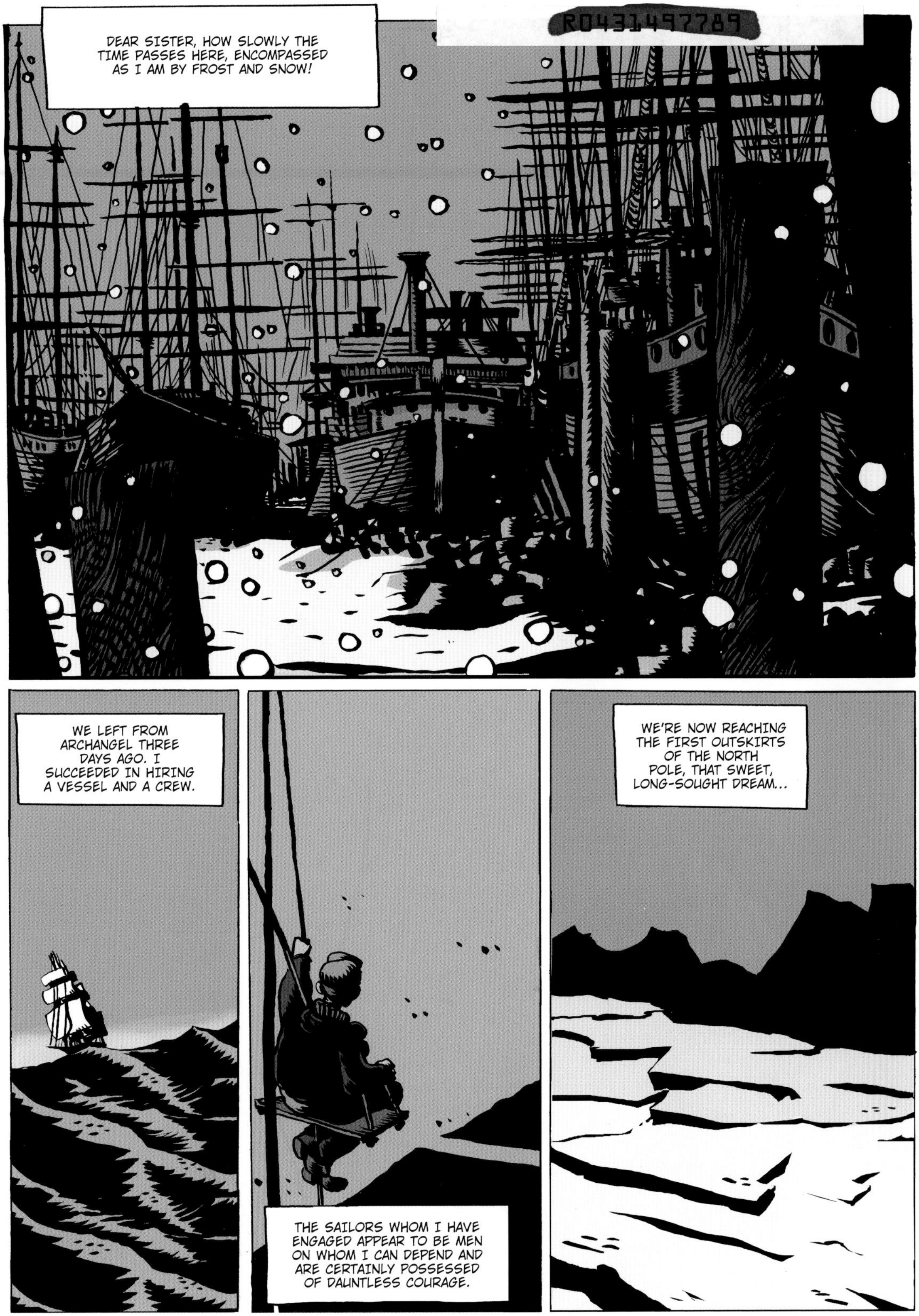
DEAR SISTER, HOW SLOWLY THE TIME PASSES HERE, ENCOMPASSED AS I AM BY FROST AND SNOW!
WE LEFT FROM ARCHANGEL THREE DAYS AGO. I SUCCEEDED IN HIRING A VESSEL AND A CREW.
THE SAILORS WHOM I HAVE ENGAGED APPEAR TO BE MEN ON WHOM I CAN DEPEND AND ARE CERTAINLY POSSESSED OF DAUNTLESS COURAGE.
WE'RE NOW REACHING THE FIRST OUTSKIRTS OF THE NORTH POLE, THAT SWEET, LONG-SOUGHT DREAM...

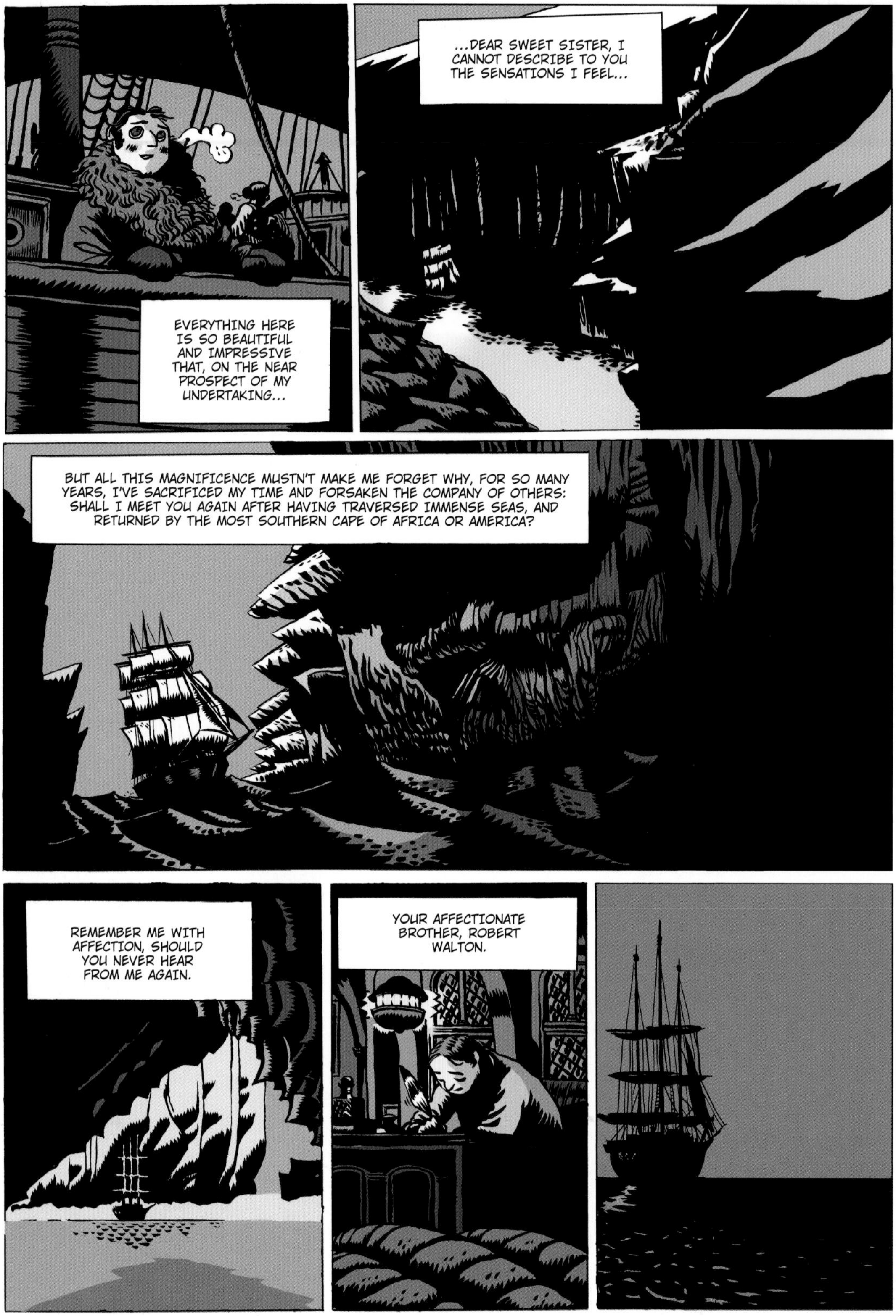
EVERYTHING HERE IS SO BEAUTIFUL AND IMPRESSIVE THAT, ON THE NEAR PROSPECT OF MY UNDERTAKING...
...DEAR SWEET SISTER, I CANNOT DESCRIBE TO YOU THE SENSATIONS I FEEL...
BUT ALL THIS MAGNIFICENCE MUSTN'T MAKE ME FORGET WHY, FOR SO MANY YEARS, I'VE SACRIFICED MY TIME AND FORSAKEN THE COMPANY OF OTHERS: SHALL I MEET YOU AGAIN AFTER HAVING TRAVERSED IMMENSE SEAS, AND RETURNED BY THE MOST SOUTHERN CAPE OF AFRICA OR AMERICA?
REMEMBER ME WITH AFFECTION, SHOULD YOU NEVER HEAR FROM ME AGAIN.
YOUR AFFECTIONATE BROTHER, ROBERT WALTON.

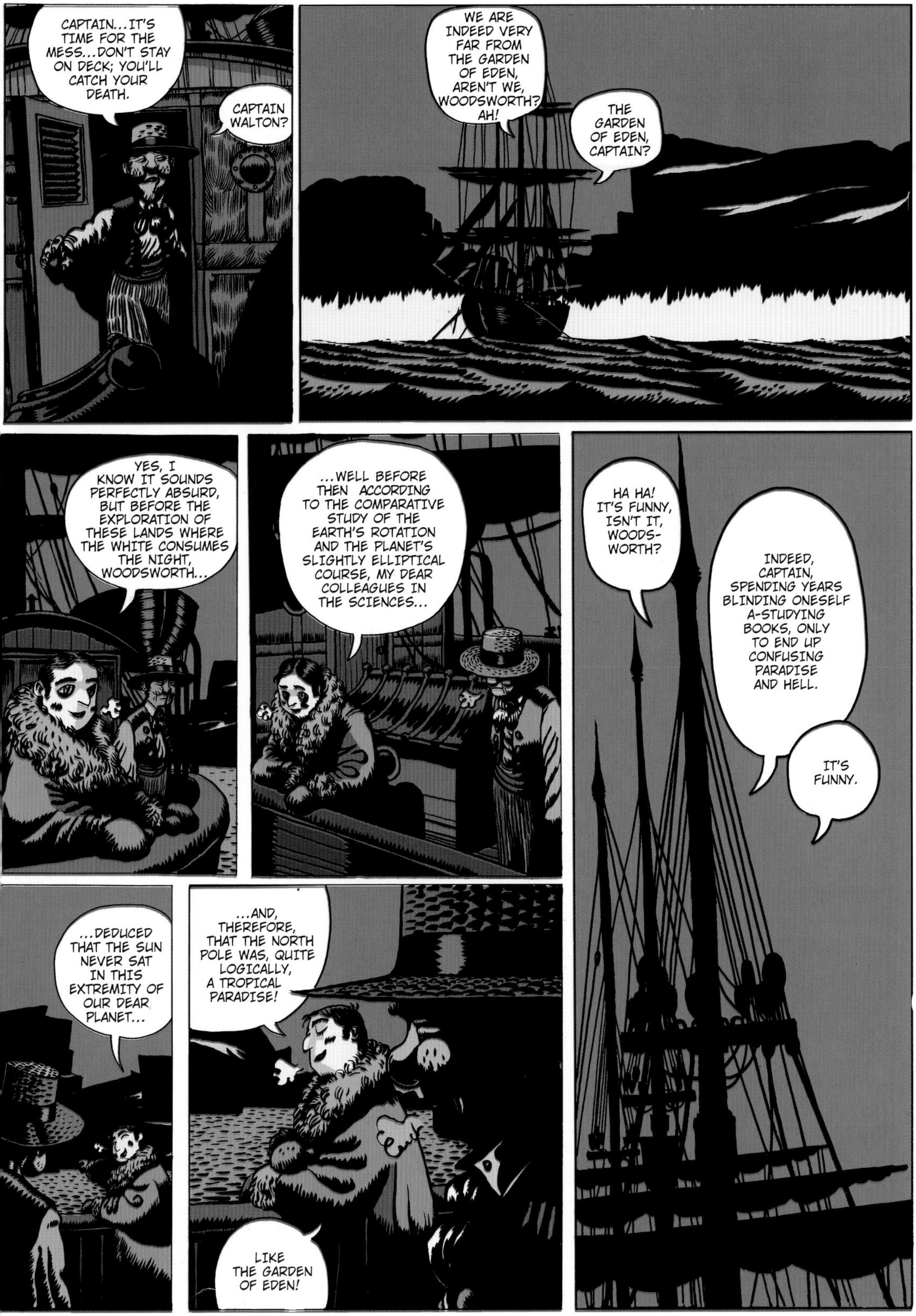
CAPTAIN...IT'S TIME FOR THE MESS...DON'T STAY ON DECK; YOU'LL CATCH YOUR DEATH.
CAPTAIN WALTON?
WE ARE INDEED VERY FAR FROM THE GARDEN OF EDEN, AREN'T WE, WOODSWORTH? AH!
THE GARDEN OF EDEN, CAPTAIN?
YES, I KNOW IT SOUNDS PERFECTLY ABSURD, BUT BEFORE THE EXPLORATION OF THESE LANDS WHERE THE WHITE CONSUMES THE NIGHT, WOODSWORTH...
...WELL BEFORE THEN ACCORDING TO THE COMPARATIVE STUDY OF THE EARTH'S ROTATION AND THE PLANET'S SLIGHTLY ELLIPTICAL COURSE, MY DEAR COLLEAGUES IN THE SCIENCES...
...DEDUCED THAT THE SUN NEVER SAT IN THIS EXTREMITY OF OUR DEAR PLANET...
...AND, THEREFORE, THAT THE NORTH POLE WAS, QUITE LOGICALLY, A TROPICAL PARADISE!
LIKE THE GARDEN OF EDEN!
HA HA! IT'S FUNNY, ISN'T IT, WOODS-WORTH?
INDEED, CAPTAIN, SPENDING YEARS BLINDING ONESELF A-STUDYING BOOKS, ONLY TO END UP CONFUSING PARADISE AND HELL.
IT'S FUNNY.

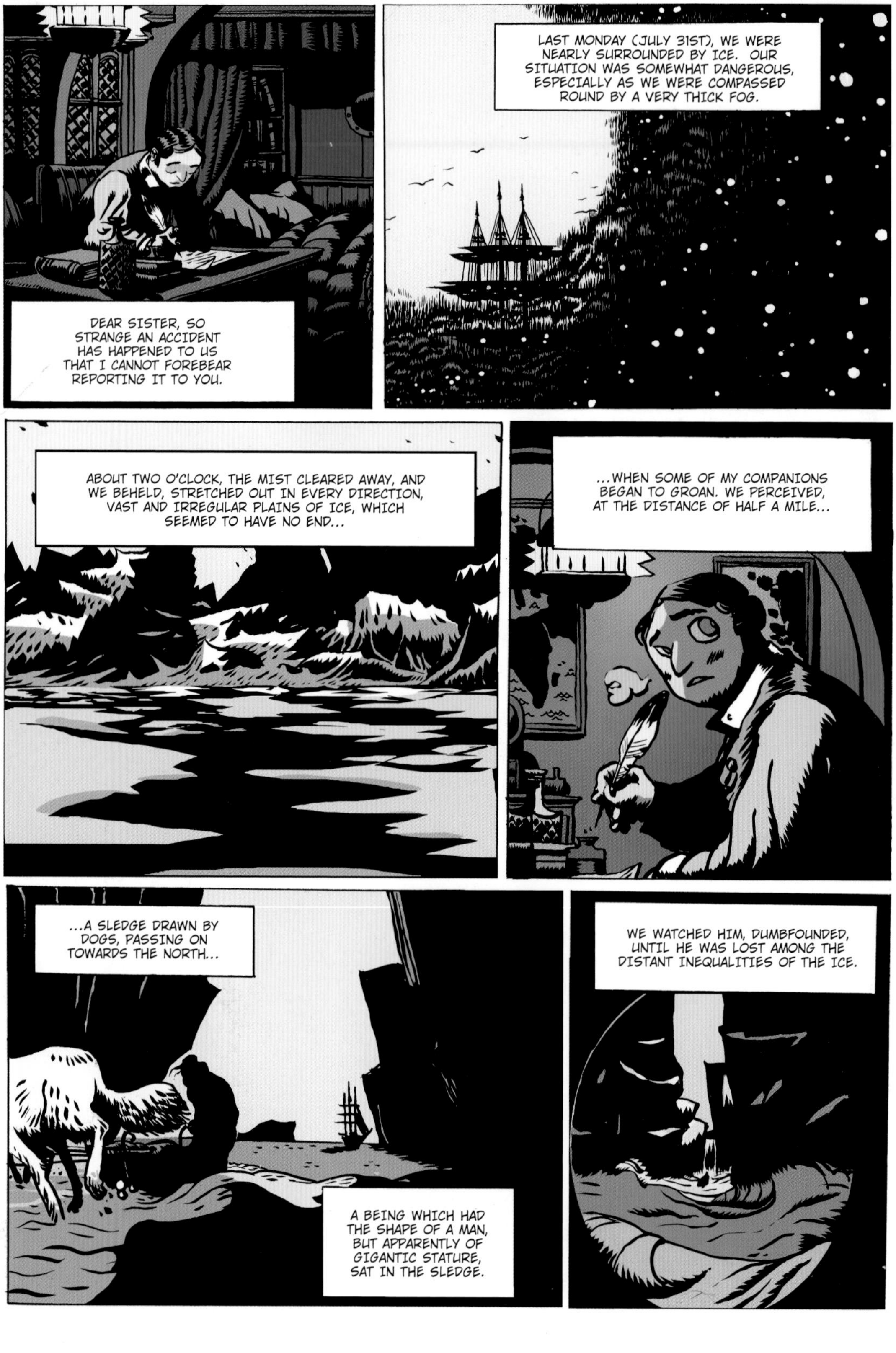
DEAR SISTER, SO STRANGE AN ACCIDENT HAS HAPPENED TO US THAT I CANNOT FOREBEAR REPORTING IT TO YOU.
LAST MONDAY (JULY 31ST), WE WERE NEARLY SURROUNDED BY ICE. OUR SITUATION WAS SOMEWHAT DANGEROUS, ESPECIALLY AS WE WERE COMPASSED ROUND BY A VERY THICK FOG.
ABOUT TWO O'CLOCK, THE MIST CLEARED AWAY, AND WE BEHELD, STRETCHED OUT IN EVERY DIRECTION, VAST AND IRREGULAR PLAINS OF ICE, WHICH SEEMED TO HAVE NO END...
...WHEN SOME OF MY COMPANIONS BEGAN TO GROAN. WE PERCEIVED, AT THE DISTANCE OF HALF A MILE...
...A SLEDGE DRAWN BY DOGS, PASSING ON TOWARDS THE NORTH...
A BEING WHICH HAD THE SHAPE OF A MAN, BUT APPARENTLY OF GIGANTIC STATURE, SAT IN THE SLEDGE.
WE WATCHED HIM, DUMBFOUNDED, UNTIL HE WAS LOST AMONG THE DISTANT INEQUALITIES OF THE ICE.

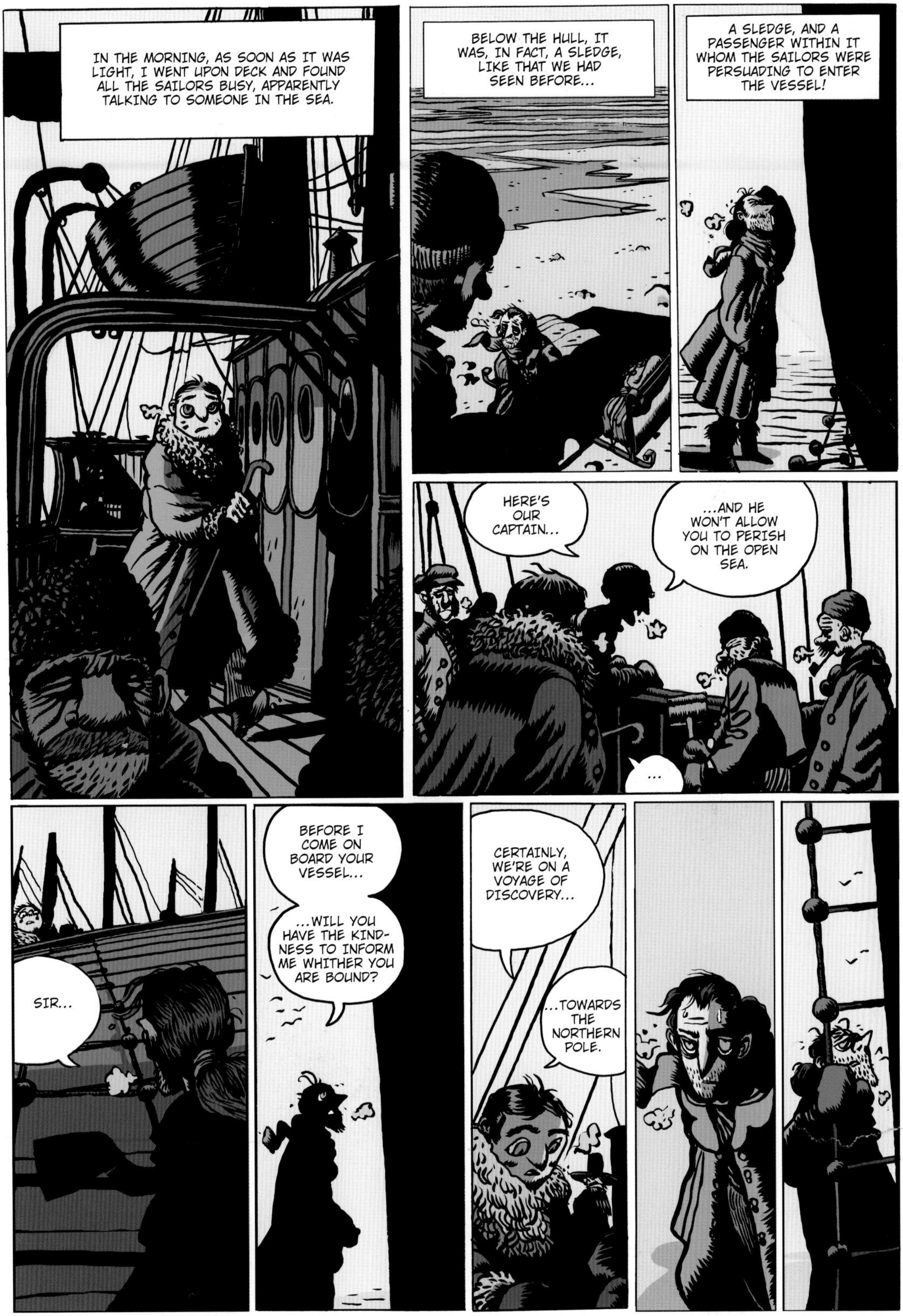
IN THE MORNING, AS SOON AS IT WAS LIGHT, I WENT UPON DECK AND FOUND ALL THE SAILORS BUSY, APPARENTLY TALKING TO SOMEONE IN THE SEA.
BELOW THE HULL, IT WAS, IN FACT, A SLEDGE, LIKE THAT WE HAD SEEN BEFORE...
A SLEDGE, AND A PASSENGER WITHIN IT WHOM THE SAILORS WERE PERSUADING TO ENTER THE VESSEL!
HERE'S OUR CAPTAIN...
...AND HE WON'T ALLOW YOU TO PERISH ON THE OPEN SEA.
...
SIR...
BEFORE I COME ON BOARD YOUR VESSEL...
...WILL YOU HAVE THE KINDNESS TO INFORM ME WHITHER YOU ARE BOUND?
CERTAINLY, WE'RE ON A VOYAGE OF DISCOVERY...
...TOWARDS THE NORTHERN POLE.

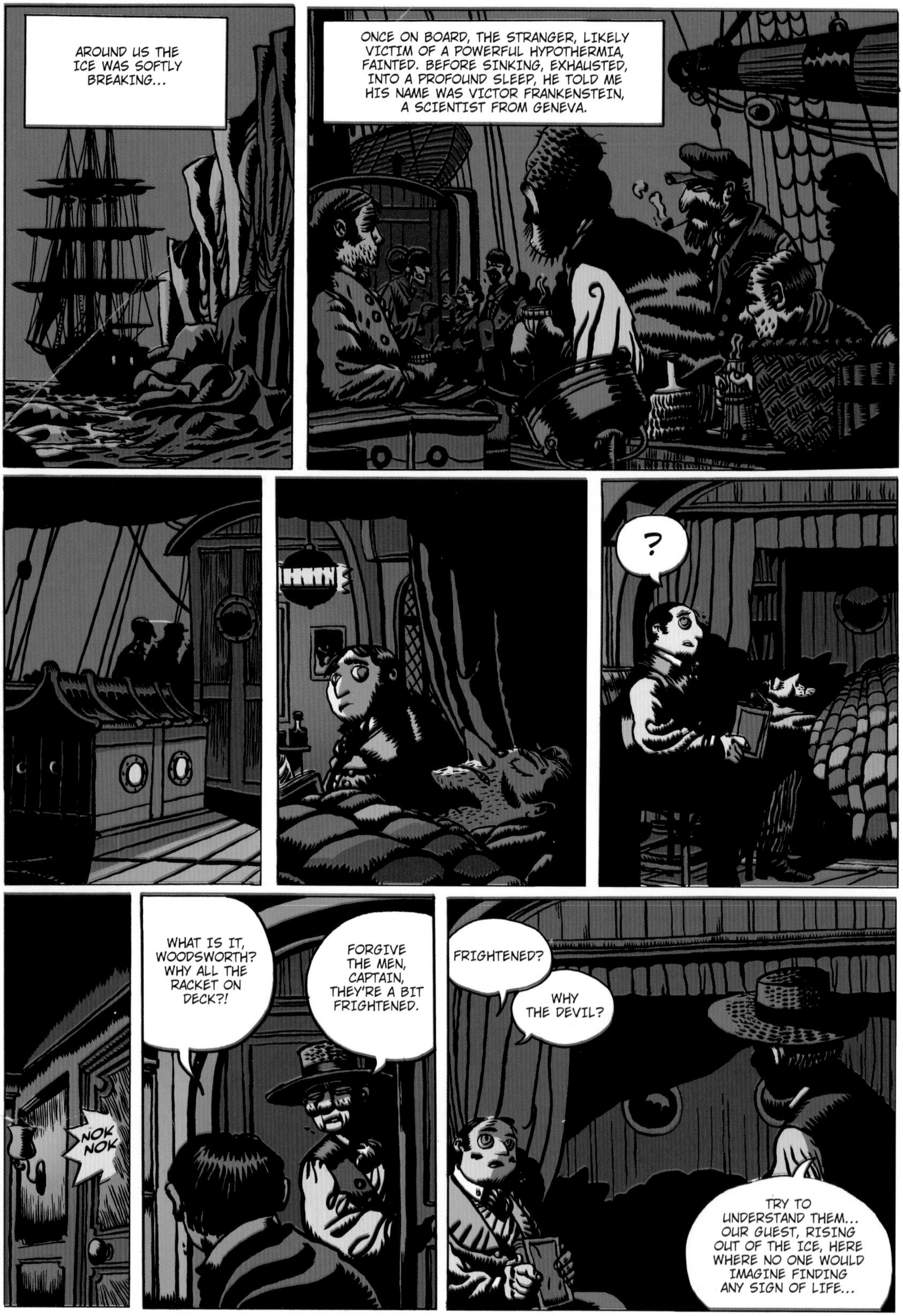
AROUND US THE ICE WAS SOFTLY BREAKING...
ONCE ON BOARD, THE STRANGER, LIKELY VICTIM OF A POWERFUL HYPOTHERMIA, FAINTED. BEFORE SINKING, EXHAUSTED, INTO A PROFOUND SLEEP, HE TOLD ME HIS NAME WAS VICTOR FRANKENSTEIN, A SCIENTIST FROM GENEVA.
?
NOK NOK
WHAT IS IT, WOODSWORTH? WHY ALL THE RACKET ON DECK?!
FORGIVE THE MEN, CAPTAIN, THEY'RE A BIT FRIGHTENED.
FRIGHTENED?
WHY THE DEVIL?
TRY TO UNDERSTAND THEM... OUR GUEST, RISING OUT OF THE ICE, HERE WHERE NO ONE WOULD IMAGINE FINDING ANY SIGN OF LIFE...

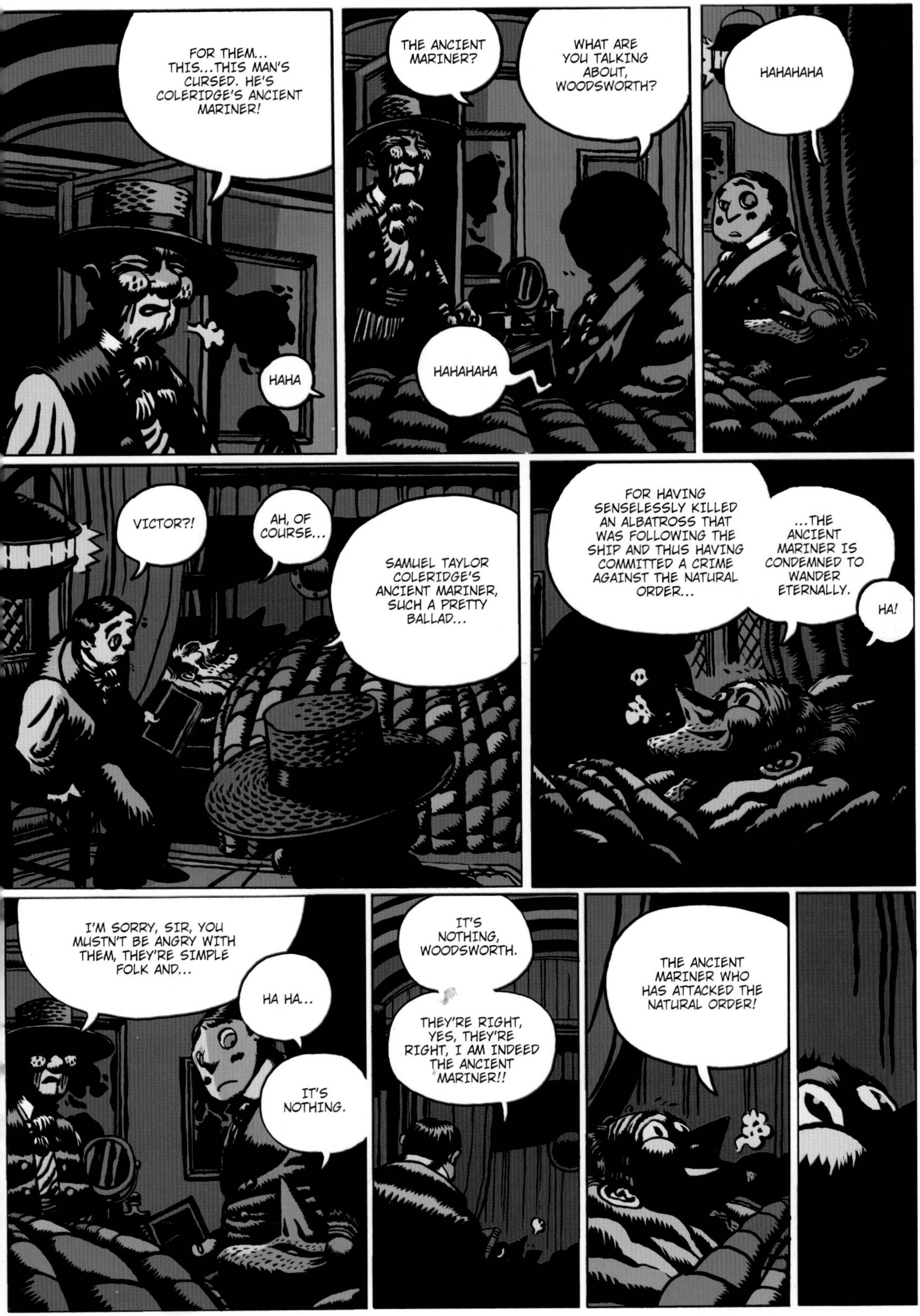
FOR THEM... THIS...THIS MAN'S CURSED. HE'S COLERIDGE'S ANCIENT MARINER!
HAHA
THE ANCIENT MARINER?
WHAT ARE YOU TALKING ABOUT, WOODSWORTH?
HAHAHAHA
HAHAHAHA
VICTOR?!
AH, OF COURSE...
SAMUEL TAYLOR COLERIDGE'S ANCIENT MARINER, SUCH A PRETTY BALLAD...
FOR HAVING SENSELESSLY KILLED AN ALBATROSS THAT WAS FOLLOWING THE SHIP AND THUS HAVING COMMITTED A CRIME AGAINST THE NATURAL ORDER...
...THE ANCIENT MARINER IS CONDEMNED TO WANDER ETERNALLY.
HA!
I'M SORRY, SIR, YOU MUSTN'T BE ANGRY WITH THEM, THEY'RE SIMPLE FOLK AND...
HA HA...
IT'S NOTHING.
IT'S NOTHING, WOODSWORTH.
THEY'RE RIGHT, YES, THEY'RE RIGHT, I AM INDEED THE ANCIENT MARINER!!
THE ANCIENT MARINER WHO HAS ATTACKED THE NATURAL ORDER!

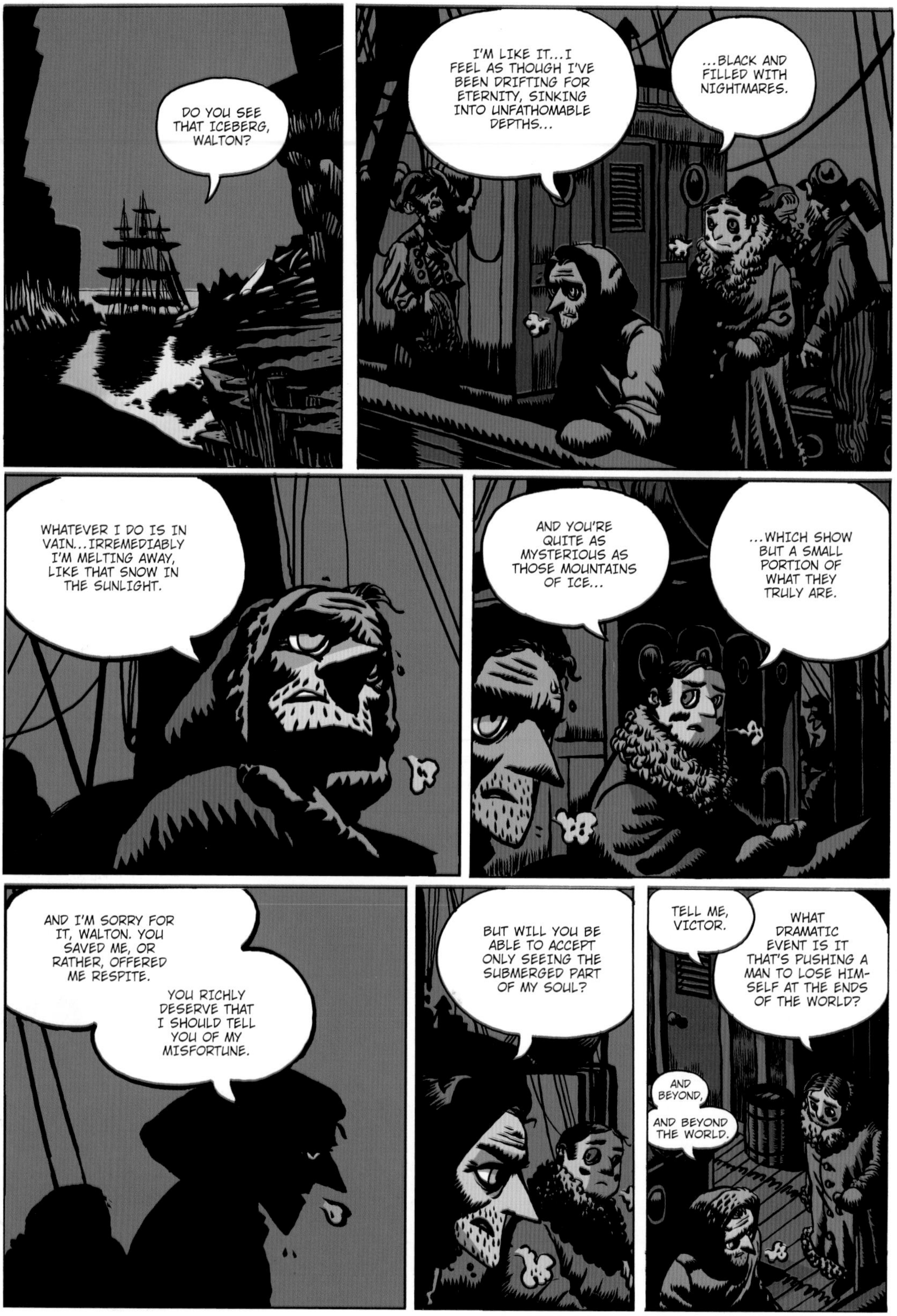
DO YOU SEE THAT ICEBERG, WALTON?
I'M LIKE IT...I FEEL AS THOUGH I'VE BEEN DRIFTING FOR ETERNITY, SINKING INTO UNFATHOMABLE DEPTHS...
...BLACK AND FILLED WITH NIGHTMARES.
WHATEVER I DO IS IN VAIN...IRREMEDIABLY I'M MELTING AWAY, LIKE THAT SNOW IN THE SUNLIGHT.
AND YOU'RE QUITE AS MYSTERIOUS AS THOSE MOUNTAINS OF ICE...
...WHICH SHOW BUT A SMALL PORTION OF WHAT THEY TRULY ARE.
AND I'M SORRY FOR IT, WALTON. YOU SAVED ME, OR RATHER, OFFERED ME RESPITE.
YOU RICHLY DESERVE THAT I SHOULD TELL YOU OF MY MISFORTUNE.
BUT WILL YOU BE ABLE TO ACCEPT ONLY SEEING THE SUBMERGED PART OF MY SOUL?
TELL ME, VICTOR.
WHAT DRAMATIC EVENT IS IT THAT'S PUSHING A MAN TO LOSE HIMSELF AT THE ENDS OF THE WORLD?
AND BEYOND,
AND BEYOND THE WORLD.

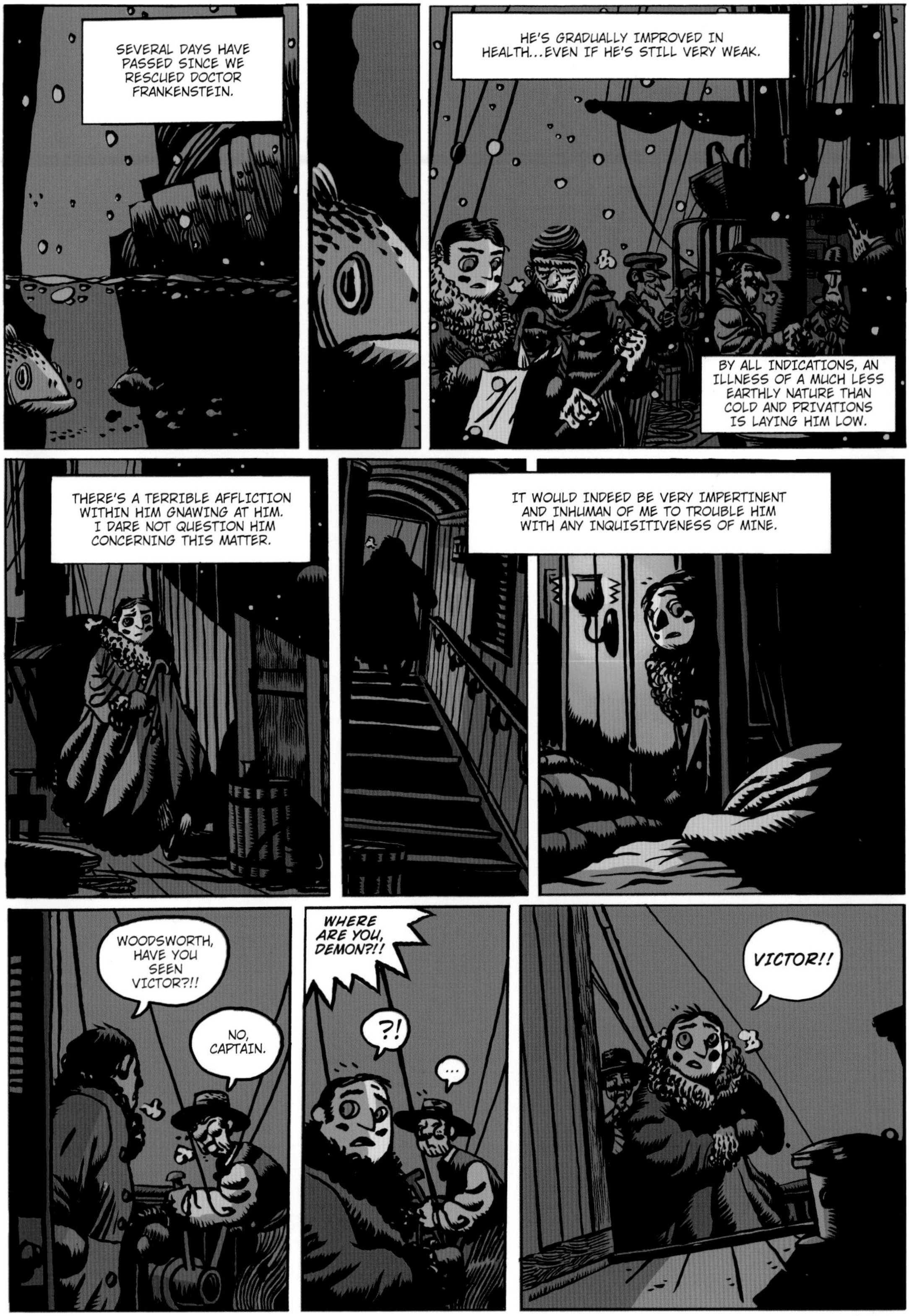
SEVERAL DAYS HAVE PASSED SINCE WE RESCUED DOCTOR FRANKENSTEIN.
HE'S GRADUALLY IMPROVED IN HEALTH...EVEN IF HE'S STILL VERY WEAK.
BY ALL INDICATIONS, AN ILLNESS OF A MUCH LESS EARTHLY NATURE THAN COLD AND PRIVATIONS IS LAYING HIM LOW.
THERE'S A TERRIBLE AFFLICTION WITHIN HIM GNAWING AT HIM. I DARE NOT QUESTION HIM CONCERNING THIS MATTER.
IT WOULD INDEED BE VERY IMPERTINENT AND INHUMAN OF ME TO TROUBLE HIM WITH ANY INQUISITIVENESS OF MINE.
WOODSWORTH, HAVE YOU SEEN VICTOR?!!
NO, CAPTAIN.
WHERE ARE YOU, DEMON?!!
?!
...
VICTOR!!

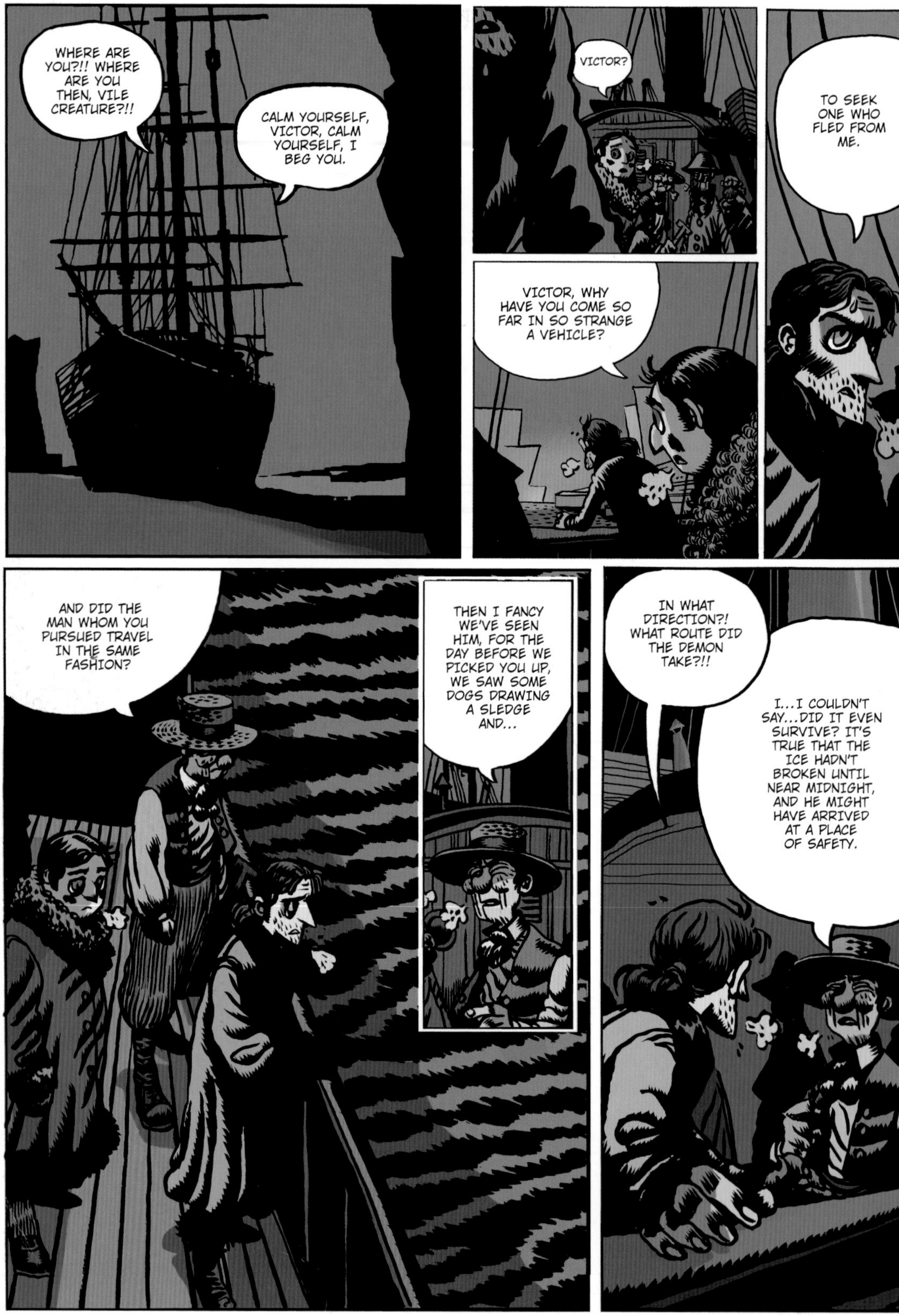
WHERE ARE YOU?!! WHERE ARE YOU THEN, VILE CREATURE?!!
CALM YOURSELF, VICTOR, CALM YOURSELF, I BEG YOU.
VICTOR?
VICTOR, WHY HAVE YOU COME SO FAR IN SO STRANGE A VEHICLE?
TO SEEK ONE WHO FLED FROM ME.
AND DID THE MAN WHOM YOU PURSUED TRAVEL IN THE SAME FASHION?
THEN I FANCY WE'VE SEEN HIM, FOR THE DAY BEFORE WE PICKED YOU UP, WE SAW SOME DOGS DRAWING A SLEDGE AND...
IN WHAT DIRECTION?! WHAT ROUTE DID THE DEMON TAKE?!!
I...I COULDN'T SAY...DID IT EVEN SURVIVE? IT'S TRUE THAT THE ICE HADN'T BROKEN UNTIL NEAR MIDNIGHT, AND HE MIGHT HAVE ARRIVED AT A PLACE OF SAFETY.

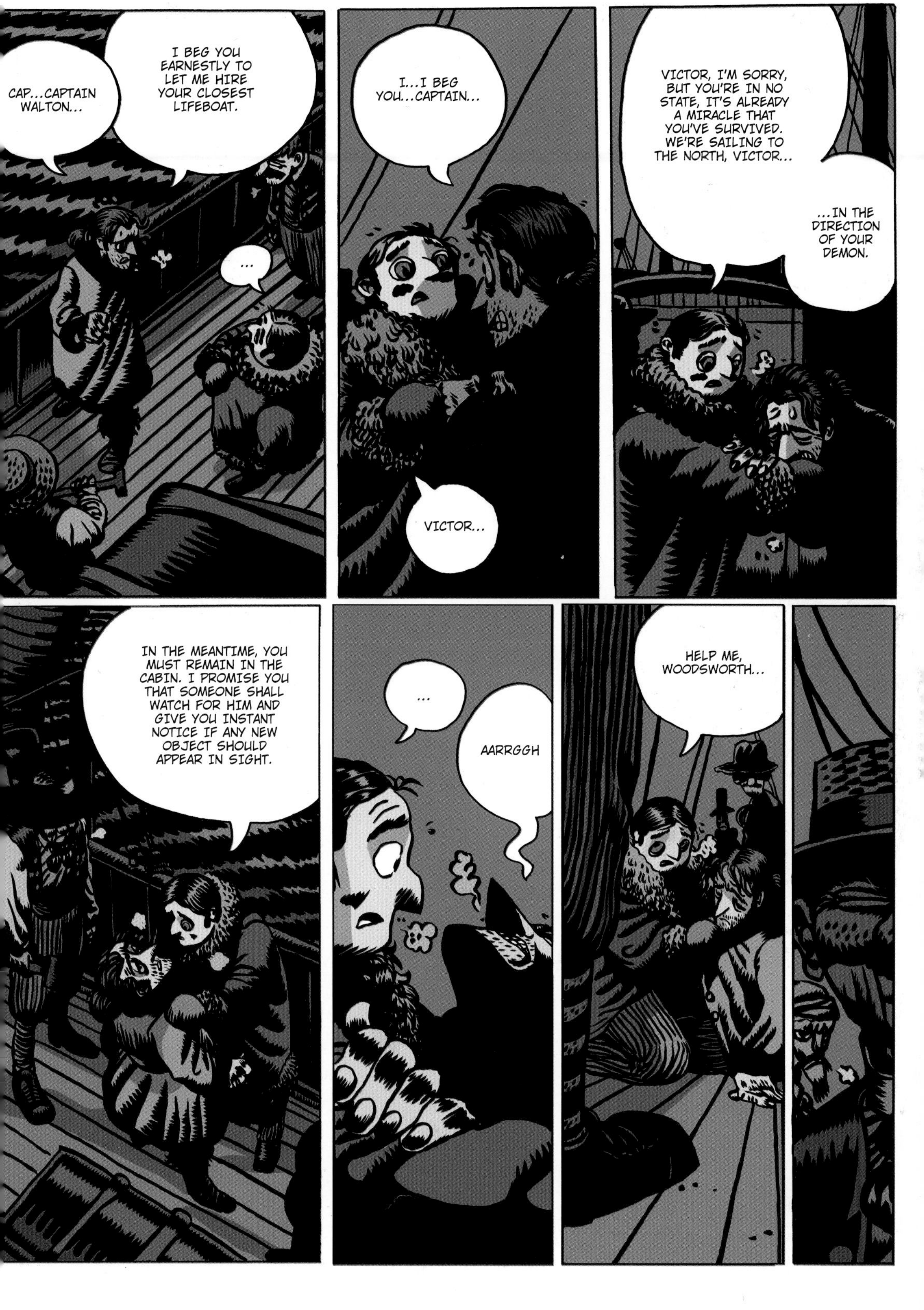

CAP...CAPTAIN WALTON...
I BEG YOU EARNESTLY TO LET ME HIRE YOUR CLOSEST LIFEBOAT.
...
I...I BEG YOU...CAPTAIN...
VICTOR...
VICTOR, I'M SORRY, BUT YOU'RE IN NO STATE, IT'S ALREADY A MIRACLE THAT YOU'VE SURVIVED. WE'RE SAILING TO THE NORTH, VICTOR...
...IN THE DIRECTION OF YOUR DEMON.
IN THE MEANTIME, YOU MUST REMAIN IN THE CABIN. I PROMISE YOU THAT SOMEONE SHALL WATCH FOR HIM AND GIVE YOU INSTANT NOTICE IF ANY NEW OBJECT SHOULD APPEAR IN SIGHT.
...
AARRGGH
HELP ME, WOODSWORTH...

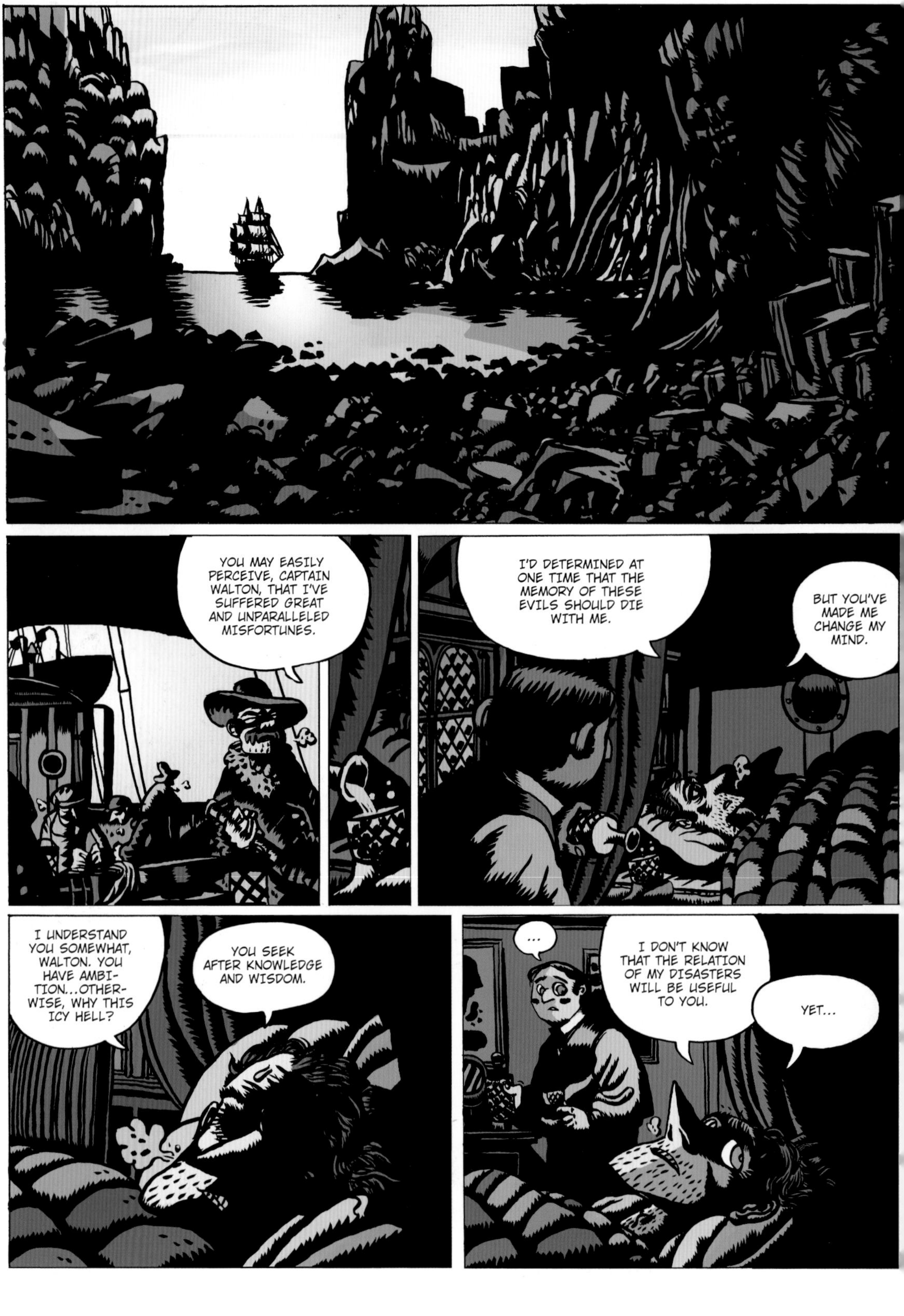
YOU MAY EASILY PERCEIVE, CAPTAIN WALTON, THAT I'VE SUFFERED GREAT AND UNPARALLELED MISFORTUNES.
I'D DETERMINED AT ONE TIME THAT THE MEMORY OF THESE EVILS SHOULD DIE WITH ME.
BUT YOU'VE MADE ME CHANGE MY MIND.
I UNDERSTAND YOU SOMEWHAT, WALTON. YOU HAVE AMBI-TION...OTHER-WISE, WHY THIS ICY HELL?
YOU SEEK AFTER KNOWLEDGE AND WISDOM.
...
I DON'T KNOW THAT THE RELATION OF MY DISASTERS WILL BE USEFUL TO YOU.
YET...

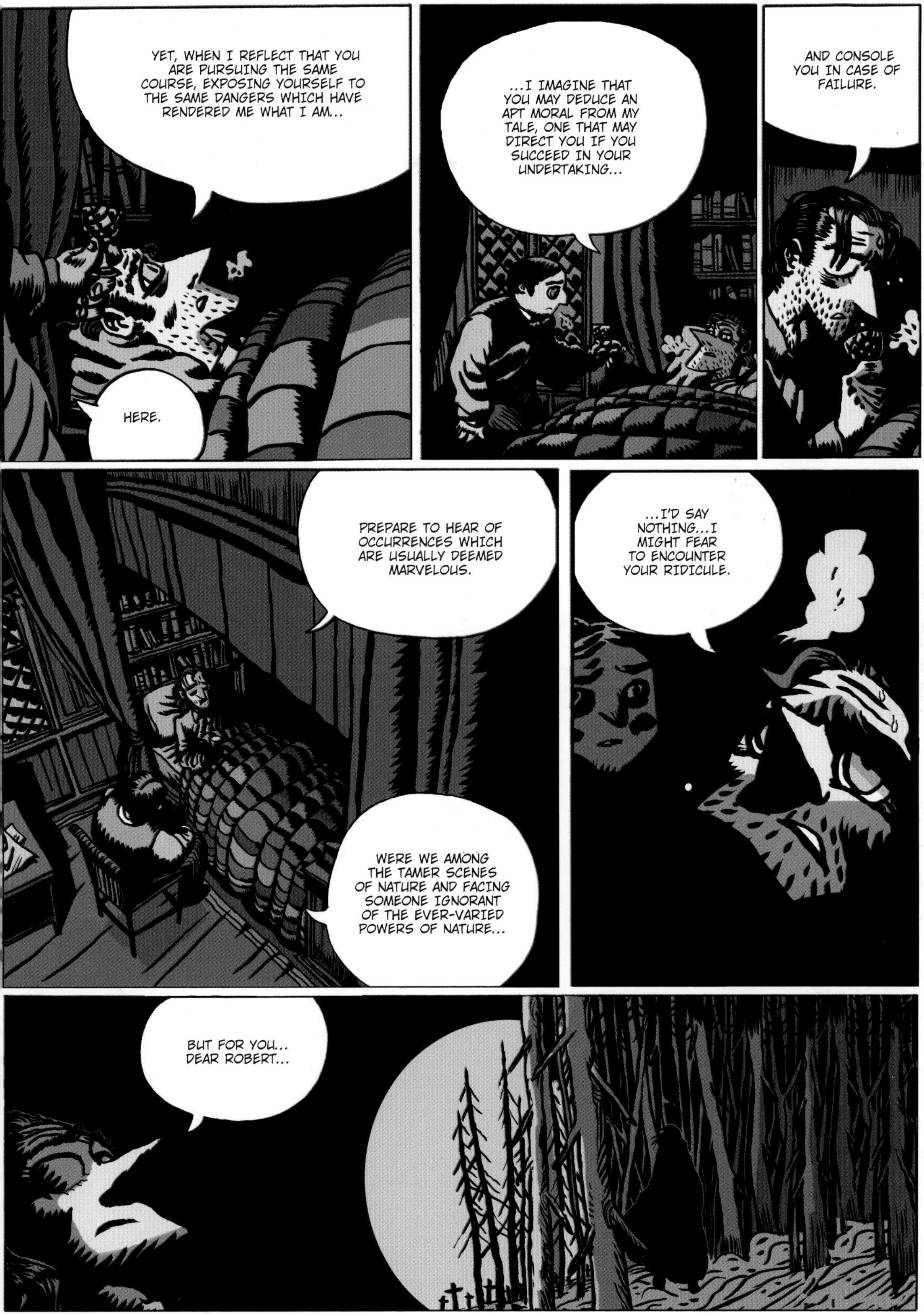
YET, WHEN I REFLECT THAT YOU ARE PURSUING THE SAME COURSE, EXPOSING YOURSELF TO THE SAME DANGERS WHICH HAVE RENDERED ME WHAT I AM...
HERE.
...I IMAGINE THAT YOU MAY DEDUCE AN APT MORAL FROM MY TALE, ONE THAT MAY DIRECT YOU IF YOU SUCCEED IN YOUR UNDERTAKING...
AND CONSOLE YOU IN CASE OF FAILURE.
PREPARE TO HEAR OF OCCURRENCES WHICH ARE USUALLY DEEMED MARVELOUS.
WERE WE AMONG THE TAMER SCENES OF NATURE AND FACING SOMEONE IGNORANT OF THE EVER-VARIED POWERS OF NATURE...
...I'D SAY NOTHING...I MIGHT FEAR TO ENCOUNTER YOUR RIDICULE.
BUT FOR YOU... DEAR ROBERT...

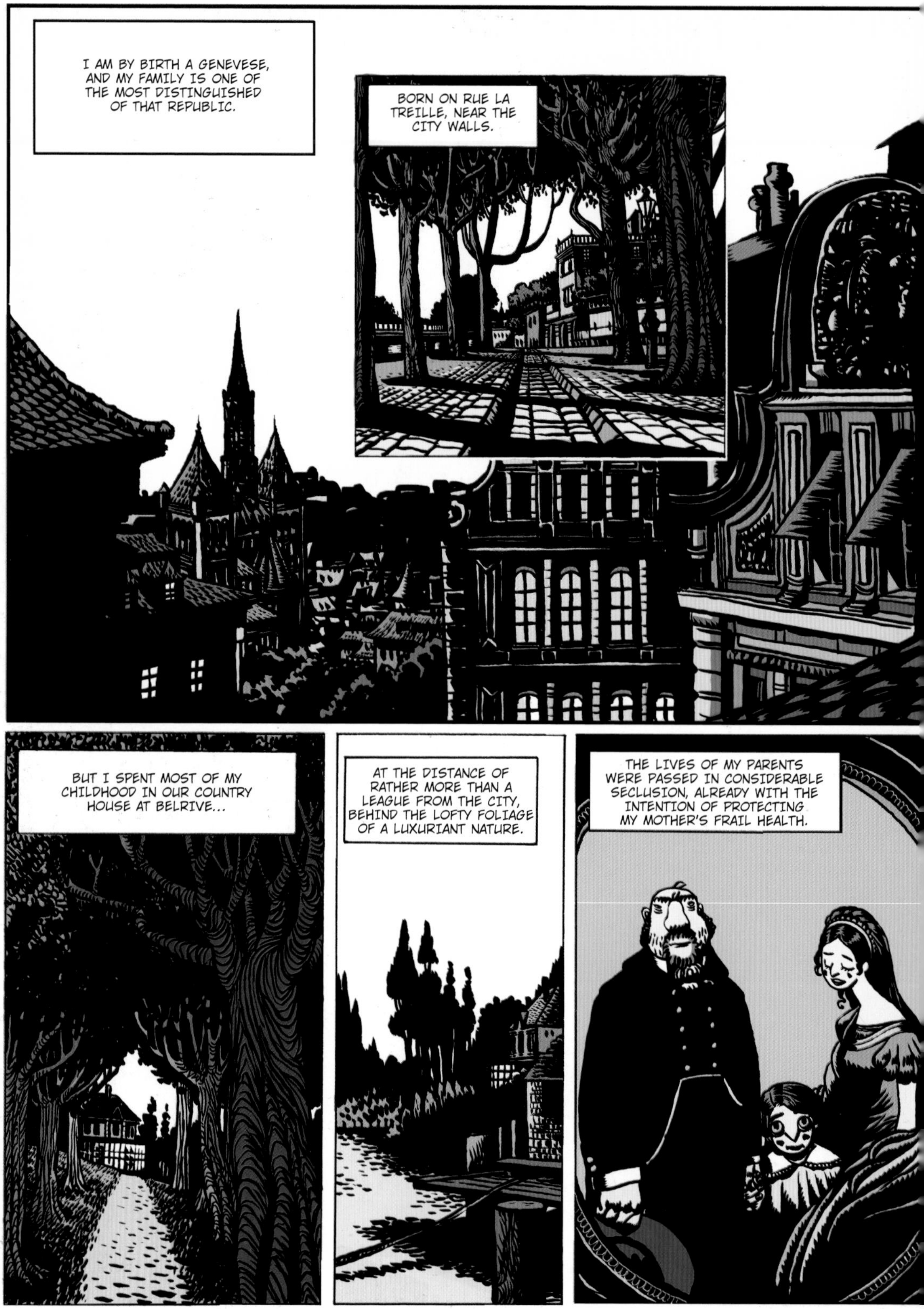
I AM BY BIRTH A GENEVESE, AND MY FAMILY IS ONE OF THE MOST DISTINGUISHED OF THAT REPUBLIC.
BORN ON RUE LA TREILLE, NEAR THE CITY WALLS.
BUT I SPENT MOST OF MY CHILDHOOD IN OUR COUNTRY HOUSE AT BELRIVE...
AT THE DISTANCE OF RATHER MORE THAN A LEAGUE FROM THE CITY, BEHIND THE LOFTY FOLIAGE OF A LUXURIANT NATURE.
THE LIVES OF MY PARENTS WERE PASSED IN CONSIDERABLE SECLUSION, ALREADY WITH THE INTENTION OF PROTECTING MY MOTHER'S FRAIL HEALTH.

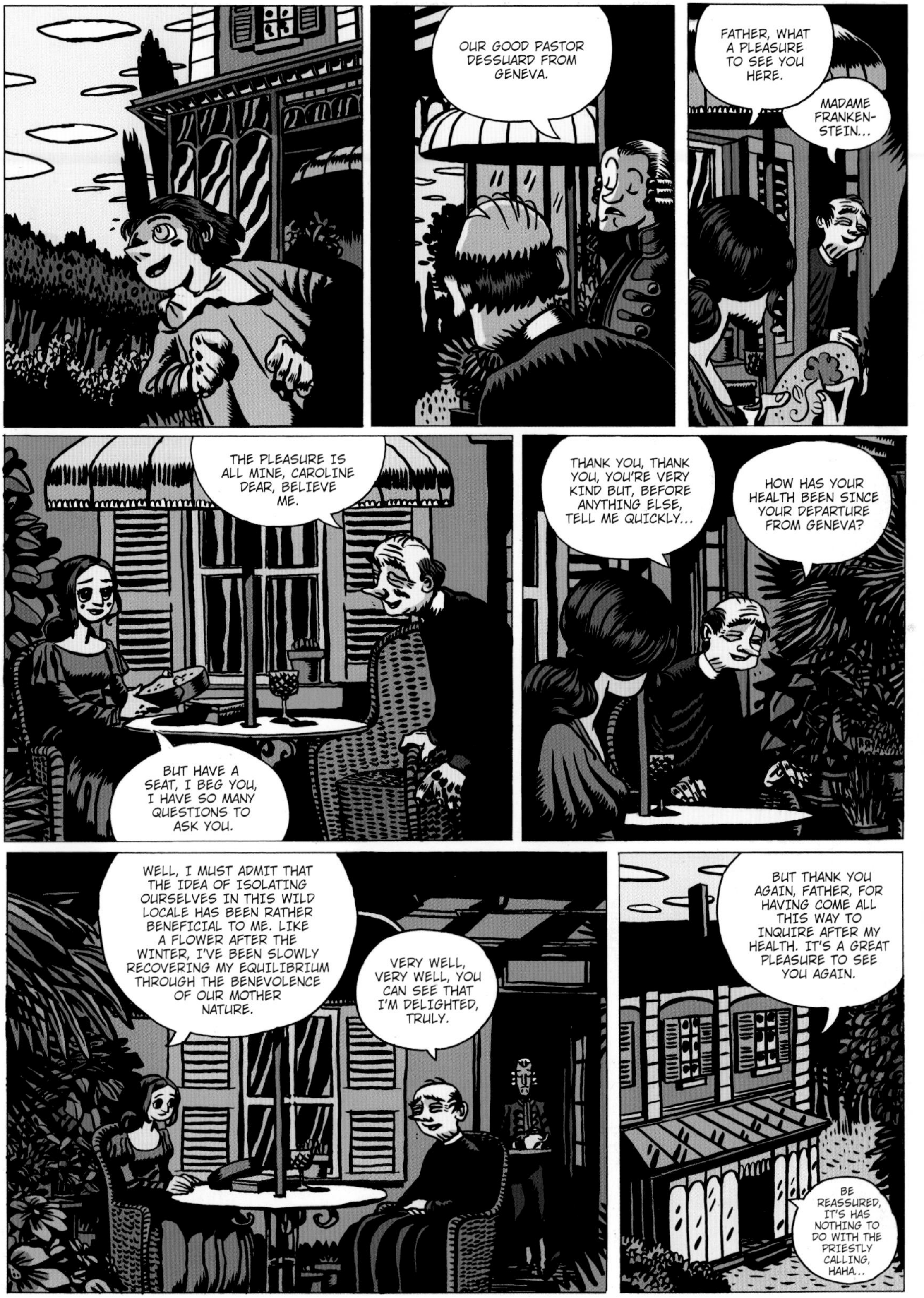
OUR GOOD PASTOR DESSUARD FROM GENEVA.
FATHER, WHAT A PLEASURE TO SEE YOU HERE.
MADAME FRANKEN-STEIN...
THE PLEASURE IS ALL MINE, CAROLINE DEAR, BELIEVE ME.
BUT HAVE A SEAT, I BEG YOU, I HAVE SO MANY QUESTIONS TO ASK YOU.
THANK YOU, THANK YOU, YOU'RE VERY KIND BUT, BEFORE ANYTHING ELSE, TELL ME QUICKLY...
HOW HAS YOUR HEALTH BEEN SINCE YOUR DEPARTURE FROM GENEVA?
WELL, I MUST ADMIT THAT THE IDEA OF ISOLATING OURSELVES IN THIS WILD LOCALE HAS BEEN RATHER BENEFICIAL TO ME. LIKE A FLOWER AFTER THE WINTER, I'VE BEEN SLOWLY RECOVERING MY EQUILIBRIUM THROUGH THE BENEVOLENCE OF OUR MOTHER NATURE.
VERY WELL, VERY WELL, YOU CAN SEE THAT I'M DELIGHTED, TRULY.
BUT THANK YOU AGAIN, FATHER, FOR HAVING COME ALL THIS WAY TO INQUIRE AFTER MY HEALTH. IT'S A GREAT PLEASURE TO SEE YOU AGAIN.
BE REASSURED, IT'S HAS NOTHING TO DO WITH THE PRIESTLY CALLING, HAHA...

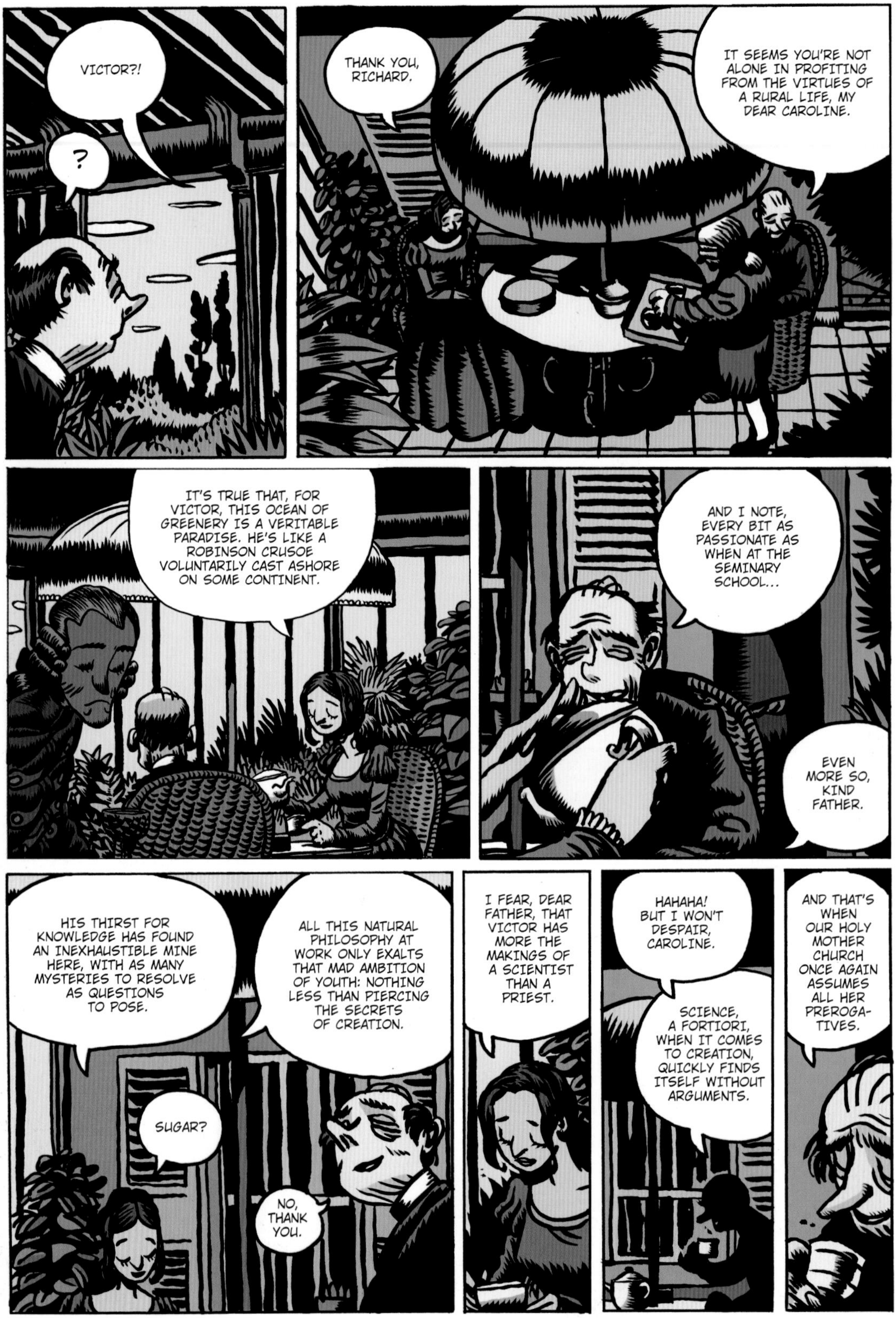
VICTOR?!
?
THANK YOU, RICHARD.
IT SEEMS YOU'RE NOT ALONE IN PROFITING FROM THE VIRTUES OF A RURAL LIFE, MY DEAR CAROLINE.
IT'S TRUE THAT, FOR VICTOR, THIS OCEAN OF GREENERY IS A VERITABLE PARADISE. HE'S LIKE A ROBINSON CRUSOE VOLUNTARILY CAST ASHORE ON SOME CONTINENT.
AND I NOTE, EVERY BIT AS PASSIONATE AS WHEN AT THE SEMINARY SCHOOL...
EVEN MORE SO, KIND FATHER.
HIS THIRST FOR KNOWLEDGE HAS FOUND AN INEXHAUSTIBLE MINE HERE, WITH AS MANY MYSTERIES TO RESOLVE AS QUESTIONS TO POSE.
ALL THIS NATURAL PHILOSOPHY AT WORK ONLY EXALTS THAT MAD AMBITION OF YOUTH: NOTHING LESS THAN PIERCING THE SECRETS OF CREATION.
SUGAR?
NO, THANK YOU.
I FEAR, DEAR FATHER, THAT VICTOR HAS MORE THE MAKINGS OF A SCIENTIST THAN A PRIEST.
HAHAHA! BUT I WON'T DESPAIR, CAROLINE.
SCIENCE, A FORTIORI, WHEN IT COMES TO CREATION, QUICKLY FINDS ITSELF WITHOUT ARGUMENTS.
AND THAT'S WHEN OUR HOLY MOTHER CHURCH ONCE AGAIN ASSUMES ALL HER PREROGA-TIVES.

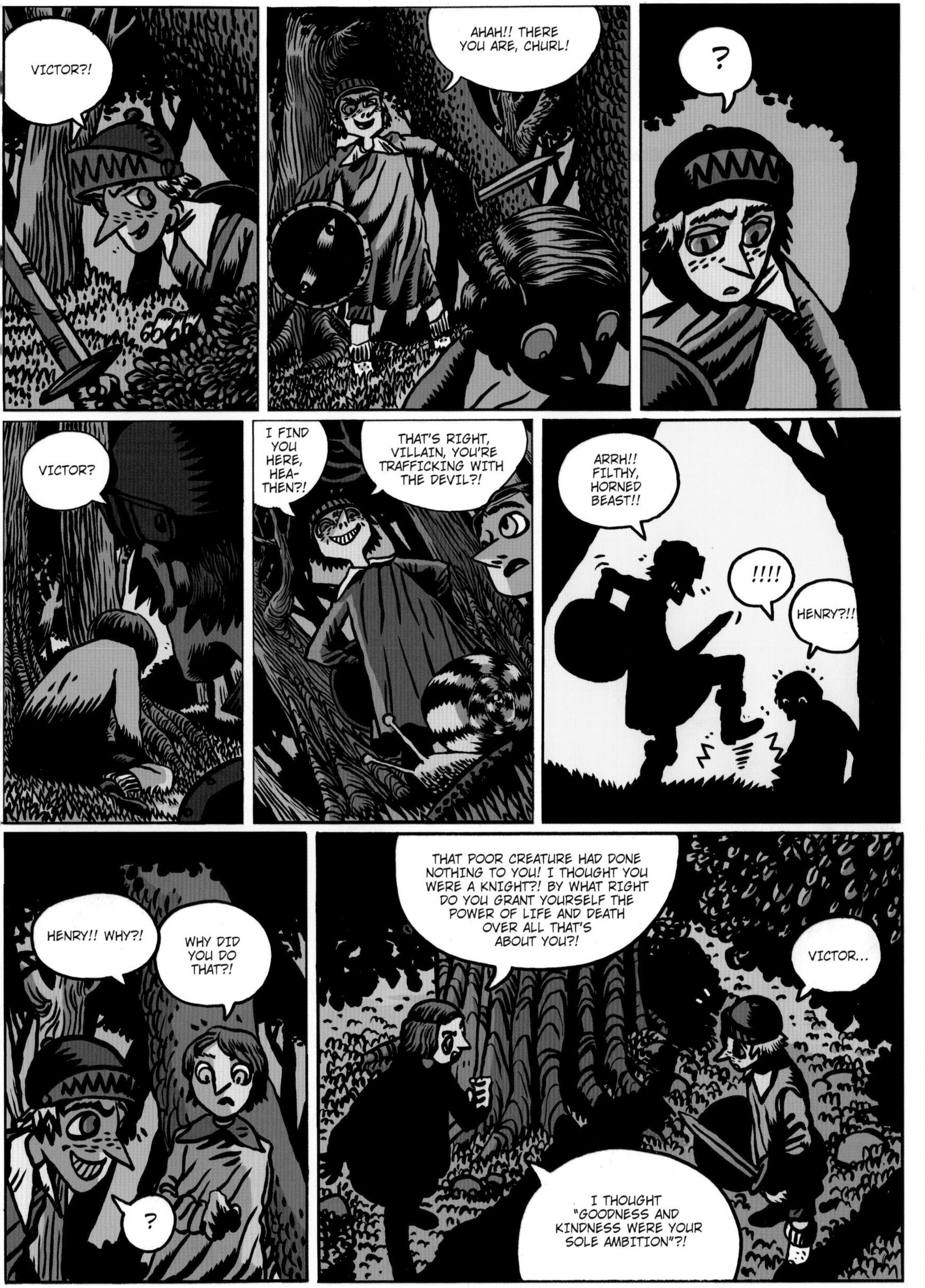
VICTOR?!
AHAH!! THERE YOU ARE, CHURL!
?
VICTOR?
I FIND YOU HERE, HEA-THEN?!
THAT'S RIGHT, VILLAIN, YOU'RE TRAFFICKING WITH THE DEVIL?!
ARRH!! FILTHY, HORNED BEAST!!
!!!!
HENRY?!!
HENRY!! WHY?!
WHY DID YOU DO THAT?!
?
THAT POOR CREATURE HAD DONE NOTHING TO YOU! I THOUGHT YOU WERE A KNIGHT?! BY WHAT RIGHT DO YOU GRANT YOURSELF THE POWER OF LIFE AND DEATH OVER ALL THAT'S ABOUT YOU?!
VICTOR...
I THOUGHT "GOODNESS AND KINDNESS WERE YOUR SOLE AMBITION"?!

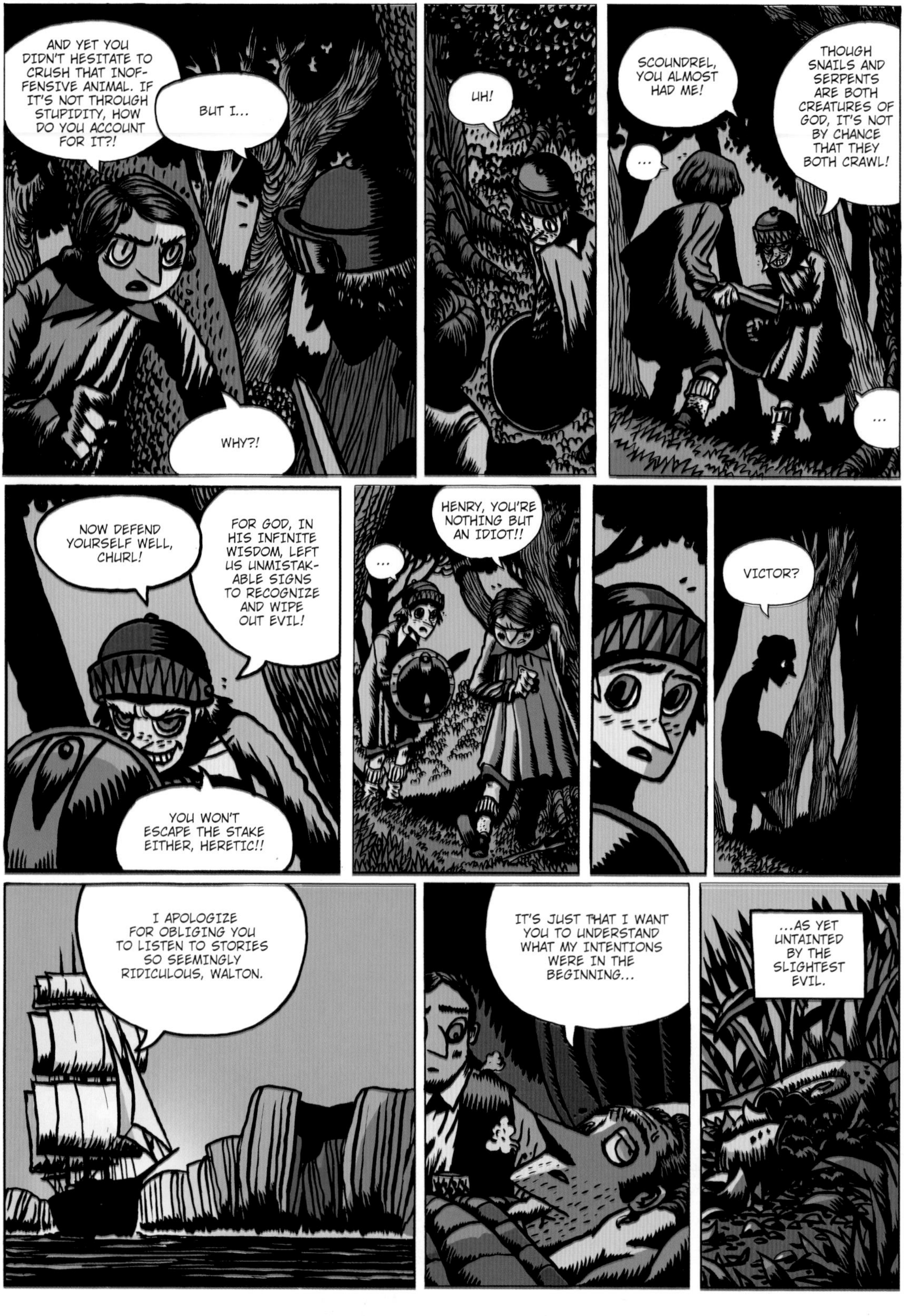
AND YET YOU DIDN'T HESITATE TO CRUSH THAT INOFFENSIVE ANIMAL. IF IT'S NOT THROUGH STUPIDITY, HOW DO YOU ACCOUNT FOR IT?!
BUT I...
WHY?!
UH!
SCOUNDREL, YOU ALMOST HAD ME!
...
THOUGH SNAILS AND SERPENTS ARE BOTH CREATURES OF GOD, IT'S NOT BY CHANCE THAT THEY BOTH CRAWL!
...
NOW DEFEND YOURSELF WELL, CHURL!
FOR GOD, IN HIS INFINITE WISDOM, LEFT US UNMISTAKABLE SIGNS TO RECOGNIZE AND WIPE OUT EVIL!
YOU WON'T ESCAPE THE STAKE EITHER, HERETIC!!
...
HENRY, YOU'RE NOTHING BUT AN IDIOT!!
VICTOR?
I APOLOGIZE FOR OBLIGING YOU TO LISTEN TO STORIES SO SEEMINGLY RIDICULOUS, WALTON.
IT'S JUST THAT I WANT YOU TO UNDERSTAND WHAT MY INTENTIONS WERE IN THE BEGINNING...
...AS YET UNTAINTED BY THE SLIGHTEST EVIL.

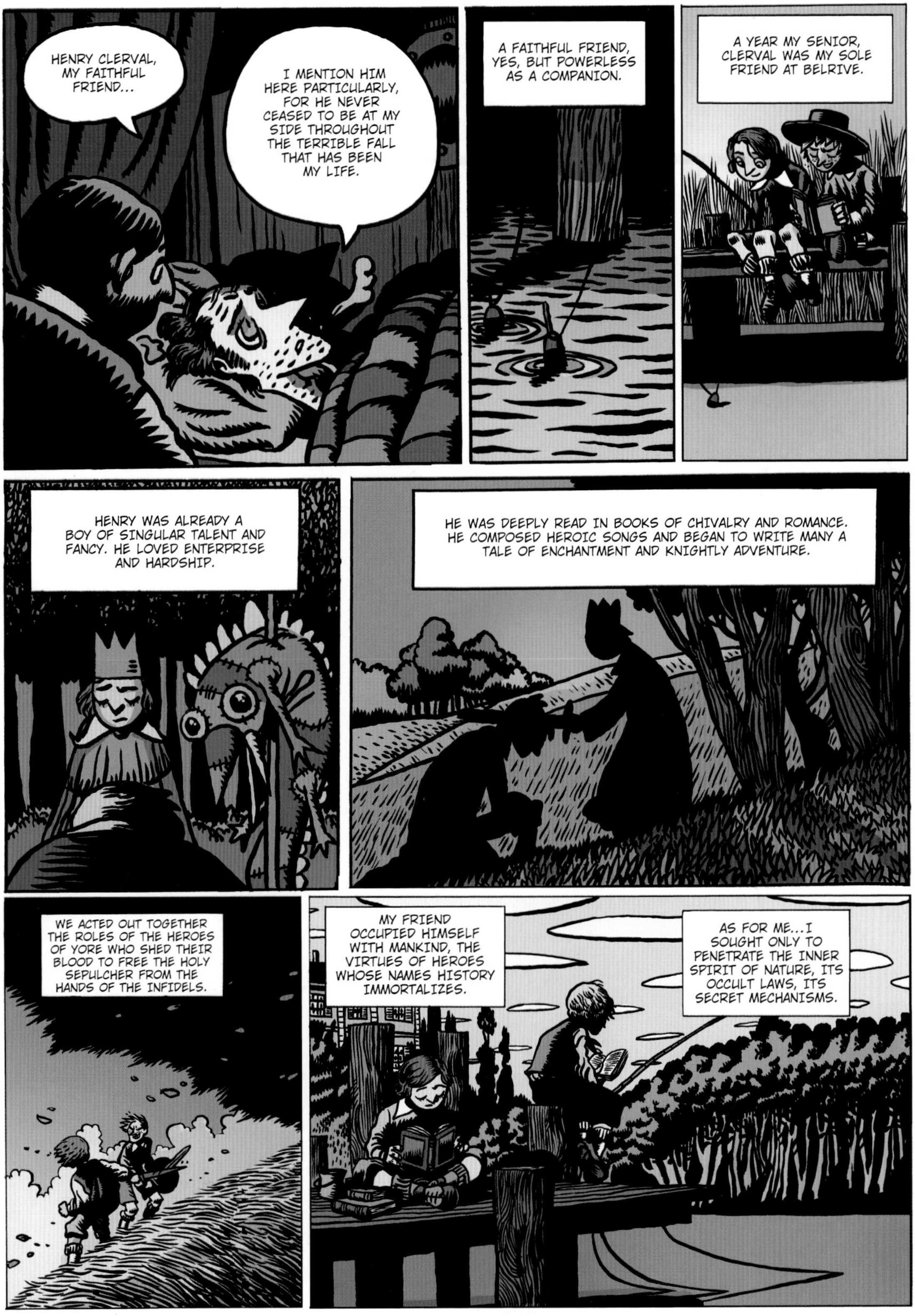
HENRY CLERVAL, MY FAITHFUL FRIEND...
I MENTION HIM HERE PARTICULARLY, FOR HE NEVER CEASED TO BE AT MY SIDE THROUGHOUT THE TERRIBLE FALL THAT HAS BEEN MY LIFE.
A FAITHFUL FRIEND, YES, BUT POWERLESS AS A COMPANION.
A YEAR MY SENIOR, CLERVAL WAS MY SOLE FRIEND AT BELRIVE.
HENRY WAS ALREADY A BOY OF SINGULAR TALENT AND FANCY. HE LOVED ENTERPRISE AND HARDSHIP.
HE WAS DEEPLY READ IN BOOKS OF CHIVALRY AND ROMANCE. HE COMPOSED HEROIC SONGS AND BEGAN TO WRITE MANY A TALE OF ENCHANTMENT AND KNIGHTLY ADVENTURE.
WE ACTED OUT TOGETHER THE ROLES OF THE HEROES OF YORE WHO SHED THEIR BLOOD TO FREE THE HOLY SEPULCHER FROM THE HANDS OF THE INFIDELS.
MY FRIEND OCCUPIED HIMSELF WITH MANKIND, THE VIRTUES OF HEROES WHOSE NAMES HISTORY IMMORTALIZES.
AS FOR ME...I SOUGHT ONLY TO PENETRATE THE INNER SPIRIT OF NATURE, ITS OCCULT LAWS, ITS SECRET MECHANISMS.

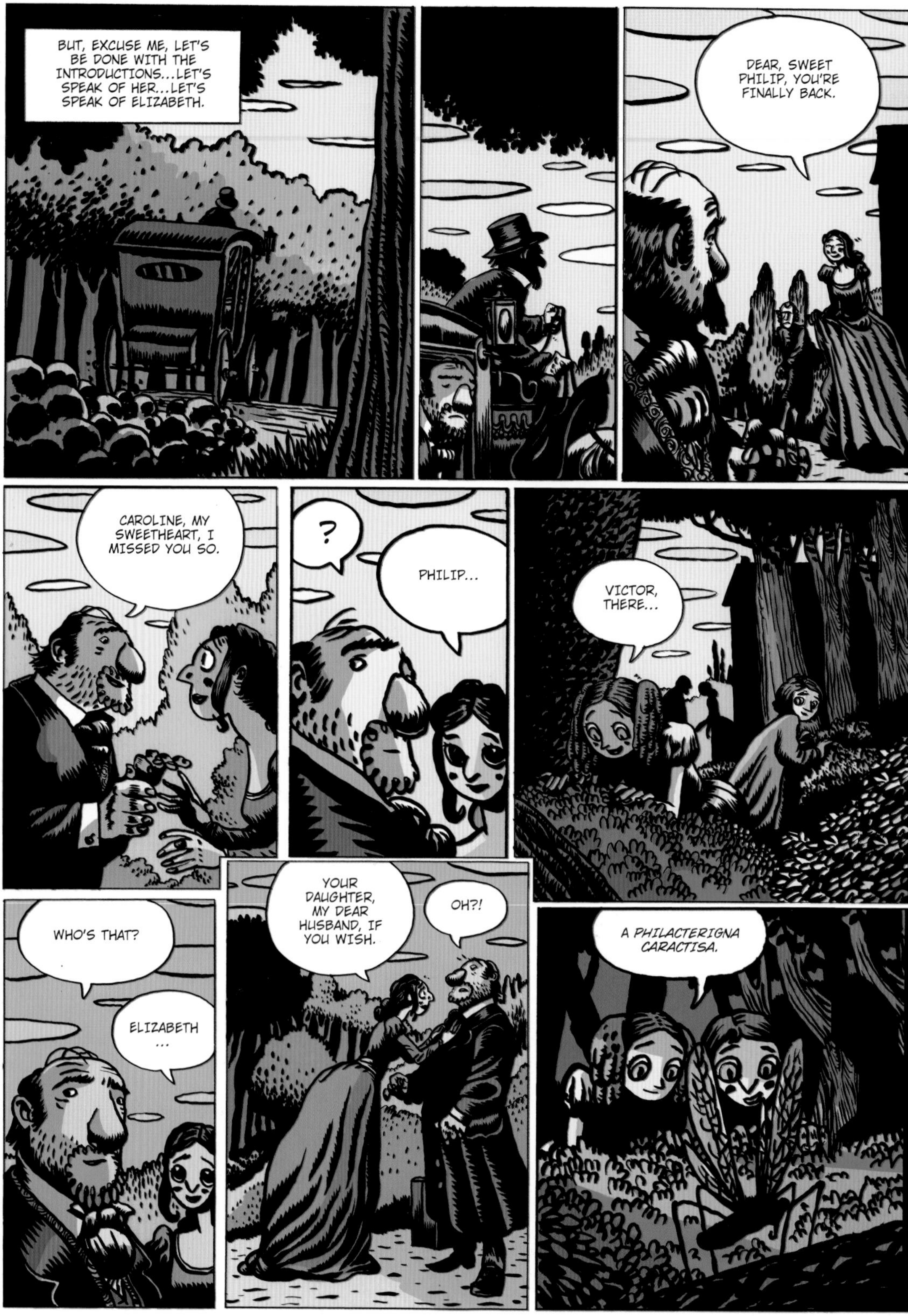
BUT, EXCUSE ME, LET'S BE DONE WITH THE INTRODUCTIONS...LET'S SPEAK OF HER...LET'S SPEAK OF ELIZABETH.
DEAR, SWEET PHILIP, YOU'RE FINALLY BACK.
CAROLINE, MY SWEETHEART, I MISSED YOU SO.
?
PHILIP...
VICTOR, THERE...
WHO'S THAT?
ELIZABETH ...
YOUR DAUGHTER, MY DEAR HUSBAND, IF YOU WISH.
OH?!
A *PHILACTERIGNA CARACTISA.*

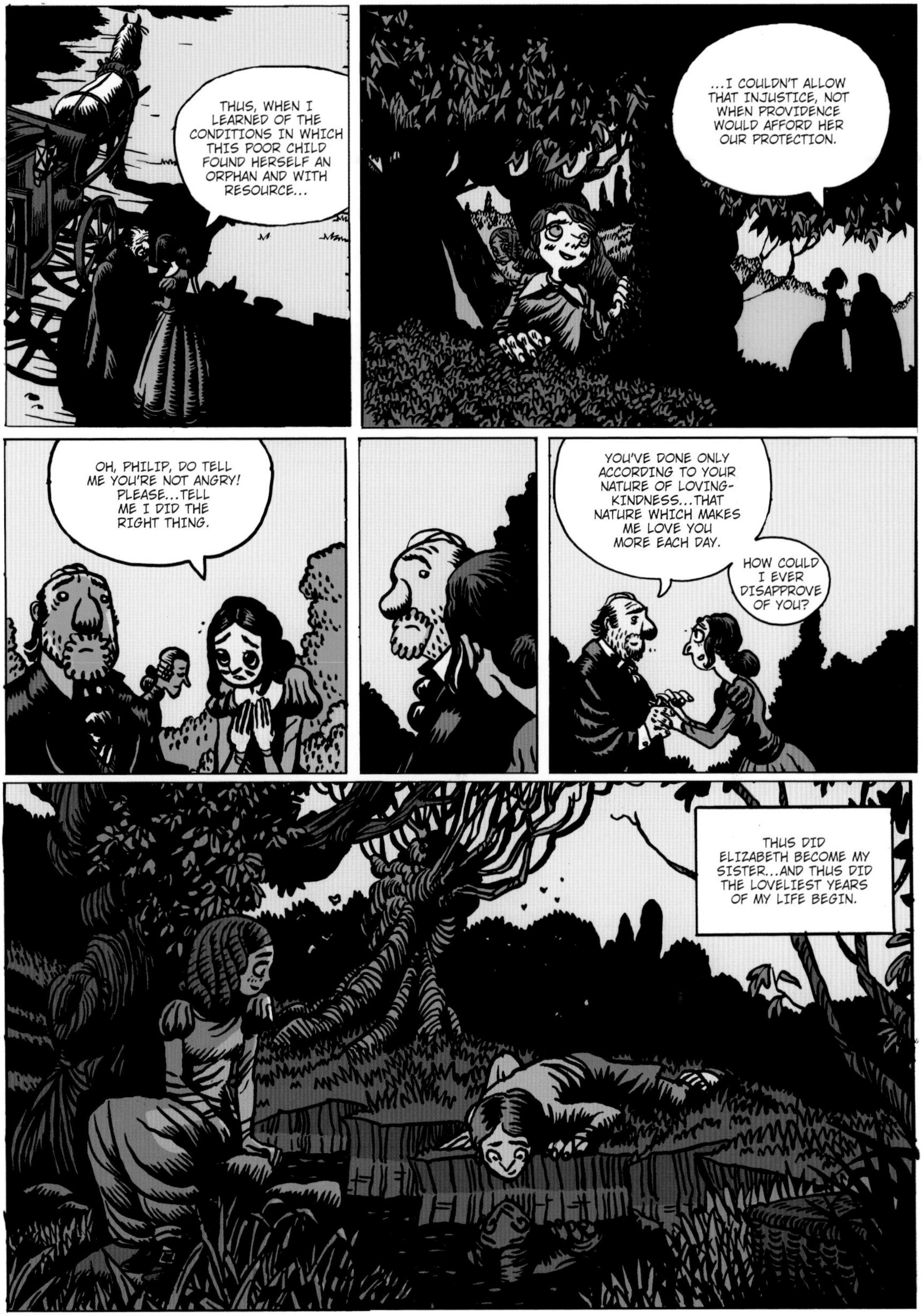
THUS, WHEN I LEARNED OF THE CONDITIONS IN WHICH THIS POOR CHILD FOUND HERSELF AN ORPHAN AND WITH RESOURCE...
...I COULDN'T ALLOW THAT INJUSTICE, NOT WHEN PROVIDENCE WOULD AFFORD HER OUR PROTECTION.
OH, PHILIP, DO TELL ME YOU'RE NOT ANGRY! PLEASE...TELL ME I DID THE RIGHT THING.
YOU'VE DONE ONLY ACCORDING TO YOUR NATURE OF LOVING-KINDNESS...THAT NATURE WHICH MAKES ME LOVE YOU MORE EACH DAY.
HOW COULD I EVER DISAPPROVE OF YOU?
THUS DID ELIZABETH BECOME MY SISTER...AND THUS DID THE LOVELIEST YEARS OF MY LIFE BEGIN.

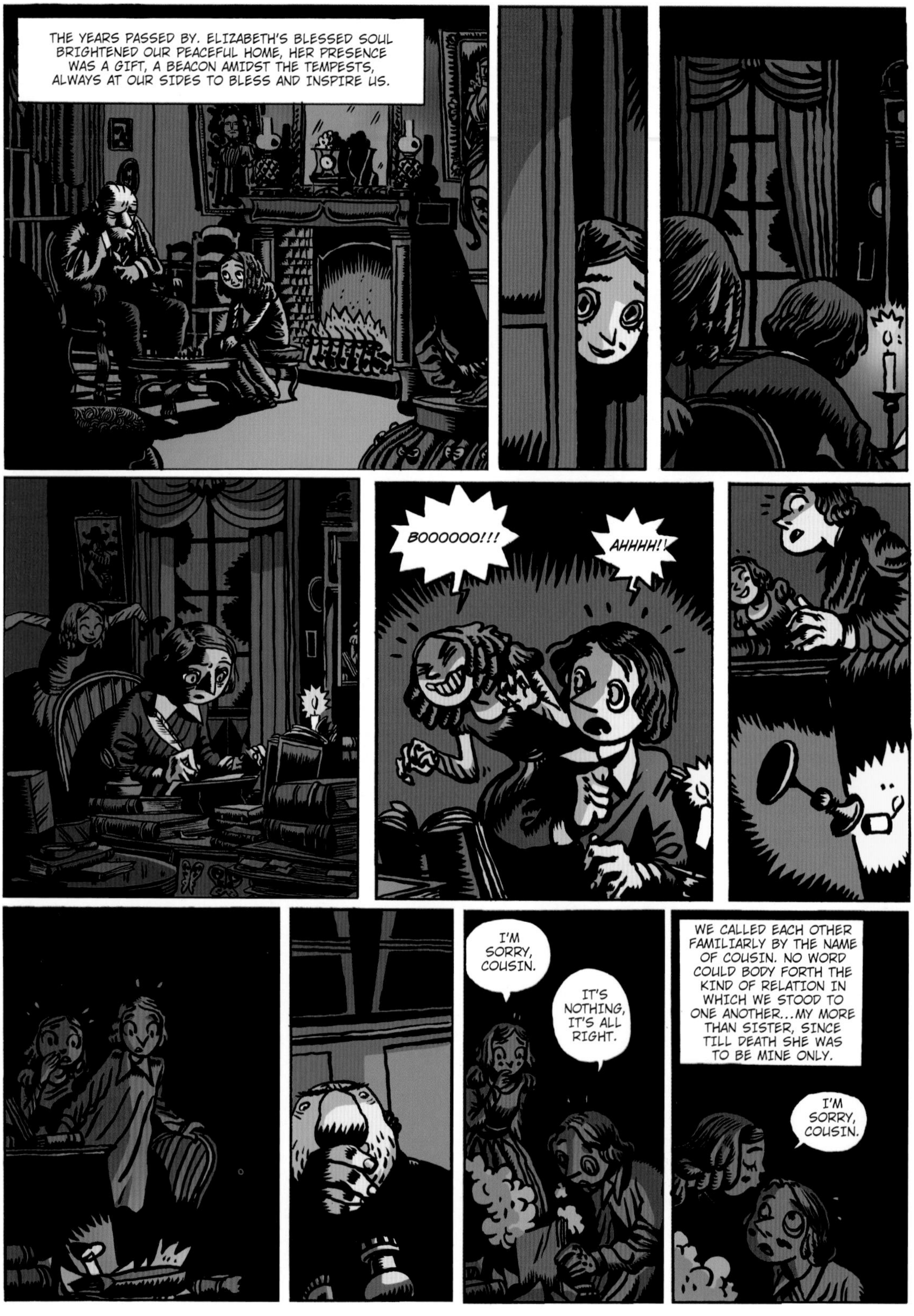
THE YEARS PASSED BY. ELIZABETH'S BLESSED SOUL BRIGHTENED OUR PEACEFUL HOME, HER PRESENCE WAS A GIFT, A BEACON AMIDST THE TEMPESTS, ALWAYS AT OUR SIDES TO BLESS AND INSPIRE US.
BOOOOOO!!!
AHHHH!!
I'M SORRY, COUSIN.
IT'S NOTHING, IT'S ALL RIGHT.
WE CALLED EACH OTHER FAMILIARLY BY THE NAME OF COUSIN. NO WORD COULD BODY FORTH THE KIND OF RELATION IN WHICH WE STOOD TO ONE ANOTHER...MY MORE THAN SISTER, SINCE TILL DEATH SHE WAS TO BE MINE ONLY.
I'M SORRY, COUSIN.

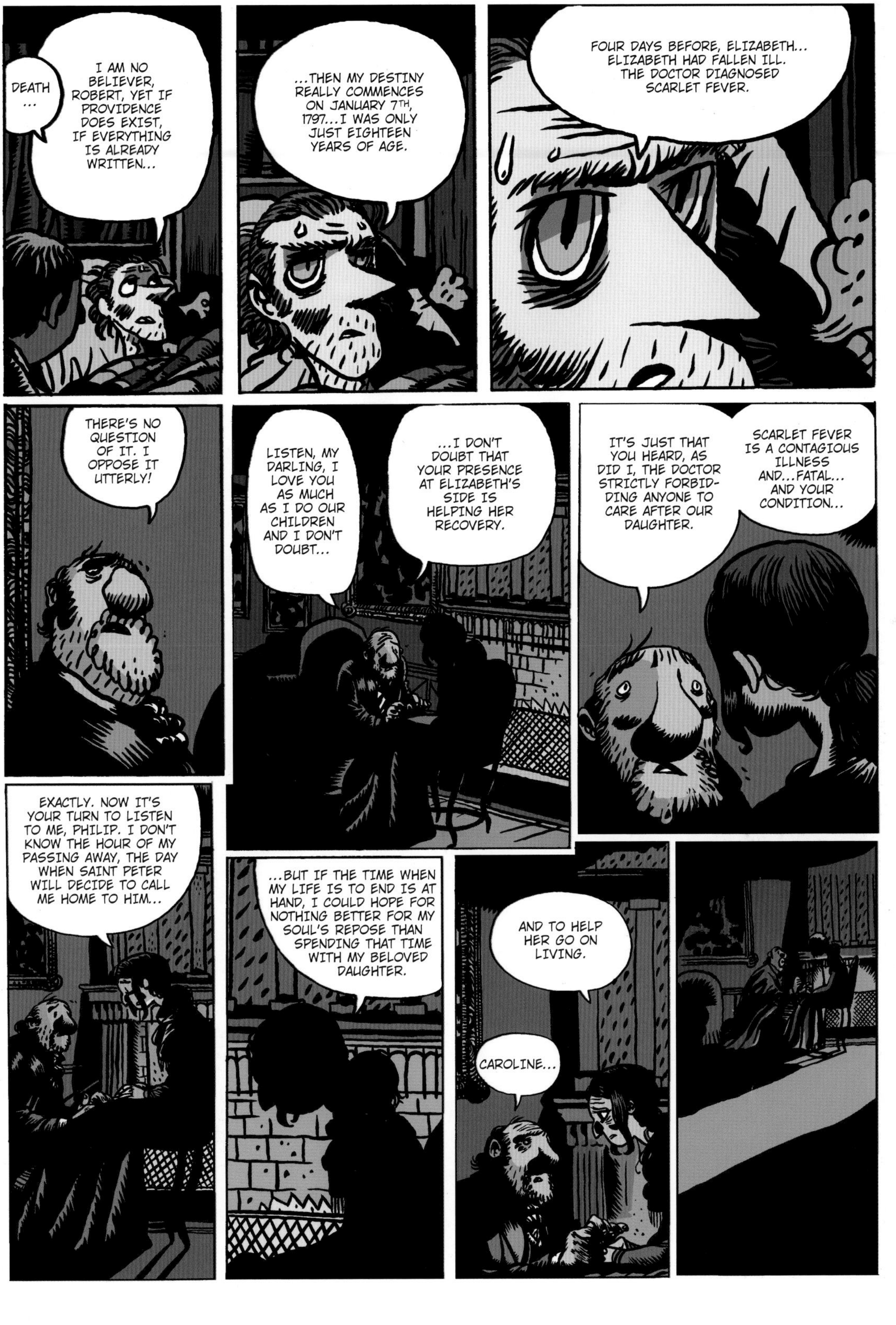
DEATH...
I AM NO BELIEVER, ROBERT, YET IF PROVIDENCE DOES EXIST, IF EVERYTHING IS ALREADY WRITTEN...
...THEN MY DESTINY REALLY COMMENCES ON JANUARY 7TH, 1797...I WAS ONLY JUST EIGHTEEN YEARS OF AGE.
FOUR DAYS BEFORE, ELIZABETH... ELIZABETH HAD FALLEN ILL. THE DOCTOR DIAGNOSED SCARLET FEVER.
THERE'S NO QUESTION OF IT. I OPPOSE IT UTTERLY!
LISTEN, MY DARLING, I LOVE YOU AS MUCH AS I DO OUR CHILDREN AND I DON'T DOUBT...
...I DON'T DOUBT THAT YOUR PRESENCE AT ELIZABETH'S SIDE IS HELPING HER RECOVERY.
IT'S JUST THAT YOU HEARD, AS DID I, THE DOCTOR STRICTLY FORBIDDING ANYONE TO CARE AFTER OUR DAUGHTER.
SCARLET FEVER IS A CONTAGIOUS ILLNESS AND...FATAL... AND YOUR CONDITION...
EXACTLY. NOW IT'S YOUR TURN TO LISTEN TO ME, PHILIP. I DON'T KNOW THE HOUR OF MY PASSING AWAY, THE DAY WHEN SAINT PETER WILL DECIDE TO CALL ME HOME TO HIM...
...BUT IF THE TIME WHEN MY LIFE IS TO END IS AT HAND, I COULD HOPE FOR NOTHING BETTER FOR MY SOUL'S REPOSE THAN SPENDING THAT TIME WITH MY BELOVED DAUGHTER.
AND TO HELP HER GO ON LIVING.
CAROLINE...

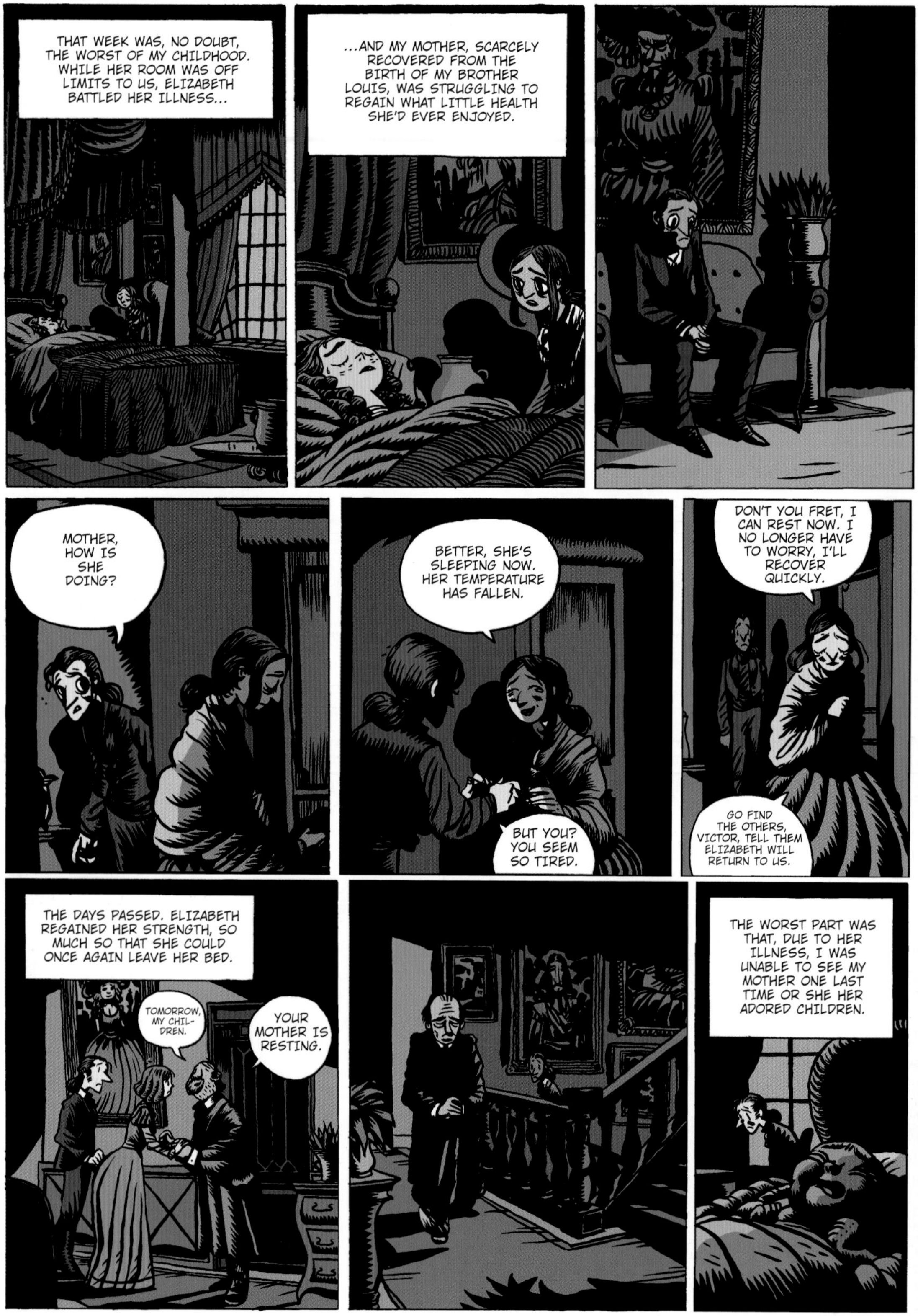
THAT WEEK WAS, NO DOUBT, THE WORST OF MY CHILDHOOD. WHILE HER ROOM WAS OFF LIMITS TO US, ELIZABETH BATTLED HER ILLNESS...
...AND MY MOTHER, SCARCELY RECOVERED FROM THE BIRTH OF MY BROTHER LOUIS, WAS STRUGGLING TO REGAIN WHAT LITTLE HEALTH SHE'D EVER ENJOYED.
MOTHER, HOW IS SHE DOING?
BETTER, SHE'S SLEEPING NOW. HER TEMPERATURE HAS FALLEN.
BUT YOU? YOU SEEM SO TIRED.
DON'T YOU FRET, I CAN REST NOW. I NO LONGER HAVE TO WORRY, I'LL RECOVER QUICKLY.
GO FIND THE OTHERS, VICTOR, TELL THEM ELIZABETH WILL RETURN TO US.
THE DAYS PASSED. ELIZABETH REGAINED HER STRENGTH, SO MUCH SO THAT SHE COULD ONCE AGAIN LEAVE HER BED.
TOMORROW, MY CHIL-DREN.
YOUR MOTHER IS RESTING.
THE WORST PART WAS THAT, DUE TO HER ILLNESS, I WAS UNABLE TO SEE MY MOTHER ONE LAST TIME OR SHE HER ADORED CHILDREN.

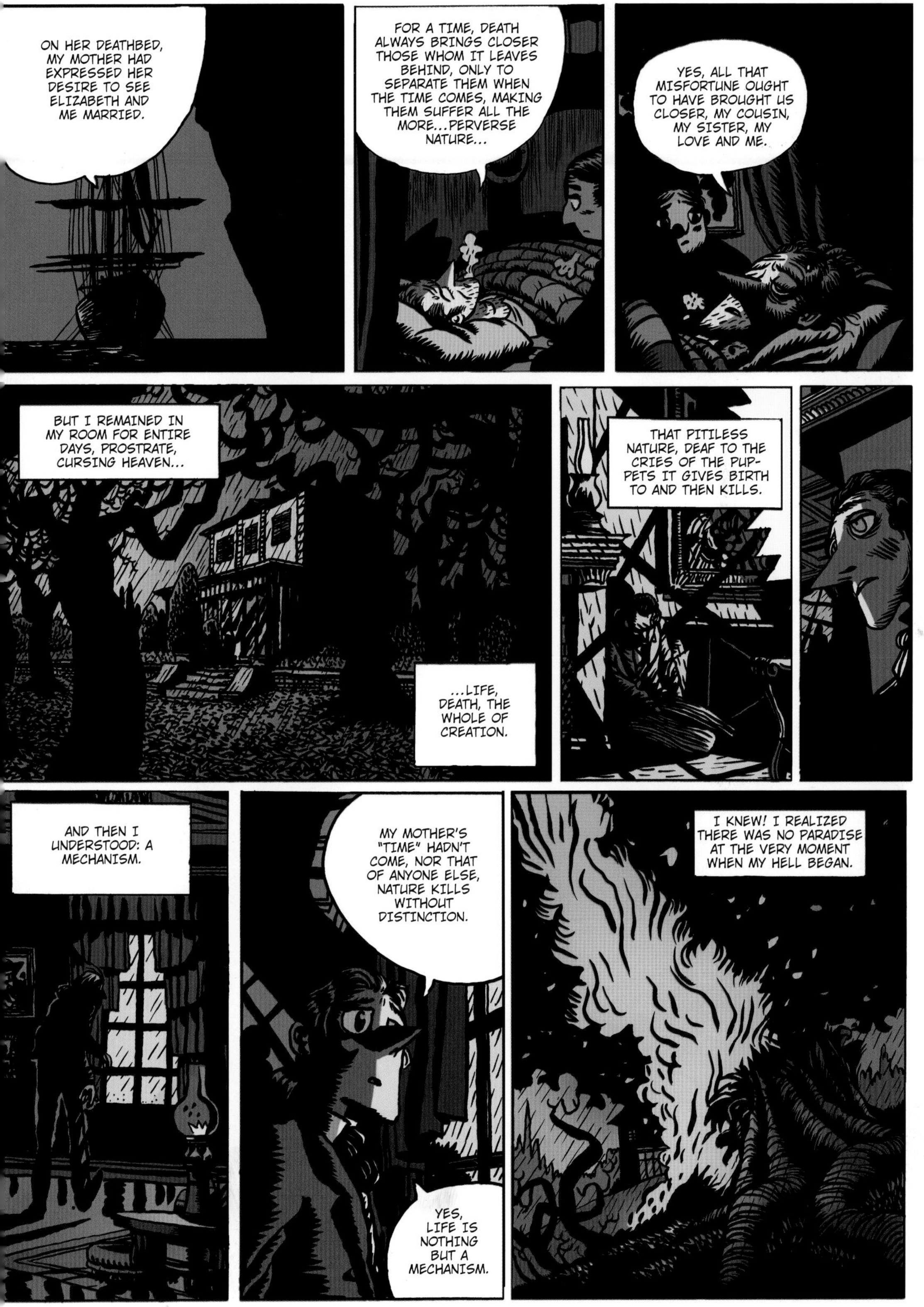
ON HER DEATHBED, MY MOTHER HAD EXPRESSED HER DESIRE TO SEE ELIZABETH AND ME MARRIED.
FOR A TIME, DEATH ALWAYS BRINGS CLOSER THOSE WHOM IT LEAVES BEHIND, ONLY TO SEPARATE THEM WHEN THE TIME COMES, MAKING THEM SUFFER ALL THE MORE...PERVERSE NATURE...
YES, ALL THAT MISFORTUNE OUGHT TO HAVE BROUGHT US CLOSER, MY COUSIN, MY SISTER, MY LOVE AND ME.
BUT I REMAINED IN MY ROOM FOR ENTIRE DAYS, PROSTRATE, CURSING HEAVEN...
...LIFE, DEATH, THE WHOLE OF CREATION.
THAT PITILESS NATURE, DEAF TO THE CRIES OF THE PUP-PETS IT GIVES BIRTH TO AND THEN KILLS.
AND THEN I UNDERSTOOD: A MECHANISM.
MY MOTHER'S "TIME" HADN'T COME, NOR THAT OF ANYONE ELSE, NATURE KILLS WITHOUT DISTINCTION.
YES, LIFE IS NOTHING BUT A MECHANISM.
I KNEW! I REALIZED THERE WAS NO PARADISE AT THE VERY MOMENT WHEN MY HELL BEGAN.

VICTOR, I DON'T UNDERSTAND. WHAT HAPPENED? WHY?

PATIENCE, WALTON, IT'S JUST AS IMPORTANT TO ME AS TO YOU THAT YOU UNDER-STAND...THAT YOU KNOW.

I TOLD YOU I'D UNDERSTOOD! PROVIDENCE, DESTINY AND EVEN THAT MUCH-PRAISED PARADISE, IT ALL EXISTED NO MORE, DEAD ALONG WITH MY DEAR MOTHER.

CRUSHED THEREAFTER BY THAT CONVICTION, THAT CERTAINTY OF THE DECEPTION, HOW COULD SUCH A HORROR BE BORNE?

IT MADE NO SENSE!

GOD NO LONGER EXISTED FROM THE DAY MY MOTHER DIED.

YOU DO UNDER-STAND, ROBERT, MY MOTHER WAS A SAINT! HA HA! SHE DID GOOD WORKS ALL HER LIFE, SO WHY?!

IT WASN'T LOGICAL OR, IF INDEED LOGICAL, IT WAS LOGICAL LIKE A MECHANISM!

YOU NO DOUBT PITY ME, ROBERT. YOU'RE FINDING OUT ABOUT THAT DAY WHEN I WENT MAD, AH! EVEN THOUGH IN REALITY, IT WAS MY REASON THAT I'D FINALLY RECOVERED.

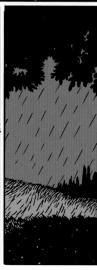

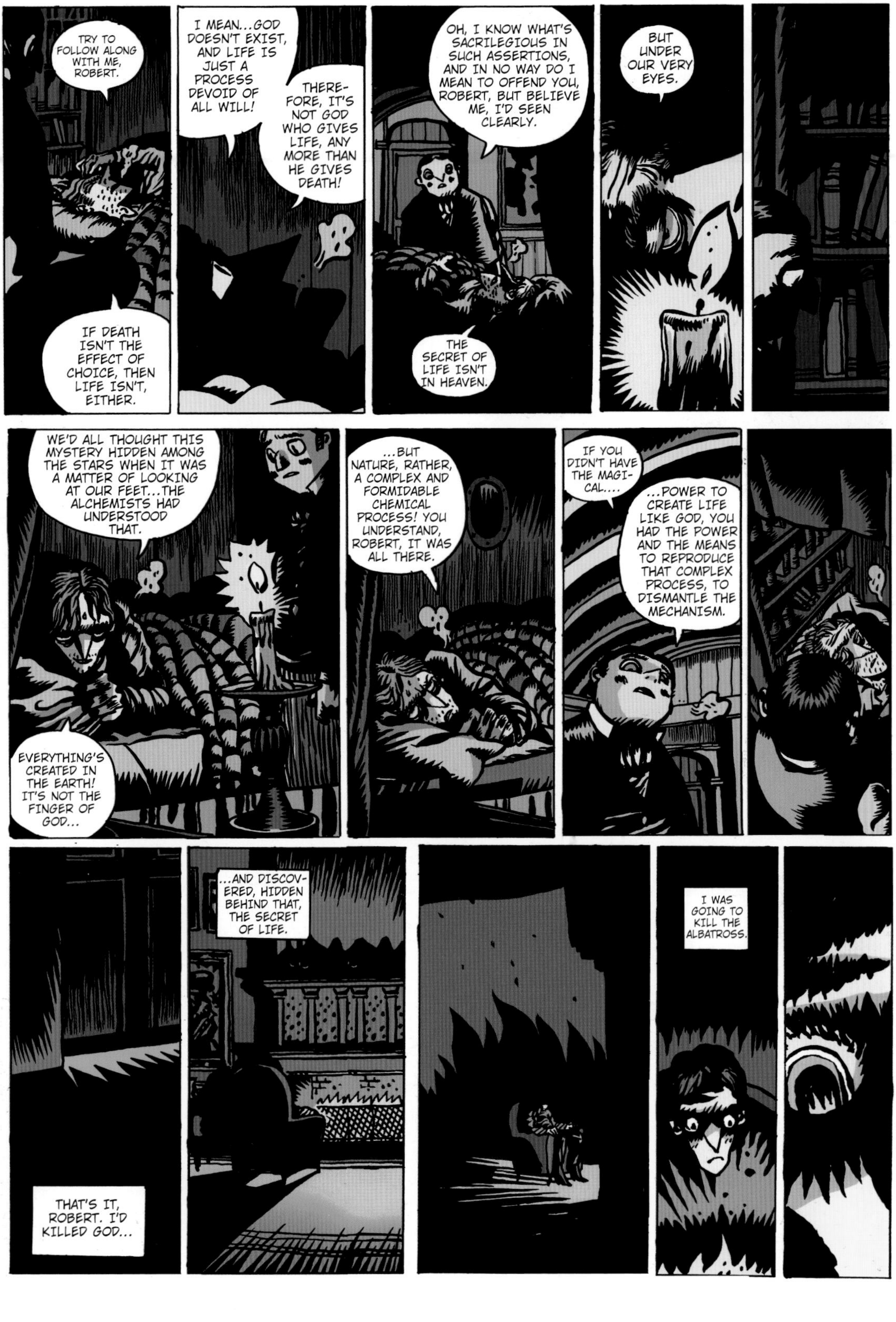
TRY TO FOLLOW ALONG WITH ME, ROBERT.
IF DEATH ISN'T THE EFFECT OF CHOICE, THEN LIFE ISN'T, EITHER.
I MEAN...GOD DOESN'T EXIST, AND LIFE IS JUST A PROCESS DEVOID OF ALL WILL!
THERE-FORE, IT'S NOT GOD WHO GIVES LIFE, ANY MORE THAN HE GIVES DEATH!
OH, I KNOW WHAT'S SACRILEGIOUS IN SUCH ASSERTIONS, AND IN NO WAY DO I MEAN TO OFFEND YOU, ROBERT, BUT BELIEVE ME, I'D SEEN CLEARLY.
THE SECRET OF LIFE ISN'T IN HEAVEN.
BUT UNDER OUR VERY EYES.
WE'D ALL THOUGHT THIS MYSTERY HIDDEN AMONG THE STARS WHEN IT WAS A MATTER OF LOOKING AT OUR FEET...THE ALCHEMISTS HAD UNDERSTOOD THAT.
EVERYTHING'S CREATED IN THE EARTH! IT'S NOT THE FINGER OF GOD...
...BUT NATURE, RATHER, A COMPLEX AND FORMIDABLE CHEMICAL PROCESS! YOU UNDERSTAND, ROBERT, IT WAS ALL THERE.
IF YOU DIDN'T HAVE THE MAGI-CAL....
...POWER TO CREATE LIFE LIKE GOD, YOU HAD THE POWER AND THE MEANS TO REPRODUCE THAT COMPLEX PROCESS, TO DISMANTLE THE MECHANISM.
THAT'S IT, ROBERT. I'D KILLED GOD...
...AND DISCOV-ERED, HIDDEN BEHIND THAT, THE SECRET OF LIFE.
I WAS GOING TO KILL THE ALBATROSS.

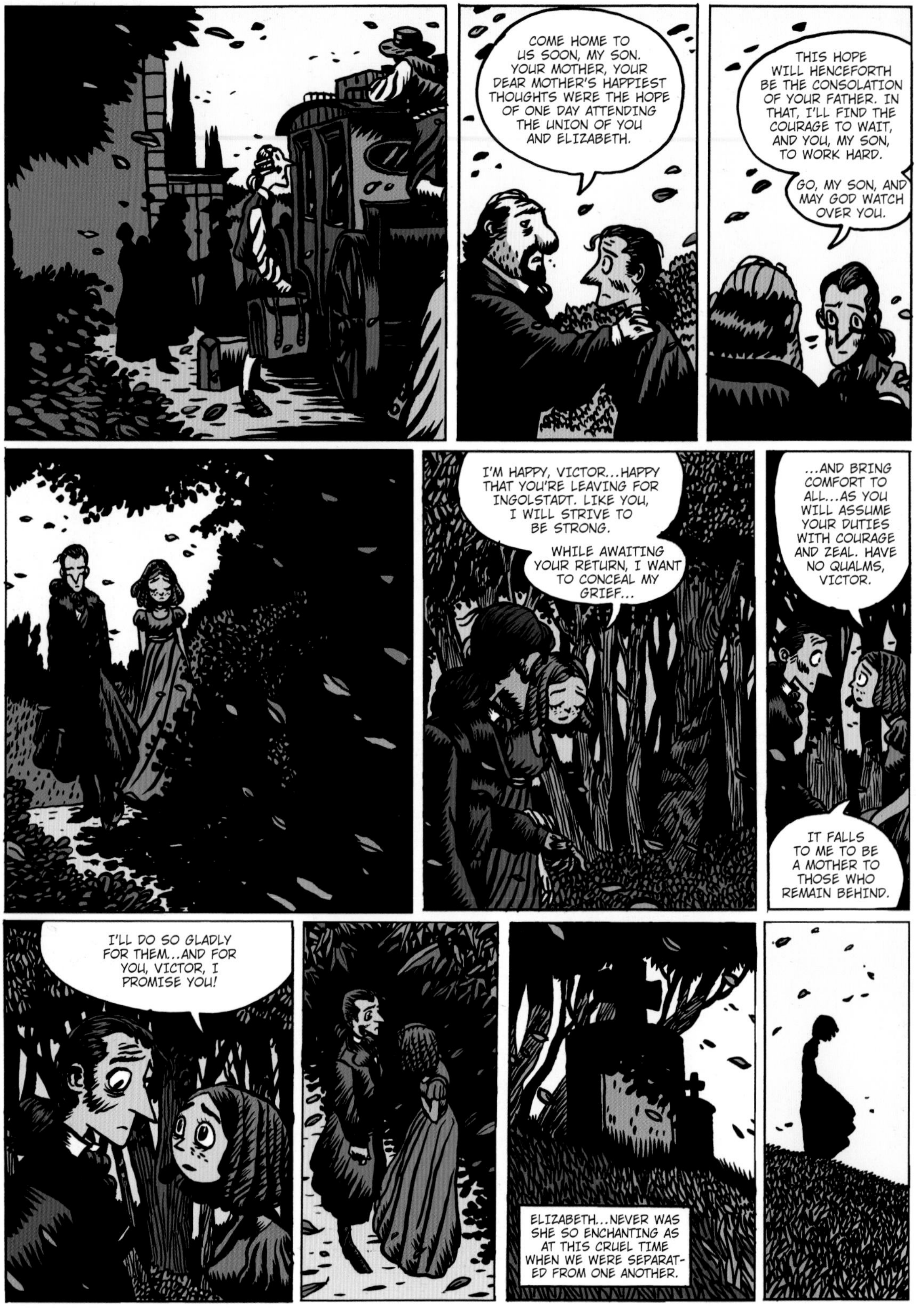
COME HOME TO US SOON, MY SON. YOUR MOTHER, YOUR DEAR MOTHER'S HAPPIEST THOUGHTS WERE THE HOPE OF ONE DAY ATTENDING THE UNION OF YOU AND ELIZABETH.
THIS HOPE WILL HENCEFORTH BE THE CONSOLATION OF YOUR FATHER. IN THAT, I'LL FIND THE COURAGE TO WAIT, AND YOU, MY SON, TO WORK HARD.
GO, MY SON, AND MAY GOD WATCH OVER YOU.
I'M HAPPY, VICTOR...HAPPY THAT YOU'RE LEAVING FOR INGOLSTADT. LIKE YOU, I WILL STRIVE TO BE STRONG.
WHILE AWAITING YOUR RETURN, I WANT TO CONCEAL MY GRIEF...
...AND BRING COMFORT TO ALL...AS YOU WILL ASSUME YOUR DUTIES WITH COURAGE AND ZEAL. HAVE NO QUALMS, VICTOR.
IT FALLS TO ME TO BE A MOTHER TO THOSE WHO REMAIN BEHIND.
I'LL DO SO GLADLY FOR THEM...AND FOR YOU, VICTOR, I PROMISE YOU!
ELIZABETH...NEVER WAS SHE SO ENCHANTING AS AT THIS CRUEL TIME WHEN WE WERE SEPARAT-ED FROM ONE ANOTHER.

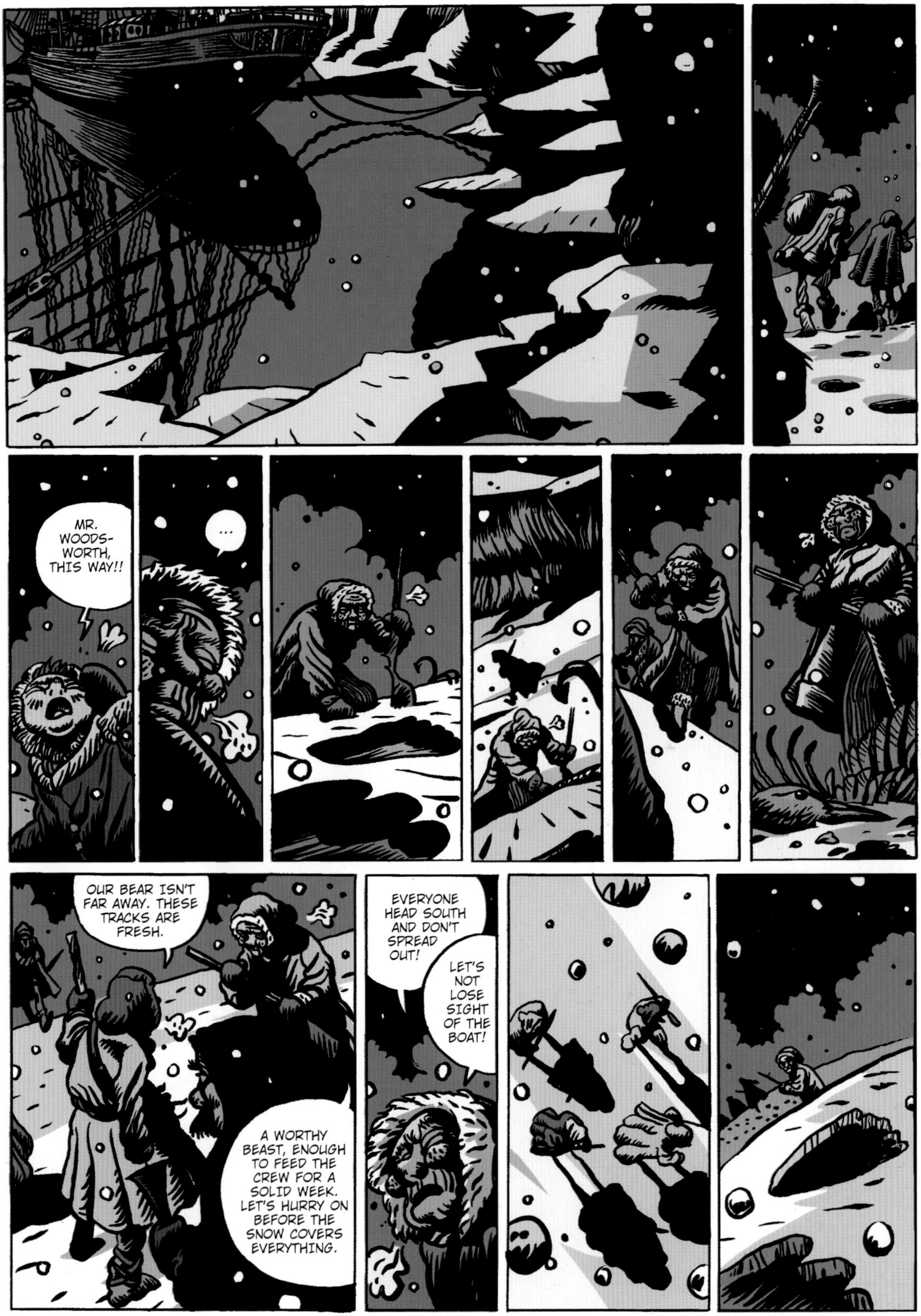
MR. WOODS-WORTH, THIS WAY!!
...
OUR BEAR ISN'T FAR AWAY. THESE TRACKS ARE FRESH.
A WORTHY BEAST, ENOUGH TO FEED THE CREW FOR A SOLID WEEK. LET'S HURRY ON BEFORE THE SNOW COVERS EVERYTHING.
EVERYONE HEAD SOUTH AND DON'T SPREAD OUT!
LET'S NOT LOSE SIGHT OF THE BOAT!

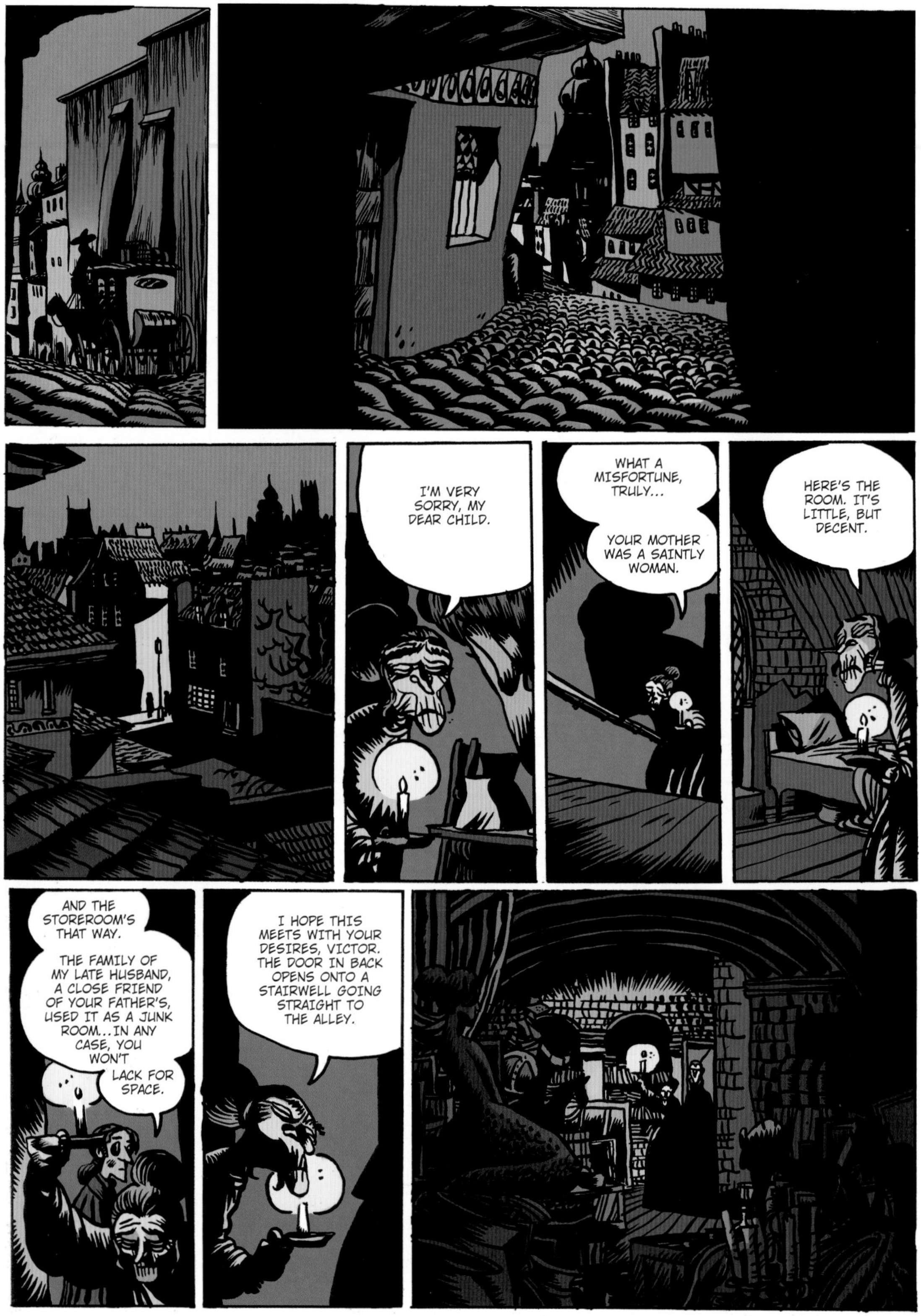
I'M VERY SORRY, MY DEAR CHILD.
WHAT A MISFORTUNE, TRULY...
YOUR MOTHER WAS A SAINTLY WOMAN.
HERE'S THE ROOM. IT'S LITTLE, BUT DECENT.
AND THE STOREROOM'S THAT WAY.
THE FAMILY OF MY LATE HUSBAND, A CLOSE FRIEND OF YOUR FATHER'S, USED IT AS A JUNK ROOM...IN ANY CASE, YOU WON'T
LACK FOR SPACE.
I HOPE THIS MEETS WITH YOUR DESIRES, VICTOR. THE DOOR IN BACK OPENS ONTO A STAIRWELL GOING STRAIGHT TO THE ALLEY.

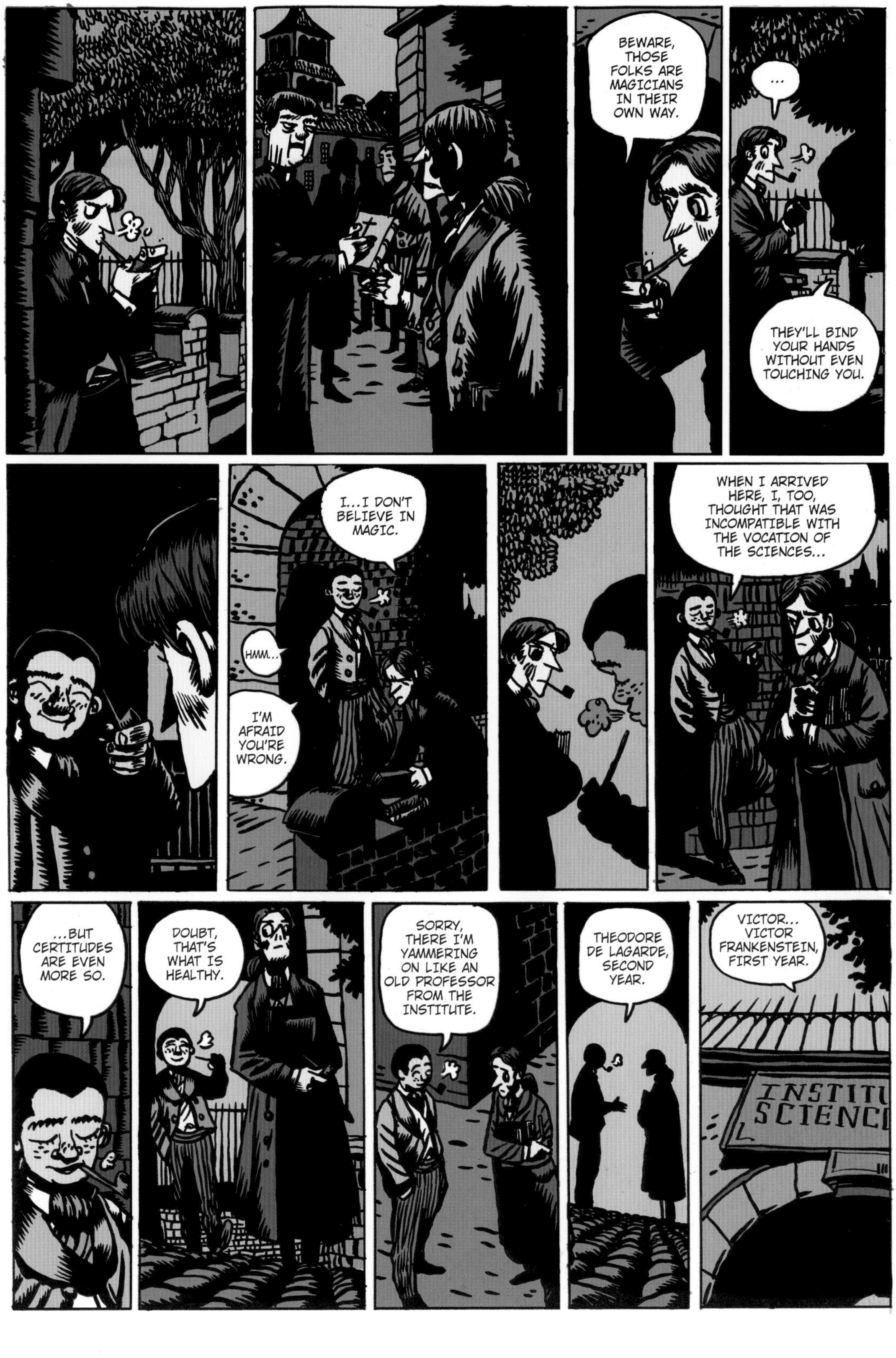
BEWARE, THOSE FOLKS ARE MAGICIANS IN THEIR OWN WAY.
...
THEY'LL BIND YOUR HANDS WITHOUT EVEN TOUCHING YOU.
I...I DON'T BELIEVE IN MAGIC.
HMM...
I'M AFRAID YOU'RE WRONG.
WHEN I ARRIVED HERE, I, TOO, THOUGHT THAT WAS INCOMPATIBLE WITH THE VOCATION OF THE SCIENCES...
...BUT CERTITUDES ARE EVEN MORE SO.
DOUBT, THAT'S WHAT IS HEALTHY.
SORRY, THERE I'M YAMMERING ON LIKE AN OLD PROFESSOR FROM THE INSTITUTE.
THEODORE DE LAGARDE, SECOND YEAR.
VICTOR... VICTOR FRANKENSTEIN, FIRST YEAR.
INSTITU
SCIENC

LASTLY, I'LL CONCLUDE WITH ONE FINAL RECOMMENDATION.

FOR A MAJORITY OF YOU, I'VE LITTLE DOUBT YOU'VE BEEN BLINDED BY THE AMBITION OF THE REVOLUTION...

...BUDDING ALCHEMISTS, DREAMING OF TRANSMUTATION AND IMMORTALITY, IT IS THUS MY DUTY TO WARN YOU... WITH SUCH A FRAME OF MIND, YOU WON'T BE ALLOWED TO REMAIN LONG IN THIS NOBLE PLACE, OUR SCHOOL, THE IMMANENT ANTENNA OF A NEW CENTURY...

... AS ENLIGHTENED AND RESPECTFUL OF TRADITION AS IT CAN BE...

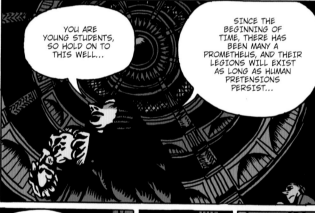

YOU ARE YOUNG STUDENTS, SO HOLD ON TO THIS WELL...

SINCE THE BEGINNING OF TIME, THERE HAS BEEN MANY A PROMETHEUS, AND THEIR LEGIONS WILL EXIST AS LONG AS HUMAN PRETENSIONS PERSIST...

...BUT RESTRAINT AND LEVEL-HEADEDNESS ARE THE PREMIER QUALITIES FOR A SCIENTIST. THEY KEEP HIM FROM SQUANDERING HIMSELF ON MAD AMBITIONS AND BEING DAZZLED BY DISCOVERIES.

NEVER FORGET, YOU YOUNG, FRESH MINDS...

KNOWLEDGE IS POWER ONLY THROUGH GOD.

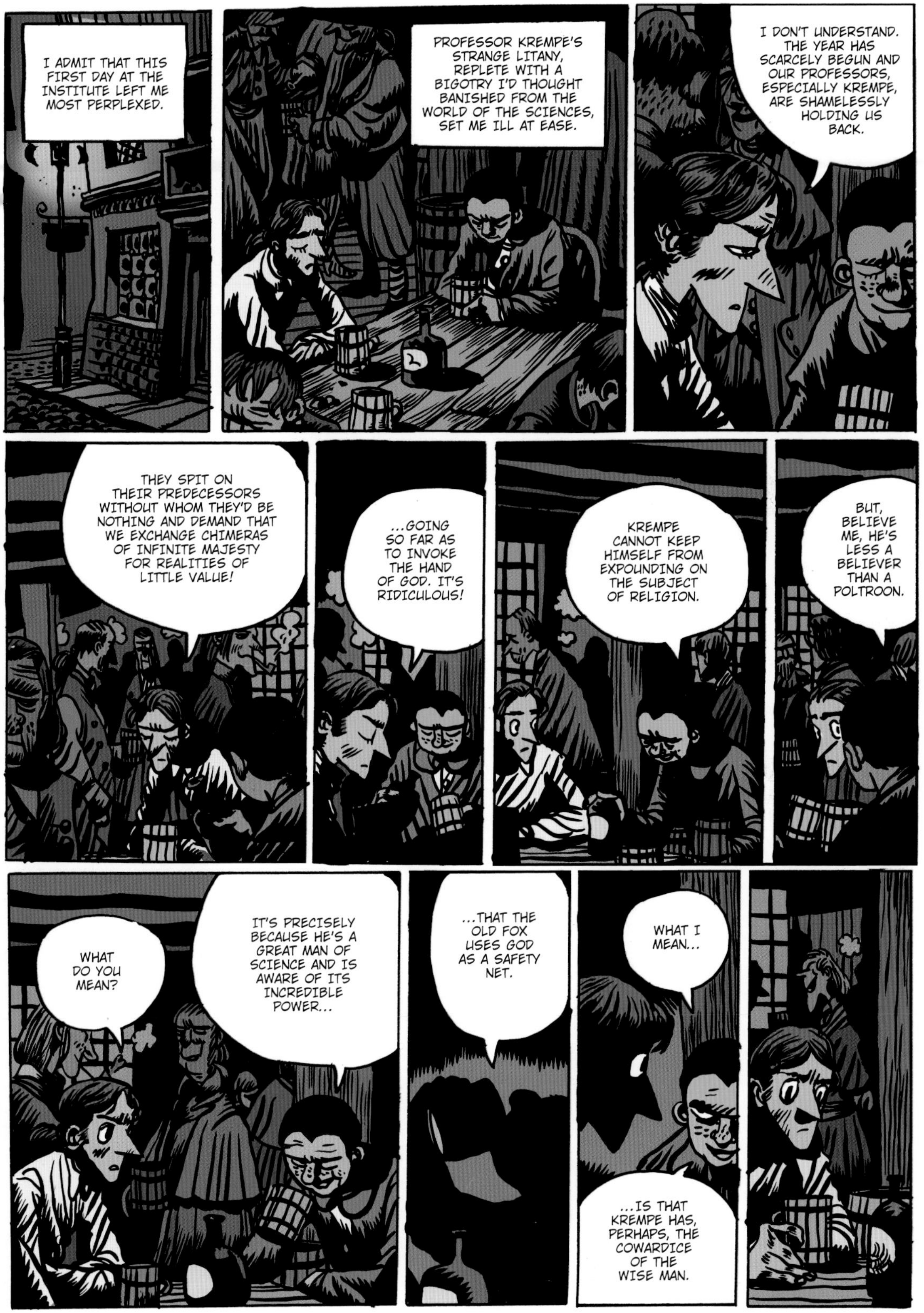
I ADMIT THAT THIS FIRST DAY AT THE INSTITUTE LEFT ME MOST PERPLEXED.
PROFESSOR KREMPE'S STRANGE LITANY, REPLETE WITH A BIGOTRY I'D THOUGHT BANISHED FROM THE WORLD OF THE SCIENCES, SET ME ILL AT EASE.
I DON'T UNDERSTAND. THE YEAR HAS SCARCELY BEGUN AND OUR PROFESSORS, ESPECIALLY KREMPE, ARE SHAMELESSLY HOLDING US BACK.
THEY SPIT ON THEIR PREDECESSORS WITHOUT WHOM THEY'D BE NOTHING AND DEMAND THAT WE EXCHANGE CHIMERAS OF INFINITE MAJESTY FOR REALITIES OF LITTLE VALUE!
...GOING SO FAR AS TO INVOKE THE HAND OF GOD. IT'S RIDICULOUS!
KREMPE CANNOT KEEP HIMSELF FROM EXPOUNDING ON THE SUBJECT OF RELIGION.
BUT, BELIEVE ME, HE'S LESS A BELIEVER THAN A POLTROON.
WHAT DO YOU MEAN?
IT'S PRECISELY BECAUSE HE'S A GREAT MAN OF SCIENCE AND IS AWARE OF ITS INCREDIBLE POWER...
...THAT THE OLD FOX USES GOD AS A SAFETY NET.
WHAT I MEAN...
...IS THAT KREMPE HAS, PERHAPS, THE COWARDICE OF THE WISE MAN.

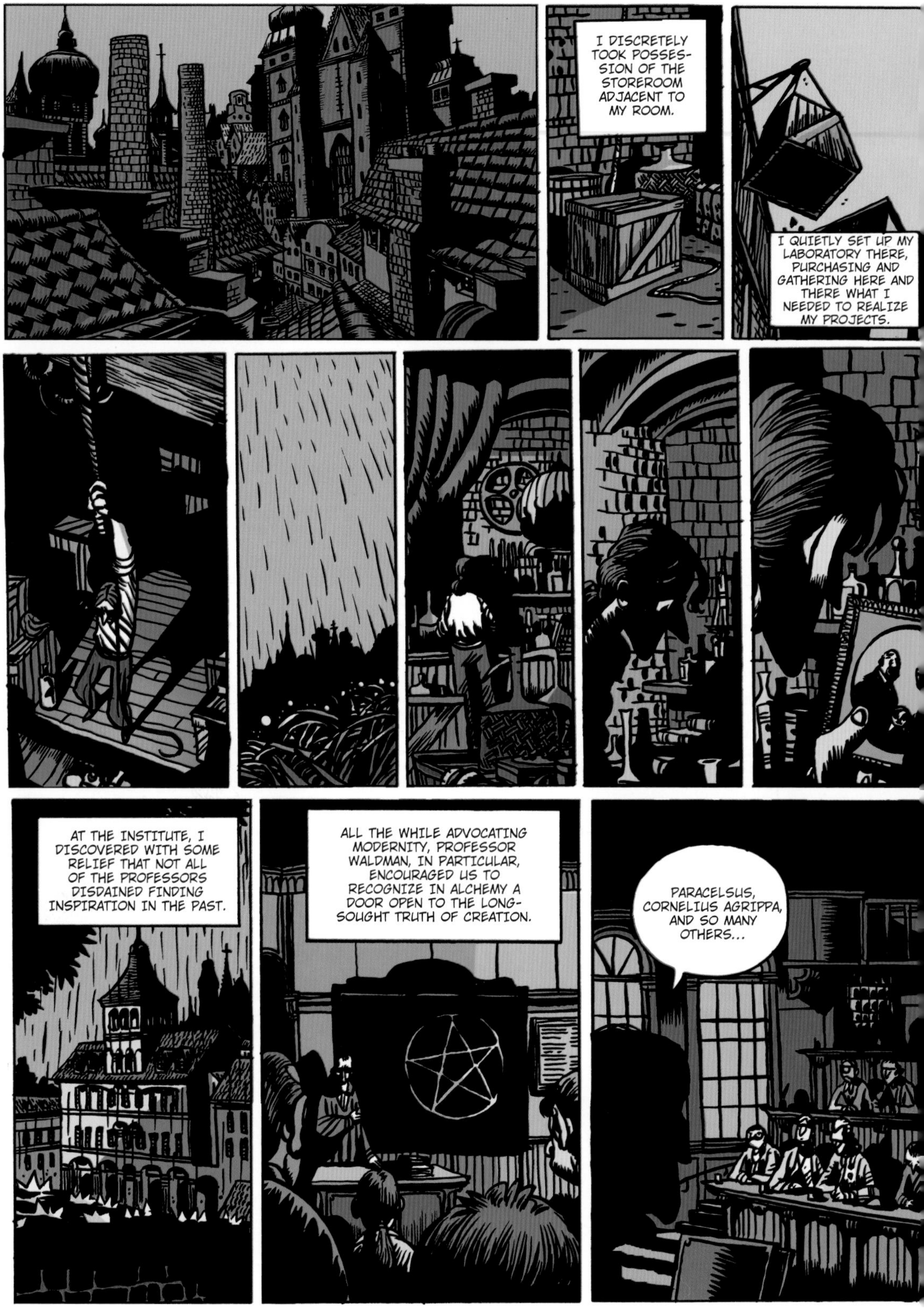
I DISCRETELY TOOK POSSESSION OF THE STOREROOM ADJACENT TO MY ROOM.
I QUIETLY SET UP MY LABORATORY THERE, PURCHASING AND GATHERING HERE AND THERE WHAT I NEEDED TO REALIZE MY PROJECTS.
AT THE INSTITUTE, I DISCOVERED WITH SOME RELIEF THAT NOT ALL OF THE PROFESSORS DISDAINED FINDING INSPIRATION IN THE PAST.
ALL THE WHILE ADVOCATING MODERNITY, PROFESSOR WALDMAN, IN PARTICULAR, ENCOURAGED US TO RECOGNIZE IN ALCHEMY A DOOR OPEN TO THE LONG-SOUGHT TRUTH OF CREATION.
PARACELSUS, CORNELIUS AGRIPPA, AND SO MANY OTHERS...

IT'S TRUE...

THE ANCIENT TEACHERS OF THIS SCIENCE PROMISED IMPOSSIBILITIES AND PERFORMED NOTHING.

THE MODERN MASTERS PROMISE VERY LITTLE. THEY KNOW THAT METALS CANNOT BE TRANSMUTED AND THAT THE ELIXIR OF LIFE IS A CHIMERA.

IT MAY BE THAT THE ALCHEMISTS PROVED NOTHING...

BUT THEY OPENED THE WAY TO THE HEAVENS.

PUSHED BY THEIR THIRST FOR KNOWLEDGE, THEY PENETRATED INTO THE TINIEST RECESSES OF NATURE.

THESE WERE MEN TO WHOSE INDEFATIGABLE ZEAL MODERN PHILOSOPHERS WERE INDEBTED FOR MOST OF THE FOUNDATIONS OF THEIR KNOWLEDGE.

BEING A SCIENTIST TODAY...DOESN'T IMPLY MAKING AN ABSTRACTION OF THE PAST...TO BE THRIFTY ABOUT THE DREAMS THAT PRECEDED US...

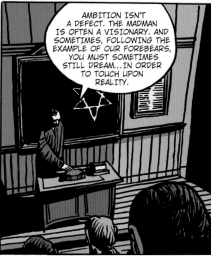

AMBITION ISN'T A DEFECT. THE MADMAN IS OFTEN A VISIONARY. AND SOMETIMES, FOLLOWING THE EXAMPLE OF OUR FOREBEARS, YOU MUST SOMETIMES STILL DREAM...IN ORDER TO TOUCH UPON REALITY.

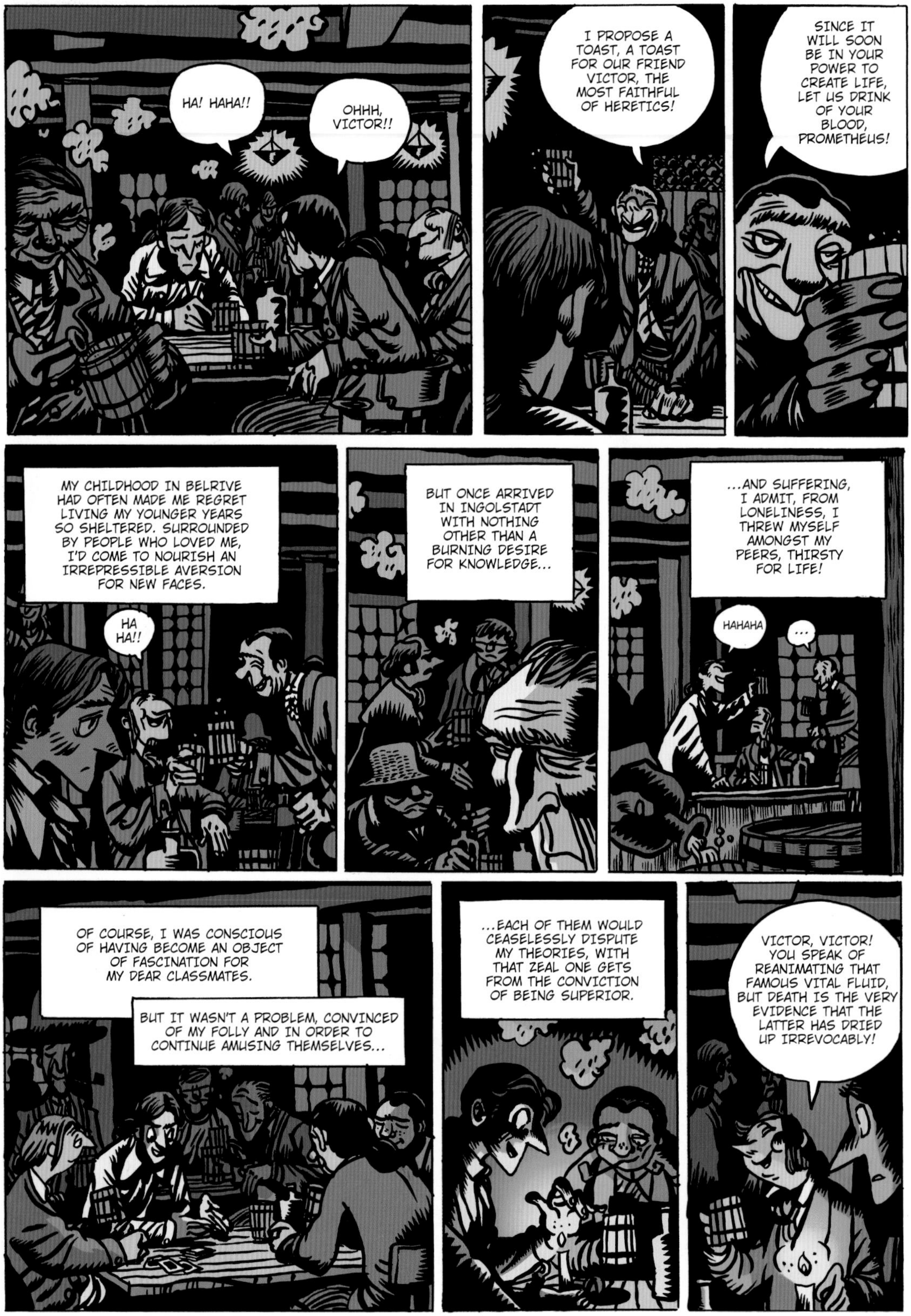
HA! HAHA!!
OHHH, VICTOR!!
I PROPOSE A TOAST, A TOAST FOR OUR FRIEND VICTOR, THE MOST FAITHFUL OF HERETICS!
SINCE IT WILL SOON BE IN YOUR POWER TO CREATE LIFE, LET US DRINK OF YOUR BLOOD, PROMETHEUS!
MY CHILDHOOD IN BELRIVE HAD OFTEN MADE ME REGRET LIVING MY YOUNGER YEARS SO SHELTERED. SURROUNDED BY PEOPLE WHO LOVED ME, I'D COME TO NOURISH AN IRREPRESSIBLE AVERSION FOR NEW FACES.
HA HA!!
BUT ONCE ARRIVED IN INGOLSTADT WITH NOTHING OTHER THAN A BURNING DESIRE FOR KNOWLEDGE...
...AND SUFFERING, I ADMIT, FROM LONELINESS, I THREW MYSELF AMONGST MY PEERS, THIRSTY FOR LIFE!
HAHAHA
...
OF COURSE, I WAS CONSCIOUS OF HAVING BECOME AN OBJECT OF FASCINATION FOR MY DEAR CLASSMATES.
BUT IT WASN'T A PROBLEM, CONVINCED OF MY FOLLY AND IN ORDER TO CONTINUE AMUSING THEMSELVES...
...EACH OF THEM WOULD CEASELESSLY DISPUTE MY THEORIES, WITH THAT ZEAL ONE GETS FROM THE CONVICTION OF BEING SUPERIOR.
VICTOR, VICTOR! YOU SPEAK OF REANIMATING THAT FAMOUS VITAL FLUID, BUT DEATH IS THE VERY EVIDENCE THAT THE LATTER HAS DRIED UP IRREVOCABLY!

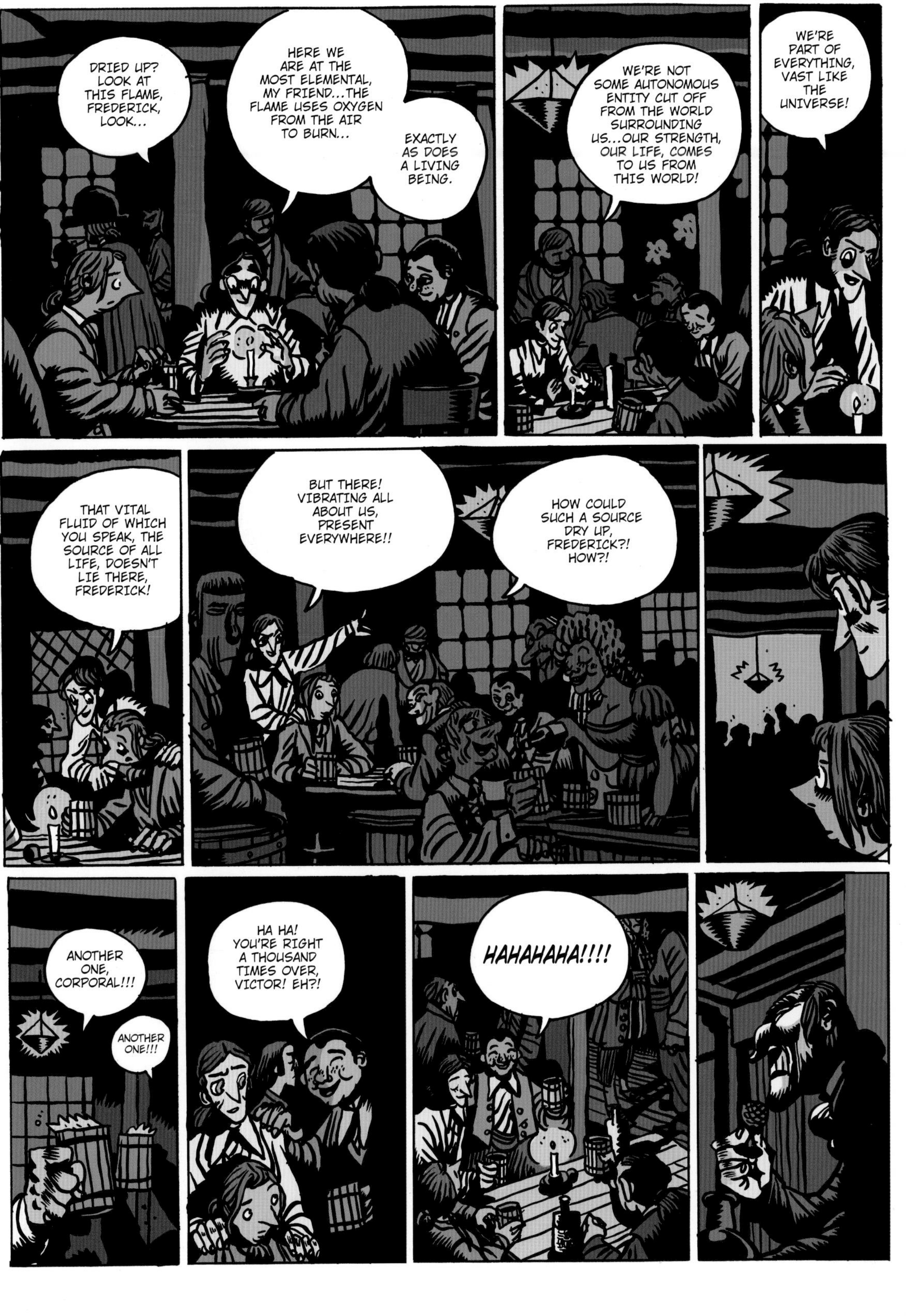
DRIED UP? LOOK AT THIS FLAME, FREDERICK, LOOK...
HERE WE ARE AT THE MOST ELEMENTAL, MY FRIEND...THE FLAME USES OXYGEN FROM THE AIR TO BURN...
EXACTLY AS DOES A LIVING BEING.
WE'RE NOT SOME AUTONOMOUS ENTITY CUT OFF FROM THE WORLD SURROUNDING US...OUR STRENGTH, OUR LIFE, COMES TO US FROM THIS WORLD!
WE'RE PART OF EVERYTHING, VAST LIKE THE UNIVERSE!
THAT VITAL FLUID OF WHICH YOU SPEAK, THE SOURCE OF ALL LIFE, DOESN'T LIE THERE, FREDERICK!
BUT THERE! VIBRATING ALL ABOUT US, PRESENT EVERYWHERE!!
HOW COULD SUCH A SOURCE DRY UP, FREDERICK?! HOW?!
ANOTHER ONE, CORPORAL!!!
ANOTHER ONE!!!
HA HA! YOU'RE RIGHT A THOUSAND TIMES OVER, VICTOR! EH?!
HAHAHAHA!!!!

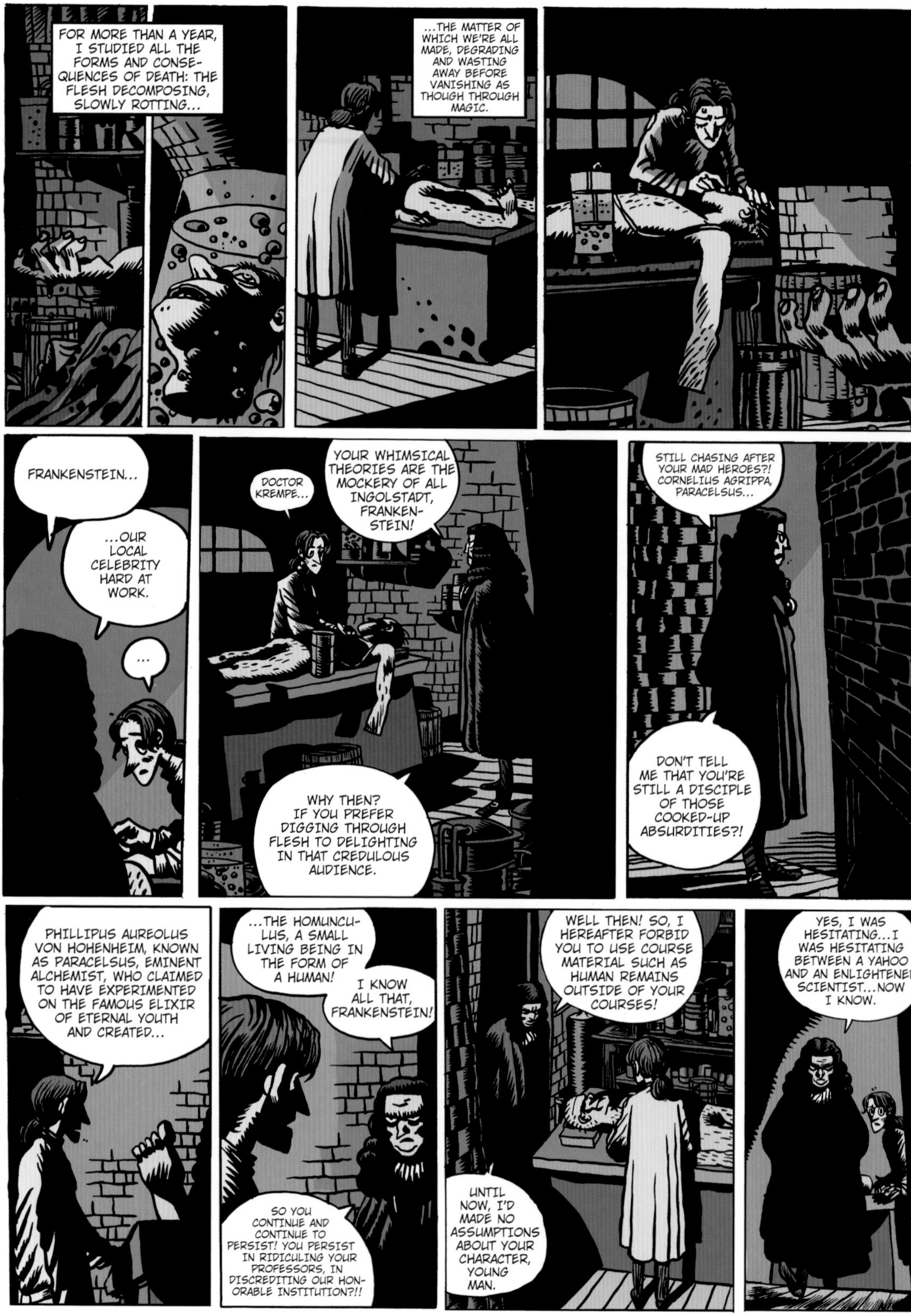
FOR MORE THAN A YEAR, I STUDIED ALL THE FORMS AND CONSEQUENCES OF DEATH: THE FLESH DECOMPOSING, SLOWLY ROTTING...
...THE MATTER OF WHICH WE'RE ALL MADE, DEGRADING AND WASTING AWAY BEFORE VANISHING AS THOUGH THROUGH MAGIC.
FRANKENSTEIN...
...OUR LOCAL CELEBRITY HARD AT WORK.
...
DOCTOR KREMPE...
YOUR WHIMSICAL THEORIES ARE THE MOCKERY OF ALL INGOLSTADT, FRANKENSTEIN!
WHY THEN? IF YOU PREFER DIGGING THROUGH FLESH TO DELIGHTING IN THAT CREDULOUS AUDIENCE.
STILL CHASING AFTER YOUR MAD HEROES?! CORNELIUS AGRIPPA, PARACELSUS...
DON'T TELL ME THAT YOU'RE STILL A DISCIPLE OF THOSE COOKED-UP ABSURDITIES?!
PHILLIPUS AUREOLUS VON HOHENHEIM, KNOWN AS PARACELSUS, EMINENT ALCHEMIST, WHO CLAIMED TO HAVE EXPERIMENTED ON THE FAMOUS ELIXIR OF ETERNAL YOUTH AND CREATED...
...THE HOMUNCULUS, A SMALL LIVING BEING IN THE FORM OF A HUMAN!
I KNOW ALL THAT, FRANKENSTEIN!
SO YOU CONTINUE AND CONTINUE TO PERSIST! YOU PERSIST IN RIDICULING YOUR PROFESSORS, IN DISCREDITING OUR HONORABLE INSTITUTION?!!
WELL THEN! SO, I HEREAFTER FORBID YOU TO USE COURSE MATERIAL SUCH AS HUMAN REMAINS OUTSIDE OF YOUR COURSES!
UNTIL NOW, I'D MADE NO ASSUMPTIONS ABOUT YOUR CHARACTER, YOUNG MAN.
YES, I WAS HESITATING...I WAS HESITATING BETWEEN A YAHOO AND AN ENLIGHTENED SCIENTIST...NOW I KNOW.

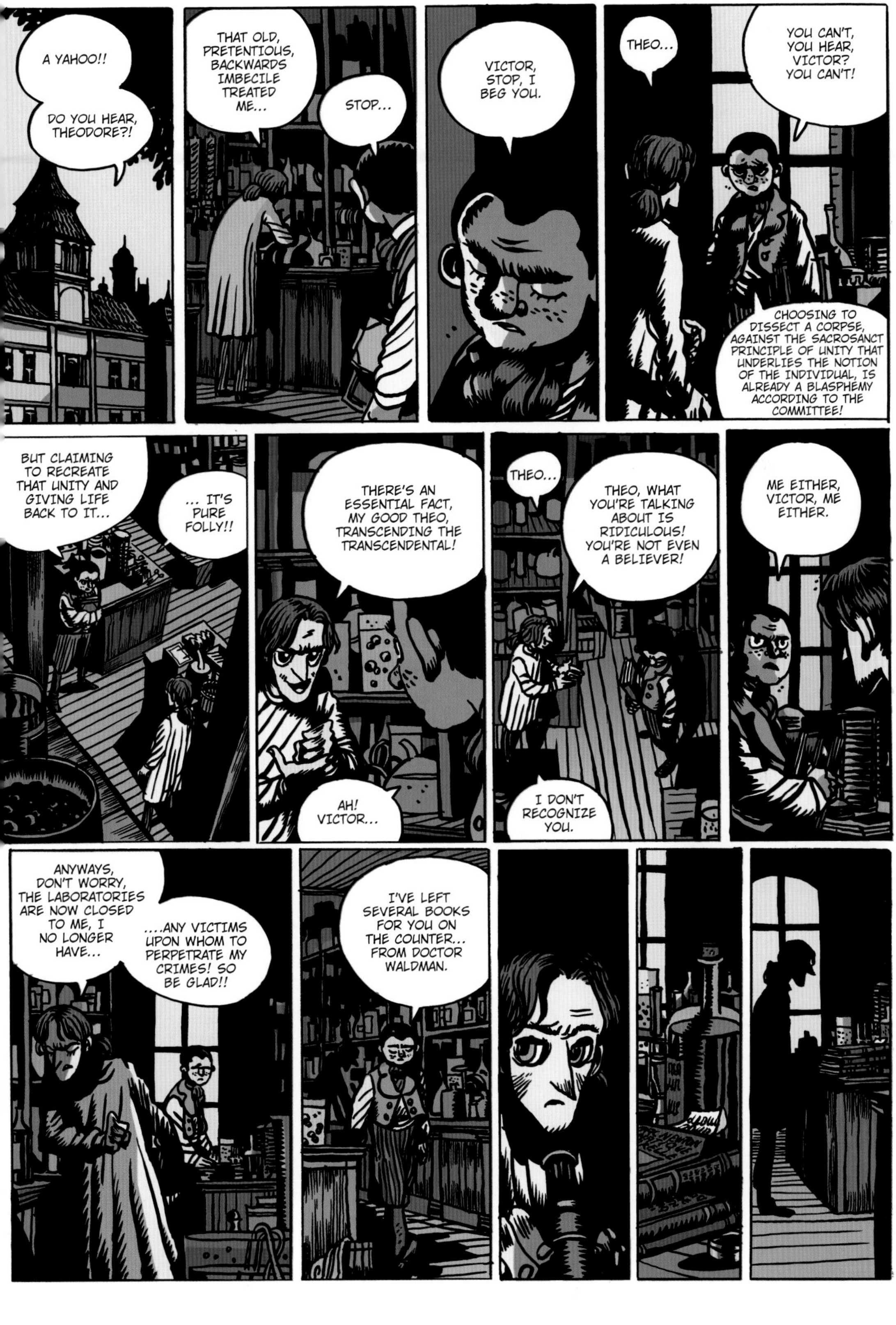
A YAHOO!!
DO YOU HEAR, THEODORE?!
THAT OLD, PRETENTIOUS, BACKWARDS IMBECILE TREATED ME...
STOP...
VICTOR, STOP, I BEG YOU.
THEO...
YOU CAN'T, YOU HEAR, VICTOR? YOU CAN'T!
CHOOSING TO DISSECT A CORPSE, AGAINST THE SACROSANCT PRINCIPLE OF UNITY THAT UNDERLIES THE NOTION OF THE INDIVIDUAL, IS ALREADY A BLASPHEMY ACCORDING TO THE COMMITTEE!
BUT CLAIMING TO RECREATE THAT UNITY AND GIVING LIFE BACK TO IT...
... IT'S PURE FOLLY!!
THERE'S AN ESSENTIAL FACT, MY GOOD THEO, TRANSCENDING THE TRANSCENDENTAL!
AH! VICTOR...
THEO...
THEO, WHAT YOU'RE TALKING ABOUT IS RIDICULOUS! YOU'RE NOT EVEN A BELIEVER!
I DON'T RECOGNIZE YOU.
ME EITHER, VICTOR, ME EITHER.
ANYWAYS, DON'T WORRY, THE LABORATORIES ARE NOW CLOSED TO ME, I NO LONGER HAVE...
....ANY VICTIMS UPON WHOM TO PERPETRATE MY CRIMES! SO BE GLAD!!
I'VE LEFT SEVERAL BOOKS FOR YOU ON THE COUNTER... FROM DOCTOR WALDMAN.

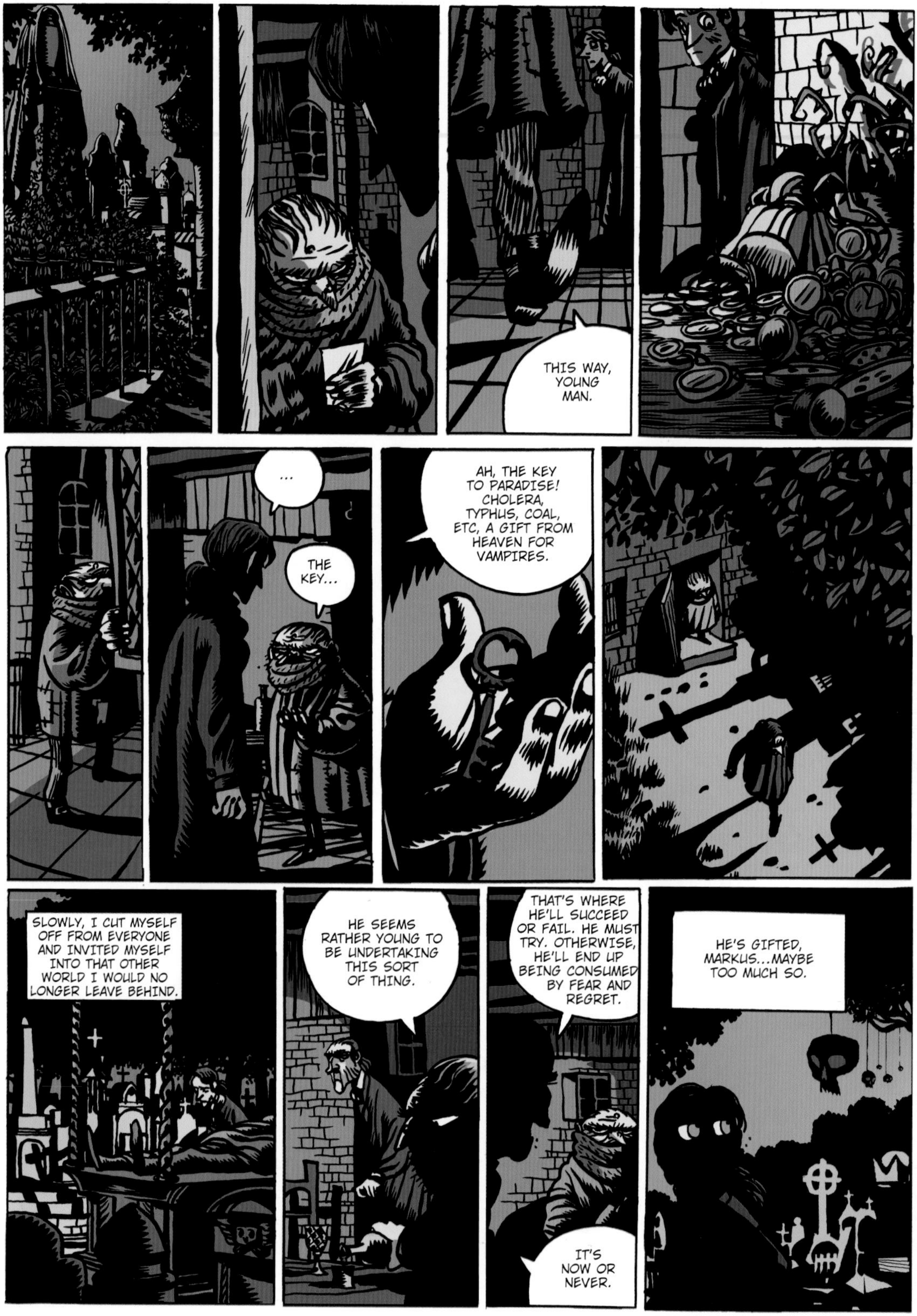
THIS WAY, YOUNG MAN.
...
THE KEY...
AH, THE KEY TO PARADISE! CHOLERA, TYPHUS, COAL, ETC, A GIFT FROM HEAVEN FOR VAMPIRES.
SLOWLY, I CUT MYSELF OFF FROM EVERYONE AND INVITED MYSELF INTO THAT OTHER WORLD I WOULD NO LONGER LEAVE BEHIND.
HE SEEMS RATHER YOUNG TO BE UNDERTAKING THIS SORT OF THING.
THAT'S WHERE HE'LL SUCCEED OR FAIL. HE MUST TRY. OTHERWISE, HE'LL END UP BEING CONSUMED BY FEAR AND REGRET.
IT'S NOW OR NEVER.
HE'S GIFTED, MARKUS...MAYBE TOO MUCH SO.

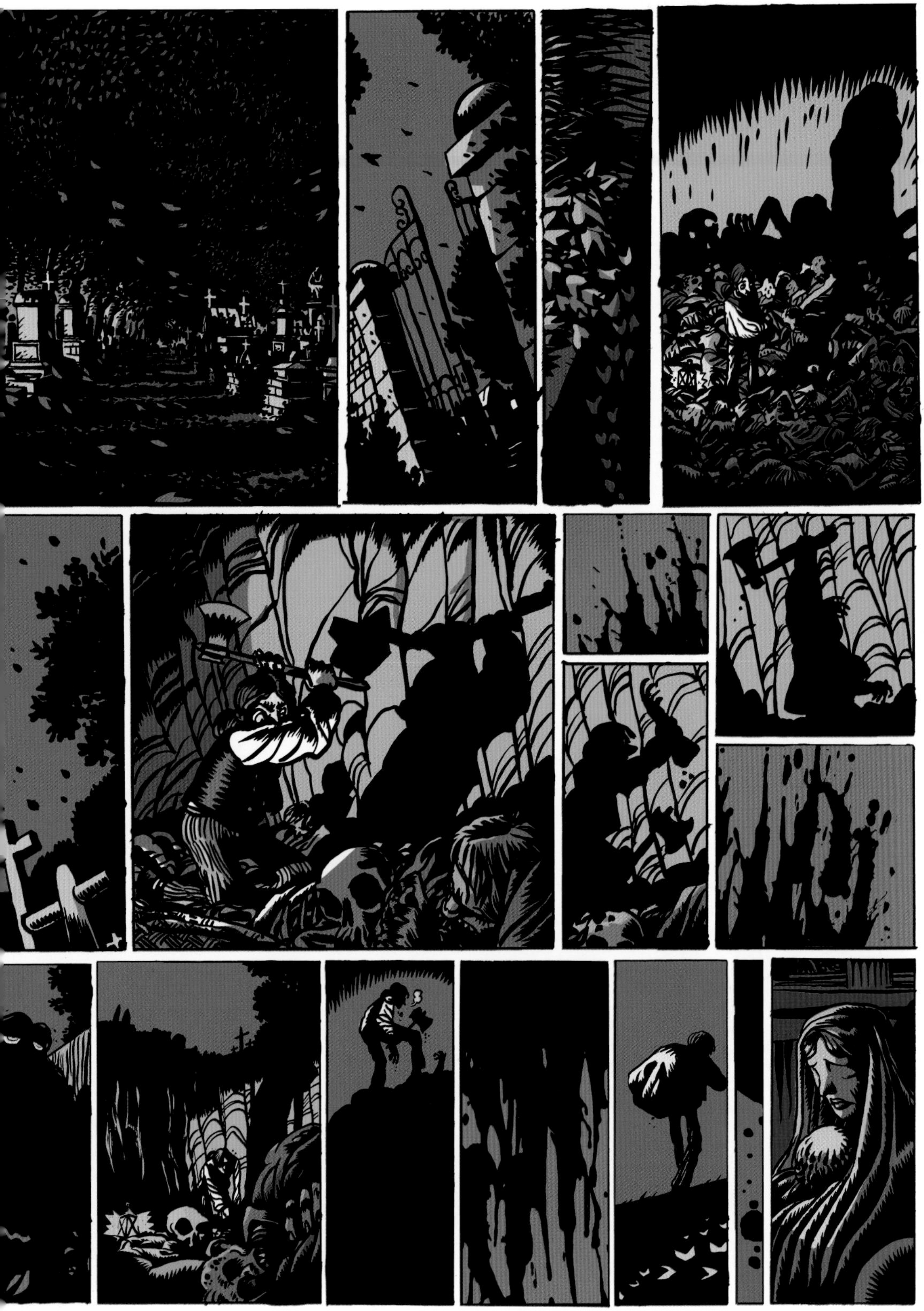

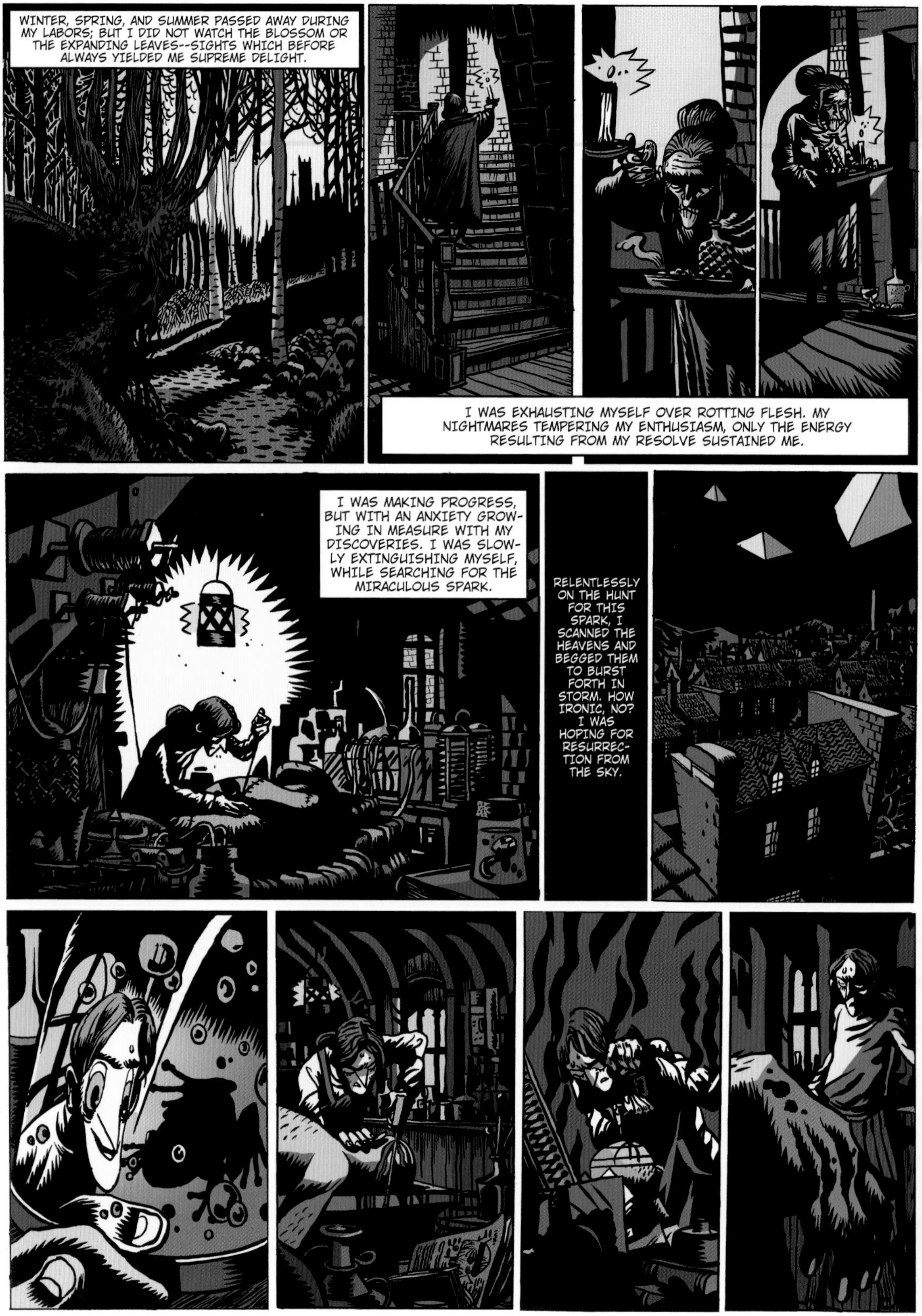

WINTER, SPRING, AND SUMMER PASSED AWAY DURING MY LABORS; BUT I DID NOT WATCH THE BLOSSOM OR THE EXPANDING LEAVES--SIGHTS WHICH BEFORE ALWAYS YIELDED ME SUPREME DELIGHT.
I WAS EXHAUSTING MYSELF OVER ROTTING FLESH. MY NIGHTMARES TEMPERING MY ENTHUSIASM, ONLY THE ENERGY RESULTING FROM MY RESOLVE SUSTAINED ME.
I WAS MAKING PROGRESS, BUT WITH AN ANXIETY GROWING IN MEASURE WITH MY DISCOVERIES. I WAS SLOWLY EXTINGUISHING MYSELF, WHILE SEARCHING FOR THE MIRACULOUS SPARK.
RELENTLESSLY ON THE HUNT FOR THIS SPARK, I SCANNED THE HEAVENS AND BEGGED THEM TO BURST FORTH IN STORM. HOW IRONIC, NO? I WAS HOPING FOR RESURRECTION FROM THE SKY.

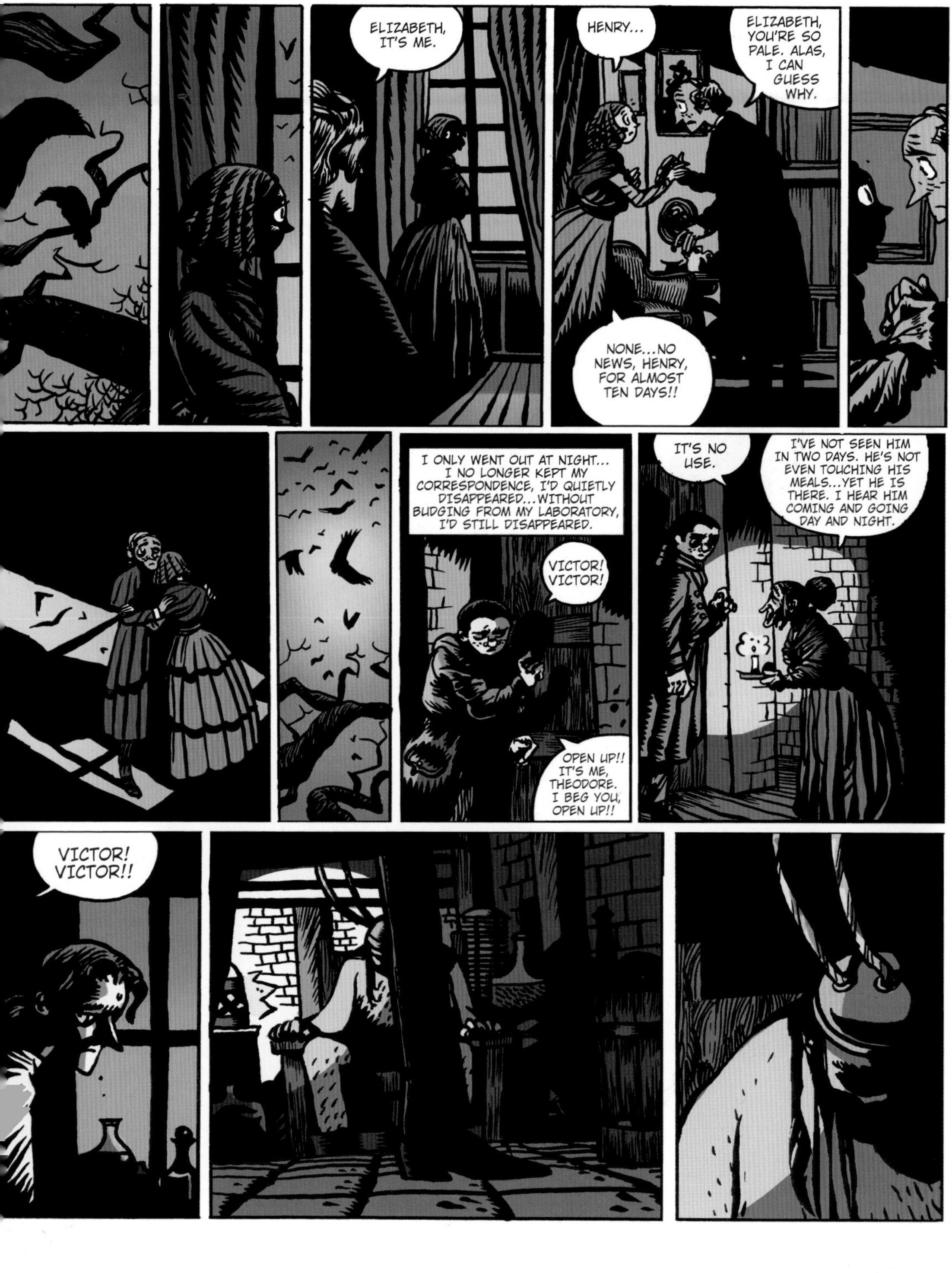
ELIZABETH, IT'S ME.
HENRY...
ELIZABETH, YOU'RE SO PALE. ALAS, I CAN GUESS WHY.
NONE...NO NEWS, HENRY, FOR ALMOST TEN DAYS!!
I ONLY WENT OUT AT NIGHT... I NO LONGER KEPT MY CORRESPONDENCE, I'D QUIETLY DISAPPEARED...WITHOUT BUDGING FROM MY LABORATORY, I'D STILL DISAPPEARED.
VICTOR! VICTOR!
OPEN UP!! IT'S ME, THEODORE. I BEG YOU, OPEN UP!!
IT'S NO USE.
I'VE NOT SEEN HIM IN TWO DAYS. HE'S NOT EVEN TOUCHING HIS MEALS...YET HE IS THERE. I HEAR HIM COMING AND GOING DAY AND NIGHT.
VICTOR! VICTOR!!

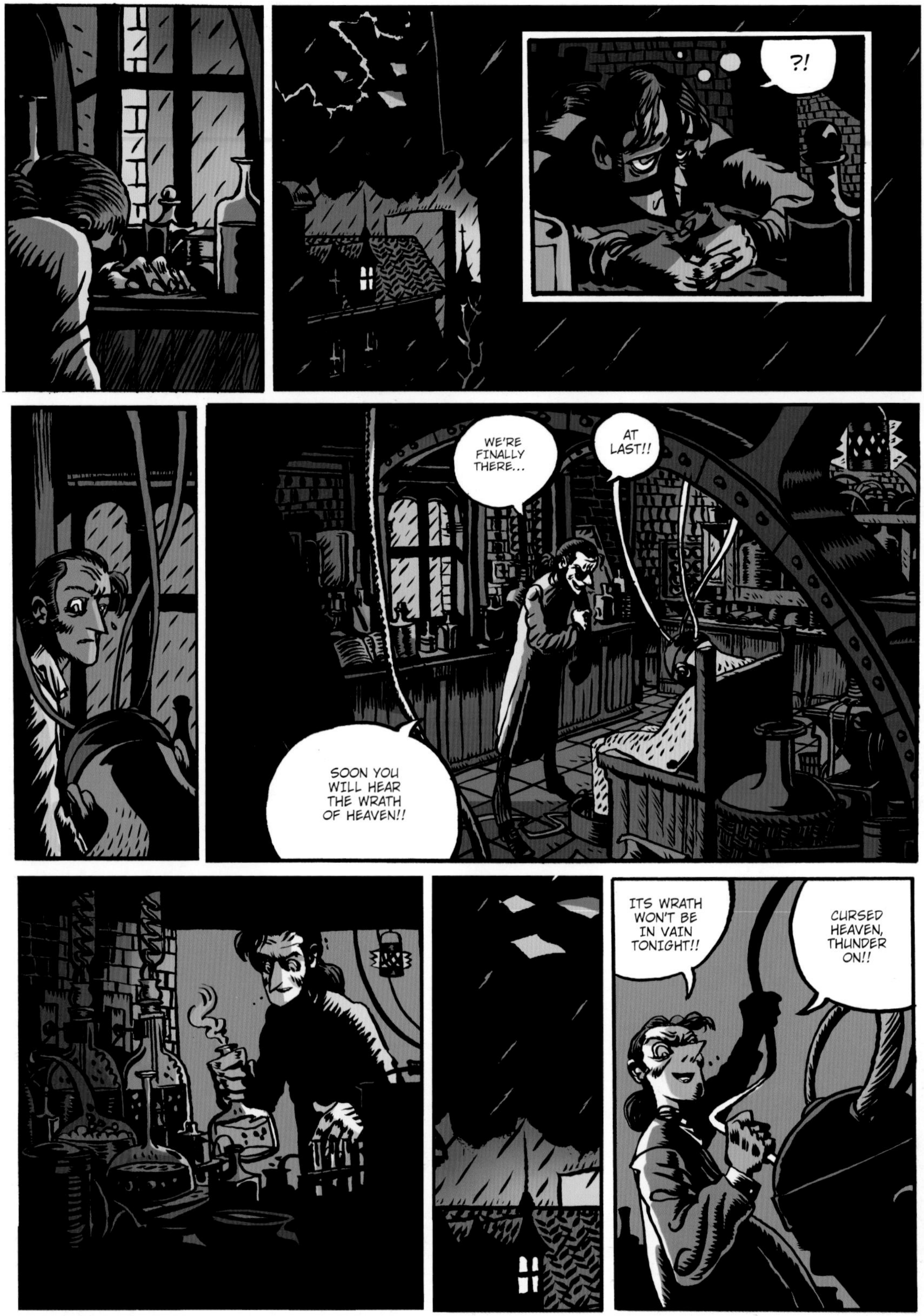
?!
WE'RE FINALLY THERE...
AT LAST!!
SOON YOU WILL HEAR THE WRATH OF HEAVEN!!
ITS WRATH WON'T BE IN VAIN TONIGHT!!
CURSED HEAVEN, THUNDER ON!!

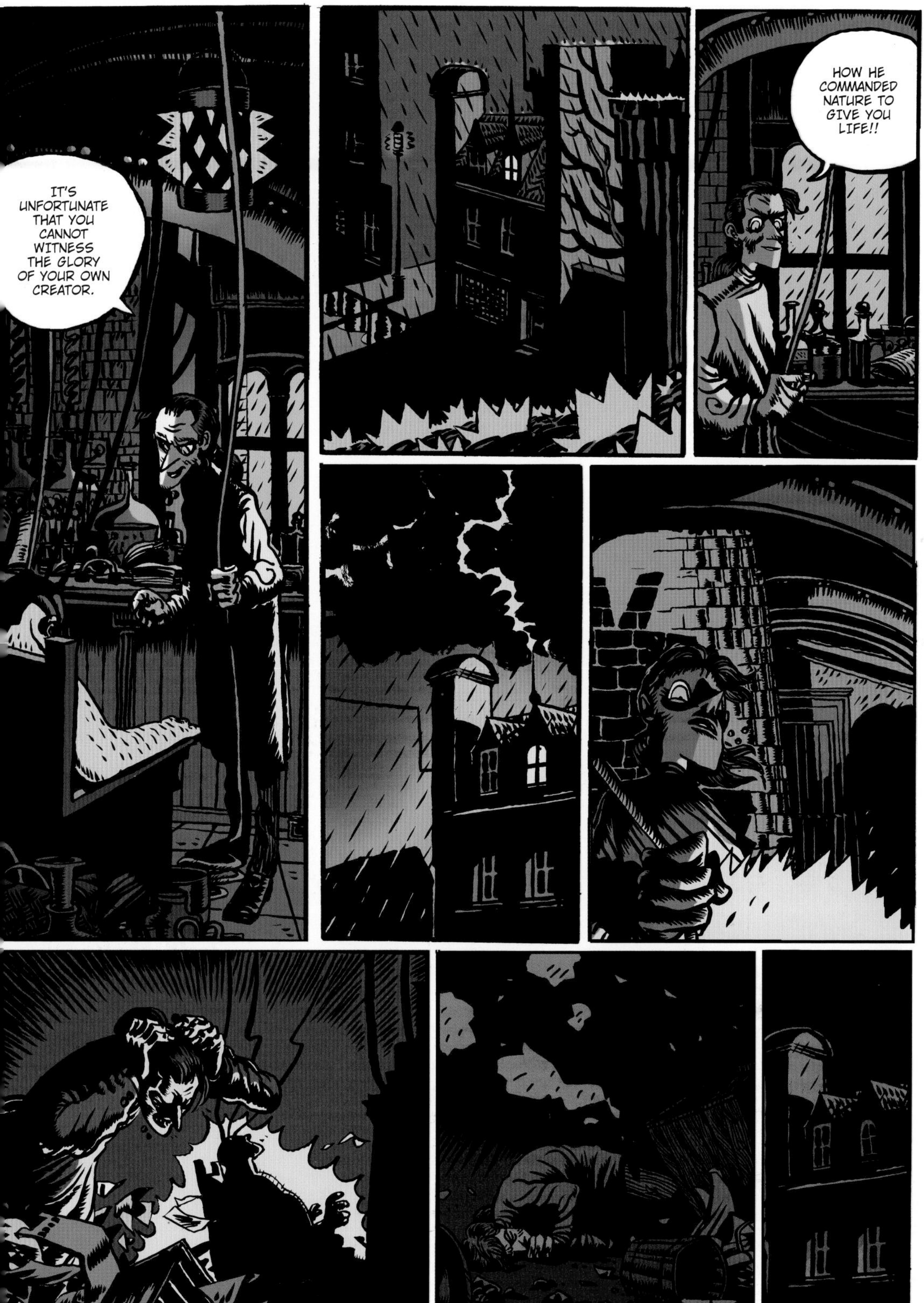
IT'S UNFORTUNATE THAT YOU CANNOT WITNESS THE GLORY OF YOUR OWN CREATOR.
HOW HE COMMANDED NATURE TO GIVE YOU LIFE!!

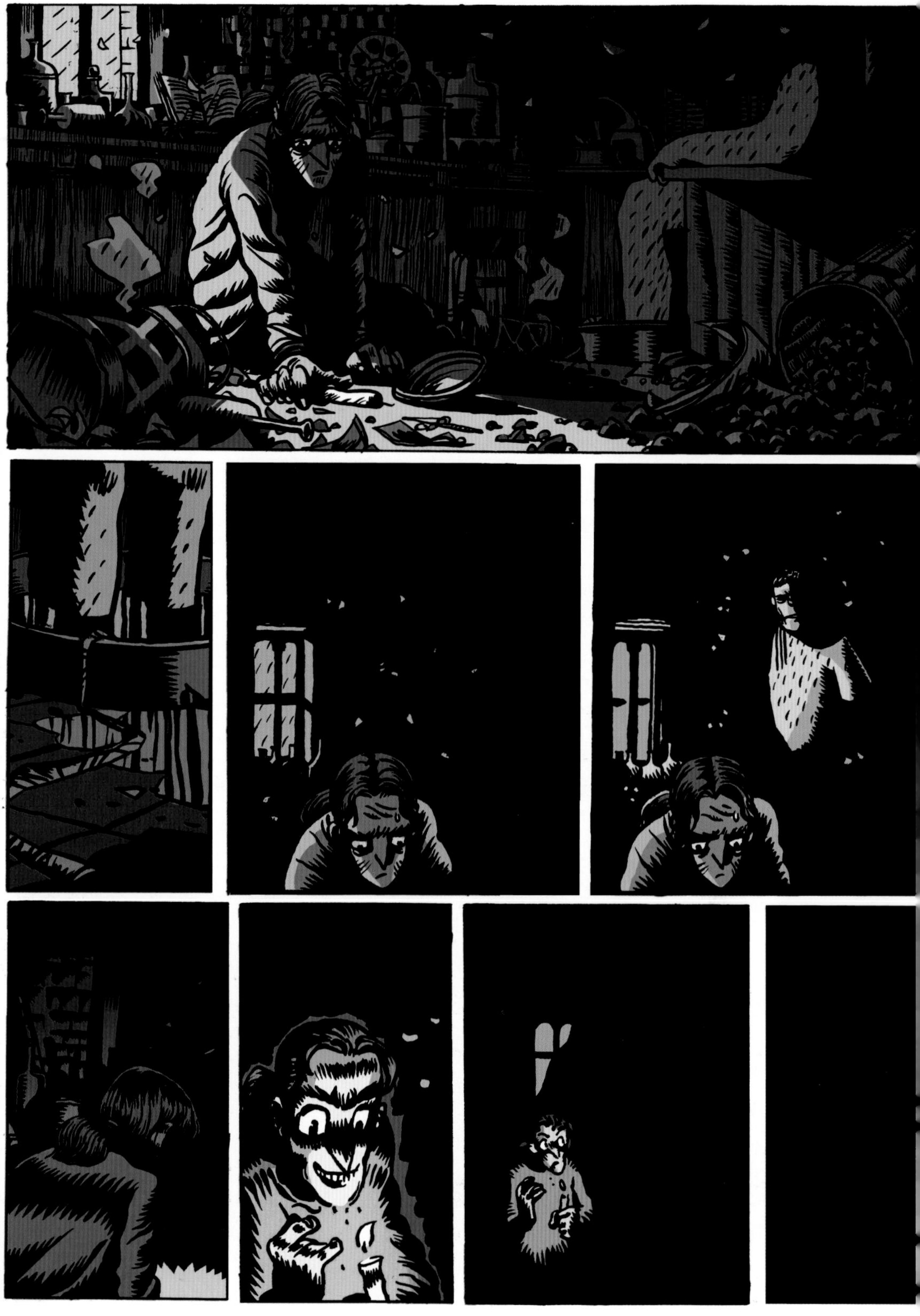

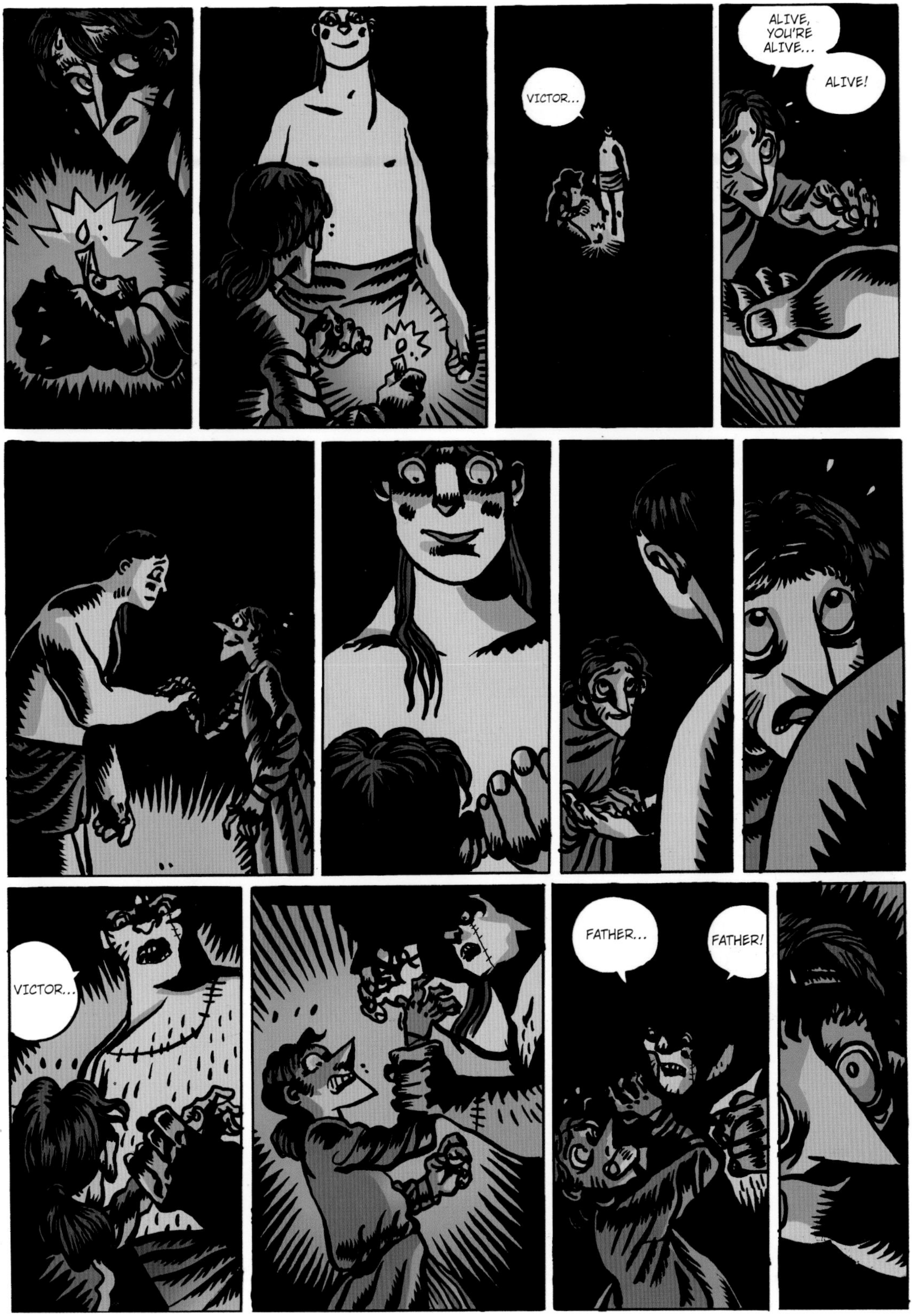
VICTOR...
ALIVE, YOU'RE ALIVE...
ALIVE!
VICTOR...
FATHER...
FATHER!

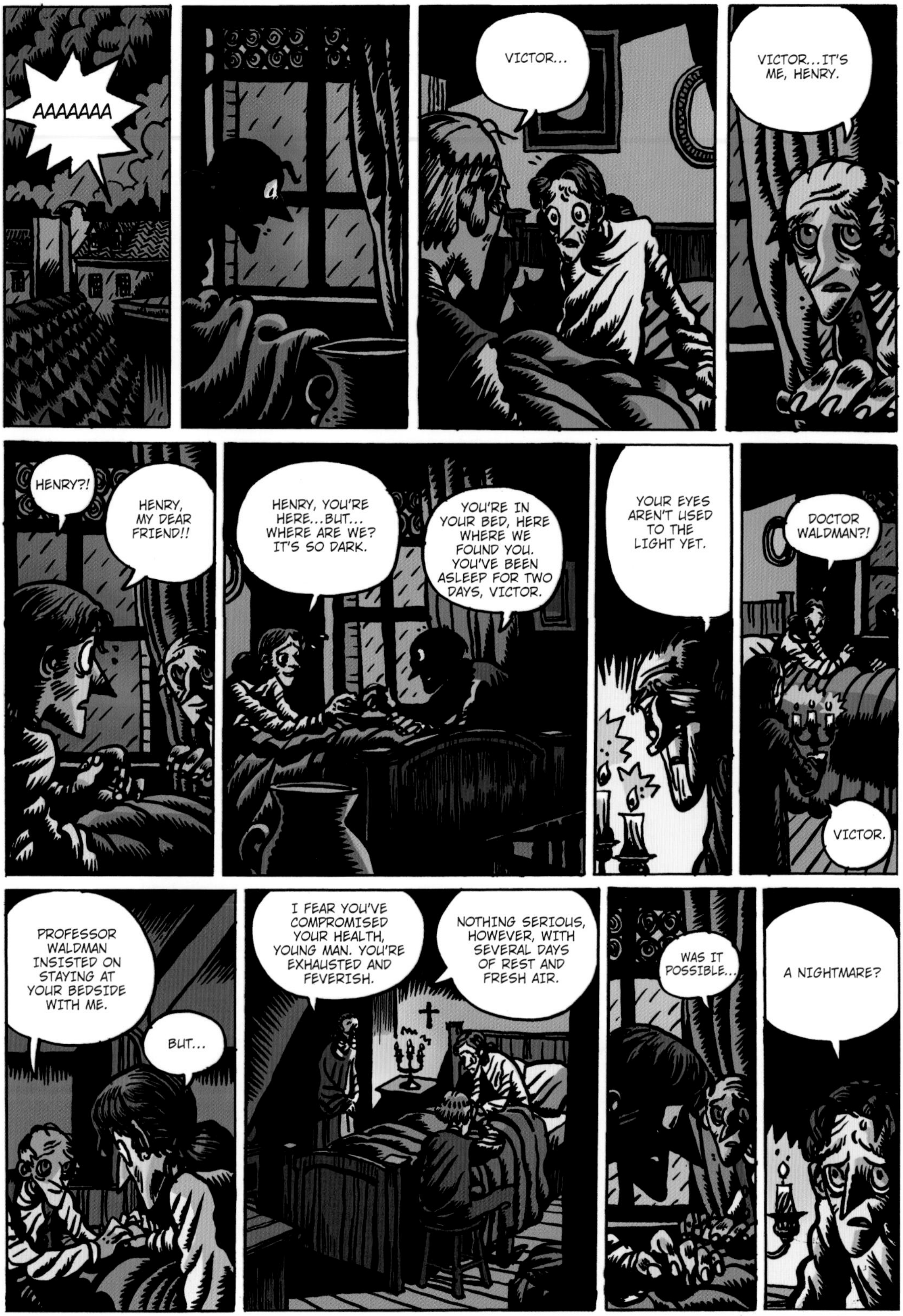
AAAAAAA
VICTOR...
VICTOR...IT'S ME, HENRY.
HENRY?!
HENRY, MY DEAR FRIEND!!
HENRY, YOU'RE HERE...BUT... WHERE ARE WE? IT'S SO DARK.
YOU'RE IN YOUR BED, HERE WHERE WE FOUND YOU. YOU'VE BEEN ASLEEP FOR TWO DAYS, VICTOR.
YOUR EYES AREN'T USED TO THE LIGHT YET.
DOCTOR WALDMAN?!
VICTOR.
PROFESSOR WALDMAN INSISTED ON STAYING AT YOUR BEDSIDE WITH ME.
BUT...
I FEAR YOU'VE COMPROMISED YOUR HEALTH, YOUNG MAN. YOU'RE EXHAUSTED AND FEVERISH.
NOTHING SERIOUS, HOWEVER, WITH SEVERAL DAYS OF REST AND FRESH AIR.
WAS IT POSSIBLE...
A NIGHTMARE?

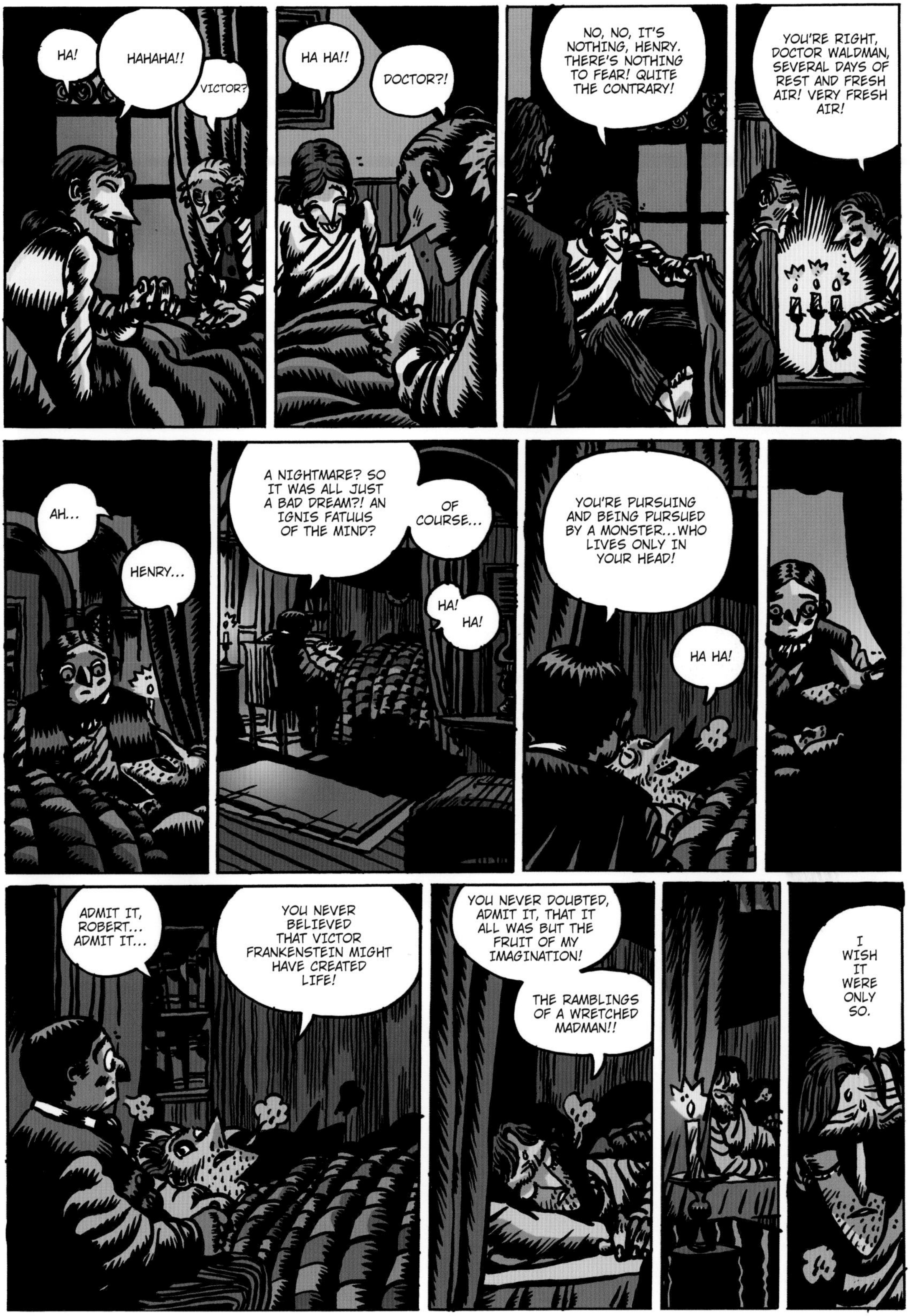
HA!
HAHAHA!!
VICTOR?
HA HA!!
DOCTOR?!
NO, NO, IT'S NOTHING, HENRY. THERE'S NOTHING TO FEAR! QUITE THE CONTRARY!
YOU'RE RIGHT, DOCTOR WALDMAN, SEVERAL DAYS OF REST AND FRESH AIR! VERY FRESH AIR!
AH...
HENRY...
A NIGHTMARE? SO IT WAS ALL JUST A BAD DREAM?! AN IGNIS FATUUS OF THE MIND?
OF COURSE...
HA!
HA!
YOU'RE PURSUING AND BEING PURSUED BY A MONSTER...WHO LIVES ONLY IN YOUR HEAD!
HA HA!
ADMIT IT, ROBERT... ADMIT IT...
YOU NEVER BELIEVED THAT VICTOR FRANKENSTEIN MIGHT HAVE CREATED LIFE!
YOU NEVER DOUBTED, ADMIT IT, THAT IT ALL WAS BUT THE FRUIT OF MY IMAGINATION!
THE RAMBLINGS OF A WRETCHED MADMAN!!
I WISH IT WERE ONLY SO.

HENRY STAYED AT MY BEDSIDE THE LENGTH OF MY CONVALESCENCE. THAT DAY, I PERSUADED HENRY TO MAKE AN OUT-ING, THAT INGOLSTADT'S OUTDOORS WOULD BE BENEFICIAL TO ME.

YOUR FEVER HAS SUBSIDED.

IT WAS A PRETEXT TO GET OUT OF MY BED AND HAVE A CHANCE TO VISIT MY LABORATORY, ABANDONED SINCE THAT NIGHTMARISH NIGHT.

THE IRONY, ROBERT, IS THAT AT THE MOMENT WHEN I WAS OPENING THE LABORATORY DOOR, I'D MADE THE DECISION TO ABANDON MY MAD RESEARCH...

...AND I WAS CONGRATULATING MYSELF FOR HAVING DONE SO BEFORE IT WAS TOO LATE.

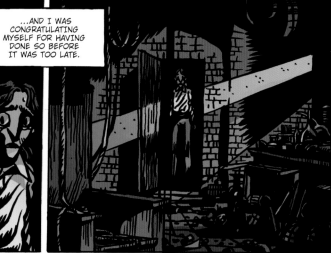

VICTOR?

I CONFESSED NOTHING TO HENRY, IT WAS USE-LESS TO DO SO. IN ANY CASE, I'D NOT HAVE FOUND THE STRENGTH TO PERSUADE HIM...

...NOT BELIEVING IT MYSELF.

MY FRIEND DECIDED TO TAKE ME BACK TO GENEVA, PERSUADED THAT AT THAT JUNCTURE, THE AFFECTIONS OF MY LOVED ONES WAS THE BEST REMEDY FOR MY STRANGE AFFLICTION.

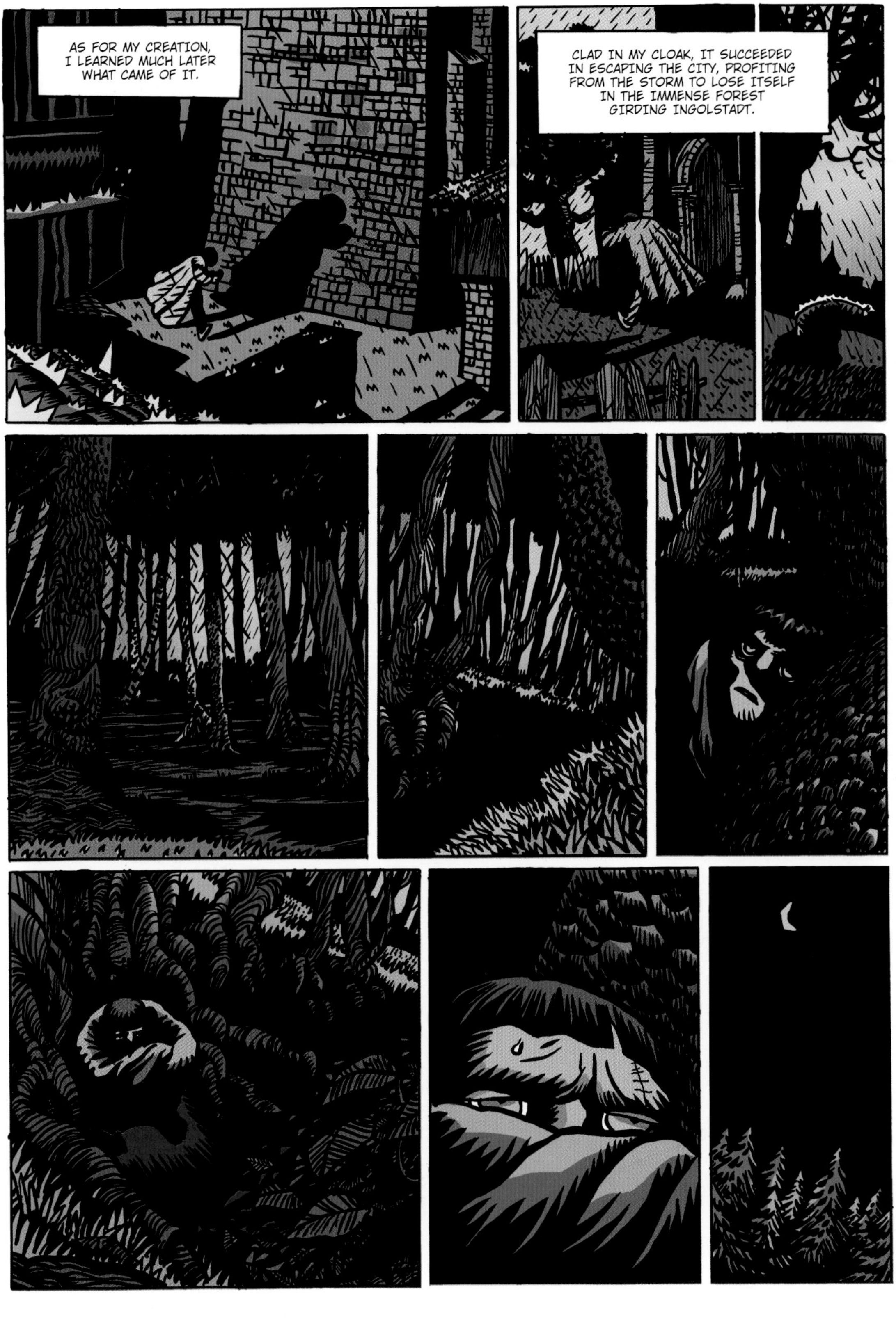
AS FOR MY CREATION, I LEARNED MUCH LATER WHAT CAME OF IT.
CLAD IN MY CLOAK, IT SUCCEEDED IN ESCAPING THE CITY, PROFITING FROM THE STORM TO LOSE ITSELF IN THE IMMENSE FOREST GIRDING INGOLSTADT.

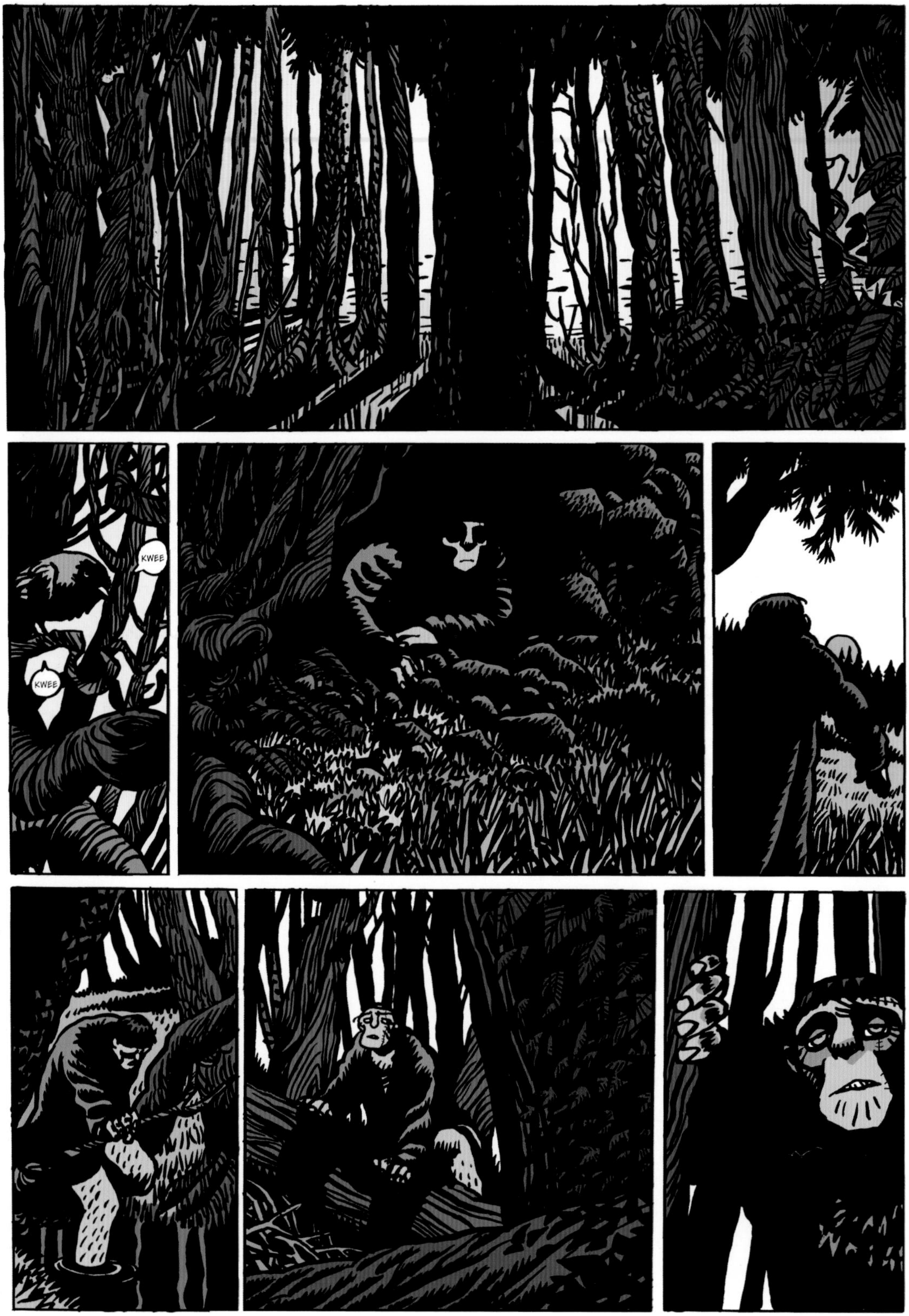
KWEE
KWEE

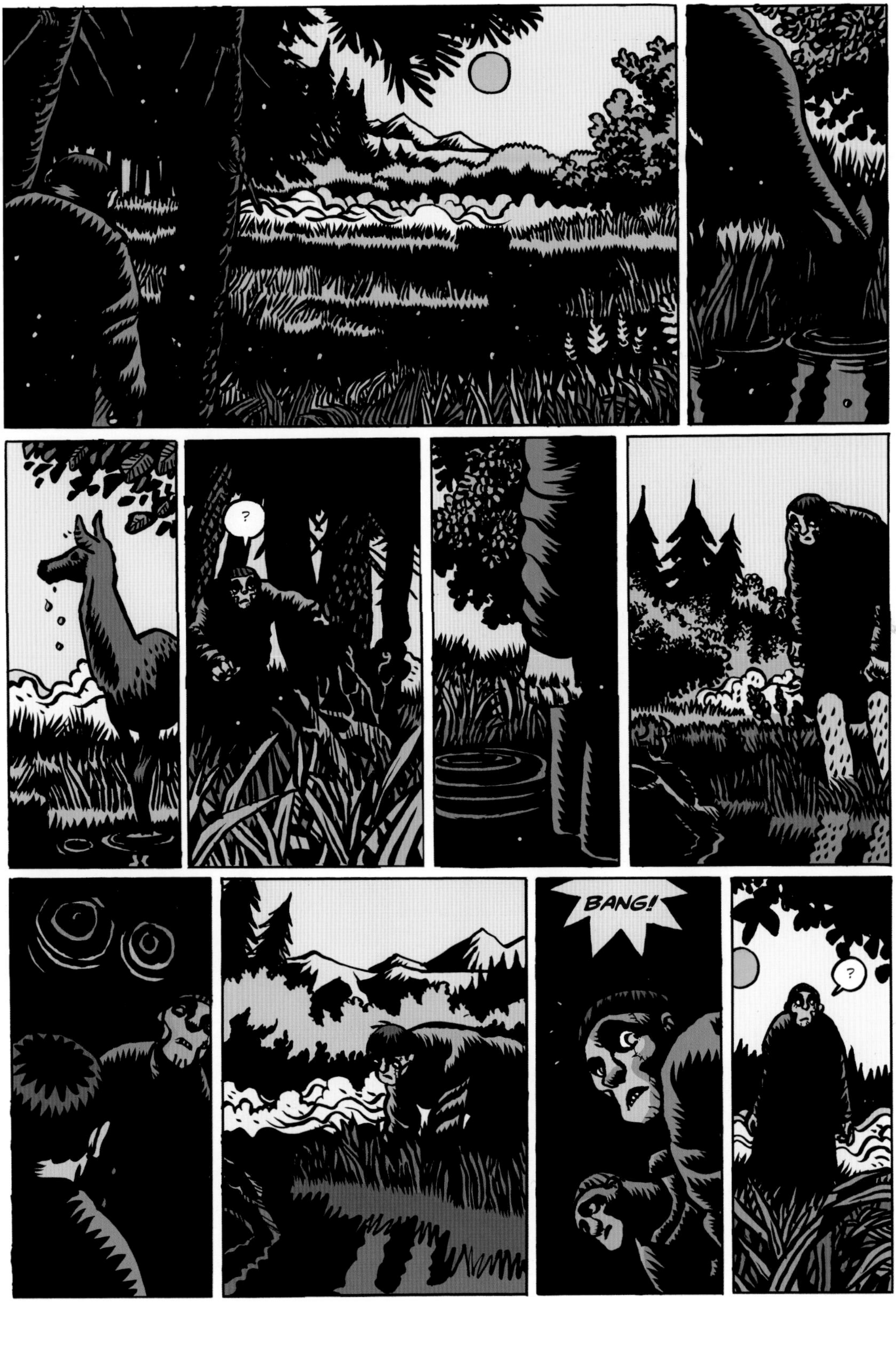
?
BANG!
?

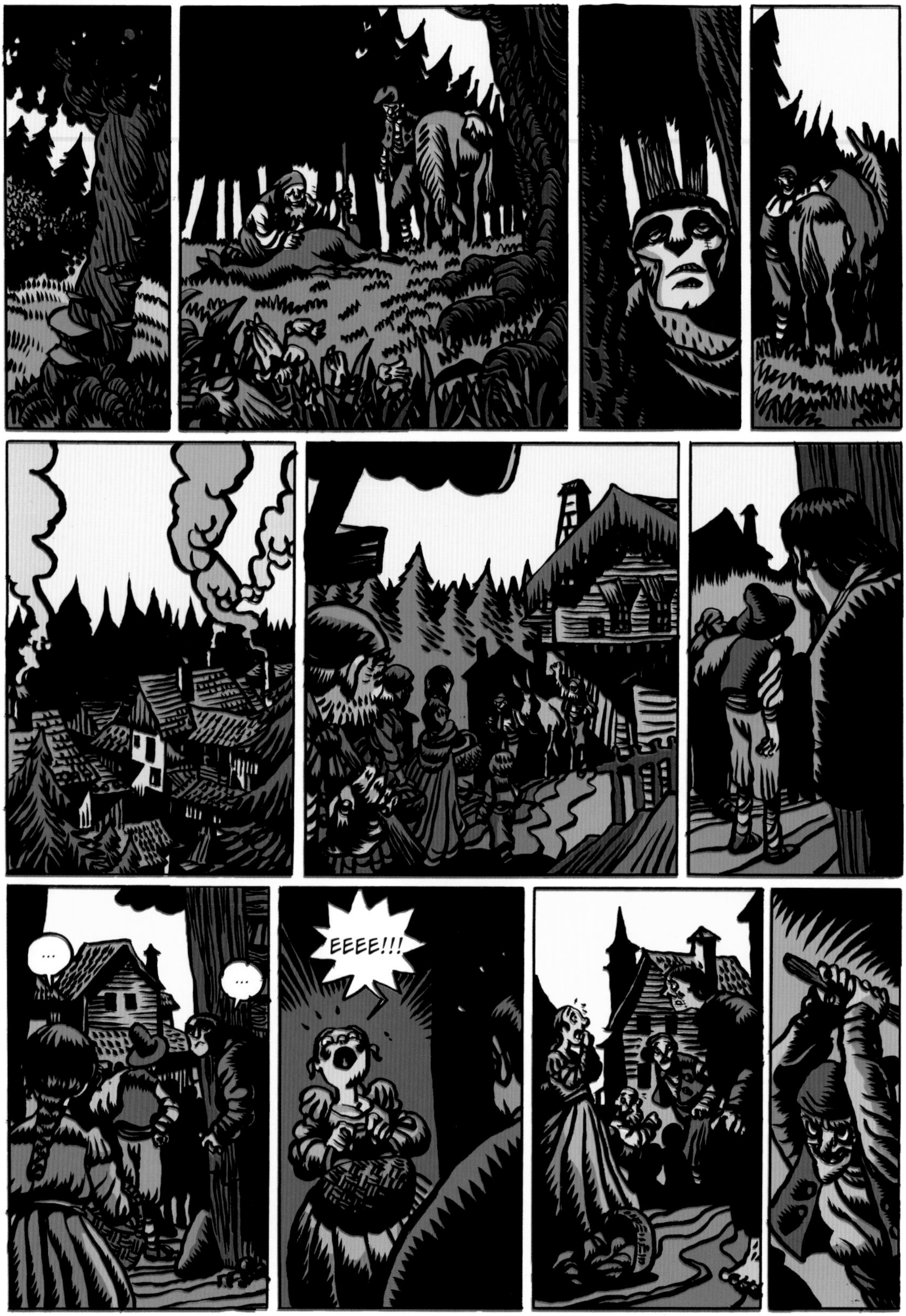
...
...
EEEE!!!

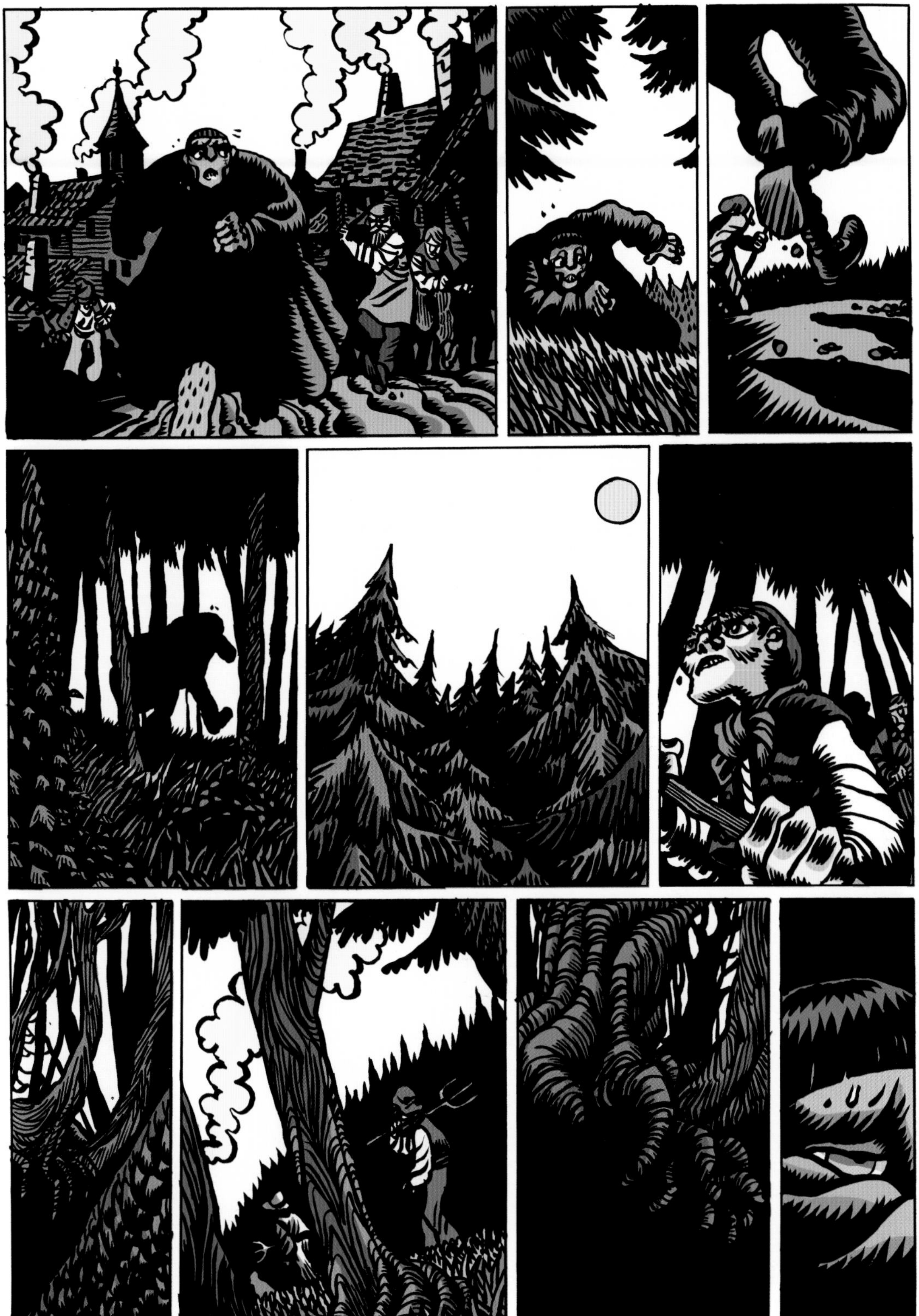

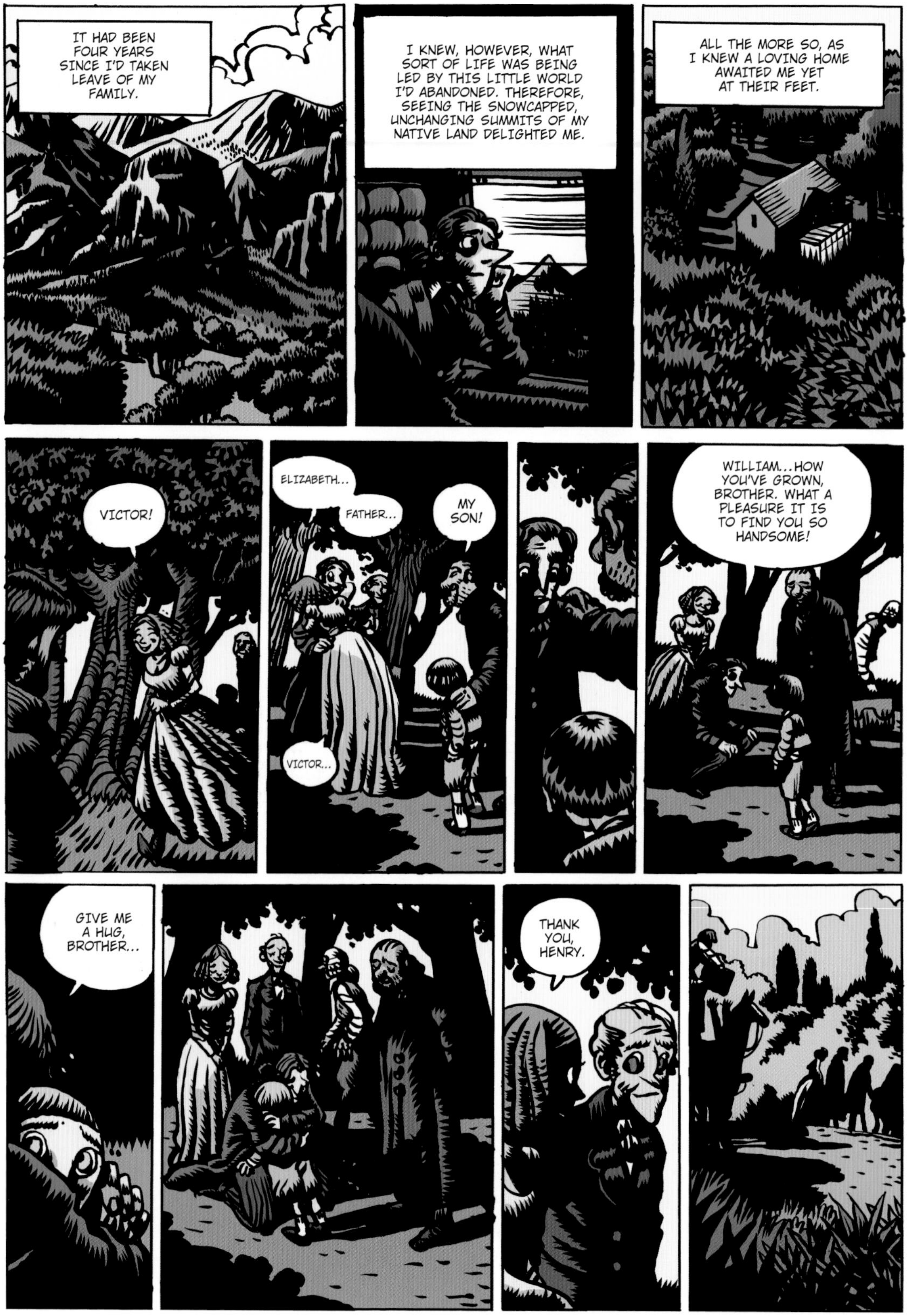
IT HAD BEEN FOUR YEARS SINCE I'D TAKEN LEAVE OF MY FAMILY.
I KNEW, HOWEVER, WHAT SORT OF LIFE WAS BEING LED BY THIS LITTLE WORLD I'D ABANDONED. THEREFORE, SEEING THE SNOWCAPPED, UNCHANGING SUMMITS OF MY NATIVE LAND DELIGHTED ME.
ALL THE MORE SO, AS I KNEW A LOVING HOME AWAITED ME YET AT THEIR FEET.
VICTOR!
ELIZABETH...
FATHER...
MY SON!
VICTOR...
WILLIAM...HOW YOU'VE GROWN, BROTHER. WHAT A PLEASURE IT IS TO FIND YOU SO HANDSOME!
GIVE ME A HUG, BROTHER...
THANK YOU, HENRY.

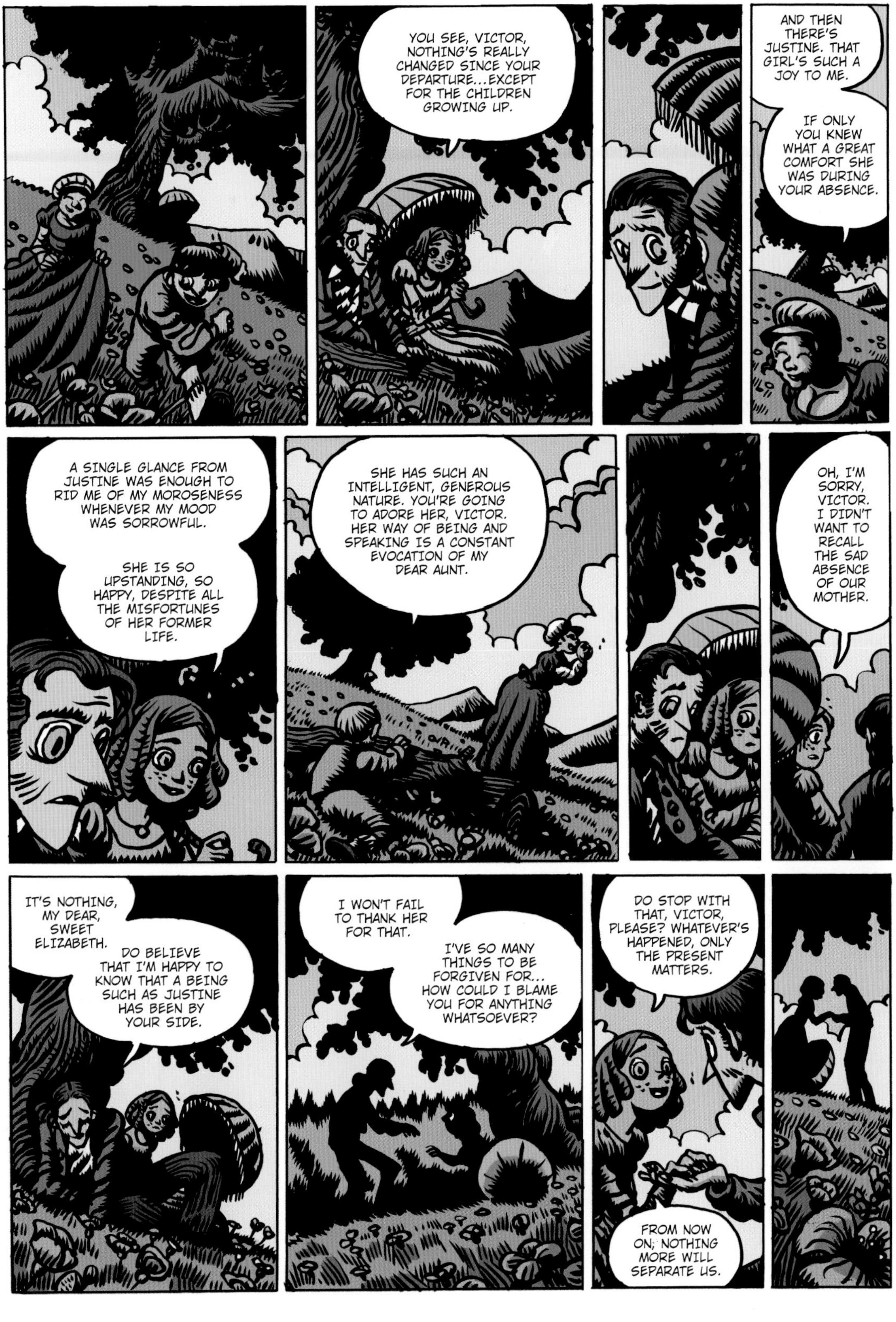
YOU SEE, VICTOR, NOTHING'S REALLY CHANGED SINCE YOUR DEPARTURE...EXCEPT FOR THE CHILDREN GROWING UP.
AND THEN THERE'S JUSTINE. THAT GIRL'S SUCH A JOY TO ME.
IF ONLY YOU KNEW WHAT A GREAT COMFORT SHE WAS DURING YOUR ABSENCE.
A SINGLE GLANCE FROM JUSTINE WAS ENOUGH TO RID ME OF MY MOROSENESS WHENEVER MY MOOD WAS SORROWFUL.
SHE IS SO UPSTANDING, SO HAPPY, DESPITE ALL THE MISFORTUNES OF HER FORMER LIFE.
SHE HAS SUCH AN INTELLIGENT, GENEROUS NATURE. YOU'RE GOING TO ADORE HER, VICTOR. HER WAY OF BEING AND SPEAKING IS A CONSTANT EVOCATION OF MY DEAR AUNT.
OH, I'M SORRY, VICTOR. I DIDN'T WANT TO RECALL THE SAD ABSENCE OF OUR MOTHER.
IT'S NOTHING, MY DEAR, SWEET ELIZABETH.
DO BELIEVE THAT I'M HAPPY TO KNOW THAT A BEING SUCH AS JUSTINE HAS BEEN BY YOUR SIDE.
I WON'T FAIL TO THANK HER FOR THAT.
I'VE SO MANY THINGS TO BE FORGIVEN FOR... HOW COULD I BLAME YOU FOR ANYTHING WHATSOEVER?
DO STOP WITH THAT, VICTOR, PLEASE? WHATEVER'S HAPPENED, ONLY THE PRESENT MATTERS.
FROM NOW ON, NOTHING MORE WILL SEPARATE US.

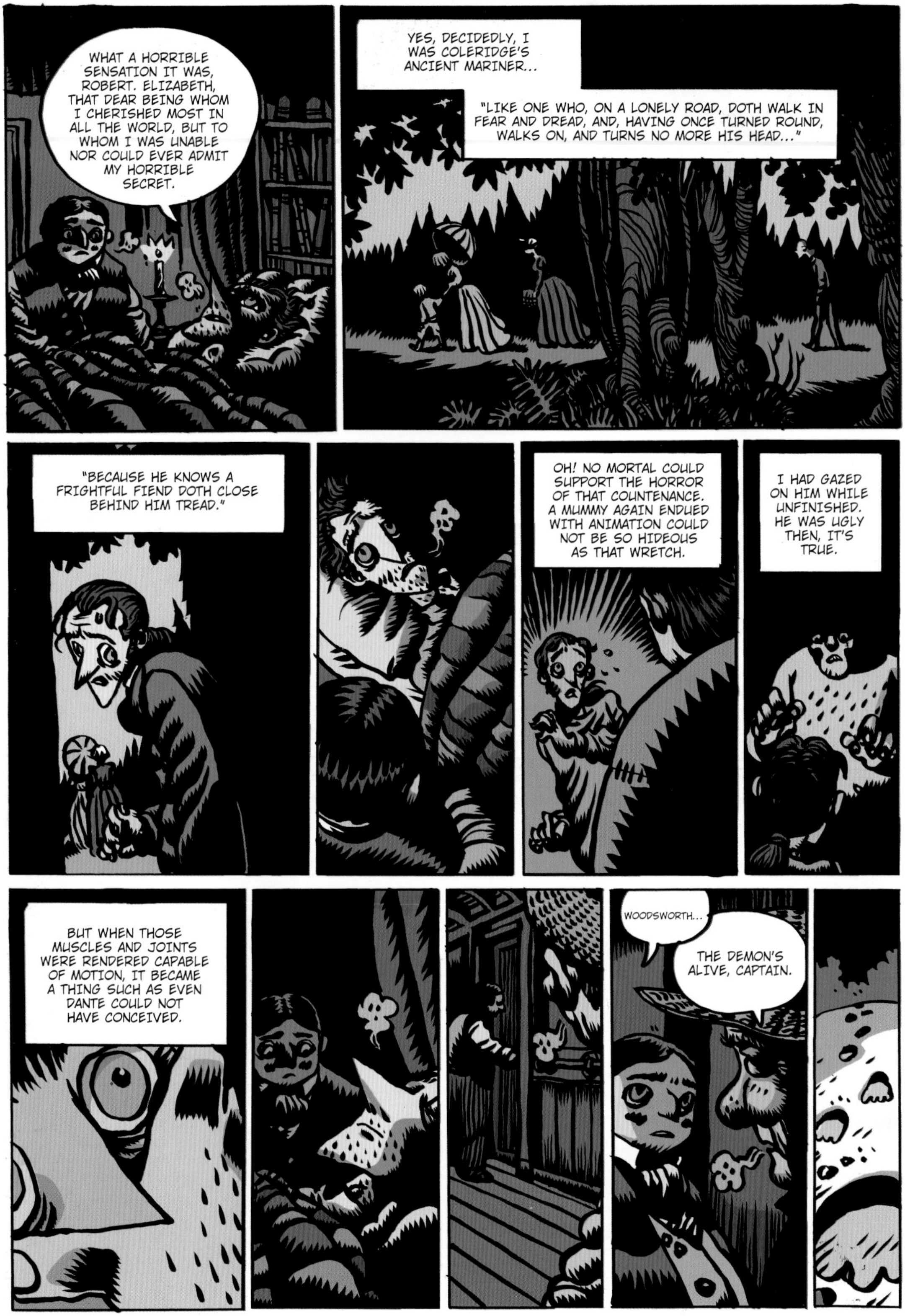
WHAT A HORRIBLE SENSATION IT WAS, ROBERT. ELIZABETH, THAT DEAR BEING WHOM I CHERISHED MOST IN ALL THE WORLD, BUT TO WHOM I WAS UNABLE NOR COULD EVER ADMIT MY HORRIBLE SECRET.
YES, DECIDEDLY, I WAS COLERIDGE'S ANCIENT MARINER...
"LIKE ONE WHO, ON A LONELY ROAD, DOTH WALK IN FEAR AND DREAD, AND, HAVING ONCE TURNED ROUND, WALKS ON, AND TURNS NO MORE HIS HEAD..."
"BECAUSE HE KNOWS A FRIGHTFUL FIEND DOTH CLOSE BEHIND HIM TREAD."
OH! NO MORTAL COULD SUPPORT THE HORROR OF THAT COUNTENANCE. A MUMMY AGAIN ENDUED WITH ANIMATION COULD NOT BE SO HIDEOUS AS THAT WRETCH.
I HAD GAZED ON HIM WHILE UNFINISHED. HE WAS UGLY THEN, IT'S TRUE.
BUT WHEN THOSE MUSCLES AND JOINTS WERE RENDERED CAPABLE OF MOTION, IT BECAME A THING SUCH AS EVEN DANTE COULD NOT HAVE CONCEIVED.
WOODSWORTH...
THE DEMON'S ALIVE, CAPTAIN.

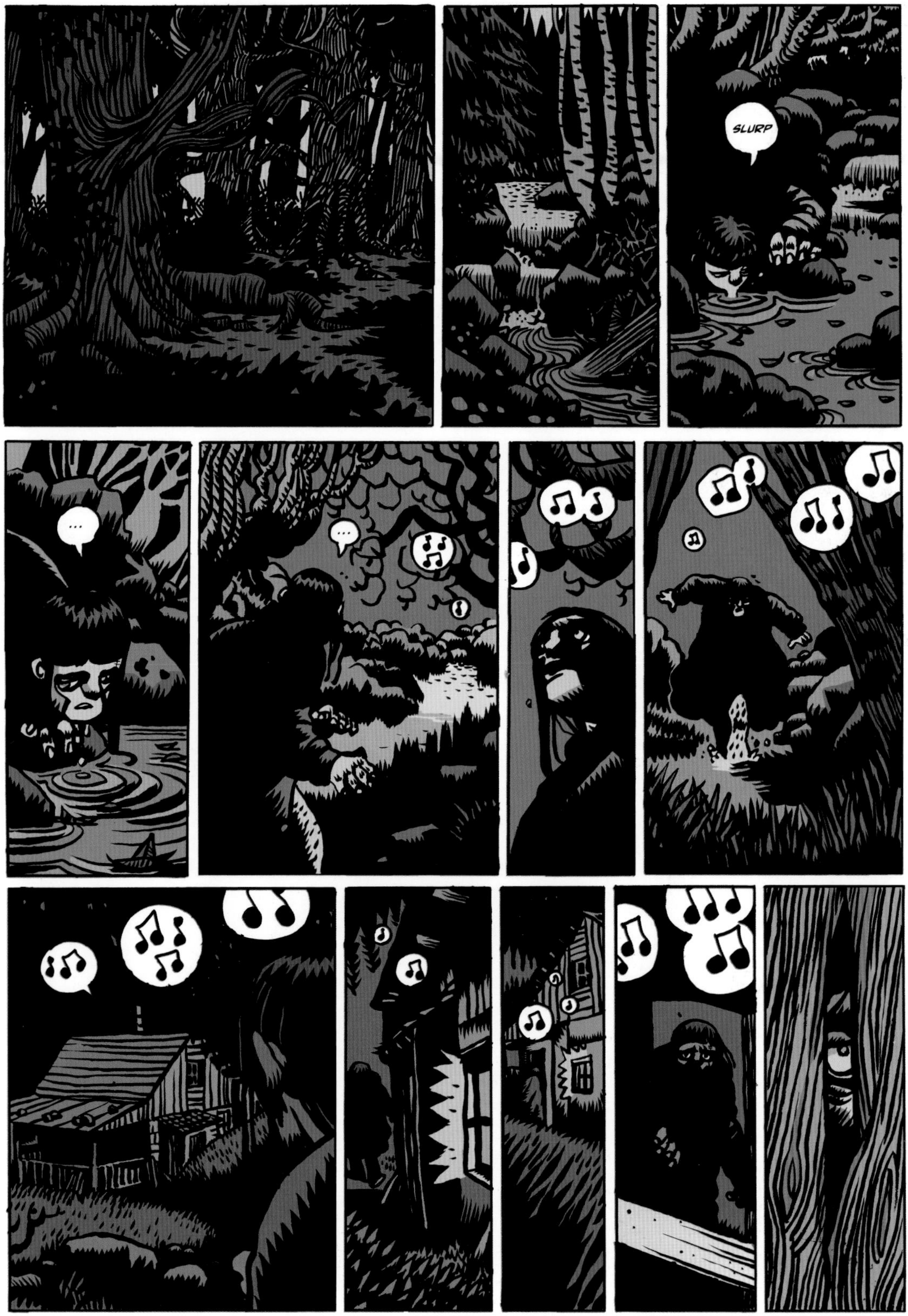
SLURP
...
...

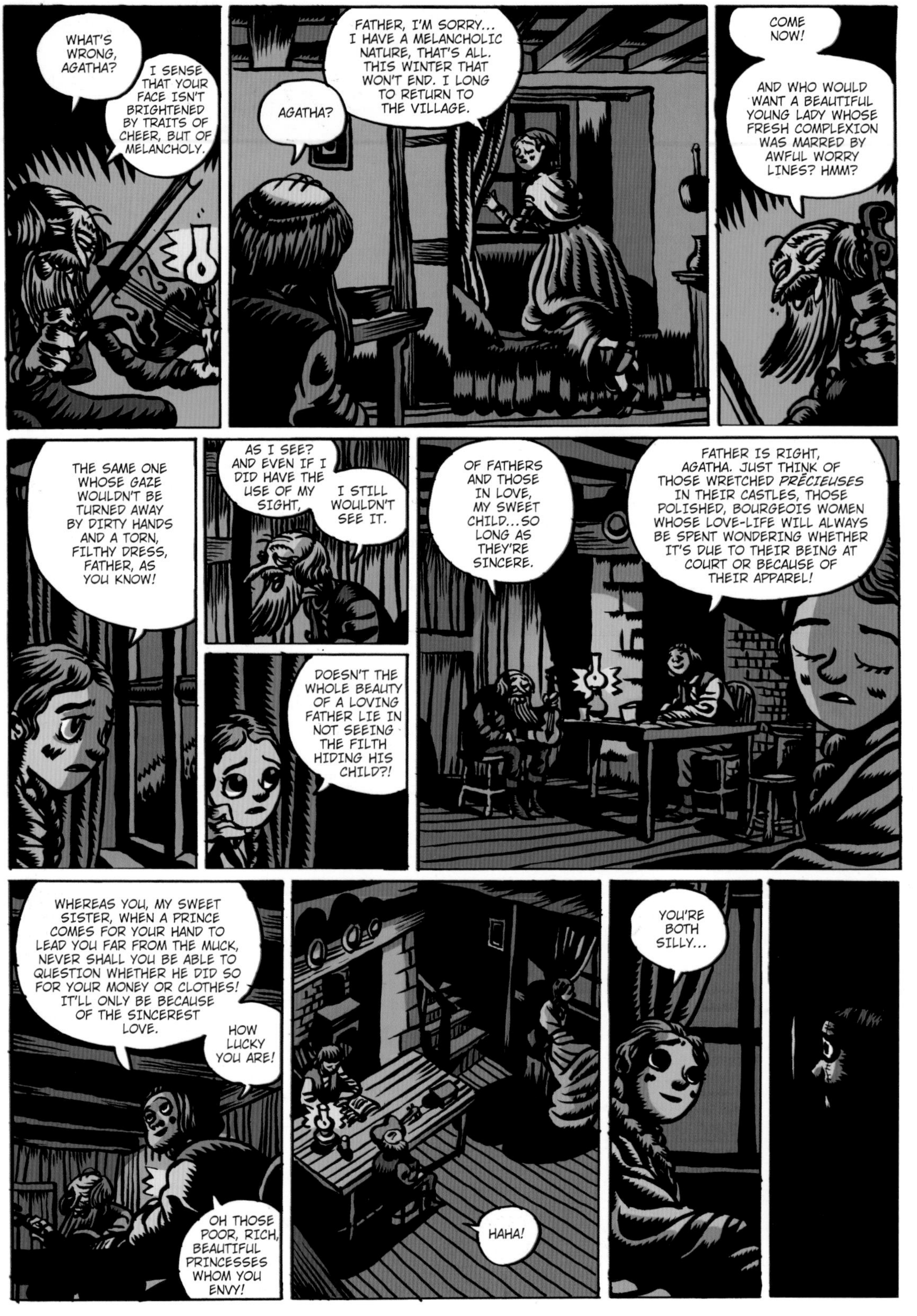
WHAT'S WRONG, AGATHA?
I SENSE THAT YOUR FACE ISN'T BRIGHTENED BY TRAITS OF CHEER, BUT OF MELANCHOLY.
AGATHA?
FATHER, I'M SORRY... I HAVE A MELANCHOLIC NATURE, THAT'S ALL. THIS WINTER THAT WON'T END. I LONG TO RETURN TO THE VILLAGE.
COME NOW!
AND WHO WOULD WANT A BEAUTIFUL YOUNG LADY WHOSE FRESH COMPLEXION WAS MARRED BY AWFUL WORRY LINES? HMM?
THE SAME ONE WHOSE GAZE WOULDN'T BE TURNED AWAY BY DIRTY HANDS AND A TORN, FILTHY DRESS, FATHER, AS YOU KNOW!
AS I SEE? AND EVEN IF I DID HAVE THE USE OF MY SIGHT,
I STILL WOULDN'T SEE IT.
DOESN'T THE WHOLE BEAUTY OF A LOVING FATHER LIE IN NOT SEEING THE FILTH HIDING HIS CHILD?!
OF FATHERS AND THOSE IN LOVE, MY SWEET CHILD...SO LONG AS THEY'RE SINCERE.
FATHER IS RIGHT, AGATHA. JUST THINK OF THOSE WRETCHED *PRÉCIEUSES* IN THEIR CASTLES, THOSE POLISHED, BOURGEOIS WOMEN WHOSE LOVE-LIFE WILL ALWAYS BE SPENT WONDERING WHETHER IT'S DUE TO THEIR BEING AT COURT OR BECAUSE OF THEIR APPAREL!
WHEREAS YOU, MY SWEET SISTER, WHEN A PRINCE COMES FOR YOUR HAND TO LEAD YOU FAR FROM THE MUCK, NEVER SHALL YOU BE ABLE TO QUESTION WHETHER HE DID SO FOR YOUR MONEY OR CLOTHES! IT'LL ONLY BE BECAUSE OF THE SINCEREST LOVE.
HOW LUCKY YOU ARE!
OH THOSE POOR, RICH, BEAUTIFUL PRINCESSES WHOM YOU ENVY!
HAHA!
YOU'RE BOTH SILLY...

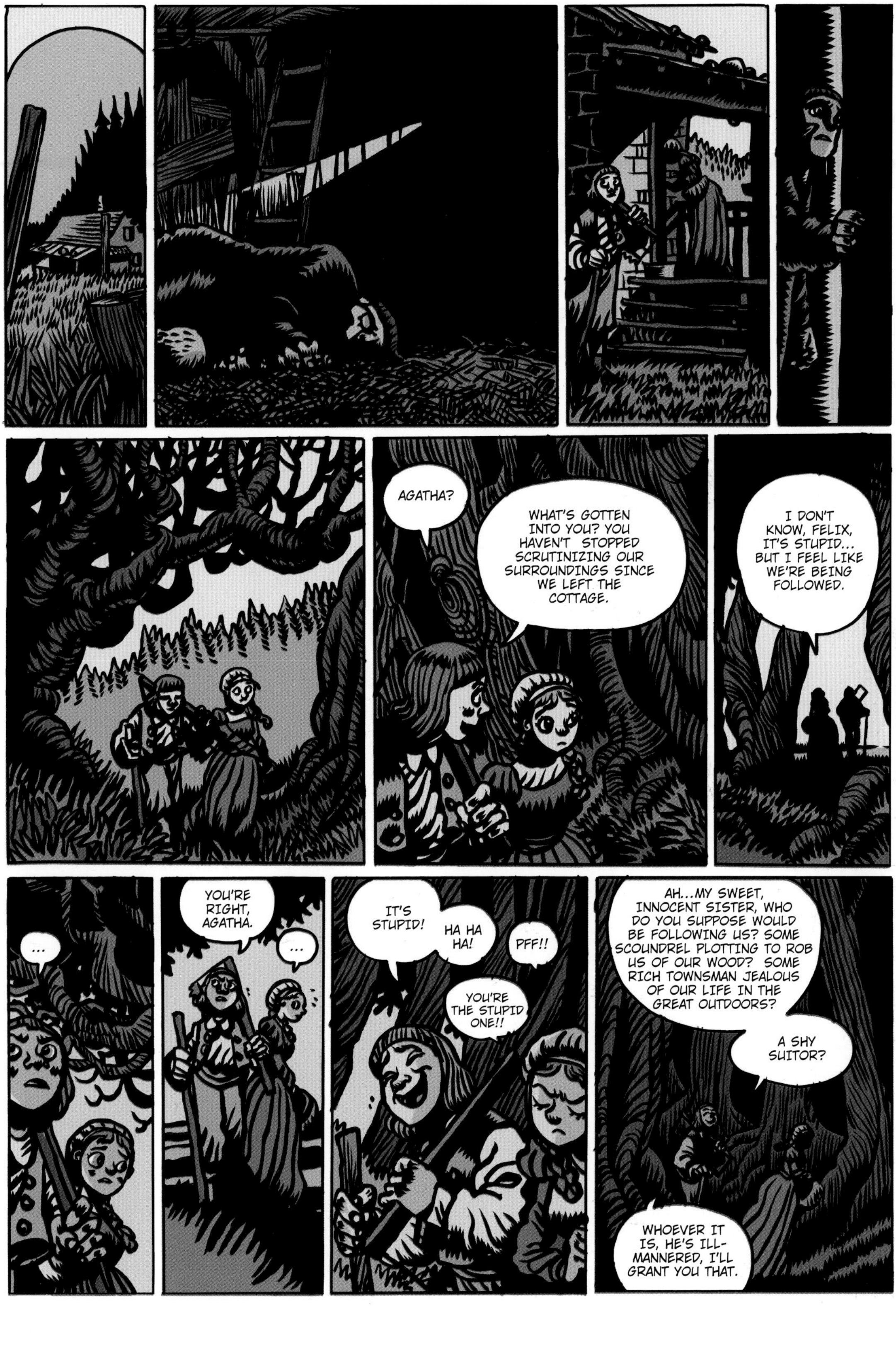

AGATHA?
WHAT'S GOTTEN INTO YOU? YOU HAVEN'T STOPPED SCRUTINIZING OUR SURROUNDINGS SINCE WE LEFT THE COTTAGE.
I DON'T KNOW, FELIX, IT'S STUPID... BUT I FEEL LIKE WE'RE BEING FOLLOWED.
...
YOU'RE RIGHT, AGATHA.
...
IT'S STUPID!
HA HA HA!
PFF!!
YOU'RE THE STUPID ONE!!
AH...MY SWEET, INNOCENT SISTER, WHO DO YOU SUPPOSE WOULD BE FOLLOWING US? SOME SCOUNDREL PLOTTING TO ROB US OF OUR WOOD? SOME RICH TOWNSMAN JEALOUS OF OUR LIFE IN THE GREAT OUTDOORS?
A SHY SUITOR?
WHOEVER IT IS, HE'S ILL-MANNERED, I'LL GRANT YOU THAT.

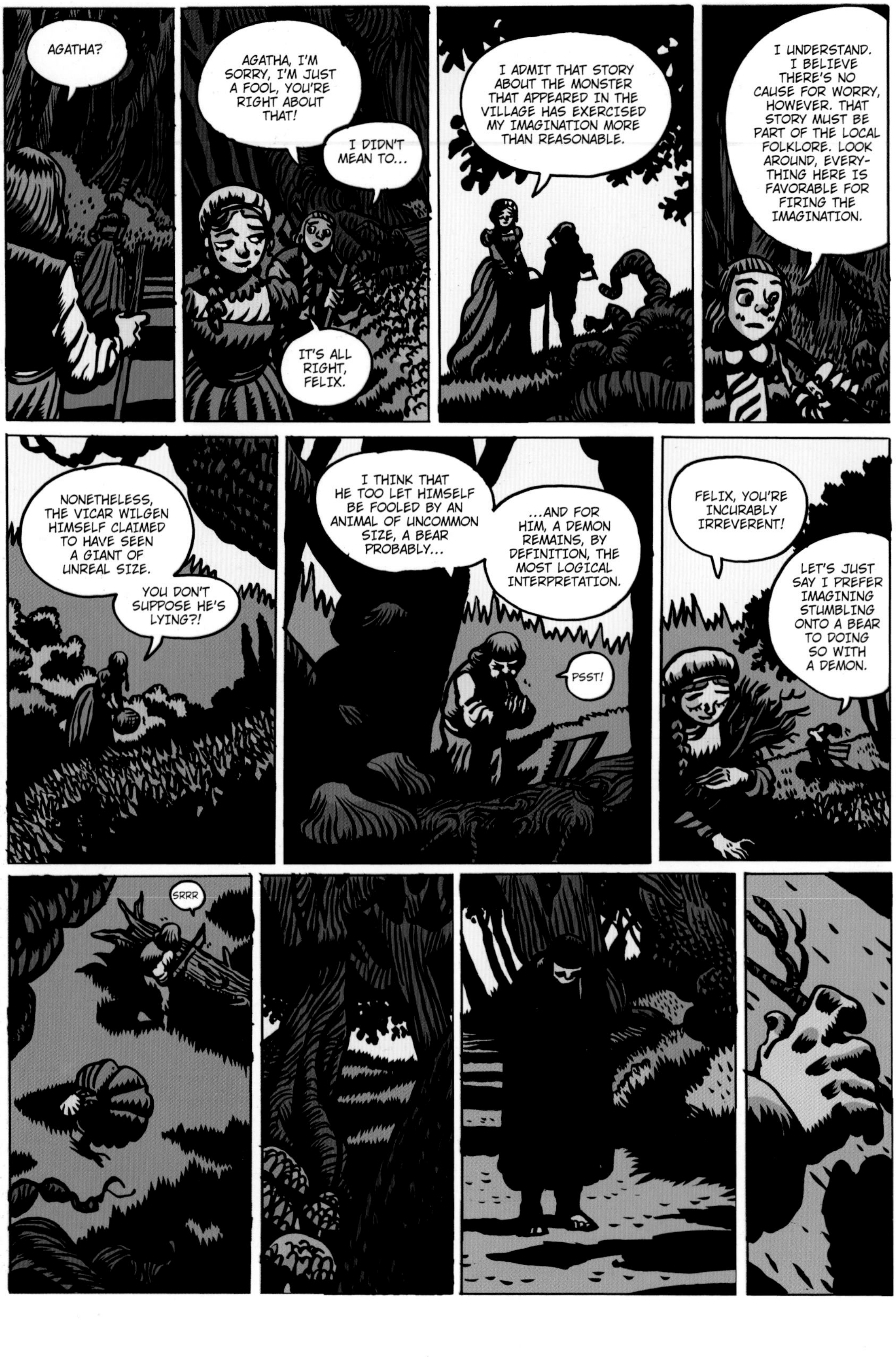
AGATHA?
AGATHA, I'M SORRY, I'M JUST A FOOL, YOU'RE RIGHT ABOUT THAT!
I DIDN'T MEAN TO...
IT'S ALL RIGHT, FELIX.
I ADMIT THAT STORY ABOUT THE MONSTER THAT APPEARED IN THE VILLAGE HAS EXERCISED MY IMAGINATION MORE THAN REASONABLE.
I UNDERSTAND. I BELIEVE THERE'S NO CAUSE FOR WORRY, HOWEVER. THAT STORY MUST BE PART OF THE LOCAL FOLKLORE. LOOK AROUND, EVERY-THING HERE IS FAVORABLE FOR FIRING THE IMAGINATION.
NONETHELESS, THE VICAR WILGEN HIMSELF CLAIMED TO HAVE SEEN A GIANT OF UNREAL SIZE.
YOU DON'T SUPPOSE HE'S LYING?!
I THINK THAT HE TOO LET HIMSELF BE FOOLED BY AN ANIMAL OF UNCOMMON SIZE, A BEAR PROBABLY...
...AND FOR HIM, A DEMON REMAINS, BY DEFINITION, THE MOST LOGICAL INTERPRETATION.
PSST!
FELIX, YOU'RE INCURABLY IRREVERENT!
LET'S JUST SAY I PREFER IMAGINING STUMBLING ONTO A BEAR TO DOING SO WITH A DEMON.
SRRR

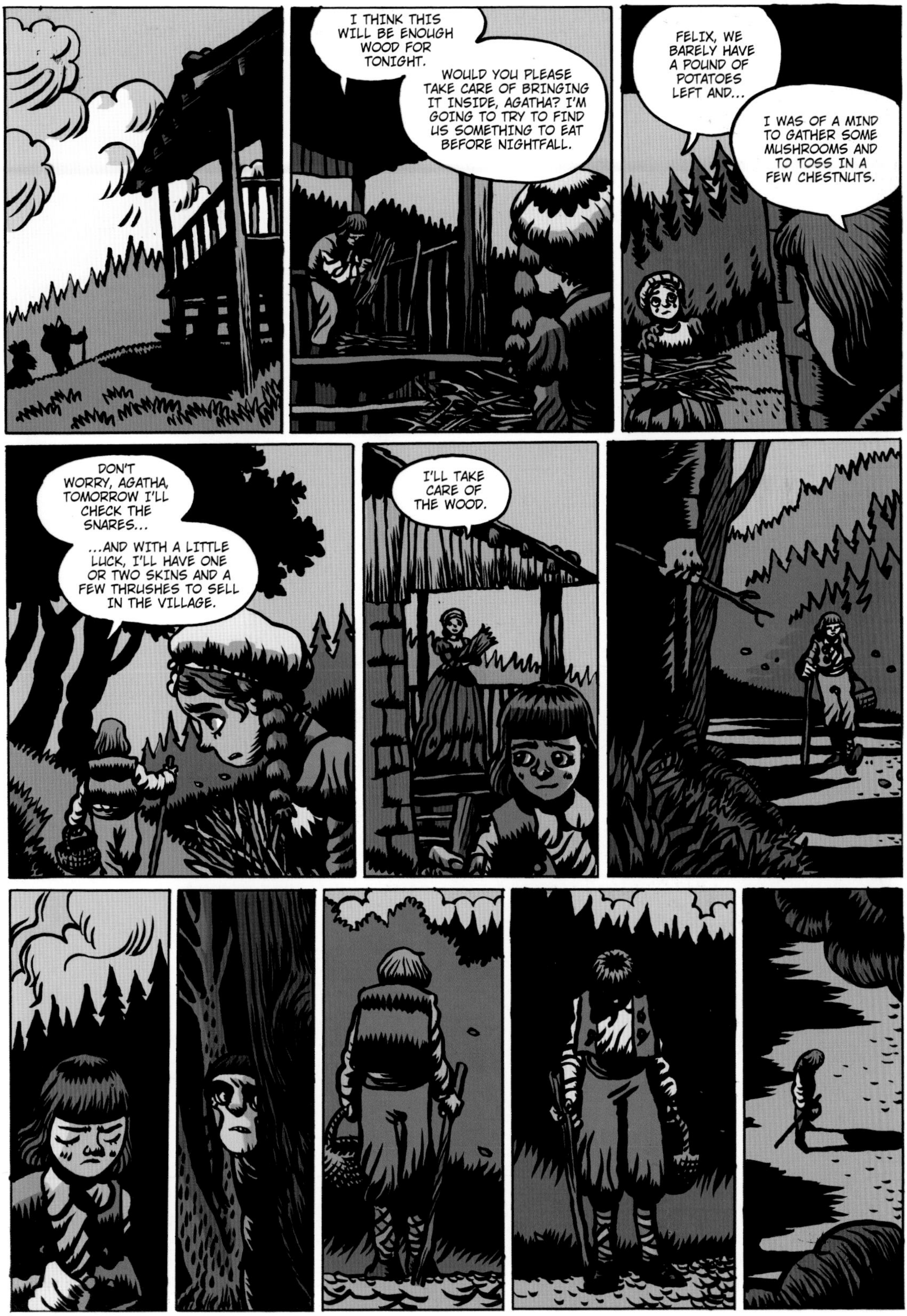
I THINK THIS WILL BE ENOUGH WOOD FOR TONIGHT.
WOULD YOU PLEASE TAKE CARE OF BRINGING IT INSIDE, AGATHA? I'M GOING TO TRY TO FIND US SOMETHING TO EAT BEFORE NIGHTFALL.
FELIX, WE BARELY HAVE A POUND OF POTATOES LEFT AND...
I WAS OF A MIND TO GATHER SOME MUSHROOMS AND TO TOSS IN A FEW CHESTNUTS.
DON'T WORRY, AGATHA, TOMORROW I'LL CHECK THE SNARES...
...AND WITH A LITTLE LUCK, I'LL HAVE ONE OR TWO SKINS AND A FEW THRUSHES TO SELL IN THE VILLAGE.
I'LL TAKE CARE OF THE WOOD.

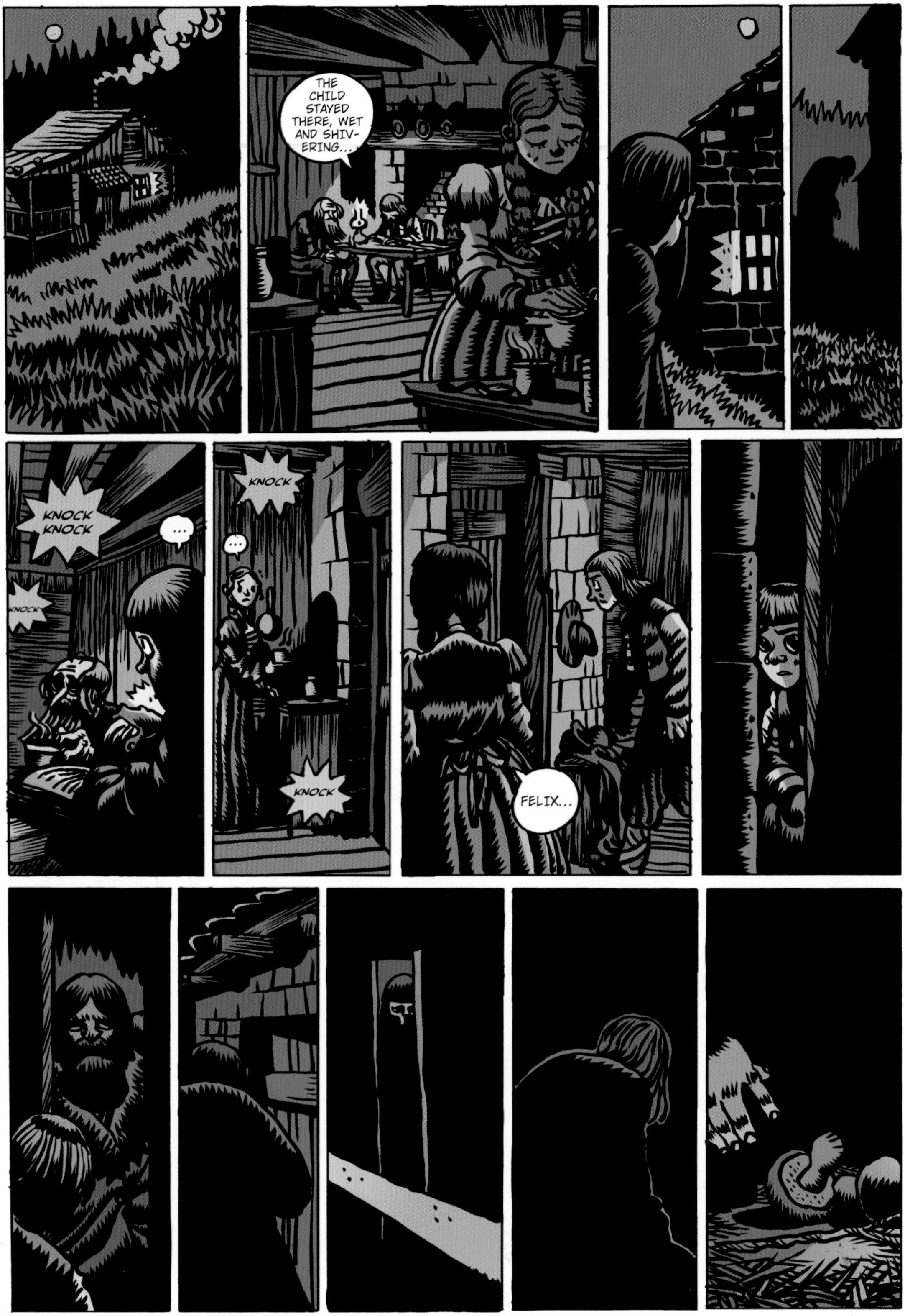

THE CHILD STAYED THERE, WET AND SHIVERING...
KNOCK KNOCK
KNOCK
...
KNOCK
...
KNOCK
FELIX...

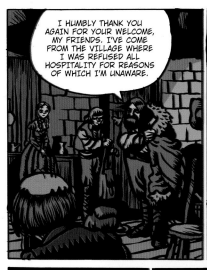

I HUMBLY THANK YOU AGAIN FOR YOUR WELCOME, MY FRIENDS. I'VE COME FROM THE VILLAGE WHERE I WAS REFUSED ALL HOSPITALITY FOR REASONS OF WHICH I'M UNAWARE.

YOU MUSTN'T BE ANGRY WITH OUR VILLAGE NEIGHBORS. FOR SOME WEEKS NOW, AT NIGHTFALL, THEIR DOORS REMAIN OBSTINATELY CLOSED, BECAUSE THERE'S RUMOR OF A STRANGE CREATURE HAUNTING THE UNDERBRUSH.

A FUNNY ANIMAL, IN TRUTH, OF AN EXCEPTIONAL SIZE, WHICH SEVERAL PEOPLE HAVE SEEN PROWLING ABOUT THE AREA.

A BEAR?

THAT'S DELAYING ITS HIBERNATION FOR THE WINTER? I DOUBT IT.

TOO BAD.

YOU'RE A HUNTER, AREN'T YOU?

WHATEVER THE CASE, LET'S LEAVE THIS CREATURE WHEREVER IT IS. FOR NOW, LET'S TRY TO WARM UP OUR FRIEND THE BEST WE CAN, CHILDREN.

AGATHA, A FEW MUSHROOMS FOR OUR FRIEND.

FELIX, WOULD YOU BE SO KIND AS TO READ US A STORY?

THANKS...

LET'S SEE...

THIS STORY TAKES PLACE IN THE YEAR OF OUR LORD 1516, DEEP IN THE BLACK FOREST OF FRAÜHINEIM. THE MOST DISMAL OF COLD, DESOLATE FORESTS...

...WHERE IT'S STILL TOLD THAT, LIVING THERE...

...IS A TERRIBLE, BLACK CREATURE THAT, AT THE WANING OF SUN--ALTHOUGH LIGHT NEVER WOULD FILTER INTO HIS LANDS--WOULD DEPART TO HAUNT THE BORDERS OF HIS DOMAIN...ON THE HUNT FOR POOR, WANDERING SOULS...

...FOLK FORGETFUL OF THE LEGENDS AND MYTHS OF THE COUNTRY OF FRAÜHINEIM.

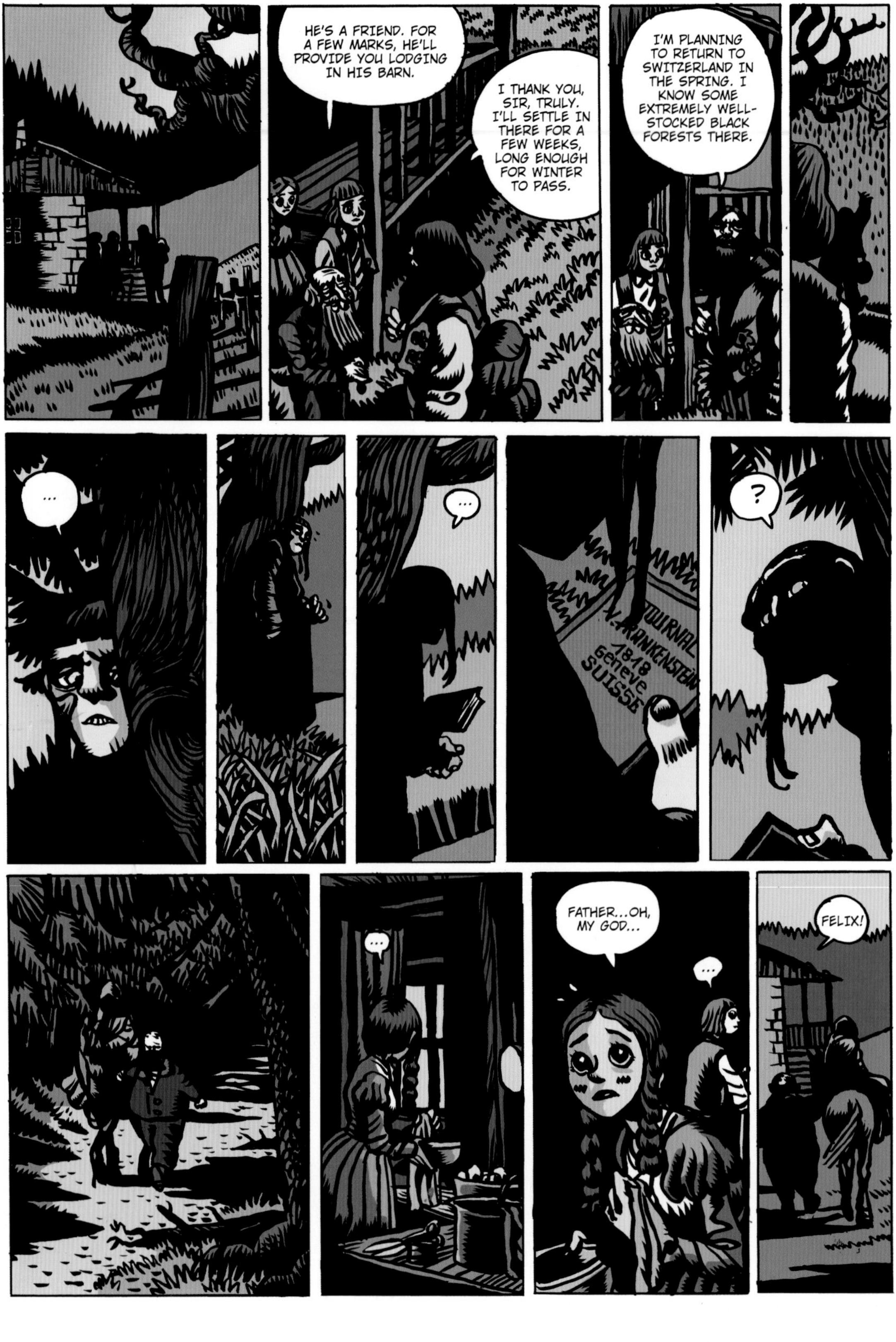
HE'S A FRIEND. FOR A FEW MARKS, HE'LL PROVIDE YOU LODGING IN HIS BARN.
I THANK YOU, SIR, TRULY. I'LL SETTLE IN THERE FOR A FEW WEEKS, LONG ENOUGH FOR WINTER TO PASS.
I'M PLANNING TO RETURN TO SWITZERLAND IN THE SPRING. I KNOW SOME EXTREMELY WELL-STOCKED BLACK FORESTS THERE.
...
...
JOURNAL
V. FRANKENSTEIN
1818
Geneve
SUISSE
?
...
FATHER...OH, MY GOD...
...
FELIX!

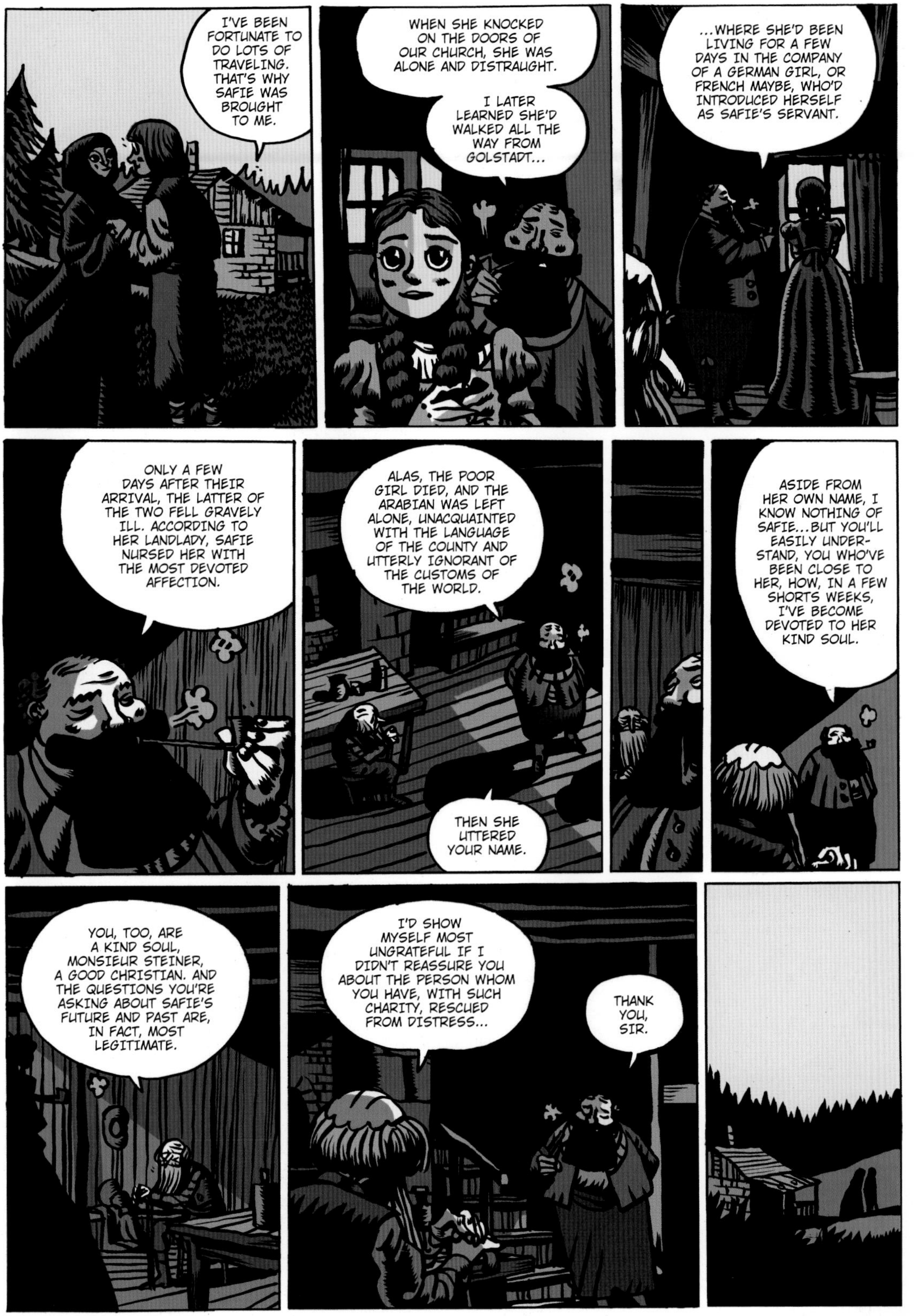
I'VE BEEN FORTUNATE TO DO LOTS OF TRAVELING. THAT'S WHY SAFIE WAS BROUGHT TO ME.
WHEN SHE KNOCKED ON THE DOORS OF OUR CHURCH, SHE WAS ALONE AND DISTRAUGHT.
I LATER LEARNED SHE'D WALKED ALL THE WAY FROM GOLSTADT...
...WHERE SHE'D BEEN LIVING FOR A FEW DAYS IN THE COMPANY OF A GERMAN GIRL, OR FRENCH MAYBE, WHO'D INTRODUCED HERSELF AS SAFIE'S SERVANT.
ONLY A FEW DAYS AFTER THEIR ARRIVAL, THE LATTER OF THE TWO FELL GRAVELY ILL. ACCORDING TO HER LANDLADY, SAFIE NURSED HER WITH THE MOST DEVOTED AFFECTION.
ALAS, THE POOR GIRL DIED, AND THE ARABIAN WAS LEFT ALONE, UNACQUAINTED WITH THE LANGUAGE OF THE COUNTY AND UTTERLY IGNORANT OF THE CUSTOMS OF THE WORLD.
THEN SHE UTTERED YOUR NAME.
ASIDE FROM HER OWN NAME, I KNOW NOTHING OF SAFIE...BUT YOU'LL EASILY UNDER-STAND, YOU WHO'VE BEEN CLOSE TO HER, HOW, IN A FEW SHORTS WEEKS, I'VE BECOME DEVOTED TO HER KIND SOUL.
YOU, TOO, ARE A KIND SOUL, MONSIEUR STEINER, A GOOD CHRISTIAN. AND THE QUESTIONS YOU'RE ASKING ABOUT SAFIE'S FUTURE AND PAST ARE, IN FACT, MOST LEGITIMATE.
I'D SHOW MYSELF MOST UNGRATEFUL IF I DIDN'T REASSURE YOU ABOUT THE PERSON WHOM YOU HAVE, WITH SUCH CHARITY, RESCUED FROM DISTRESS...
THANK YOU, SIR.

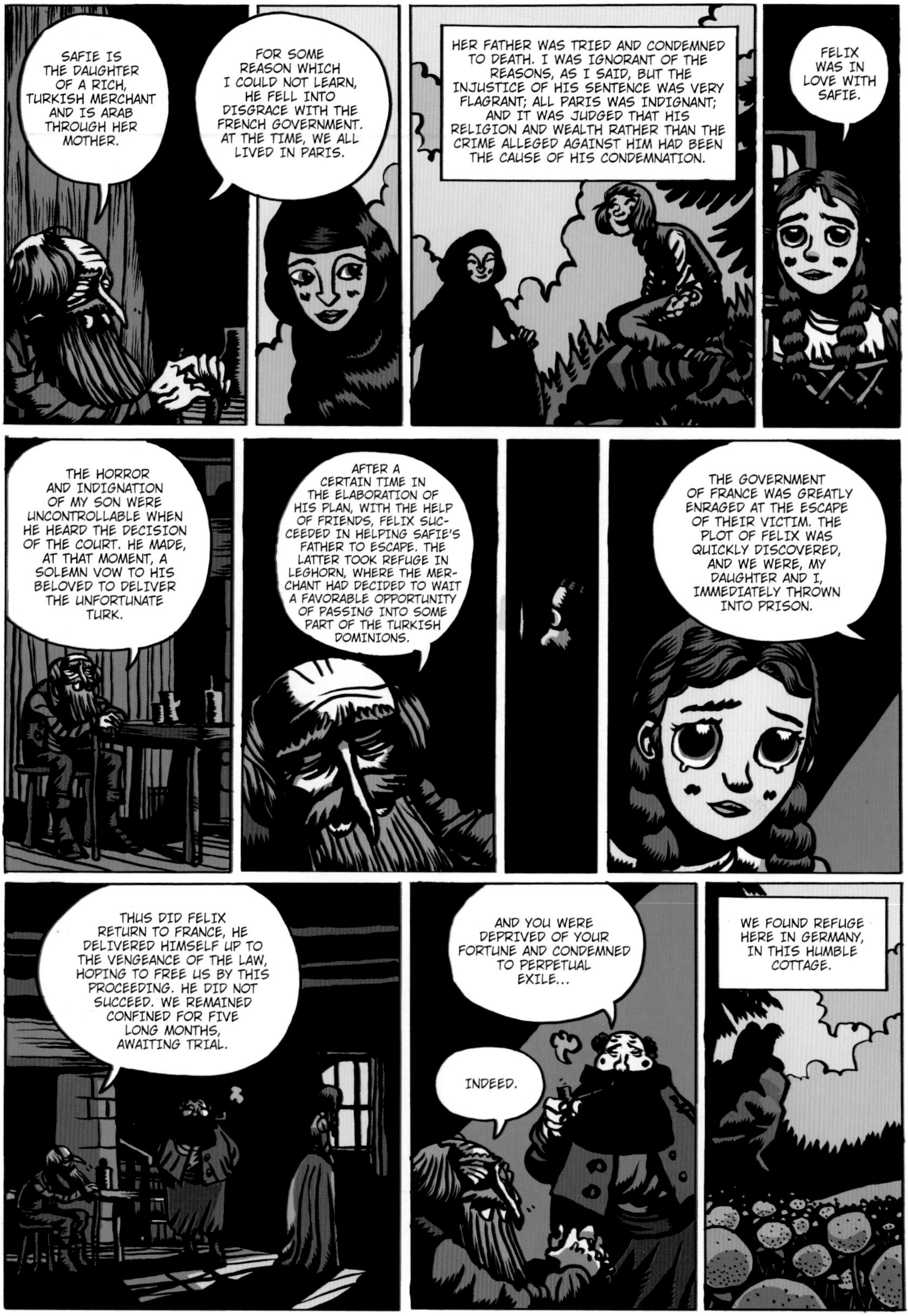
SAFIE IS THE DAUGHTER OF A RICH, TURKISH MERCHANT AND IS ARAB THROUGH HER MOTHER.
FOR SOME REASON WHICH I COULD NOT LEARN, HE FELL INTO DISGRACE WITH THE FRENCH GOVERNMENT. AT THE TIME, WE ALL LIVED IN PARIS.
HER FATHER WAS TRIED AND CONDEMNED TO DEATH. I WAS IGNORANT OF THE REASONS, AS I SAID, BUT THE INJUSTICE OF HIS SENTENCE WAS VERY FLAGRANT; ALL PARIS WAS INDIGNANT; AND IT WAS JUDGED THAT HIS RELIGION AND WEALTH RATHER THAN THE CRIME ALLEGED AGAINST HIM HAD BEEN THE CAUSE OF HIS CONDEMNATION.
FELIX WAS IN LOVE WITH SAFIE.
THE HORROR AND INDIGNATION OF MY SON WERE UNCONTROLLABLE WHEN HE HEARD THE DECISION OF THE COURT. HE MADE, AT THAT MOMENT, A SOLEMN VOW TO HIS BELOVED TO DELIVER THE UNFORTUNATE TURK.
AFTER A CERTAIN TIME IN THE ELABORATION OF HIS PLAN, WITH THE HELP OF FRIENDS, FELIX SUCCEEDED IN HELPING SAFIE'S FATHER TO ESCAPE. THE LATTER TOOK REFUGE IN LEGHORN, WHERE THE MERCHANT HAD DECIDED TO WAIT A FAVORABLE OPPORTUNITY OF PASSING INTO SOME PART OF THE TURKISH DOMINIONS.
THE GOVERNMENT OF FRANCE WAS GREATLY ENRAGED AT THE ESCAPE OF THEIR VICTIM. THE PLOT OF FELIX WAS QUICKLY DISCOVERED, AND WE WERE, MY DAUGHTER AND I, IMMEDIATELY THROWN INTO PRISON.
THUS DID FELIX RETURN TO FRANCE, HE DELIVERED HIMSELF UP TO THE VENGEANCE OF THE LAW, HOPING TO FREE US BY THIS PROCEEDING. HE DID NOT SUCCEED. WE REMAINED CONFINED FOR FIVE LONG MONTHS, AWAITING TRIAL.
AND YOU WERE DEPRIVED OF YOUR FORTUNE AND CONDEMNED TO PERPETUAL EXILE...
INDEED.
WE FOUND REFUGE HERE IN GERMANY, IN THIS HUMBLE COTTAGE.

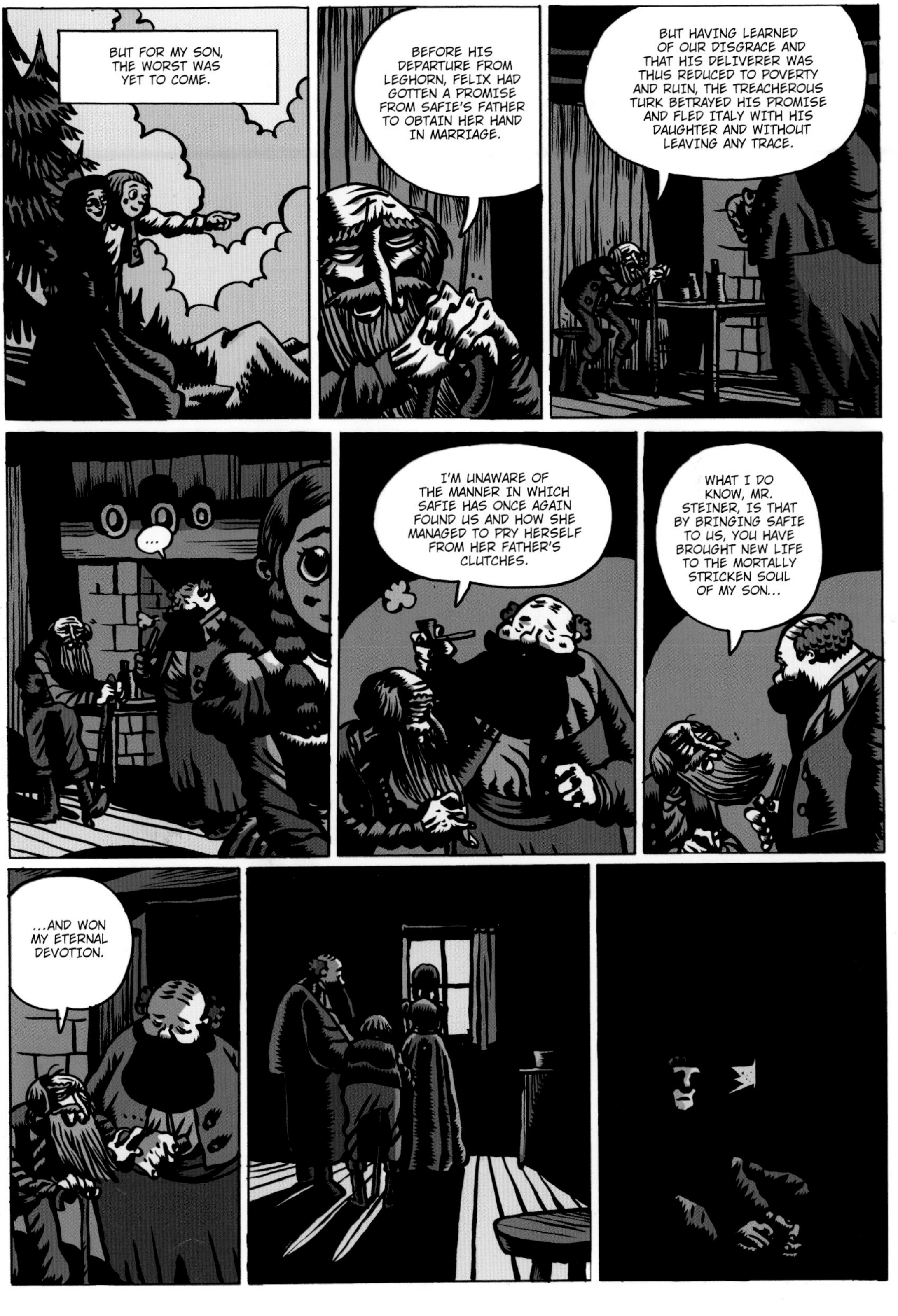
BUT FOR MY SON, THE WORST WAS YET TO COME.
BEFORE HIS DEPARTURE FROM LEGHORN, FELIX HAD GOTTEN A PROMISE FROM SAFIE'S FATHER TO OBTAIN HER HAND IN MARRIAGE.
BUT HAVING LEARNED OF OUR DISGRACE AND THAT HIS DELIVERER WAS THUS REDUCED TO POVERTY AND RUIN, THE TREACHEROUS TURK BETRAYED HIS PROMISE AND FLED ITALY WITH HIS DAUGHTER AND WITHOUT LEAVING ANY TRACE.
...
I'M UNAWARE OF THE MANNER IN WHICH SAFIE HAS ONCE AGAIN FOUND US AND HOW SHE MANAGED TO PRY HERSELF FROM HER FATHER'S CLUTCHES.
WHAT I DO KNOW, MR. STEINER, IS THAT BY BRINGING SAFIE TO US, YOU HAVE BROUGHT NEW LIFE TO THE MORTALLY STRICKEN SOUL OF MY SON...
...AND WON MY ETERNAL DEVOTION.

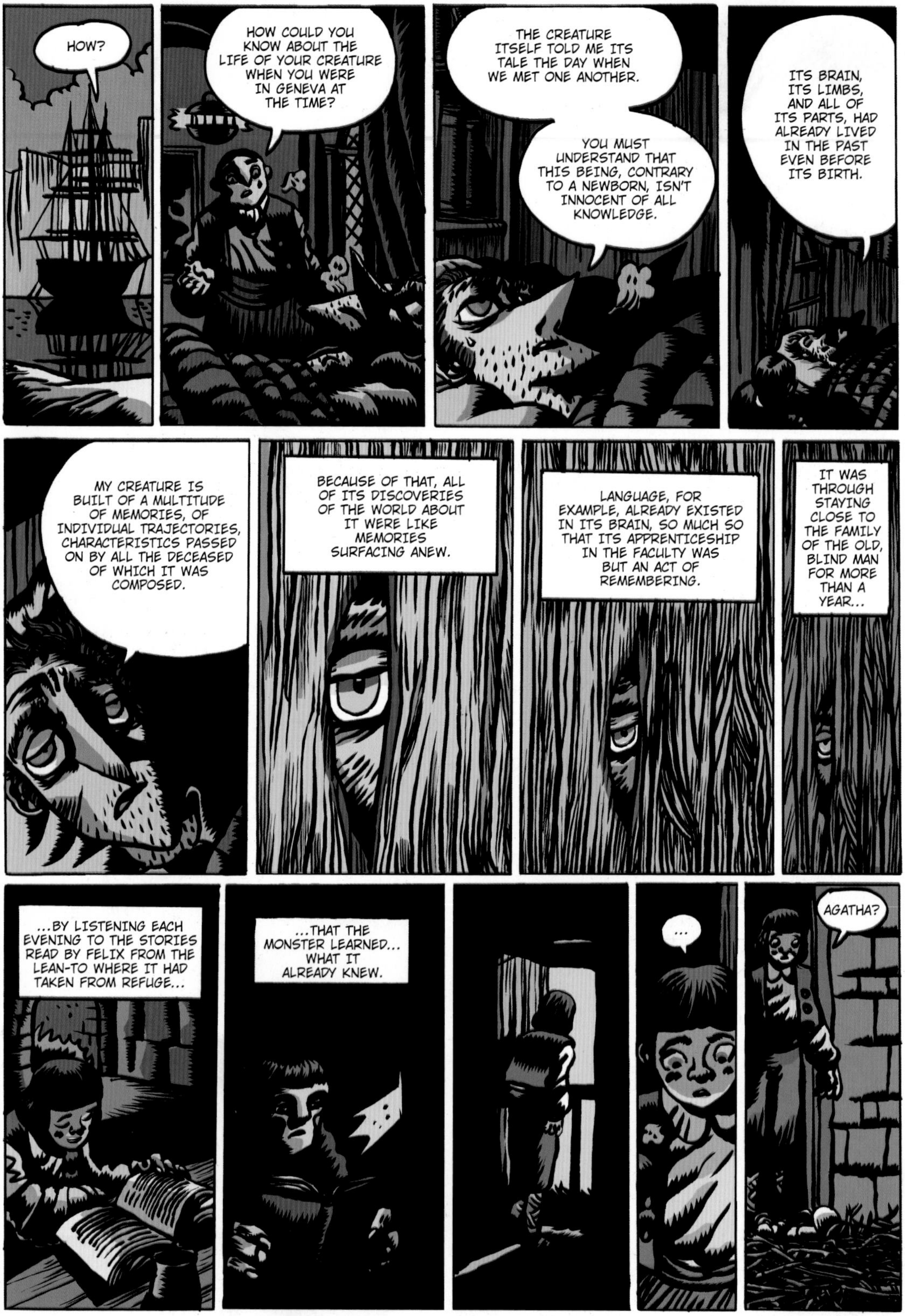
HOW?
HOW COULD YOU KNOW ABOUT THE LIFE OF YOUR CREATURE WHEN YOU WERE IN GENEVA AT THE TIME?
THE CREATURE ITSELF TOLD ME ITS TALE THE DAY WHEN WE MET ONE ANOTHER.
YOU MUST UNDERSTAND THAT THIS BEING, CONTRARY TO A NEWBORN, ISN'T INNOCENT OF ALL KNOWLEDGE.
ITS BRAIN, ITS LIMBS, AND ALL OF ITS PARTS, HAD ALREADY LIVED IN THE PAST EVEN BEFORE ITS BIRTH.
MY CREATURE IS BUILT OF A MULTITUDE OF MEMORIES, OF INDIVIDUAL TRAJECTORIES, CHARACTERISTICS PASSED ON BY ALL THE DECEASED OF WHICH IT WAS COMPOSED.
BECAUSE OF THAT, ALL OF ITS DISCOVERIES OF THE WORLD ABOUT IT WERE LIKE MEMORIES SURFACING ANEW.
LANGUAGE, FOR EXAMPLE, ALREADY EXISTED IN ITS BRAIN, SO MUCH SO THAT ITS APPRENTICESHIP IN THE FACULTY WAS BUT AN ACT OF REMEMBERING.
IT WAS THROUGH STAYING CLOSE TO THE FAMILY OF THE OLD, BLIND MAN FOR MORE THAN A YEAR...
...BY LISTENING EACH EVENING TO THE STORIES READ BY FELIX FROM THE LEAN-TO WHERE IT HAD TAKEN FROM REFUGE...
...THAT THE MONSTER LEARNED... WHAT IT ALREADY KNEW.
...
AGATHA?

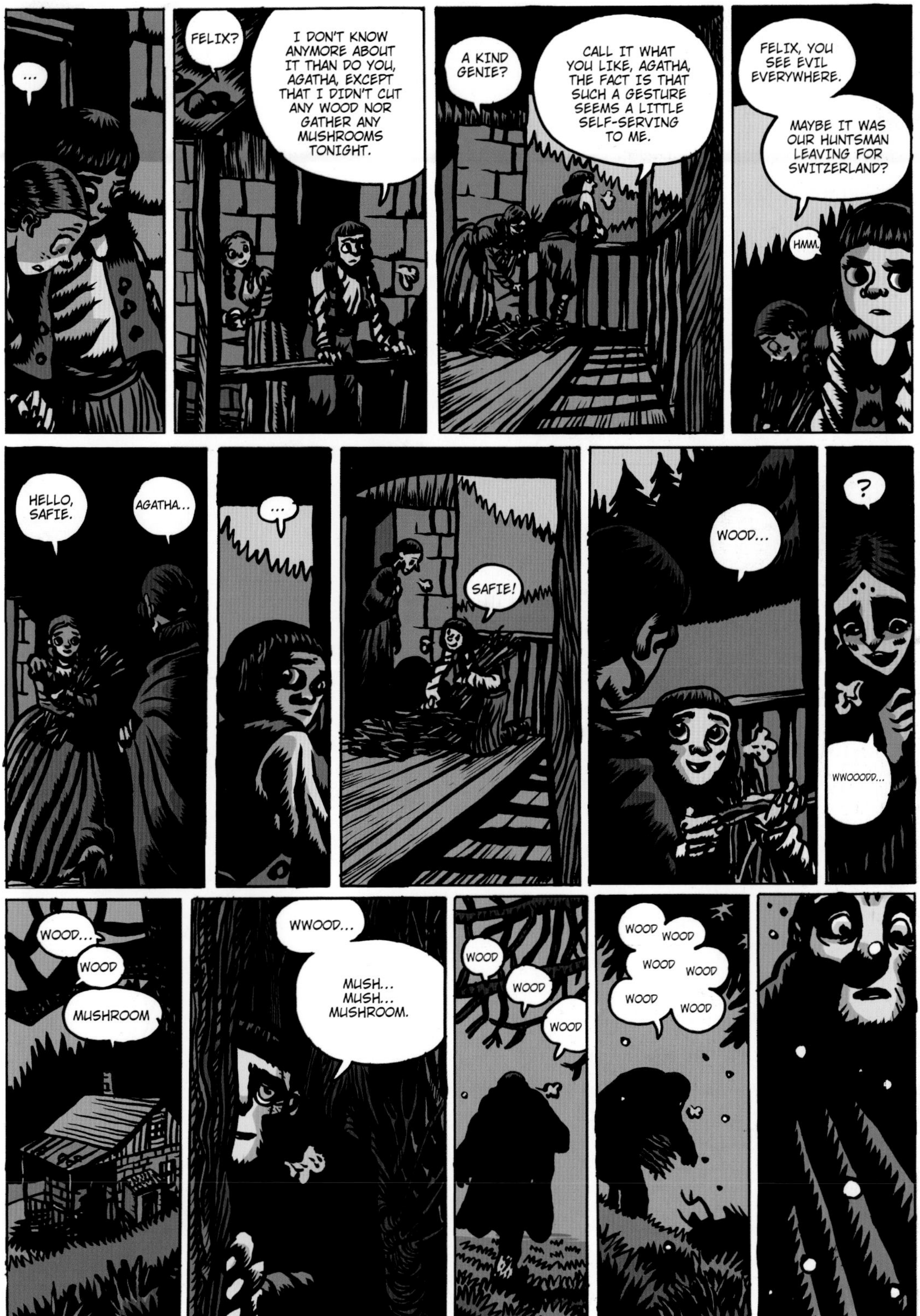
...
FELIX?
I DON'T KNOW ANYMORE ABOUT IT THAN DO YOU, AGATHA, EXCEPT THAT I DIDN'T CUT ANY WOOD NOR GATHER ANY MUSHROOMS TONIGHT.
A KIND GENIE?
CALL IT WHAT YOU LIKE, AGATHA, THE FACT IS THAT SUCH A GESTURE SEEMS A LITTLE SELF-SERVING TO ME.
FELIX, YOU SEE EVIL EVERYWHERE.
MAYBE IT WAS OUR HUNTSMAN LEAVING FOR SWITZERLAND?
HMM.
HELLO, SAFIE.
AGATHA...
...
SAFIE!
WOOD...
?
WWOOODD...
WOOD...
WOOD
MUSHROOM
WWOOD...
MUSH... MUSH... MUSHROOM.
WOOD
WOOD
WOOD
WOOD WOOD WOOD WOOD WOOD WOOD

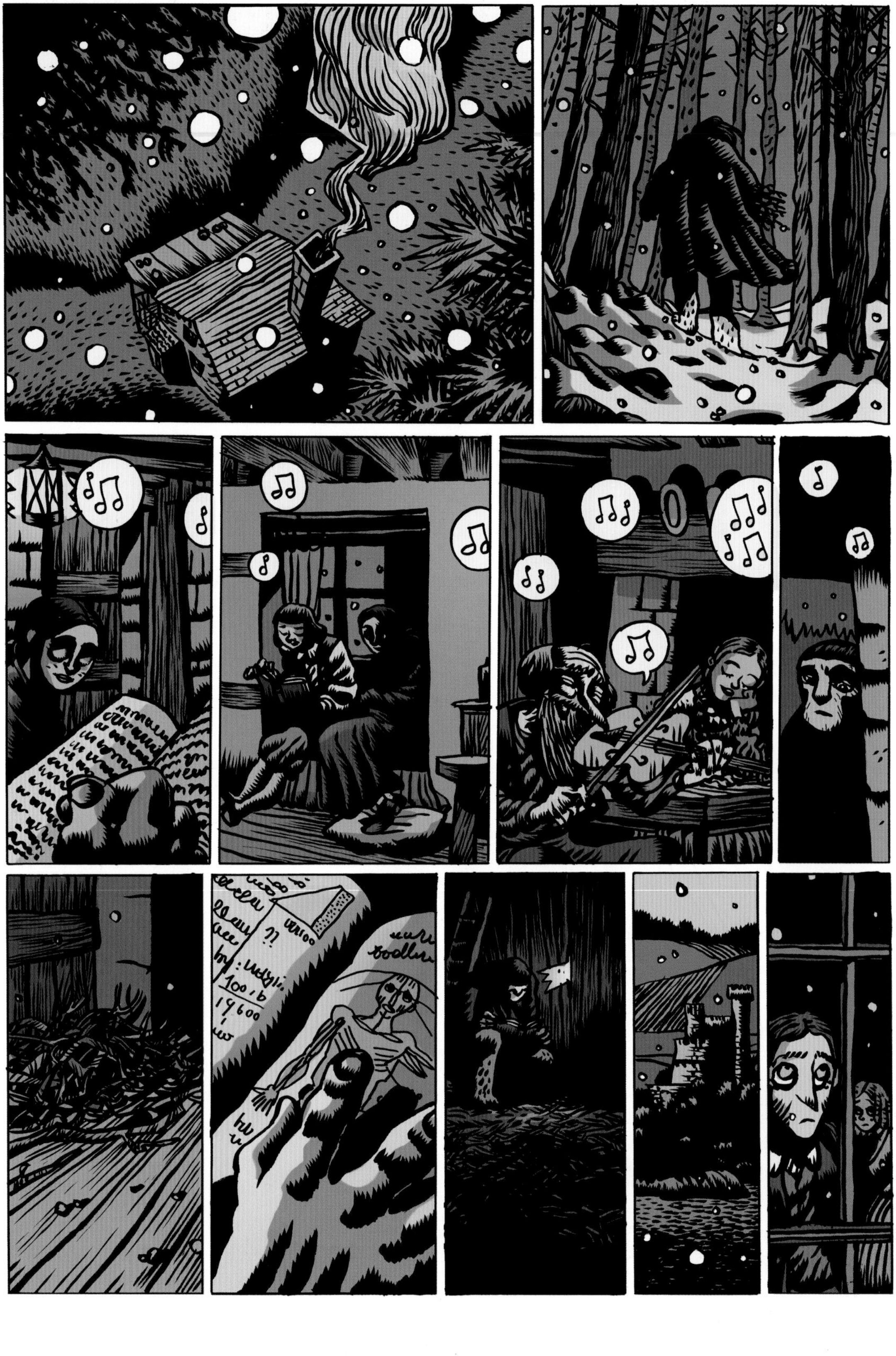

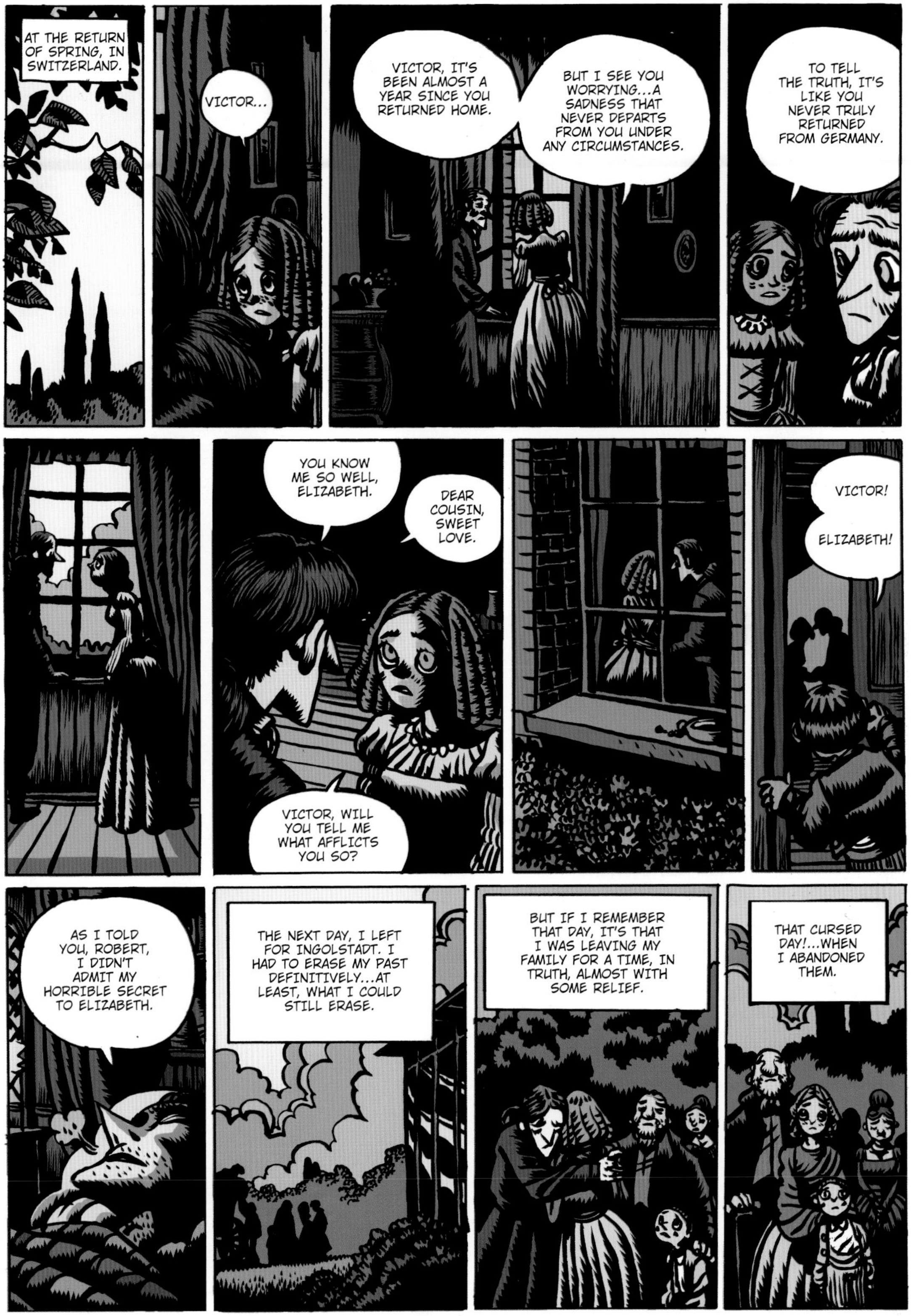
AT THE RETURN OF SPRING, IN SWITZERLAND.
VICTOR...
VICTOR, IT'S BEEN ALMOST A YEAR SINCE YOU RETURNED HOME.
BUT I SEE YOU WORRYING...A SADNESS THAT NEVER DEPARTS FROM YOU UNDER ANY CIRCUMSTANCES.
TO TELL THE TRUTH, IT'S LIKE YOU NEVER TRULY RETURNED FROM GERMANY.
YOU KNOW ME SO WELL, ELIZABETH.
DEAR COUSIN, SWEET LOVE.
VICTOR, WILL YOU TELL ME WHAT AFFLICTS YOU SO?
VICTOR!
ELIZABETH!
AS I TOLD YOU, ROBERT, I DIDN'T ADMIT MY HORRIBLE SECRET TO ELIZABETH.
THE NEXT DAY, I LEFT FOR INGOLSTADT. I HAD TO ERASE MY PAST DEFINITIVELY...AT LEAST, WHAT I COULD STILL ERASE.
BUT IF I REMEMBER THAT DAY, IT'S THAT I WAS LEAVING MY FAMILY FOR A TIME, IN TRUTH, ALMOST WITH SOME RELIEF.
THAT CURSED DAY!...WHEN I ABANDONED THEM.

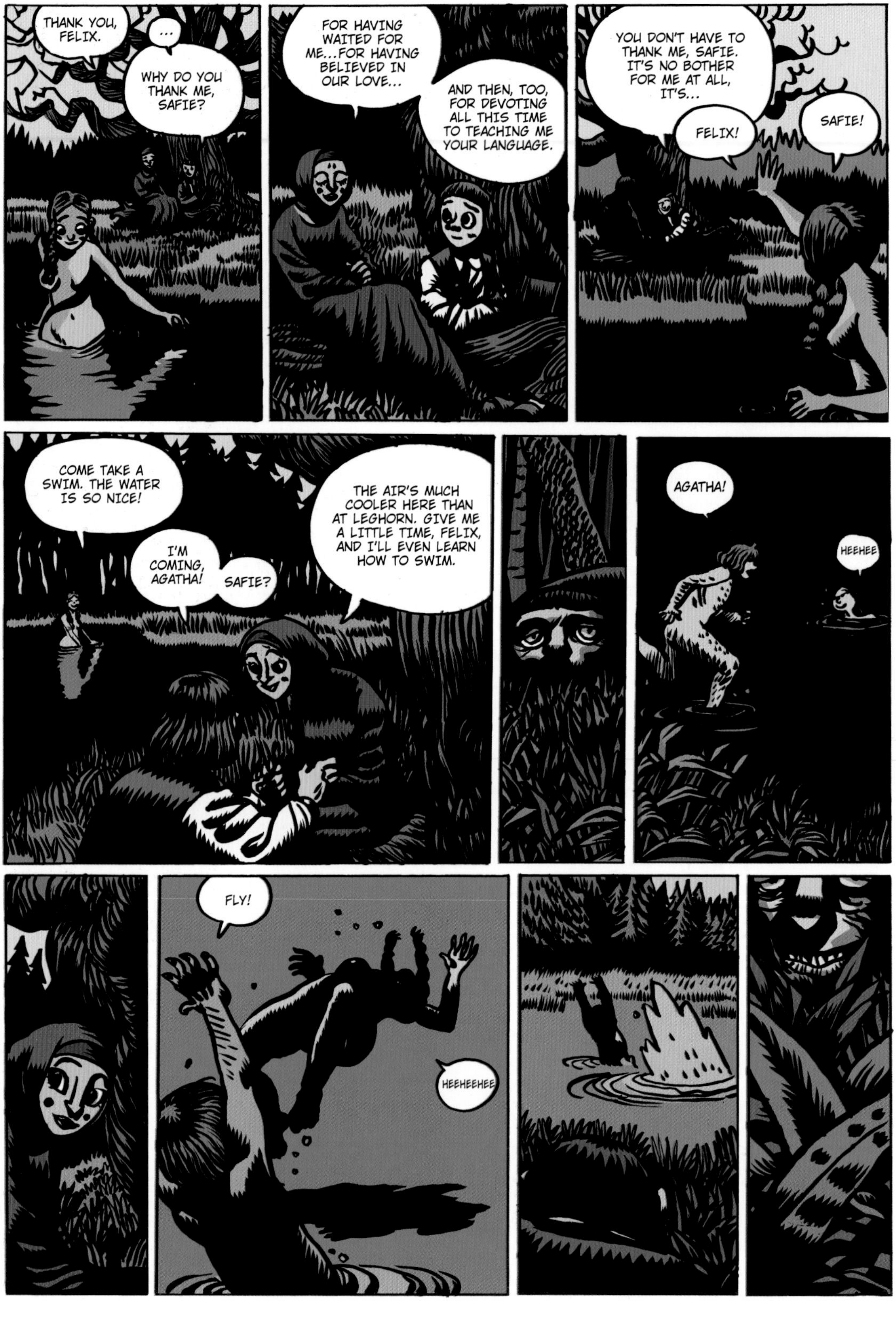
THANK YOU, FELIX.
...
WHY DO YOU THANK ME, SAFIE?
FOR HAVING WAITED FOR ME...FOR HAVING BELIEVED IN OUR LOVE...
AND THEN, TOO, FOR DEVOTING ALL THIS TIME TO TEACHING ME YOUR LANGUAGE.
YOU DON'T HAVE TO THANK ME, SAFIE. IT'S NO BOTHER FOR ME AT ALL, IT'S...
FELIX!
SAFIE!
COME TAKE A SWIM. THE WATER IS SO NICE!
I'M COMING, AGATHA!
SAFIE?
THE AIR'S MUCH COOLER HERE THAN AT LEGHORN. GIVE ME A LITTLE TIME, FELIX, AND I'LL EVEN LEARN HOW TO SWIM.
AGATHA!
HEEHEE
FLY!
HEEHEEHEE

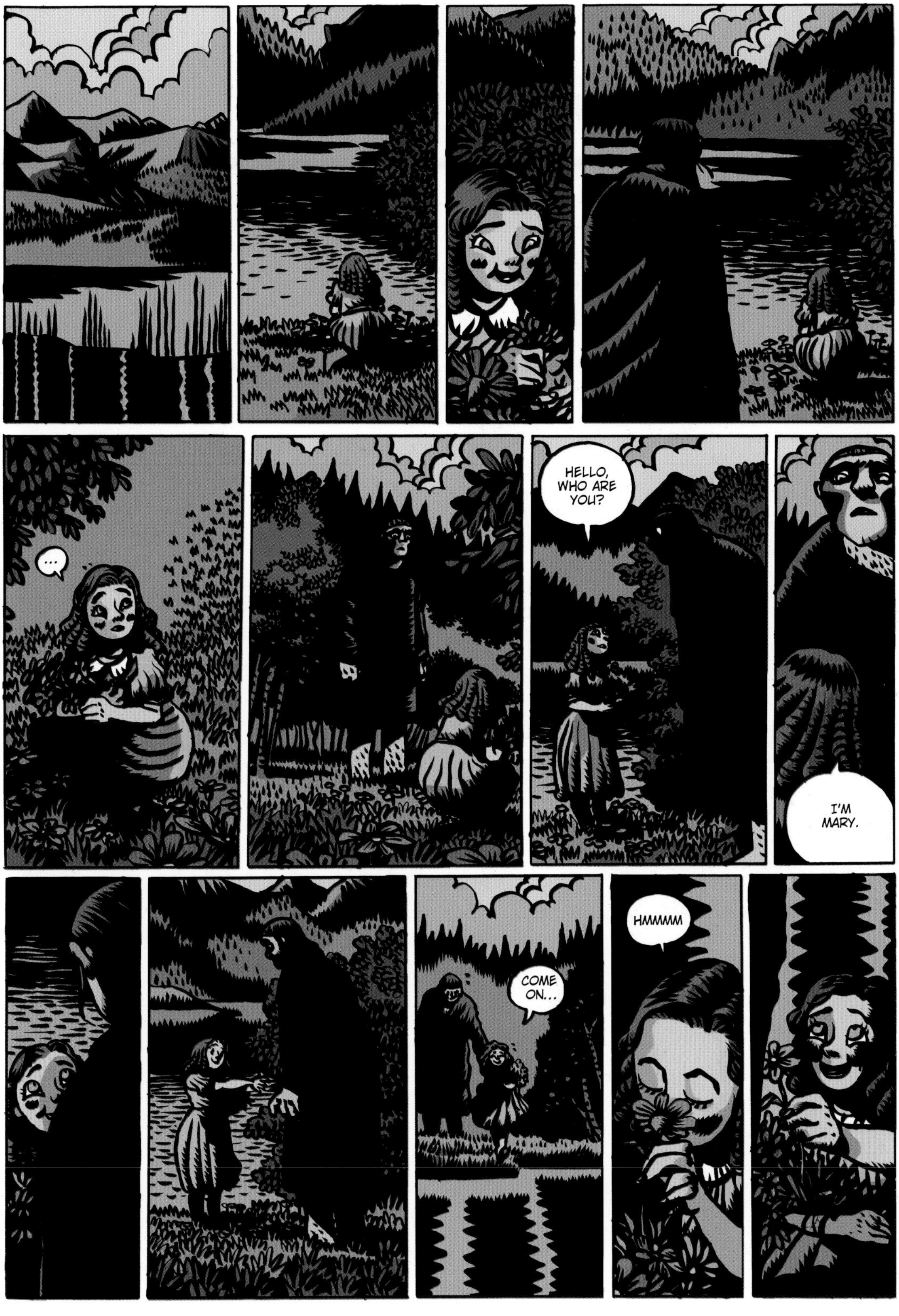
...
HELLO, WHO ARE YOU?
I'M MARY.
COME ON...
HMMMMM

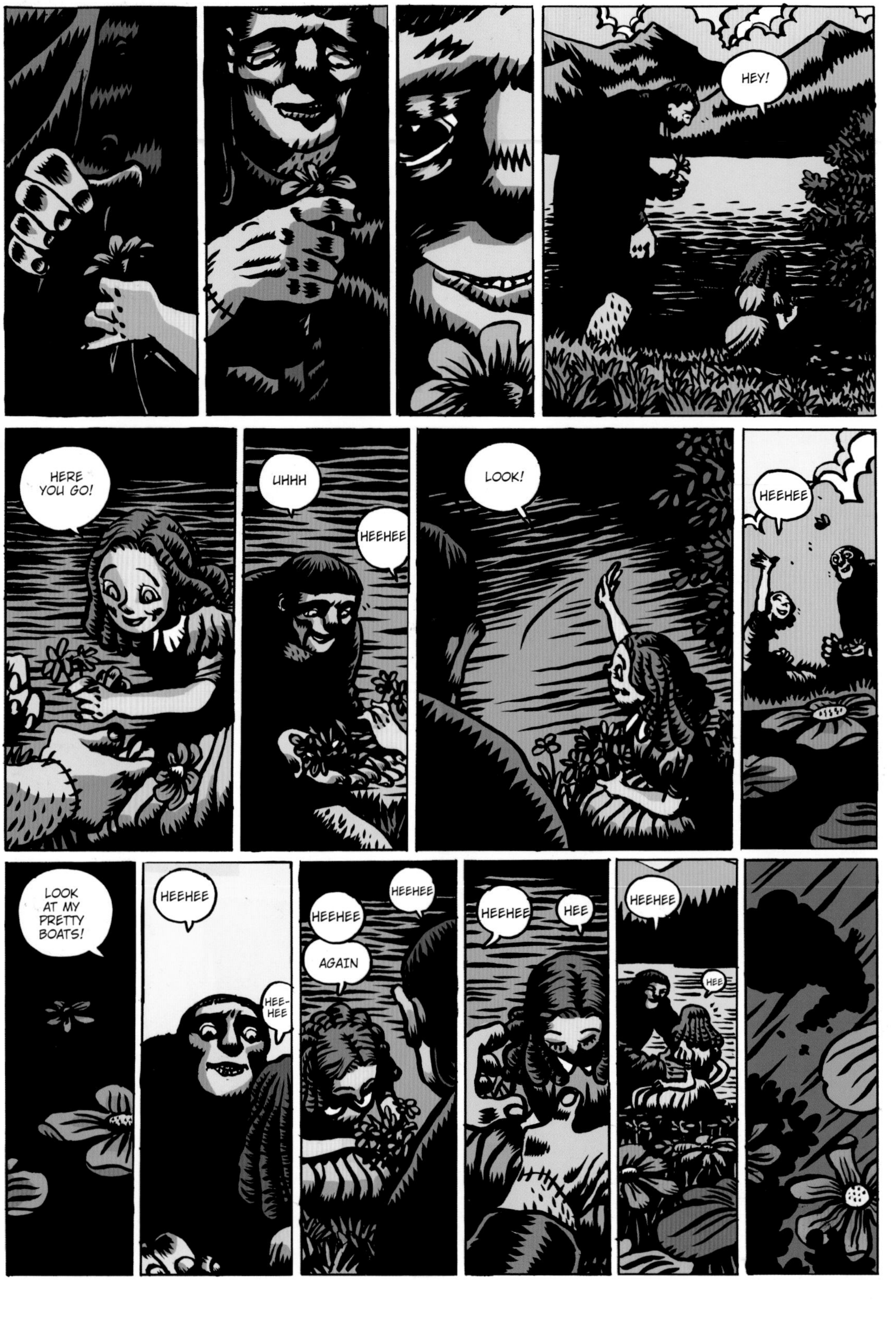
HEY!
HERE YOU GO!
UHHH
HEEHEE
LOOK!
HEEHEE
LOOK AT MY PRETTY BOATS!
HEEHEE
HEE-HEE
HEEHEE
HEEHEE
AGAIN
HEEHEE
HEE
HEEHEE
HEE

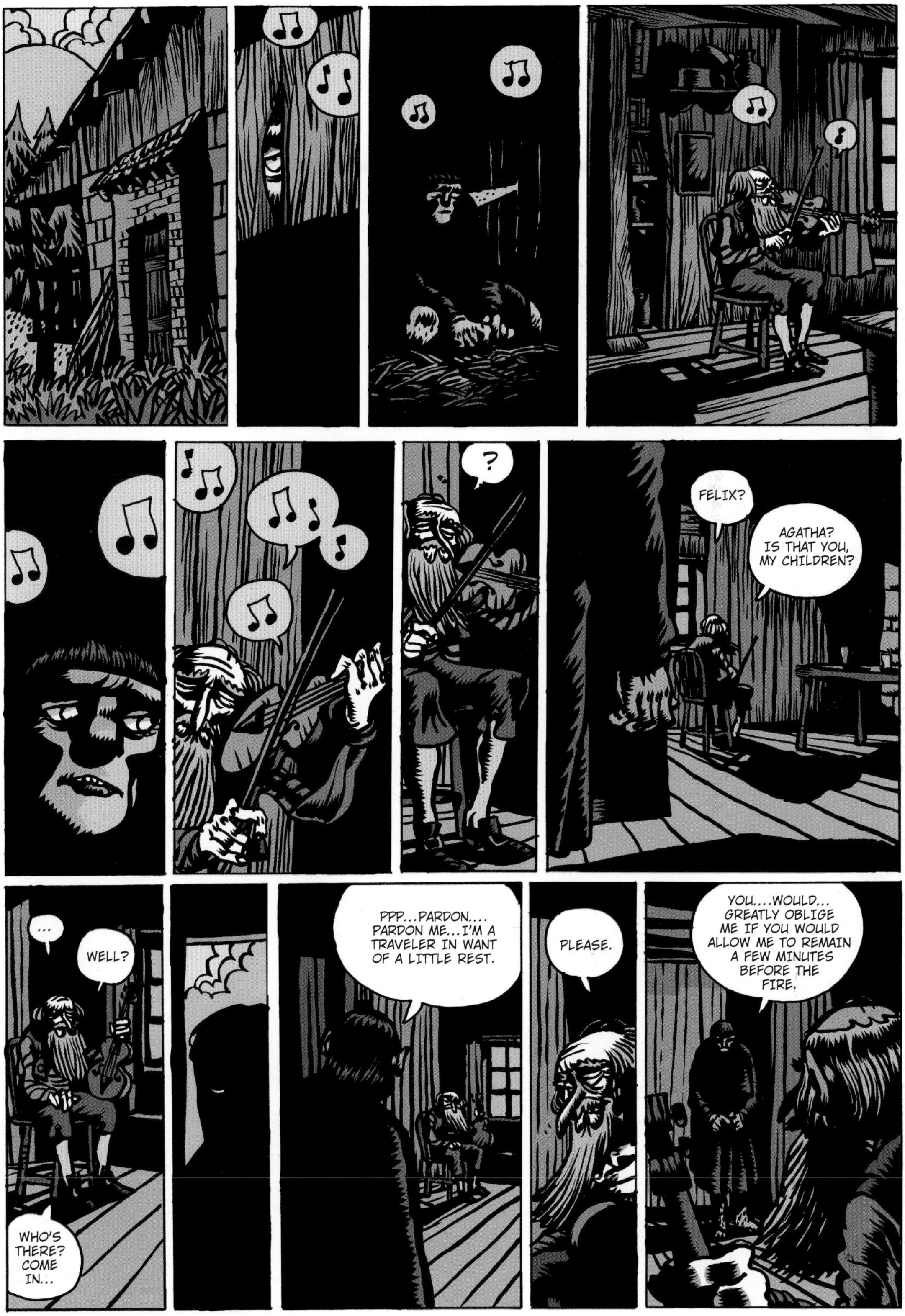

?
FELIX?
AGATHA? IS THAT YOU, MY CHILDREN?
...
WELL?
WHO'S THERE? COME IN...
PPP...PARDON.... PARDON ME...I'M A TRAVELER IN WANT OF A LITTLE REST.
PLEASE.
YOU....WOULD... GREATLY OBLIGE ME IF YOU WOULD ALLOW ME TO REMAIN A FEW MINUTES BEFORE THE FIRE.

ENTER, AND I WILL TRY TO ASSIST YOU THE BEST I CAN, BUT UNFORTUNATELY, MY CHILDREN ARE AWAY FROM HOME, AND I AM BLIND, I AM AFRAID I SHALL FIND IT DIFFICULT TO PROCURE FOOD FOR YOU.

OH, I...DO NOT TROUBLE YOURSELF, MY KIND HOST! I HAVE FOOD AND...

...IT IS WARMTH AND REST ONLY THAT I NEED!

TELL ME...

BY YOUR LANGUAGE, STRANGER, I SUPPOSE YOU ARE MY COUNTRYMAN. ARE YOU FRENCH?

NO...

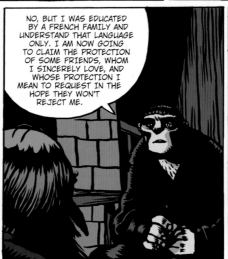

NO, BUT I WAS EDUCATED BY A FRENCH FAMILY AND UNDERSTAND THAT LANGUAGE ONLY. I AM NOW GOING TO CLAIM THE PROTECTION OF SOME FRIENDS, WHOM I SINCERELY LOVE, AND WHOSE PROTECTION I MEAN TO REQUEST IN THE HOPE THEY WON'T REJECT ME.

...

ARE THEY GERMAN?

NO...

...THEY ARE FRENCH.

I...AM AN UNFORTUNATE AND DESERTED CREATURE, MONSIEUR.

I HAVE NO RELATION OR FRIEND UPON THE EARTH. THESE AMIABLE PEOPLE TO WHOM I GO HAVE NEVER SEEN ME AND KNOW LITTLE OF ME, SUCH AS I AM.

I'M FULL OF FEARS...TORMENTED... I...BY FEAR, FOR IF I FAIL THERE, I AM AN OUTCAST IN THE WORLD FOREVER.

...

DO NOT DESPAIR.

TO BE FRIENDLESS IS INDEED TO BE UNFORTUNATE, BUT THE HEARTS OF MEN, WHEN UNPREJUDICED BY ANY OBVIOUS SELF-INTEREST, ARE FULL OF BROTHERLY LOVE AND CHARITY.

RELY, THEREFORE, ON YOUR HOPES.

AND IF THESE FRIENDS ARE GOOD AND GENEROUS BEINGS, YOU HAVE NO REASON TO DESPAIR.

THEY ARE KIND.

YES, THEY ARE THE MOST EXCELLENT CREATURES IN THE WORD. ALAS, I FEAR THEY ARE PREJUDICED AGAINST ME.

I HAVE GOOD DISPOSITIONS. MY LIFE HAS BEEN HITHERTO HARMLESS...

...BUT MY APPEARANCE, UNFORTUNATELY, IS WORKING AGAINST ME.

WHERE THEY OUGHT TO SEE A FEELING AND KIND FRIEND, THEY BEHOLD ONLY A DETESTABLE MONSTER.

THAT IS INDEED UNFORTUNATE...

BUT IF YOU ARE REALLY BLAMELESS, CANNOT YOU UNDECEIVE THEM?

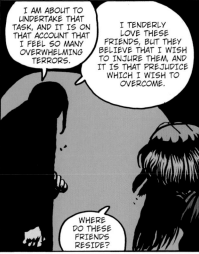

I AM ABOUT TO UNDERTAKE THAT TASK, AND IT IS ON THAT ACCOUNT THAT I FEEL SO MANY OVERWHELMING TERRORS.

I TENDERLY LOVE THESE FRIENDS, BUT THEY BELIEVE THAT I WISH TO INJURE THEM, AND IT IS THAT PREJUDICE WHICH I WISH TO OVERCOME.

WHERE DO THESE FRIENDS RESIDE?

NEAR THIS SPOT.

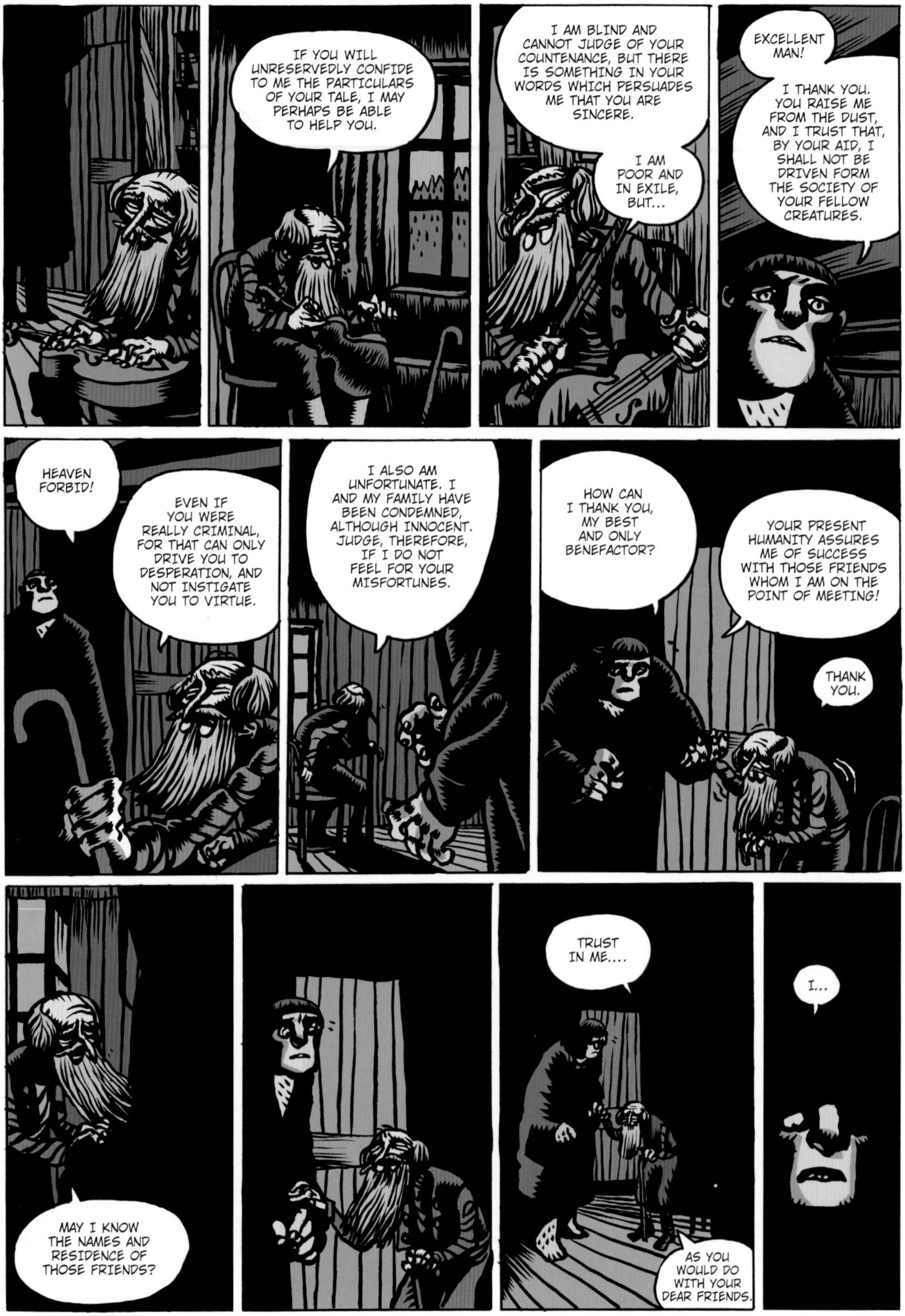

IF YOU WILL UNRESERVEDLY CONFIDE TO ME THE PARTICULARS OF YOUR TALE, I MAY PERHAPS BE ABLE TO HELP YOU.
I AM BLIND AND CANNOT JUDGE OF YOUR COUNTENANCE, BUT THERE IS SOMETHING IN YOUR WORDS WHICH PERSUADES ME THAT YOU ARE SINCERE.
I AM POOR AND IN EXILE, BUT...
EXCELLENT MAN!
I THANK YOU. YOU RAISE ME FROM THE DUST, AND I TRUST THAT, BY YOUR AID, I SHALL NOT BE DRIVEN FORM THE SOCIETY OF YOUR FELLOW CREATURES.
HEAVEN FORBID!
EVEN IF YOU WERE REALLY CRIMINAL, FOR THAT CAN ONLY DRIVE YOU TO DESPERATION, AND NOT INSTIGATE YOU TO VIRTUE.
I ALSO AM UNFORTUNATE. I AND MY FAMILY HAVE BEEN CONDEMNED, ALTHOUGH INNOCENT. JUDGE, THEREFORE, IF I DO NOT FEEL FOR YOUR MISFORTUNES.
HOW CAN I THANK YOU, MY BEST AND ONLY BENEFACTOR?
YOUR PRESENT HUMANITY ASSURES ME OF SUCCESS WITH THOSE FRIENDS WHOM I AM ON THE POINT OF MEETING!
THANK YOU.
MAY I KNOW THE NAMES AND RESIDENCE OF THOSE FRIENDS?
TRUST IN ME....
AS YOU WOULD DO WITH YOUR DEAR FRIENDS.
I...

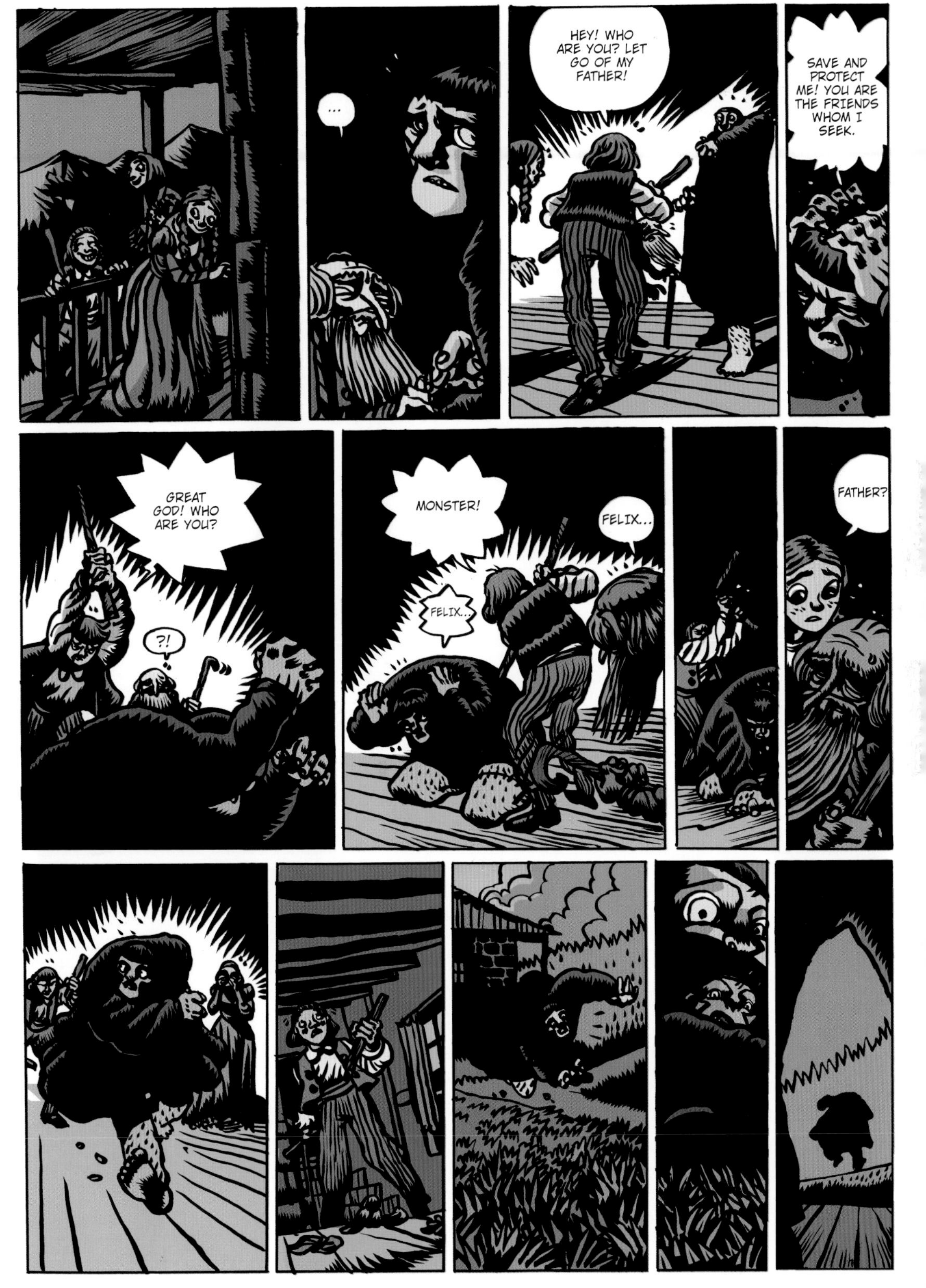
...
HEY! WHO ARE YOU? LET GO OF MY FATHER!
SAVE AND PROTECT ME! YOU ARE THE FRIENDS WHOM I SEEK.
GREAT GOD! WHO ARE YOU?
?!
MONSTER!
FELIX...
FELIX...
FATHER?

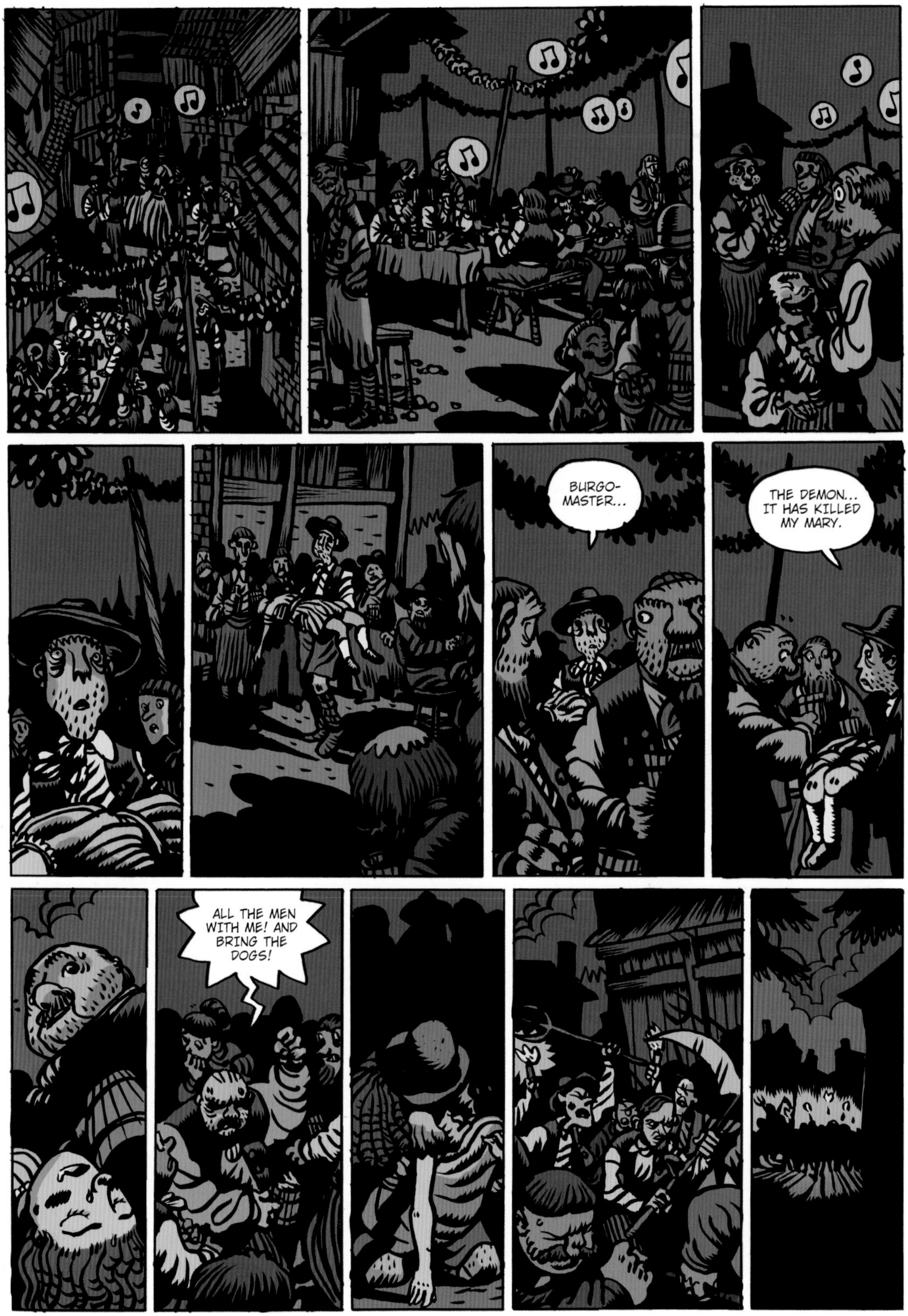
BURGO-
MASTER...
THE DEMON...
IT HAS KILLED
MY MARY.
ALL THE MEN
WITH ME! AND
BRING THE
DOGS!

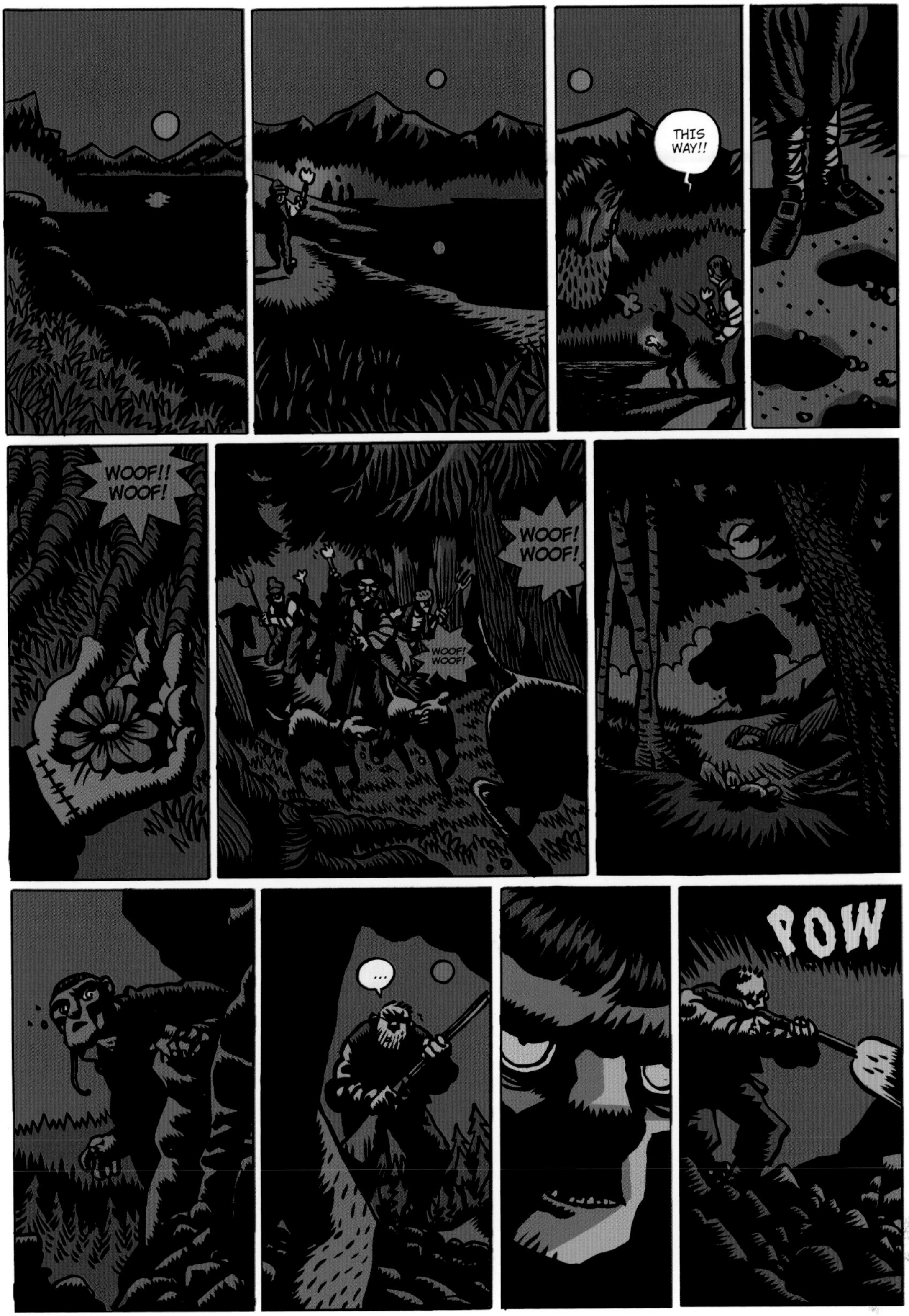
THIS WAY!!
WOOF!! WOOF!
WOOF! WOOF!
WOOF! WOOF!
...
POW

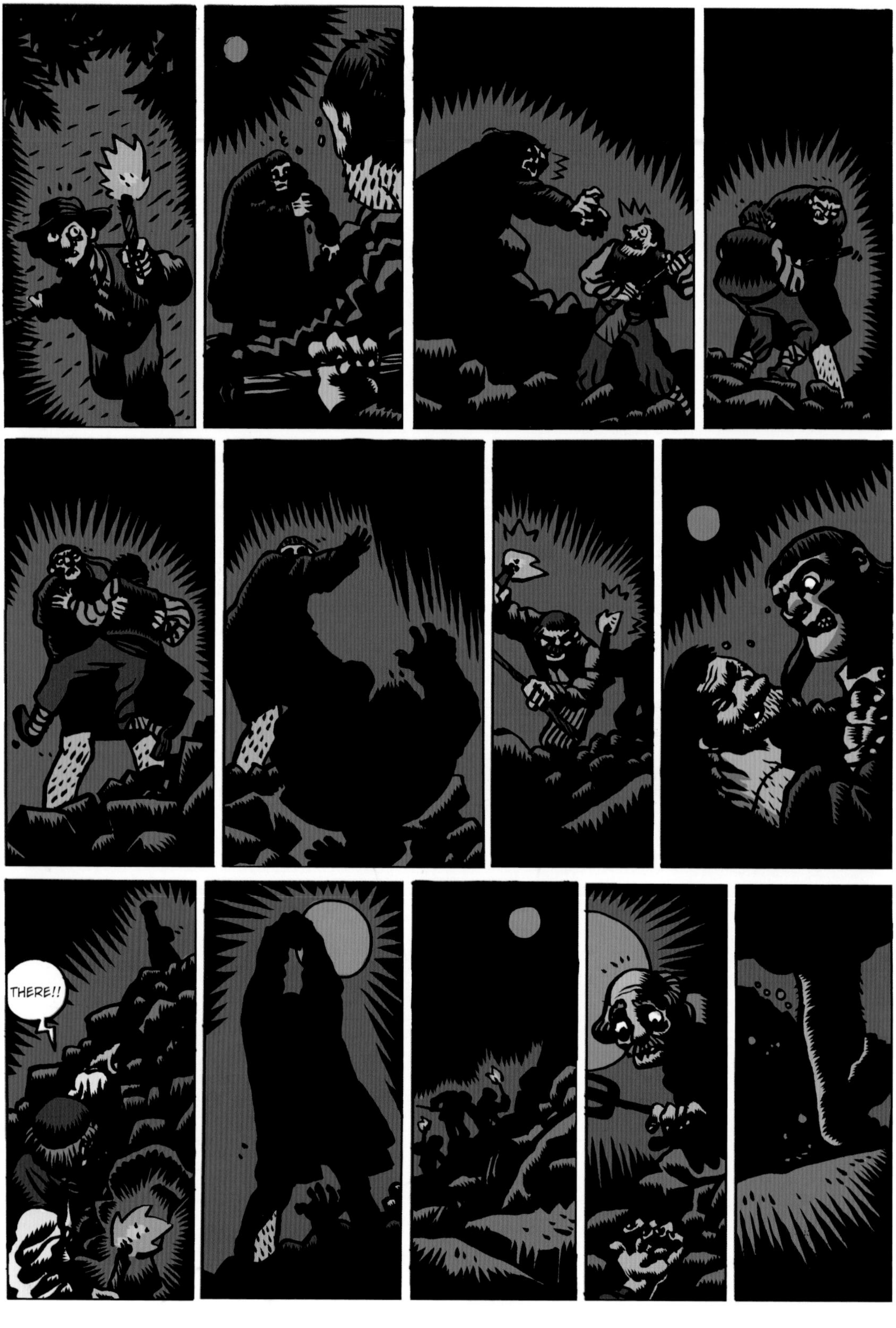
THERE!!

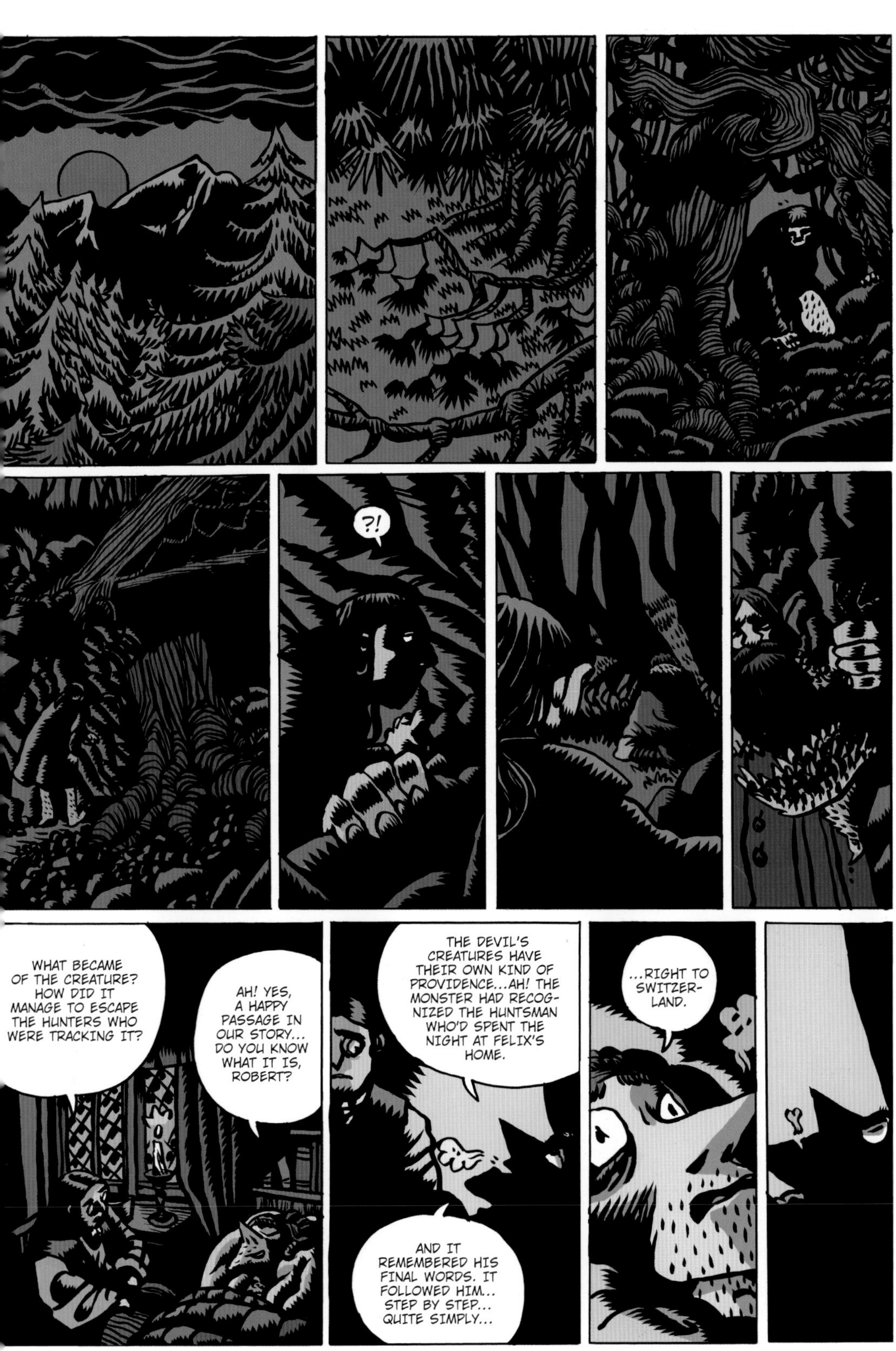
?!
WHAT BECAME OF THE CREATURE? HOW DID IT MANAGE TO ESCAPE THE HUNTERS WHO WERE TRACKING IT?
AH! YES, A HAPPY PASSAGE IN OUR STORY... DO YOU KNOW WHAT IT IS, ROBERT?
THE DEVIL'S CREATURES HAVE THEIR OWN KIND OF PROVIDENCE...AH! THE MONSTER HAD RECOGNIZED THE HUNTSMAN WHO'D SPENT THE NIGHT AT FELIX'S HOME.
AND IT REMEMBERED HIS FINAL WORDS. IT FOLLOWED HIM... STEP BY STEP... QUITE SIMPLY...
...RIGHT TO SWITZERLAND.

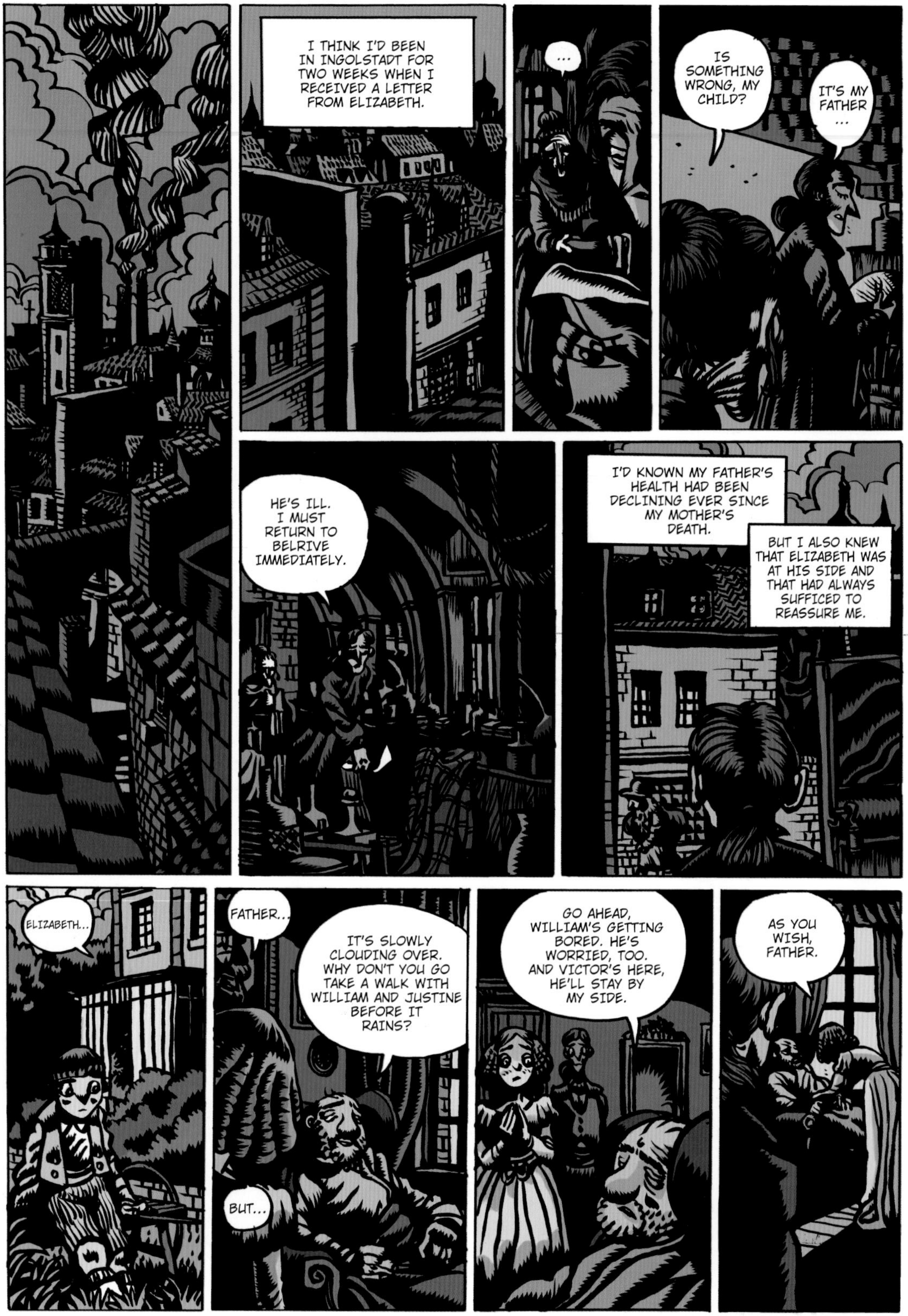
I THINK I'D BEEN IN INGOLSTADT FOR TWO WEEKS WHEN I RECEIVED A LETTER FROM ELIZABETH.
...
IS SOMETHING WRONG, MY CHILD?
IT'S MY FATHER ...
HE'S ILL. I MUST RETURN TO BELRIVE IMMEDIATELY.
I'D KNOWN MY FATHER'S HEALTH HAD BEEN DECLINING EVER SINCE MY MOTHER'S DEATH.
BUT I ALSO KNEW THAT ELIZABETH WAS AT HIS SIDE AND THAT HAD ALWAYS SUFFICED TO REASSURE ME.
ELIZABETH...
FATHER...
IT'S SLOWLY CLOUDING OVER. WHY DON'T YOU GO TAKE A WALK WITH WILLIAM AND JUSTINE BEFORE IT RAINS?
BUT...
GO AHEAD, WILLIAM'S GETTING BORED. HE'S WORRIED, TOO. AND VICTOR'S HERE, HE'LL STAY BY MY SIDE.
AS YOU WISH, FATHER.

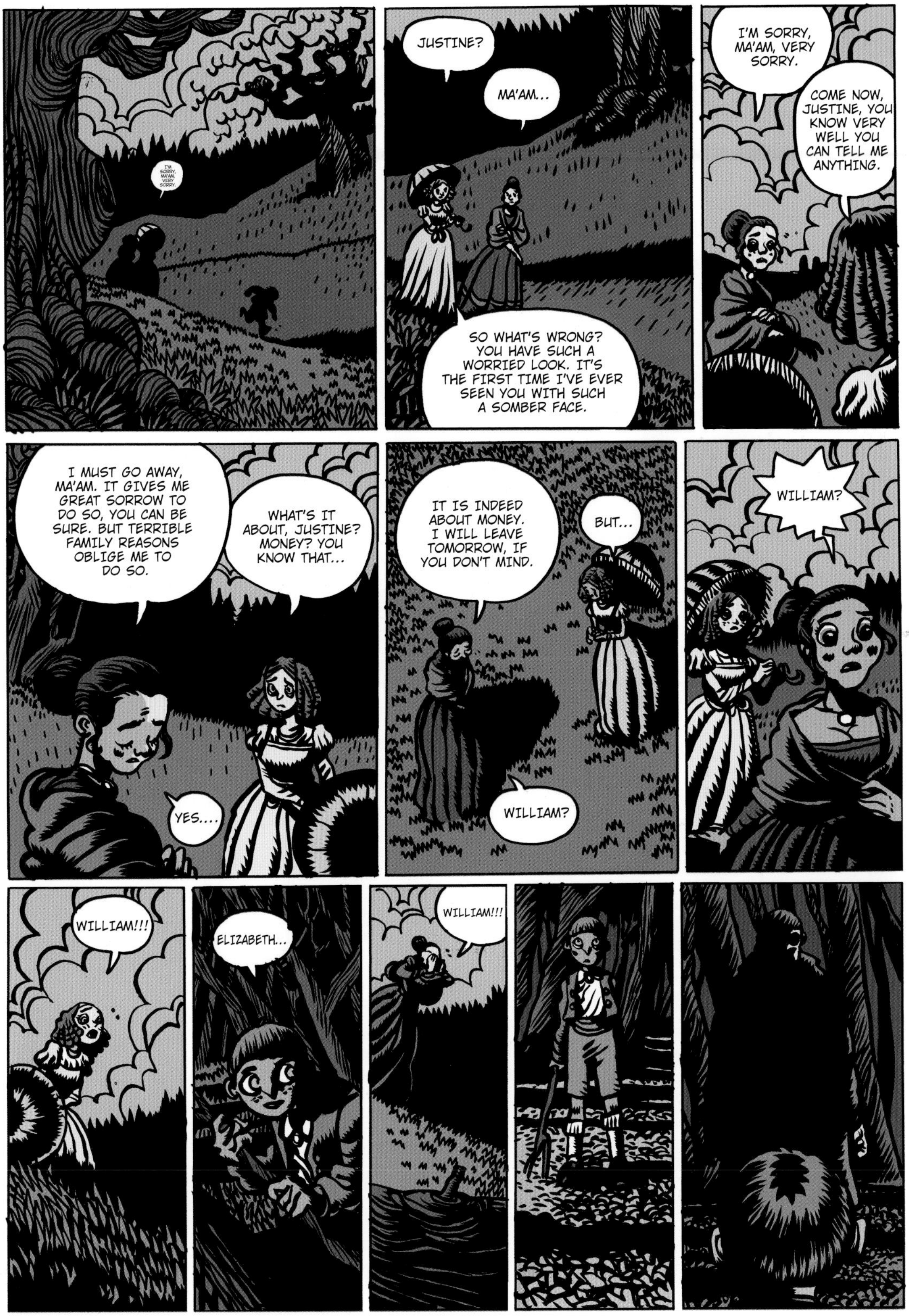
I'M SORRY, MA'AM, VERY SORRY.
JUSTINE?
MA'AM...
SO WHAT'S WRONG? YOU HAVE SUCH A WORRIED LOOK. IT'S THE FIRST TIME I'VE EVER SEEN YOU WITH SUCH A SOMBER FACE.
I'M SORRY, MA'AM, VERY SORRY.
COME NOW, JUSTINE, YOU KNOW VERY WELL YOU CAN TELL ME ANYTHING.
I MUST GO AWAY, MA'AM. IT GIVES ME GREAT SORROW TO DO SO, YOU CAN BE SURE. BUT TERRIBLE FAMILY REASONS OBLIGE ME TO DO SO.
WHAT'S IT ABOUT, JUSTINE? MONEY? YOU KNOW THAT...
YES....
IT IS INDEED ABOUT MONEY. I WILL LEAVE TOMORROW, IF YOU DON'T MIND.
BUT...
WILLIAM?
WILLIAM?
WILLIAM!!!
ELIZABETH...
WILLIAM!!!

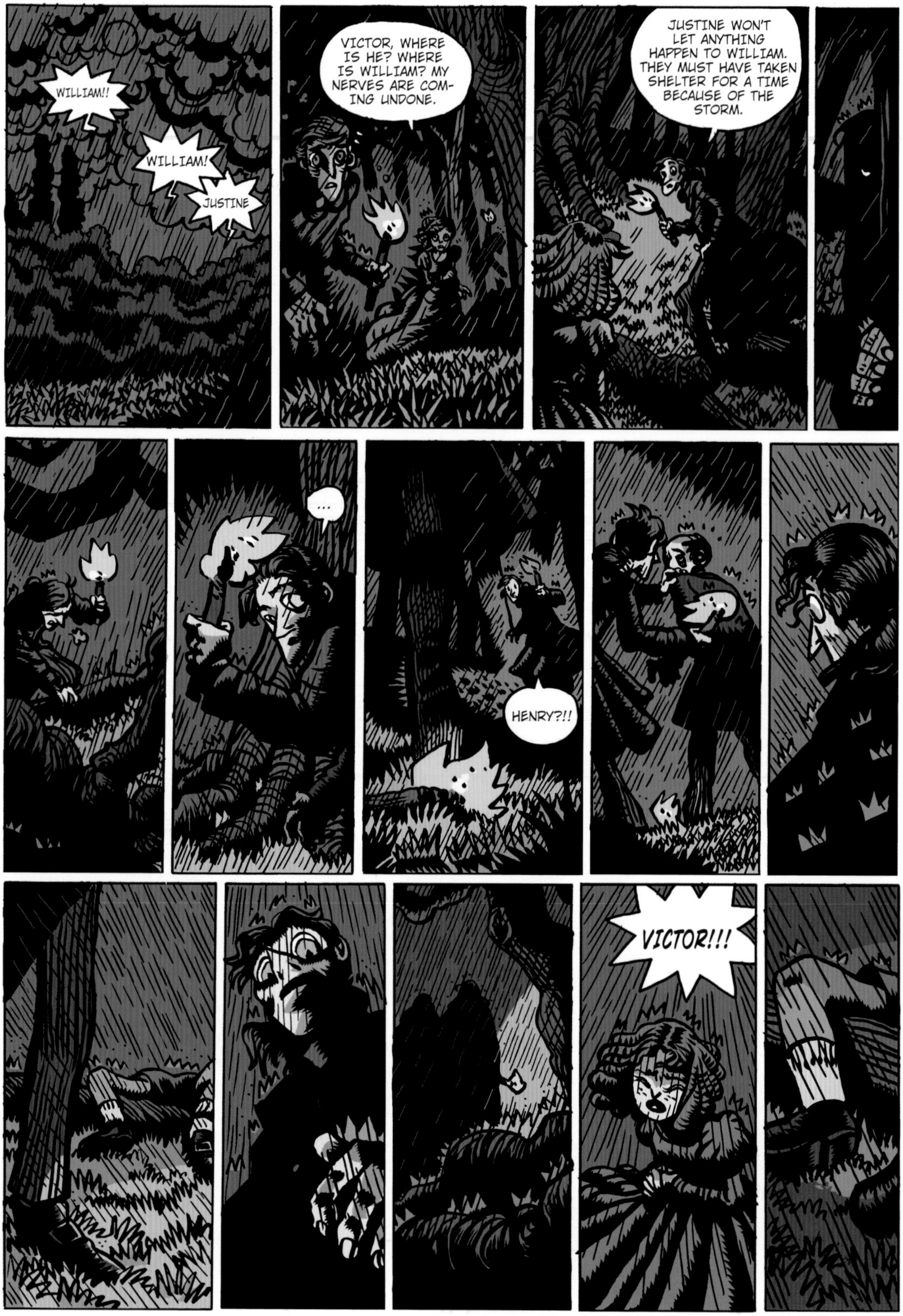
WILLIAM!!
WILLIAM!
JUSTINE
VICTOR, WHERE IS HE? WHERE IS WILLIAM? MY NERVES ARE COMING UNDONE.
JUSTINE WON'T LET ANYTHING HAPPEN TO WILLIAM. THEY MUST HAVE TAKEN SHELTER FOR A TIME BECAUSE OF THE STORM.
...
HENRY?!!
VICTOR!!!

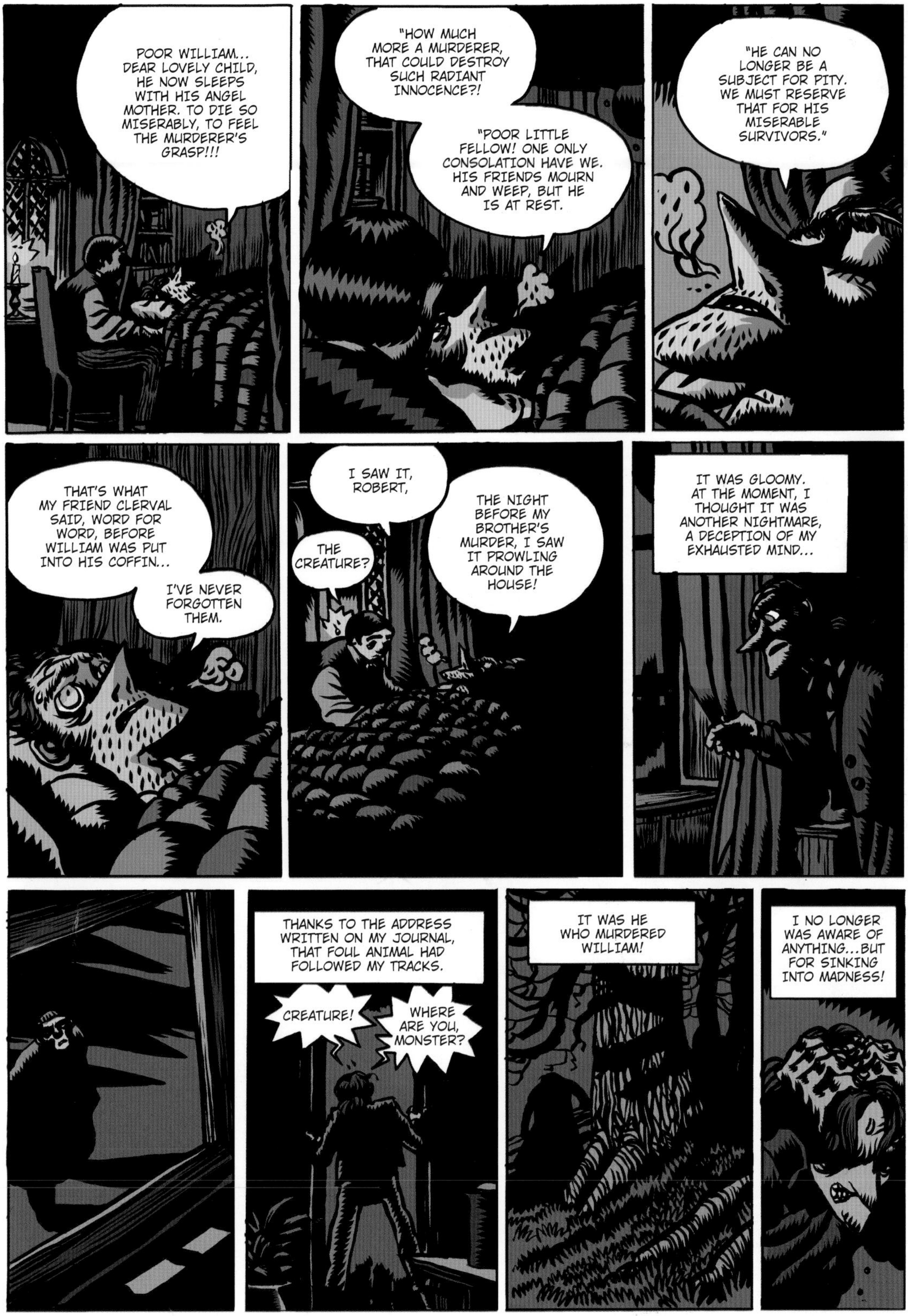
POOR WILLIAM... DEAR LOVELY CHILD, HE NOW SLEEPS WITH HIS ANGEL MOTHER. TO DIE SO MISERABLY, TO FEEL THE MURDERER'S GRASP!!!
"HOW MUCH MORE A MURDERER, THAT COULD DESTROY SUCH RADIANT INNOCENCE?!
"POOR LITTLE FELLOW! ONE ONLY CONSOLATION HAVE WE. HIS FRIENDS MOURN AND WEEP, BUT HE IS AT REST.
"HE CAN NO LONGER BE A SUBJECT FOR PITY. WE MUST RESERVE THAT FOR HIS MISERABLE SURVIVORS."
THAT'S WHAT MY FRIEND CLERVAL SAID, WORD FOR WORD, BEFORE WILLIAM WAS PUT INTO HIS COFFIN...
I'VE NEVER FORGOTTEN THEM.
I SAW IT, ROBERT,
THE CREATURE?
THE NIGHT BEFORE MY BROTHER'S MURDER, I SAW IT PROWLING AROUND THE HOUSE!
IT WAS GLOOMY. AT THE MOMENT, I THOUGHT IT WAS ANOTHER NIGHTMARE, A DECEPTION OF MY EXHAUSTED MIND...
THANKS TO THE ADDRESS WRITTEN ON MY JOURNAL, THAT FOUL ANIMAL HAD FOLLOWED MY TRACKS.
CREATURE!
WHERE ARE YOU, MONSTER?
IT WAS HE WHO MURDERED WILLIAM!
I NO LONGER WAS AWARE OF ANYTHING...BUT FOR SINKING INTO MADNESS!

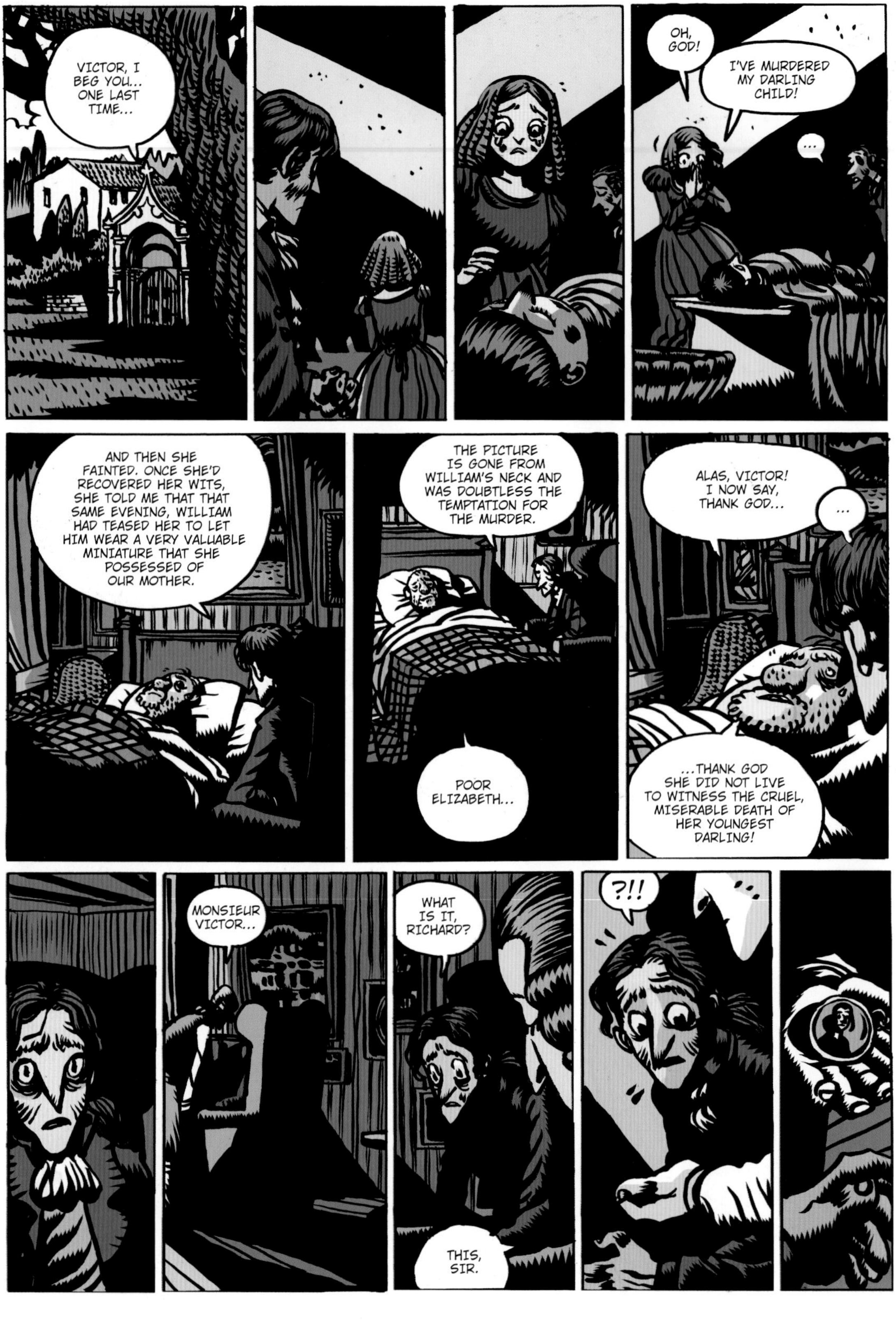
VICTOR, I BEG YOU... ONE LAST TIME...
OH, GOD!
I'VE MURDERED MY DARLING CHILD!
...
AND THEN SHE FAINTED. ONCE SHE'D RECOVERED HER WITS, SHE TOLD ME THAT THAT SAME EVENING, WILLIAM HAD TEASED HER TO LET HIM WEAR A VERY VALUABLE MINIATURE THAT SHE POSSESSED OF OUR MOTHER.
THE PICTURE IS GONE FROM WILLIAM'S NECK AND WAS DOUBTLESS THE TEMPTATION FOR THE MURDER.
POOR ELIZABETH...
ALAS, VICTOR! I NOW SAY, THANK GOD...
...
...THANK GOD SHE DID NOT LIVE TO WITNESS THE CRUEL, MISERABLE DEATH OF HER YOUNGEST DARLING!
MONSIEUR VICTOR...
WHAT IS IT, RICHARD?
THIS, SIR.
?!!

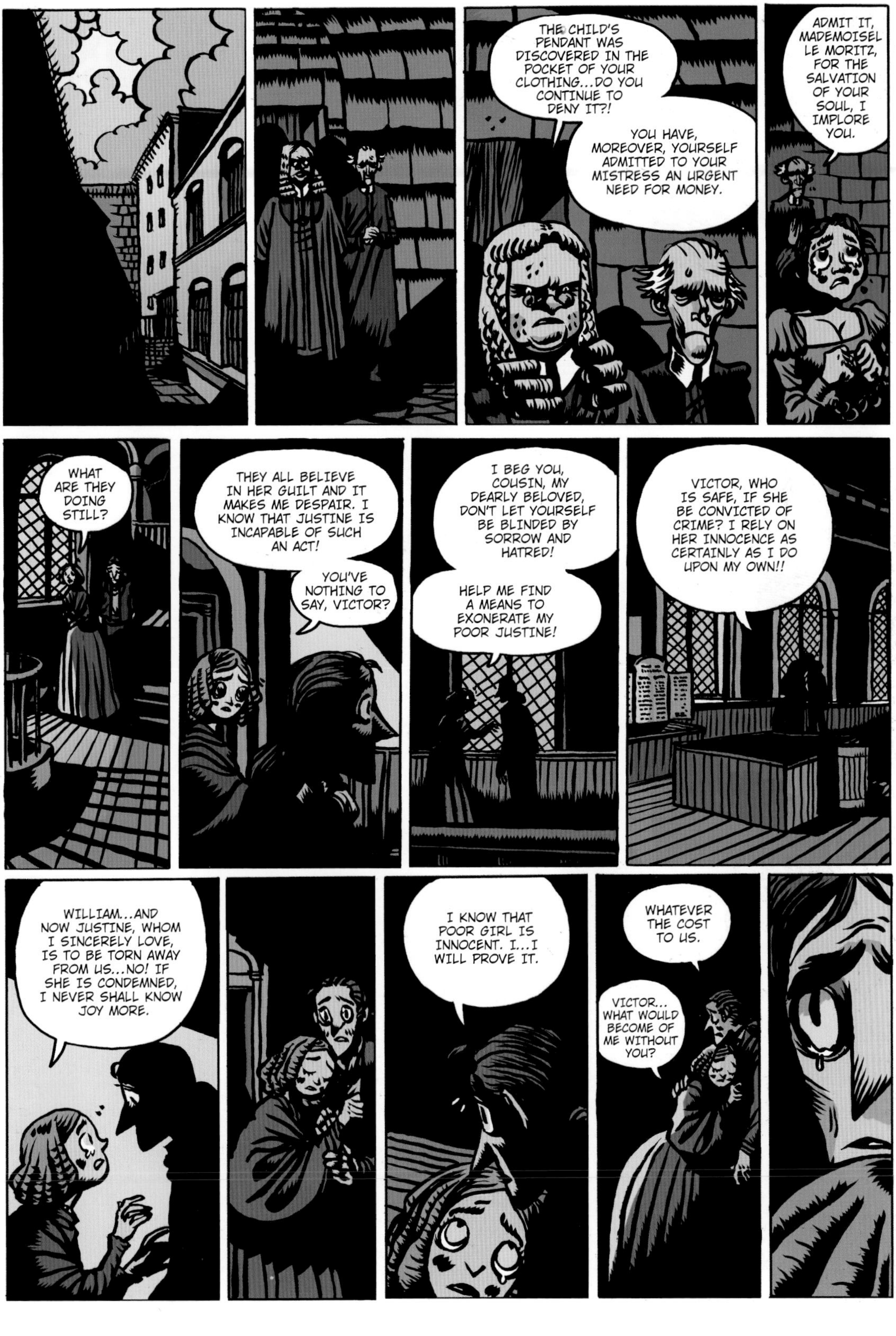
THE CHILD'S PENDANT WAS DISCOVERED IN THE POCKET OF YOUR CLOTHING...DO YOU CONTINUE TO DENY IT?!
YOU HAVE, MOREOVER, YOURSELF ADMITTED TO YOUR MISTRESS AN URGENT NEED FOR MONEY.
ADMIT IT, MADEMOISELLE MORITZ, FOR THE SALVATION OF YOUR SOUL, I IMPLORE YOU.
WHAT ARE THEY DOING STILL?
THEY ALL BELIEVE IN HER GUILT AND IT MAKES ME DESPAIR. I KNOW THAT JUSTINE IS INCAPABLE OF SUCH AN ACT!
YOU'VE NOTHING TO SAY, VICTOR?
I BEG YOU, COUSIN, MY DEARLY BELOVED, DON'T LET YOURSELF BE BLINDED BY SORROW AND HATRED!
HELP ME FIND A MEANS TO EXONERATE MY POOR JUSTINE!
VICTOR, WHO IS SAFE, IF SHE BE CONVICTED OF CRIME? I RELY ON HER INNOCENCE AS CERTAINLY AS I DO UPON MY OWN!!
WILLIAM...AND NOW JUSTINE, WHOM I SINCERELY LOVE, IS TO BE TORN AWAY FROM US...NO! IF SHE IS CONDEMNED, I NEVER SHALL KNOW JOY MORE.
I KNOW THAT POOR GIRL IS INNOCENT. I...I WILL PROVE IT.
WHATEVER THE COST TO US.
VICTOR... WHAT WOULD BECOME OF ME WITHOUT YOU?

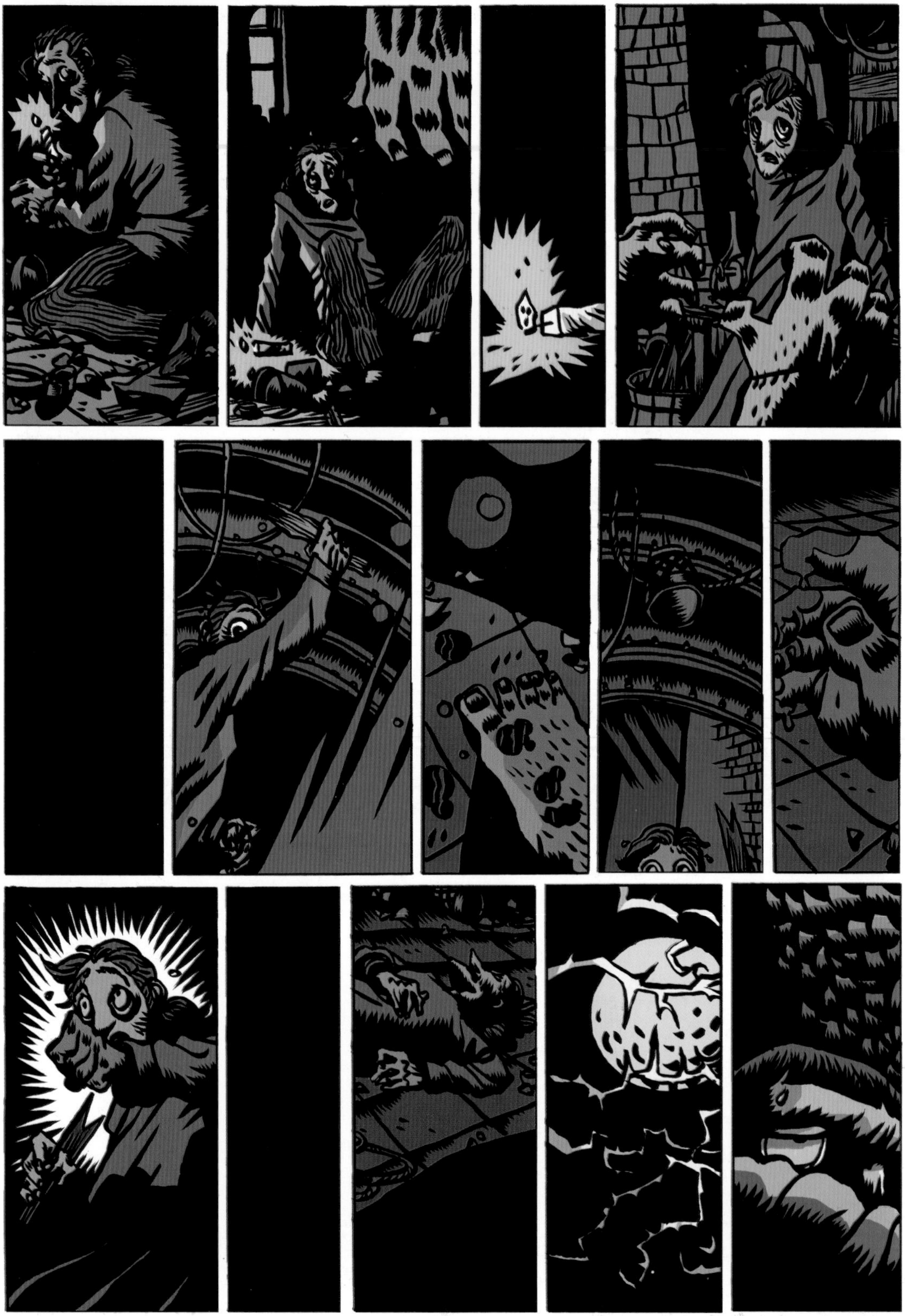

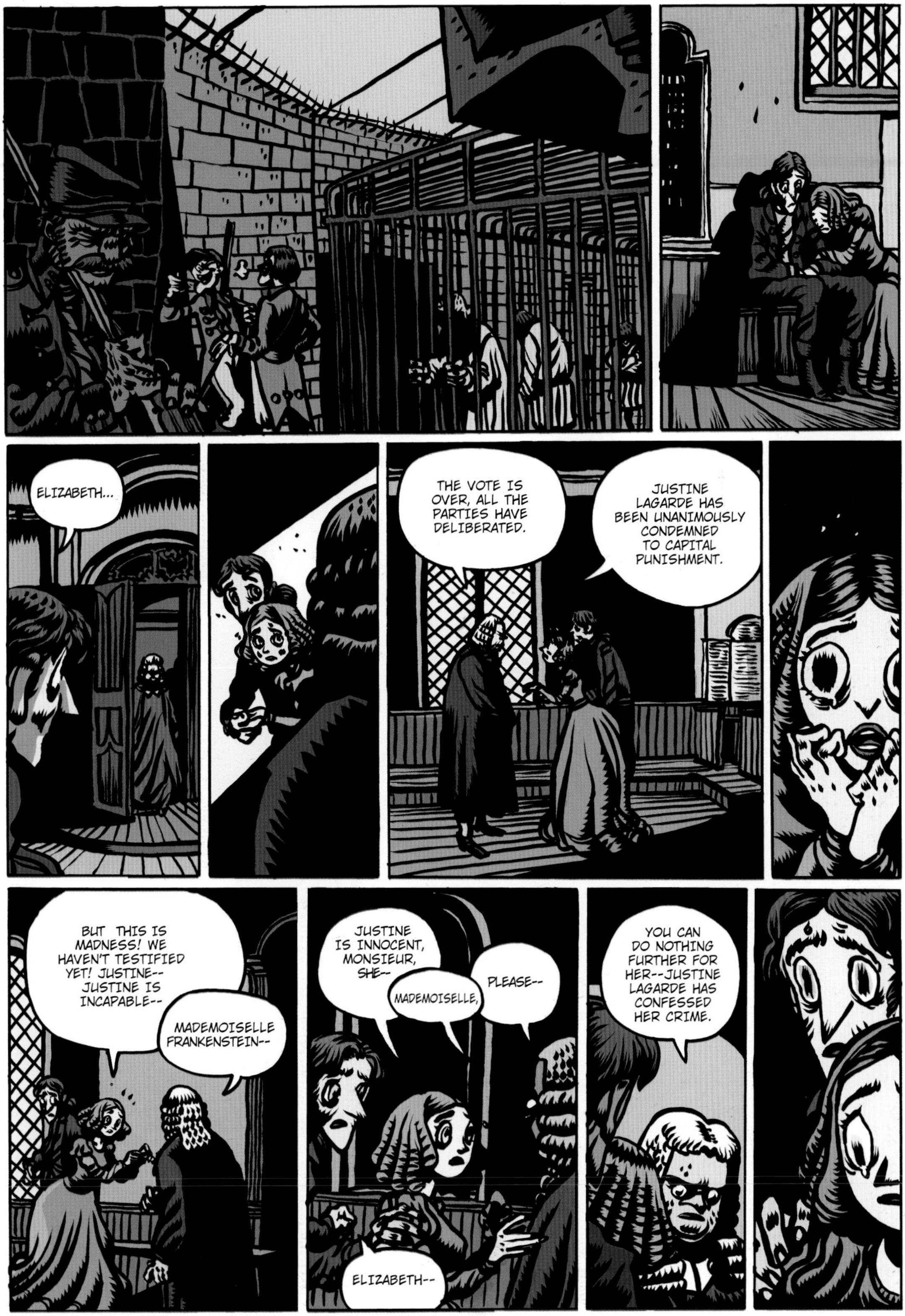
ELIZABETH...
THE VOTE IS OVER, ALL THE PARTIES HAVE DELIBERATED.
JUSTINE LAGARDE HAS BEEN UNANIMOUSLY CONDEMNED TO CAPITAL PUNISHMENT.
BUT THIS IS MADNESS! WE HAVEN'T TESTIFIED YET! JUSTINE-- JUSTINE IS INCAPABLE--
MADEMOISELLE FRANKENSTEIN--
JUSTINE IS INNOCENT, MONSIEUR, SHE--
MADEMOISELLE,
PLEASE--
ELIZABETH--
YOU CAN DO NOTHING FURTHER FOR HER--JUSTINE LAGARDE HAS CONFESSED HER CRIME.

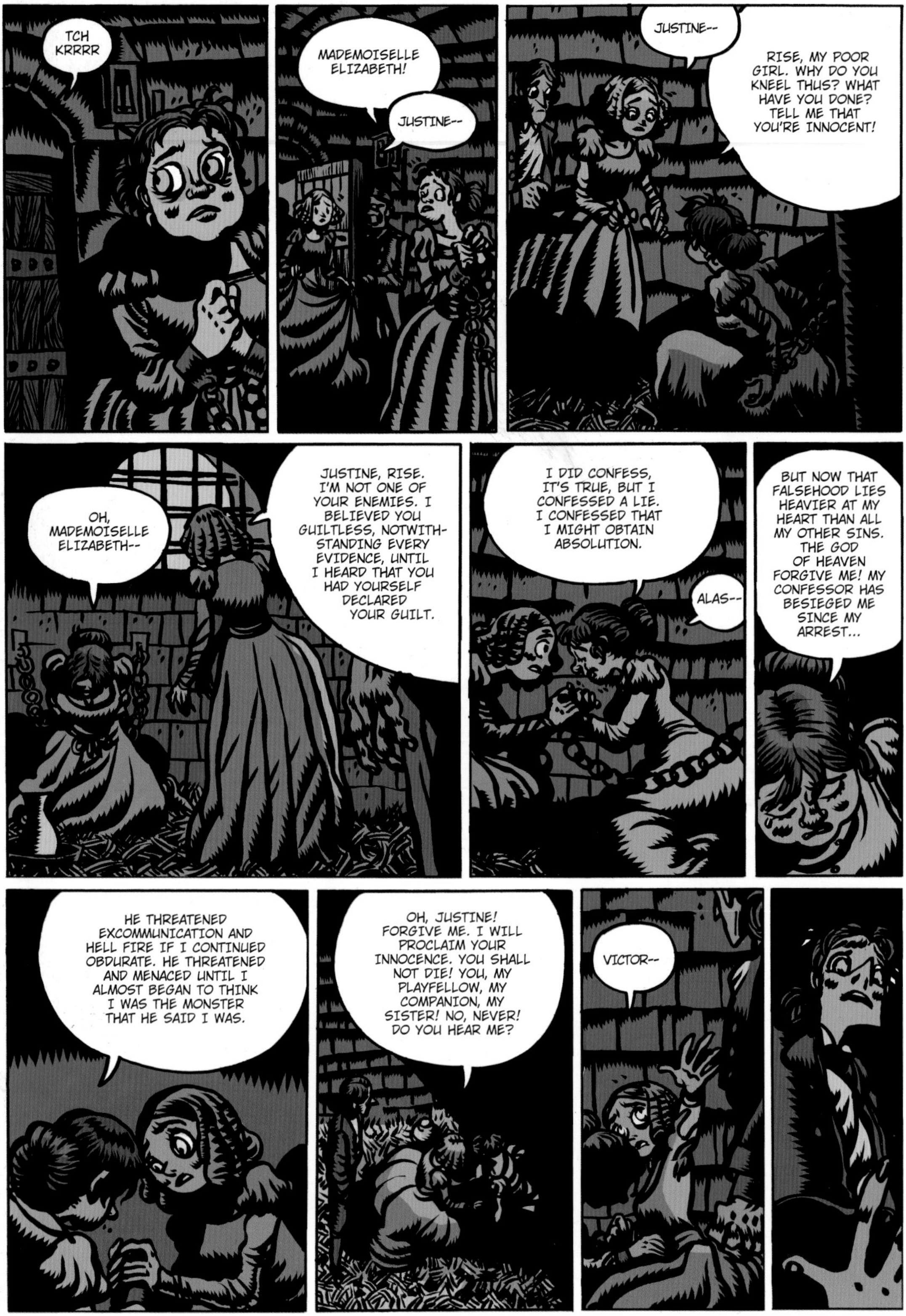
TCH KRRRR
MADEMOISELLE ELIZABETH!
JUSTINE--
JUSTINE--
RISE, MY POOR GIRL. WHY DO YOU KNEEL THUS? WHAT HAVE YOU DONE? TELL ME THAT YOU'RE INNOCENT!
OH, MADEMOISELLE ELIZABETH--
JUSTINE, RISE. I'M NOT ONE OF YOUR ENEMIES. I BELIEVED YOU GUILTLESS, NOTWITH-STANDING EVERY EVIDENCE, UNTIL I HEARD THAT YOU HAD YOURSELF DECLARED YOUR GUILT.
I DID CONFESS, IT'S TRUE, BUT I CONFESSED A LIE. I CONFESSED THAT I MIGHT OBTAIN ABSOLUTION.
ALAS--
BUT NOW THAT FALSEHOOD LIES HEAVIER AT MY HEART THAN ALL MY OTHER SINS. THE GOD OF HEAVEN FORGIVE ME! MY CONFESSOR HAS BESIEGED ME SINCE MY ARREST...
HE THREATENED EXCOMMUNICATION AND HELL FIRE IF I CONTINUED OBDURATE. HE THREATENED AND MENACED UNTIL I ALMOST BEGAN TO THINK I WAS THE MONSTER THAT HE SAID I WAS.
OH, JUSTINE! FORGIVE ME. I WILL PROCLAIM YOUR INNOCENCE. YOU SHALL NOT DIE! YOU, MY PLAYFELLOW, MY COMPANION, MY SISTER! NO, NEVER! DO YOU HEAR ME?
VICTOR--

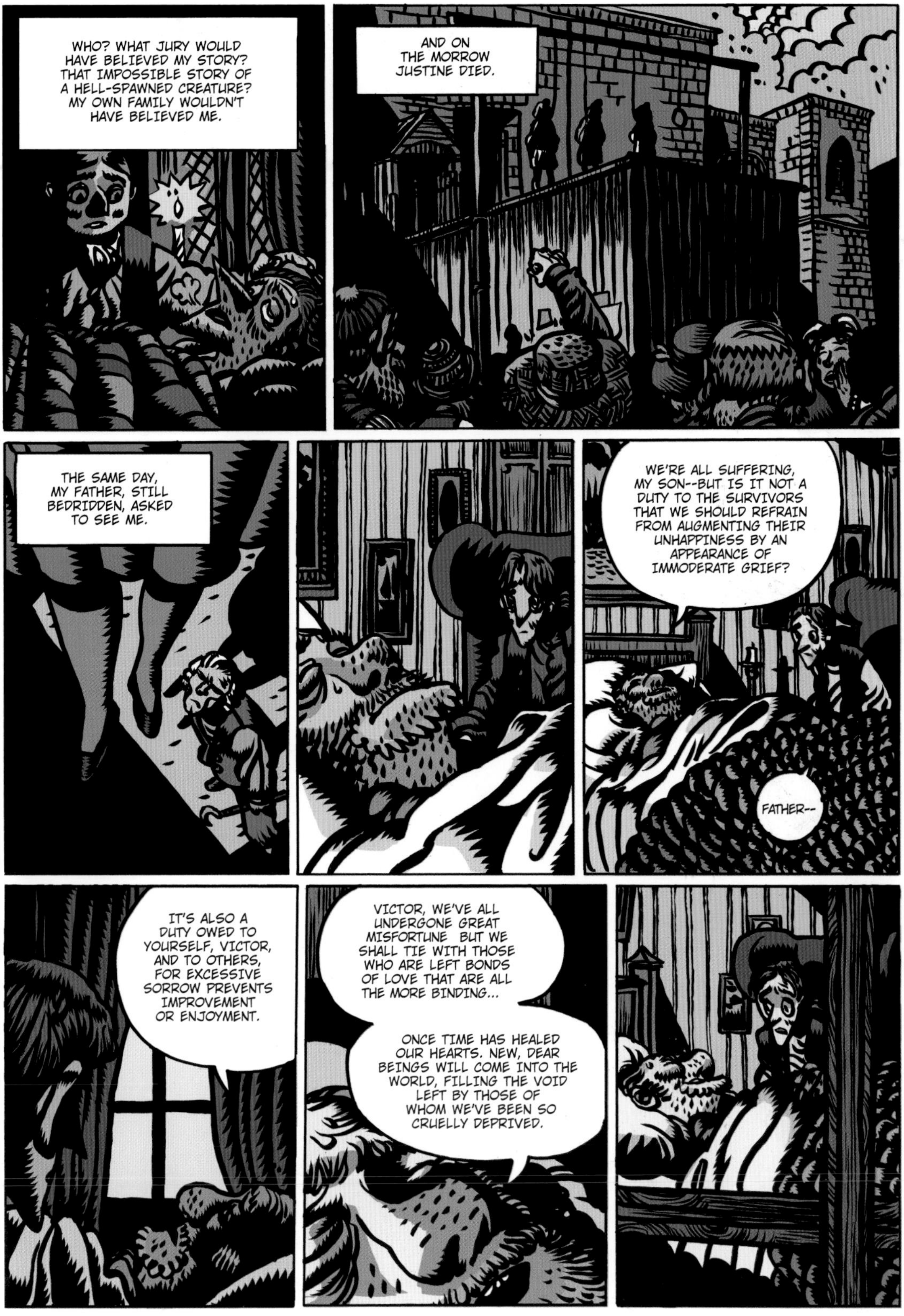
WHO? WHAT JURY WOULD HAVE BELIEVED MY STORY? THAT IMPOSSIBLE STORY OF A HELL-SPAWNED CREATURE? MY OWN FAMILY WOULDN'T HAVE BELIEVED ME.
AND ON THE MORROW JUSTINE DIED.
THE SAME DAY, MY FATHER, STILL BEDRIDDEN, ASKED TO SEE ME.
WE'RE ALL SUFFERING, MY SON--BUT IS IT NOT A DUTY TO THE SURVIVORS THAT WE SHOULD REFRAIN FROM AUGMENTING THEIR UNHAPPINESS BY AN APPEARANCE OF IMMODERATE GRIEF?
FATHER--
IT'S ALSO A DUTY OWED TO YOURSELF, VICTOR, AND TO OTHERS, FOR EXCESSIVE SORROW PREVENTS IMPROVEMENT OR ENJOYMENT.
VICTOR, WE'VE ALL UNDERGONE GREAT MISFORTUNE BUT WE SHALL TIE WITH THOSE WHO ARE LEFT BONDS OF LOVE THAT ARE ALL THE MORE BINDING...
ONCE TIME HAS HEALED OUR HEARTS. NEW, DEAR BEINGS WILL COME INTO THE WORLD, FILLING THE VOID LEFT BY THOSE OF WHOM WE'VE BEEN SO CRUELLY DEPRIVED.

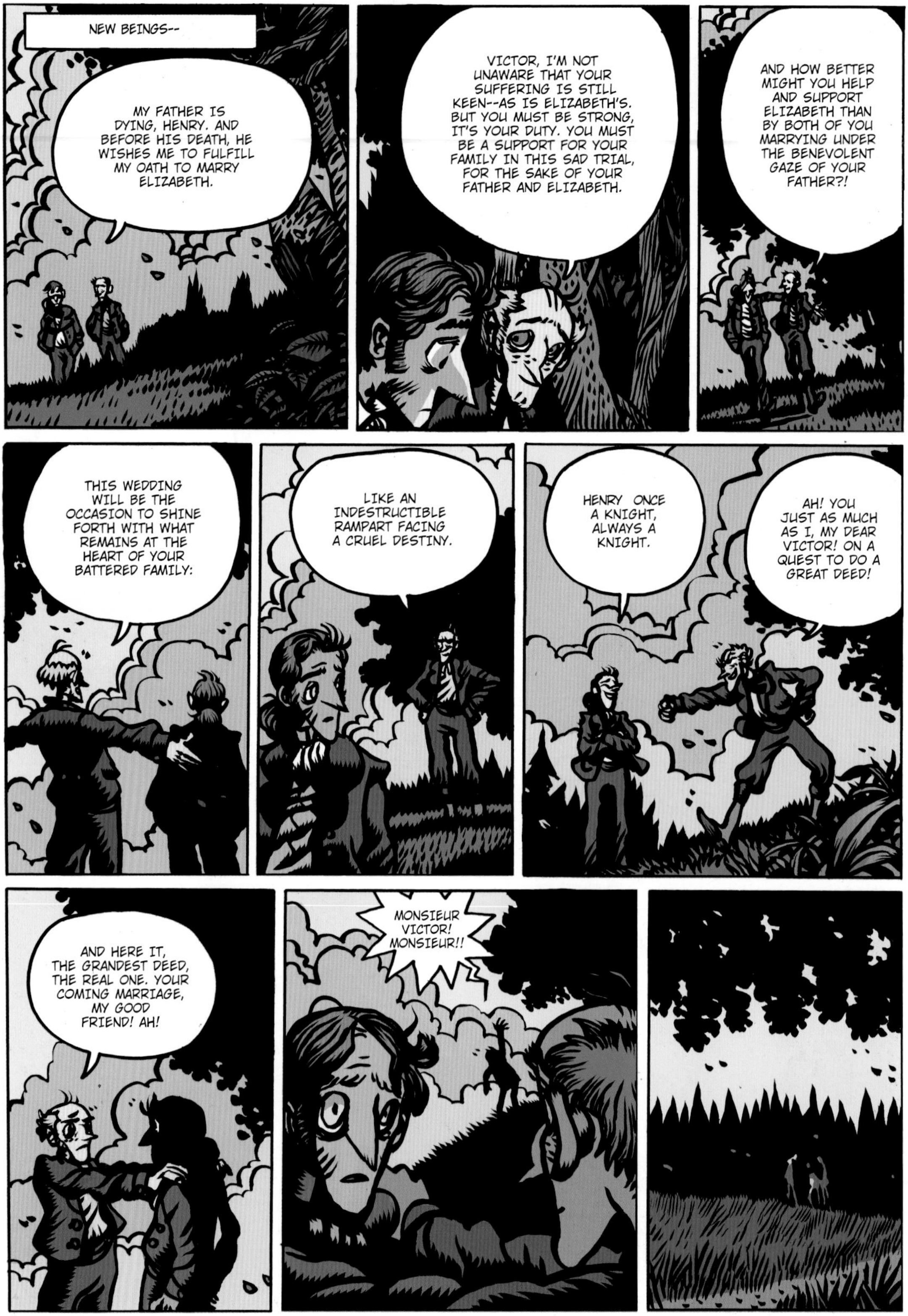
NEW BEINGS--
MY FATHER IS DYING, HENRY. AND BEFORE HIS DEATH, HE WISHES ME TO FULFILL MY OATH TO MARRY ELIZABETH.
VICTOR, I'M NOT UNAWARE THAT YOUR SUFFERING IS STILL KEEN--AS IS ELIZABETH'S. BUT YOU MUST BE STRONG, IT'S YOUR DUTY. YOU MUST BE A SUPPORT FOR YOUR FAMILY IN THIS SAD TRIAL, FOR THE SAKE OF YOUR FATHER AND ELIZABETH.
AND HOW BETTER MIGHT YOU HELP AND SUPPORT ELIZABETH THAN BY BOTH OF YOU MARRYING UNDER THE BENEVOLENT GAZE OF YOUR FATHER?!
THIS WEDDING WILL BE THE OCCASION TO SHINE FORTH WITH WHAT REMAINS AT THE HEART OF YOUR BATTERED FAMILY:
LIKE AN INDESTRUCTIBLE RAMPART FACING A CRUEL DESTINY.
HENRY ONCE A KNIGHT, ALWAYS A KNIGHT.
AH! YOU JUST AS MUCH AS I, MY DEAR VICTOR! ON A QUEST TO DO A GREAT DEED!
AND HERE IT, THE GRANDEST DEED, THE REAL ONE. YOUR COMING MARRIAGE, MY GOOD FRIEND! AH!
MONSIEUR VICTOR! MONSIEUR!!

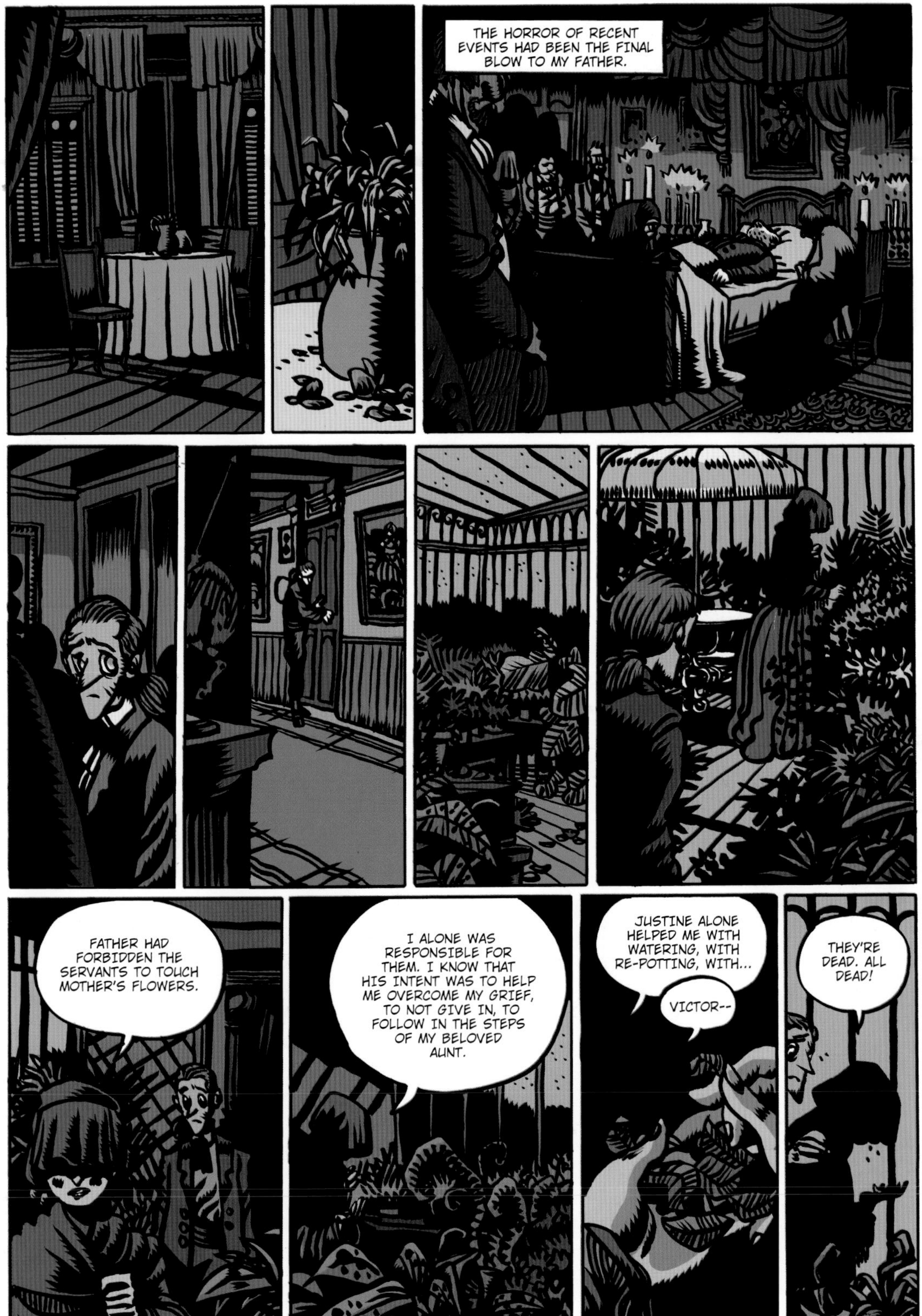
THE HORROR OF RECENT EVENTS HAD BEEN THE FINAL BLOW TO MY FATHER.
FATHER HAD FORBIDDEN THE SERVANTS TO TOUCH MOTHER'S FLOWERS.
I ALONE WAS RESPONSIBLE FOR THEM. I KNOW THAT HIS INTENT WAS TO HELP ME OVERCOME MY GRIEF, TO NOT GIVE IN, TO FOLLOW IN THE STEPS OF MY BELOVED AUNT.
JUSTINE ALONE HELPED ME WITH WATERING, WITH RE-POTTING, WITH...
VICTOR--
THEY'RE DEAD. ALL DEAD!

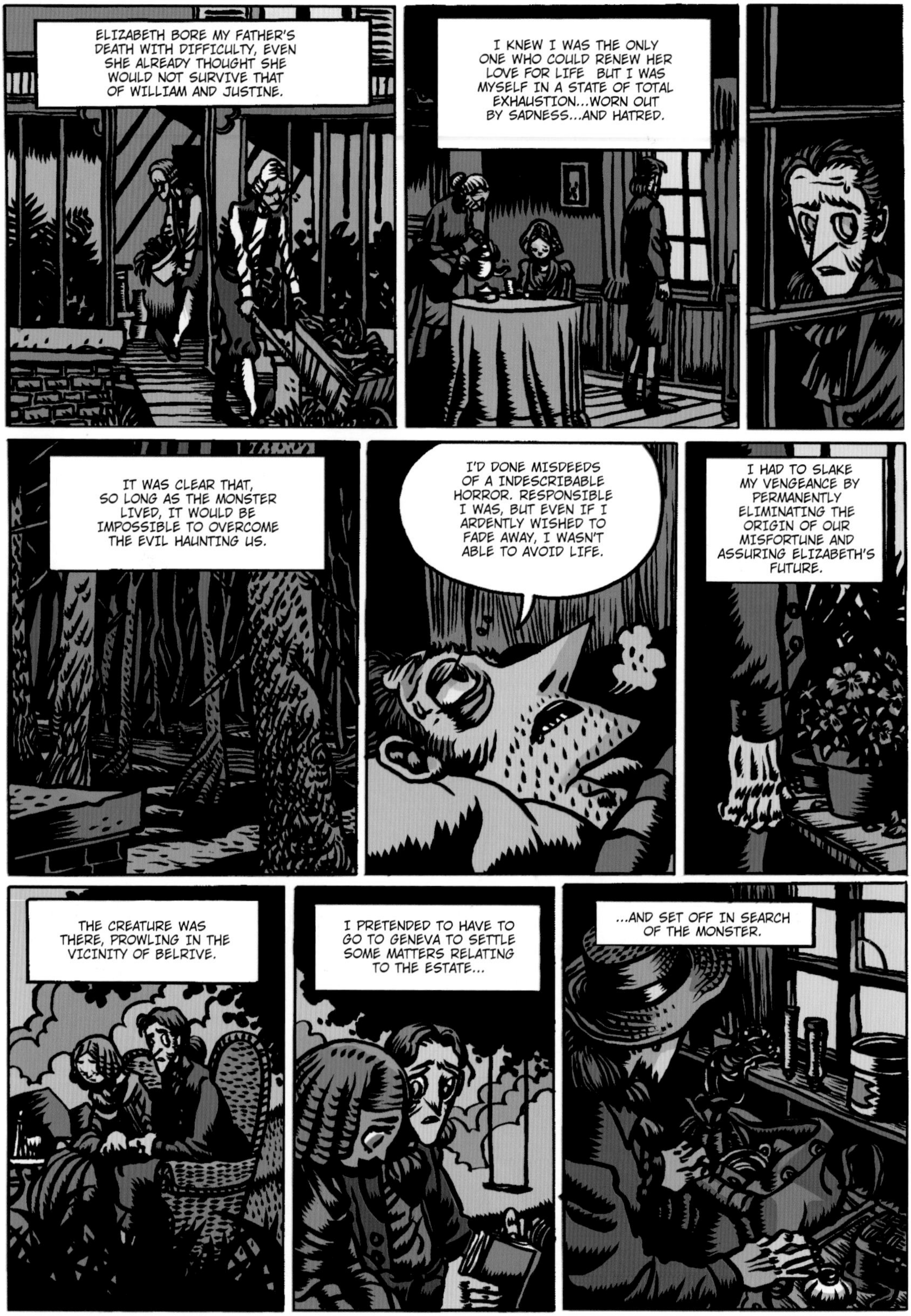
ELIZABETH BORE MY FATHER'S DEATH WITH DIFFICULTY, EVEN SHE ALREADY THOUGHT SHE WOULD NOT SURVIVE THAT OF WILLIAM AND JUSTINE.
I KNEW I WAS THE ONLY ONE WHO COULD RENEW HER LOVE FOR LIFE BUT I WAS MYSELF IN A STATE OF TOTAL EXHAUSTION...WORN OUT BY SADNESS...AND HATRED.
IT WAS CLEAR THAT, SO LONG AS THE MONSTER LIVED, IT WOULD BE IMPOSSIBLE TO OVERCOME THE EVIL HAUNTING US.
I'D DONE MISDEEDS OF A INDESCRIBABLE HORROR. RESPONSIBLE I WAS, BUT EVEN IF I ARDENTLY WISHED TO FADE AWAY, I WASN'T ABLE TO AVOID LIFE.
I HAD TO SLAKE MY VENGEANCE BY PERMANENTLY ELIMINATING THE ORIGIN OF OUR MISFORTUNE AND ASSURING ELIZABETH'S FUTURE.
THE CREATURE WAS THERE, PROWLING IN THE VICINITY OF BELRIVE.
I PRETENDED TO HAVE TO GO TO GENEVA TO SETTLE SOME MATTERS RELATING TO THE ESTATE...
...AND SET OFF IN SEARCH OF THE MONSTER.

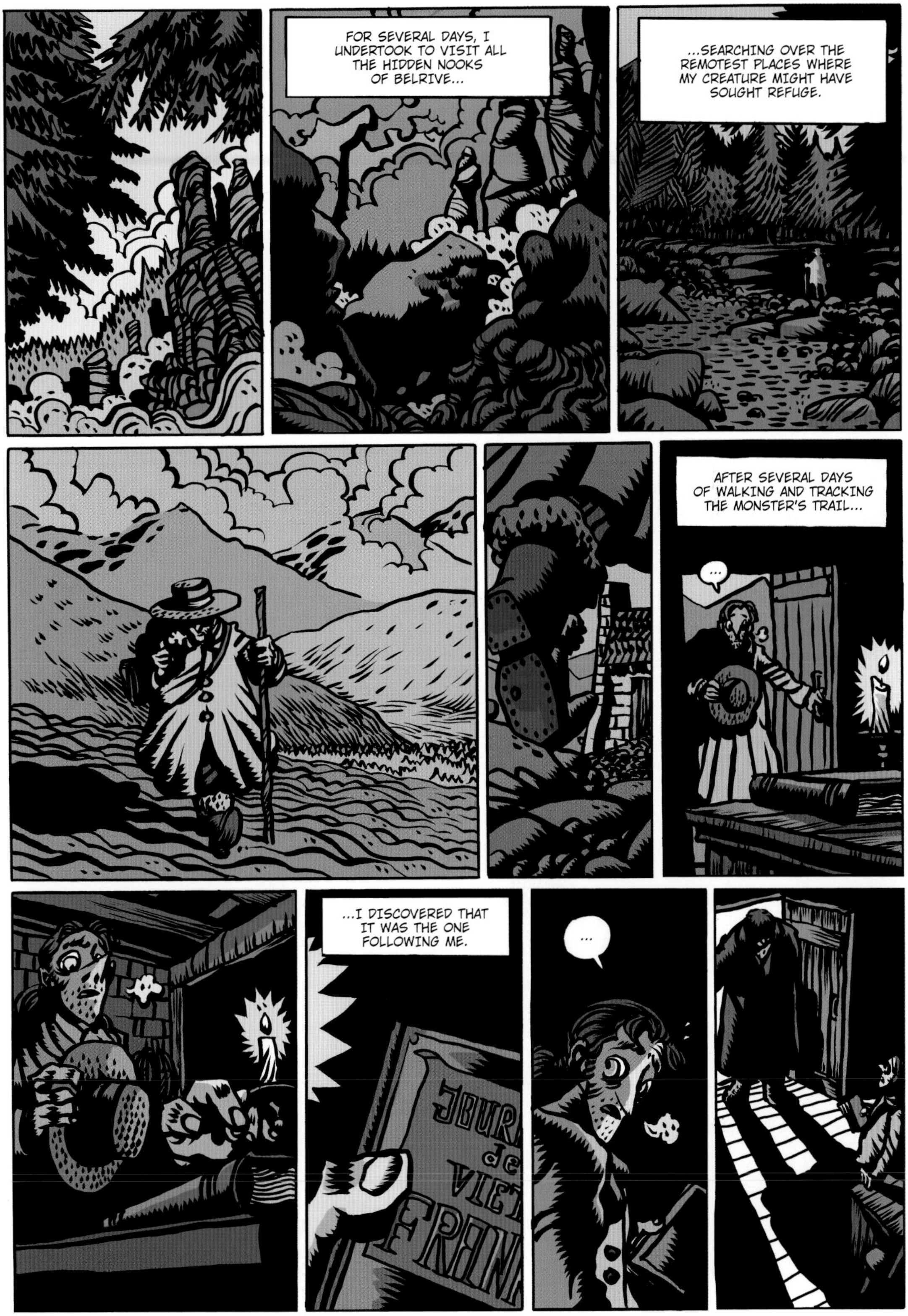

FOR SEVERAL DAYS, I UNDERTOOK TO VISIT ALL THE HIDDEN NOOKS OF BELRIVE...
...SEARCHING OVER THE REMOTEST PLACES WHERE MY CREATURE MIGHT HAVE SOUGHT REFUGE.
AFTER SEVERAL DAYS OF WALKING AND TRACKING THE MONSTER'S TRAIL...
...
...I DISCOVERED THAT IT WAS THE ONE FOLLOWING ME.
...

THE CREATURE LED YOU TO THAT ISOLATED REFUGE--WHY?

IT'S THE PLACE IT HAD CHOSEN, FAR FROM THE INHABITED WORLD, IN ORDER TO CONFRONT ITS CREATOR.

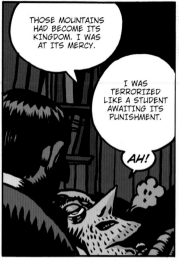

THOSE MOUNTAINS HAD BECOME ITS KINGDOM. I WAS AT ITS MERCY.

I WAS TERRORIZED LIKE A STUDENT AWAITING ITS PUNISHMENT.

AH!

WITH ME CORNERED IN ITS DEN, IT WAS FREE TO TELL ME ALL THAT IT HAD EXPERIENCED...

...SINCE THE DAY WHEN I'D ABANDONED IT ON THE THRESHOLD OF LIFE.

FOR I WAS INDEED THE FATHER, AND IT THE REPUDIATED CHILD.

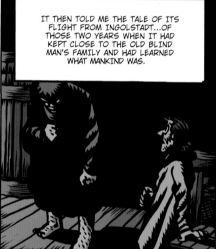

IT THEN TOLD ME THE TALE OF ITS FLIGHT FROM INGOLSTADT...OF THOSE TWO YEARS WHEN IT HAD KEPT CLOSE TO THE OLD BLIND MAN'S FAMILY AND HAD LEARNED WHAT MANKIND WAS.

AND WHAT *IT* WAS.

HOW, DESPITE ITS HOPE, IT HAD COME TO ACCEPT THAT, FOR HUMANKIND...

...IT COULD BE NOTHING OTHER THAN THIS MONSTER.

HOW IT HAD CONCEIVED OF MAKING ME PAY FOR MY COWARDICE.

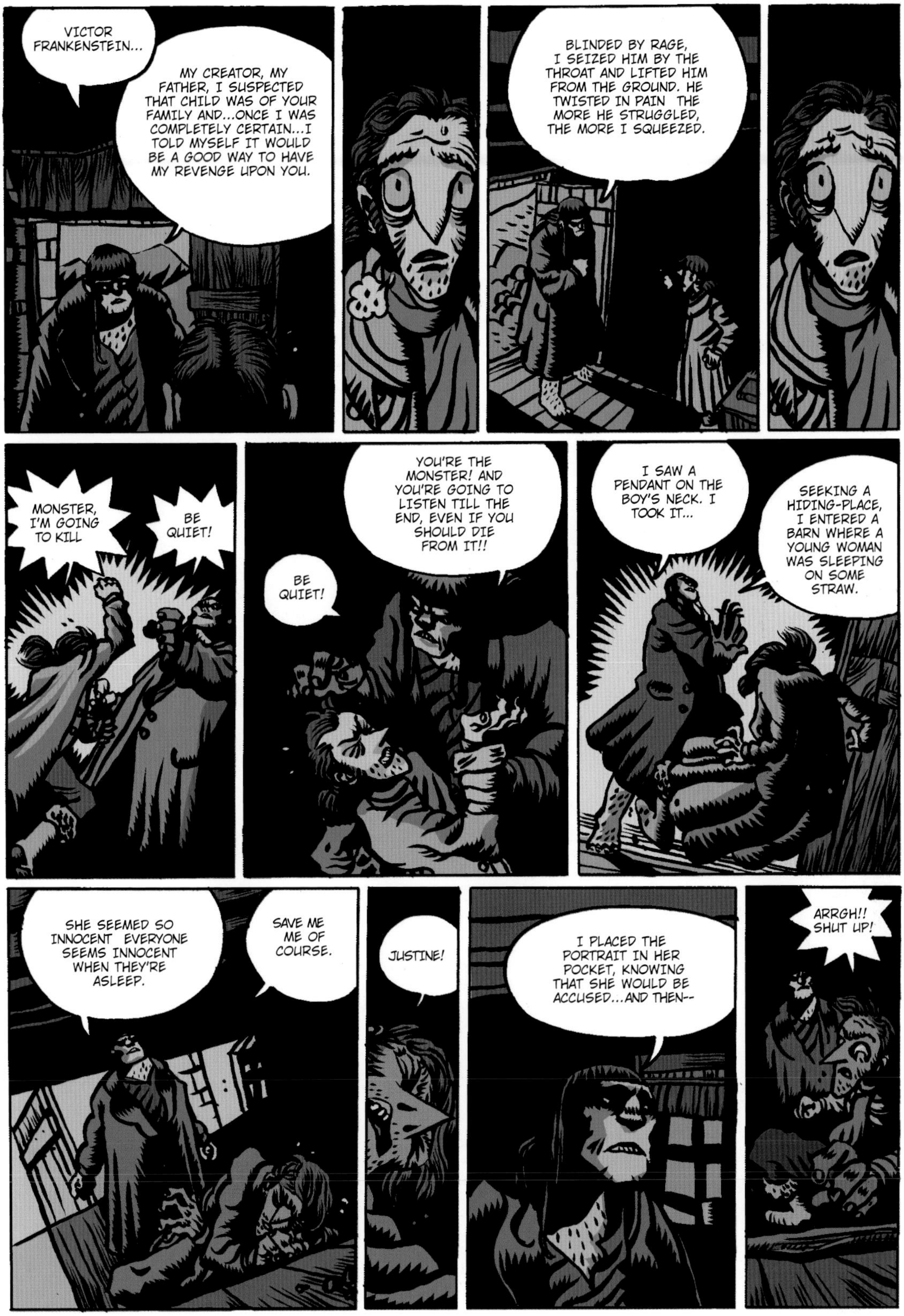
VICTOR FRANKENSTEIN...
MY CREATOR, MY FATHER, I SUSPECTED THAT CHILD WAS OF YOUR FAMILY AND...ONCE I WAS COMPLETELY CERTAIN...I TOLD MYSELF IT WOULD BE A GOOD WAY TO HAVE MY REVENGE UPON YOU.
BLINDED BY RAGE, I SEIZED HIM BY THE THROAT AND LIFTED HIM FROM THE GROUND. HE TWISTED IN PAIN THE MORE HE STRUGGLED, THE MORE I SQUEEZED.
MONSTER, I'M GOING TO KILL
BE QUIET!
YOU'RE THE MONSTER! AND YOU'RE GOING TO LISTEN TILL THE END, EVEN IF YOU SHOULD DIE FROM IT!!
BE QUIET!
I SAW A PENDANT ON THE BOY'S NECK. I TOOK IT...
SEEKING A HIDING-PLACE, I ENTERED A BARN WHERE A YOUNG WOMAN WAS SLEEPING ON SOME STRAW.
SHE SEEMED SO INNOCENT EVERYONE SEEMS INNOCENT WHEN THEY'RE ASLEEP.
SAVE ME ME OF COURSE.
JUSTINE!
I PLACED THE PORTRAIT IN HER POCKET, KNOWING THAT SHE WOULD BE ACCUSED...AND THEN--
ARRGH!! SHUT UP!

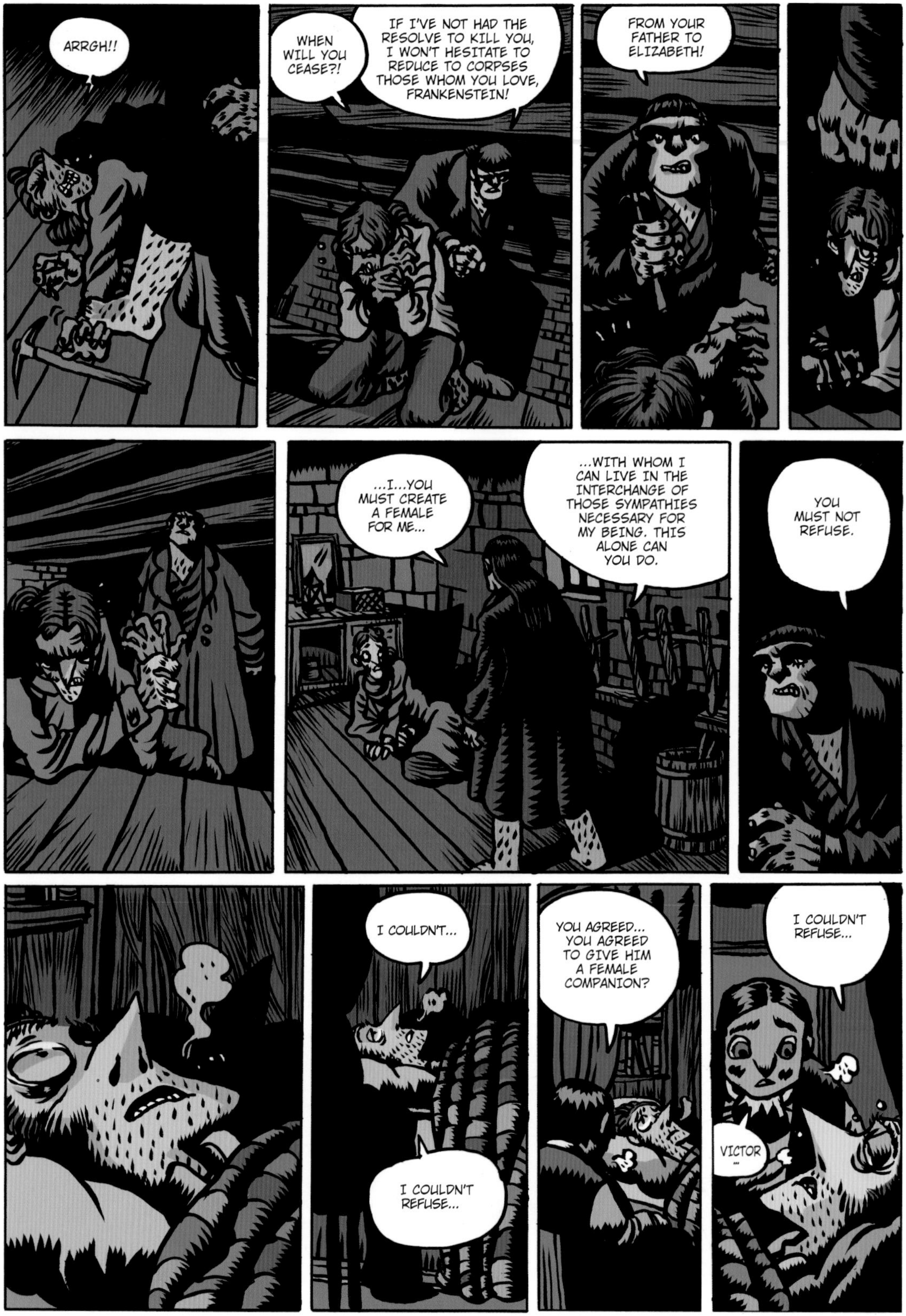
ARRGH!!
WHEN WILL YOU CEASE?!
IF I'VE NOT HAD THE RESOLVE TO KILL YOU, I WON'T HESITATE TO REDUCE TO CORPSES THOSE WHOM YOU LOVE, FRANKENSTEIN!
FROM YOUR FATHER TO ELIZABETH!
...I...YOU MUST CREATE A FEMALE FOR ME...
...WITH WHOM I CAN LIVE IN THE INTERCHANGE OF THOSE SYMPATHIES NECESSARY FOR MY BEING. THIS ALONE CAN YOU DO.
YOU MUST NOT REFUSE.
I COULDN'T...
I COULDN'T REFUSE...
YOU AGREED... YOU AGREED TO GIVE HIM A FEMALE COMPANION?
I COULDN'T REFUSE...
VICTOR...

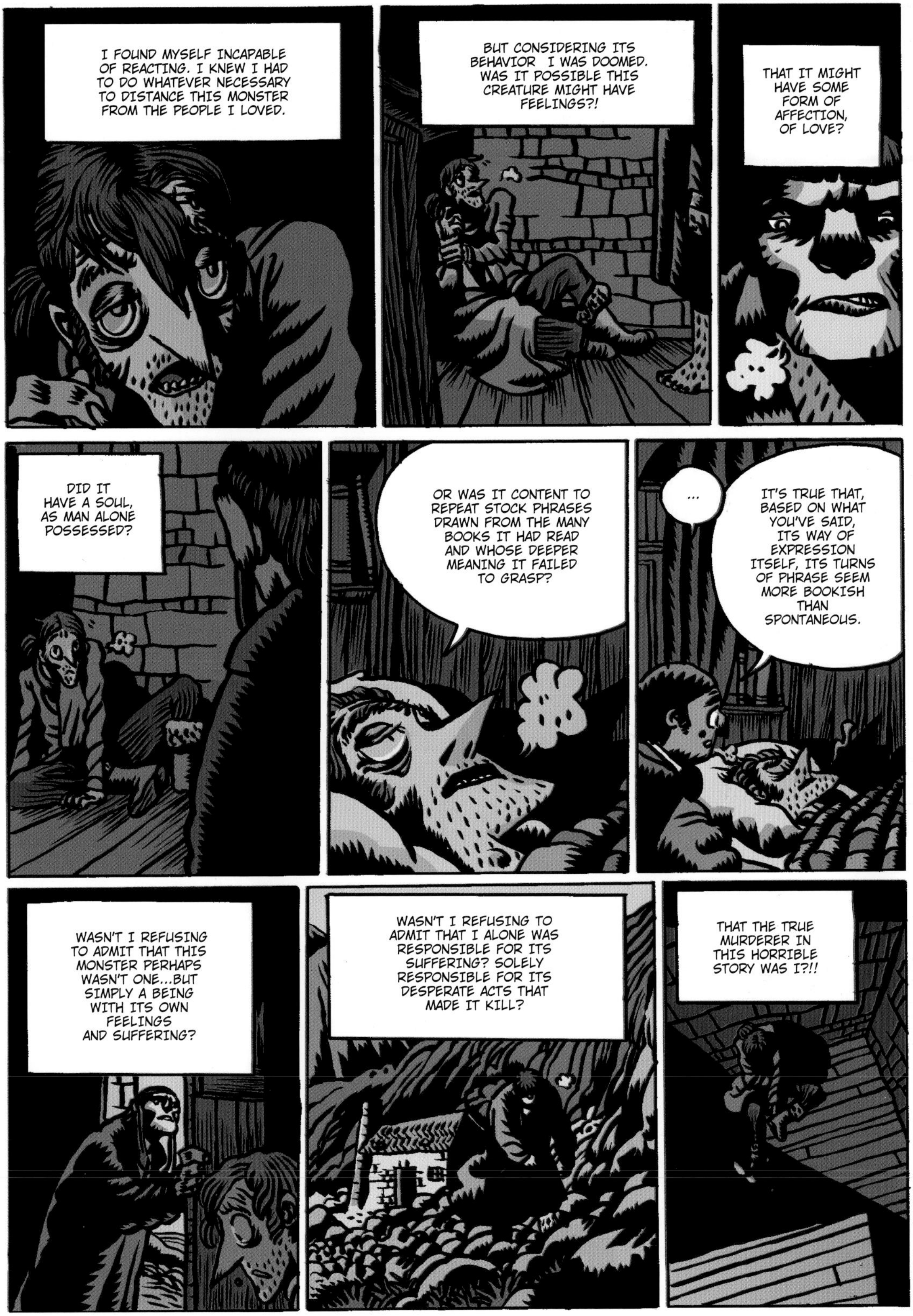
I FOUND MYSELF INCAPABLE OF REACTING. I KNEW I HAD TO DO WHATEVER NECESSARY TO DISTANCE THIS MONSTER FROM THE PEOPLE I LOVED.
BUT CONSIDERING ITS BEHAVIOR I WAS DOOMED. WAS IT POSSIBLE THIS CREATURE MIGHT HAVE FEELINGS?!
THAT IT MIGHT HAVE SOME FORM OF AFFECTION, OF LOVE?
DID IT HAVE A SOUL, AS MAN ALONE POSSESSED?
OR WAS IT CONTENT TO REPEAT STOCK PHRASES DRAWN FROM THE MANY BOOKS IT HAD READ AND WHOSE DEEPER MEANING IT FAILED TO GRASP?
...
IT'S TRUE THAT, BASED ON WHAT YOU'VE SAID, ITS WAY OF EXPRESSION ITSELF, ITS TURNS OF PHRASE SEEM MORE BOOKISH THAN SPONTANEOUS.
WASN'T I REFUSING TO ADMIT THAT THIS MONSTER PERHAPS WASN'T ONE...BUT SIMPLY A BEING WITH ITS OWN FEELINGS AND SUFFERING?
WASN'T I REFUSING TO ADMIT THAT I ALONE WAS RESPONSIBLE FOR ITS SUFFERING? SOLELY RESPONSIBLE FOR ITS DESPERATE ACTS THAT MADE IT KILL?
THAT THE TRUE MURDERER IN THIS HORRIBLE STORY WAS I?!!

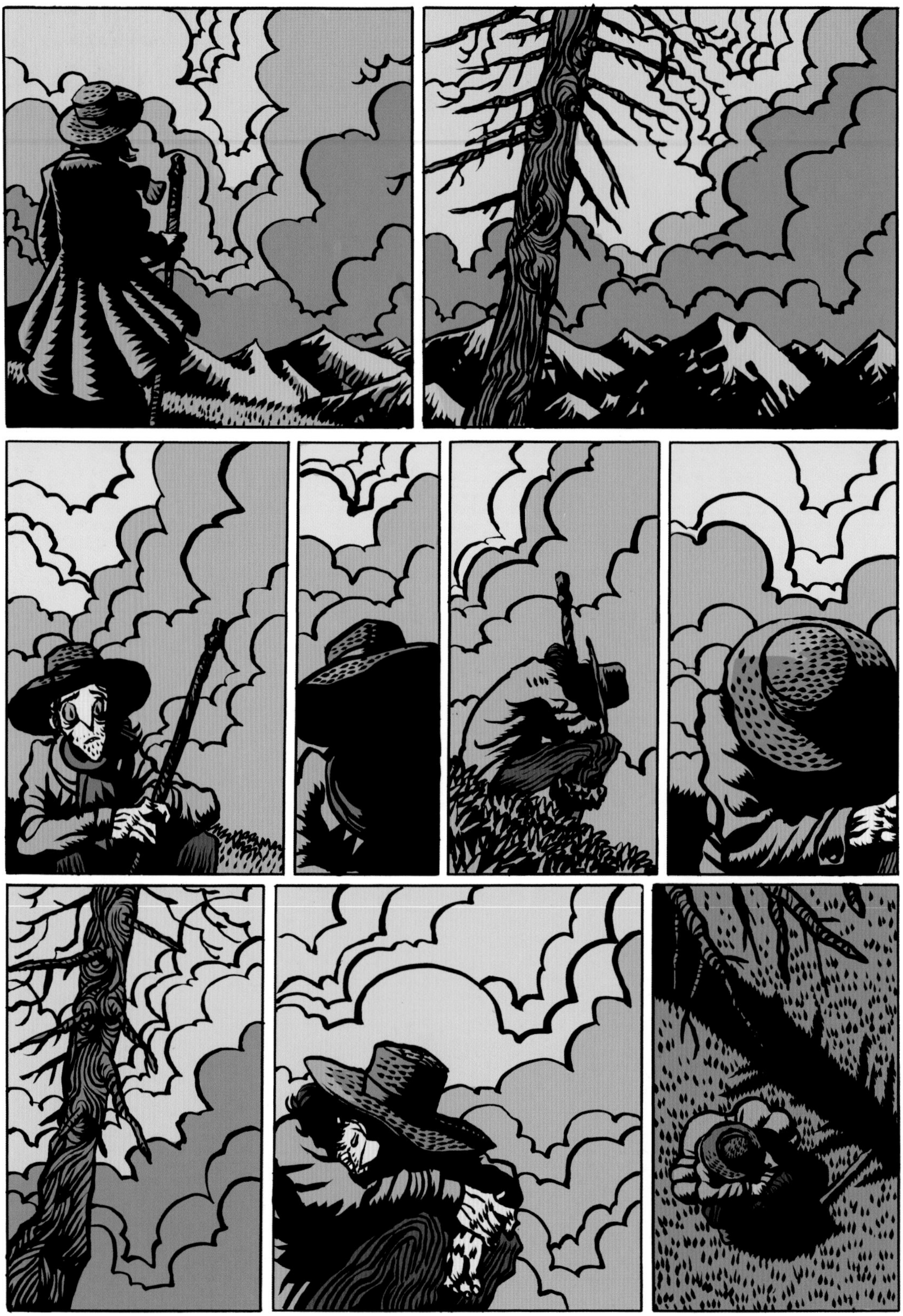

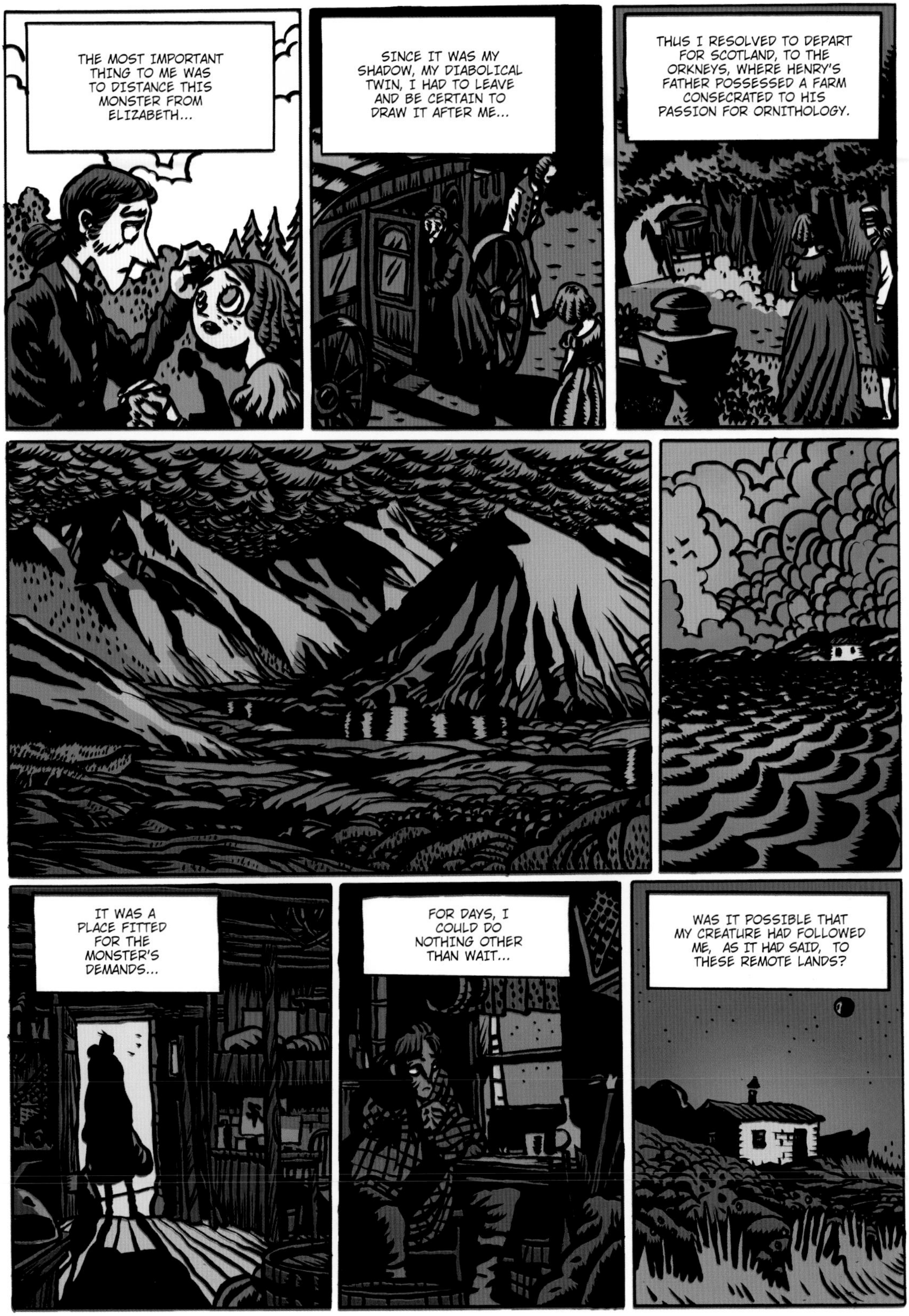
THE MOST IMPORTANT THING TO ME WAS TO DISTANCE THIS MONSTER FROM ELIZABETH...
SINCE IT WAS MY SHADOW, MY DIABOLICAL TWIN, I HAD TO LEAVE AND BE CERTAIN TO DRAW IT AFTER ME...
THUS I RESOLVED TO DEPART FOR SCOTLAND, TO THE ORKNEYS, WHERE HENRY'S FATHER POSSESSED A FARM CONSECRATED TO HIS PASSION FOR ORNITHOLOGY.
IT WAS A PLACE FITTED FOR THE MONSTER'S DEMANDS...
FOR DAYS, I COULD DO NOTHING OTHER THAN WAIT...
WAS IT POSSIBLE THAT MY CREATURE HAD FOLLOWED ME, AS IT HAD SAID, TO THESE REMOTE LANDS?

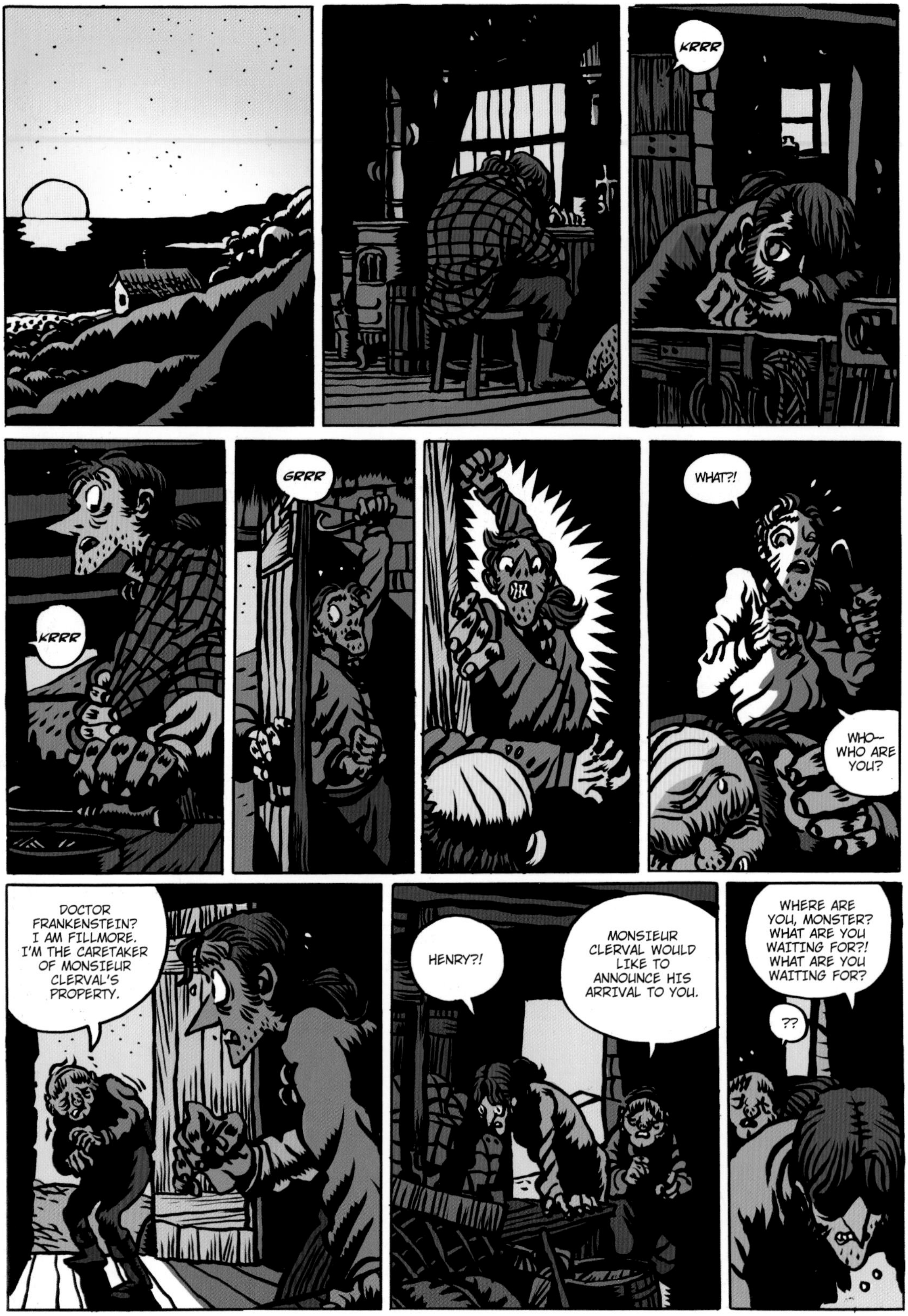
KRRR
KRRR
GRRR
WHAT?!
WHO-- WHO ARE YOU?
DOCTOR FRANKENSTEIN? I AM FILLMORE. I'M THE CARETAKER OF MONSIEUR CLERVAL'S PROPERTY.
HENRY?!
MONSIEUR CLERVAL WOULD LIKE TO ANNOUNCE HIS ARRIVAL TO YOU.
WHERE ARE YOU, MONSTER? WHAT ARE YOU WAITING FOR?! WHAT ARE YOU WAITING FOR?
??

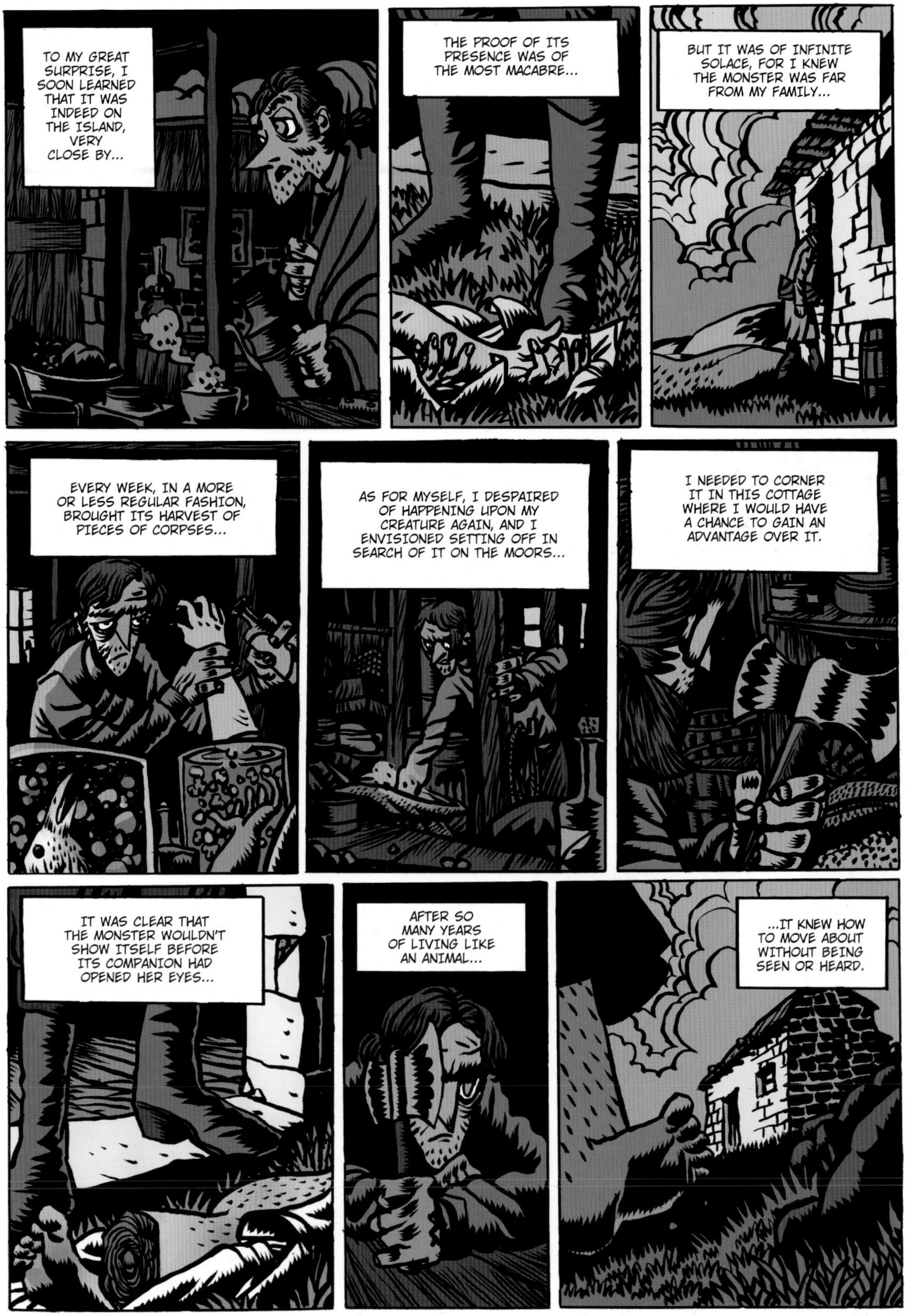
TO MY GREAT SURPRISE, I SOON LEARNED THAT IT WAS INDEED ON THE ISLAND, VERY CLOSE BY...
THE PROOF OF ITS PRESENCE WAS OF THE MOST MACABRE...
BUT IT WAS OF INFINITE SOLACE, FOR I KNEW THE MONSTER WAS FAR FROM MY FAMILY...
EVERY WEEK, IN A MORE OR LESS REGULAR FASHION, BROUGHT ITS HARVEST OF PIECES OF CORPSES...
AS FOR MYSELF, I DESPAIRED OF HAPPENING UPON MY CREATURE AGAIN, AND I ENVISIONED SETTING OFF IN SEARCH OF IT ON THE MOORS...
I NEEDED TO CORNER IT IN THIS COTTAGE WHERE I WOULD HAVE A CHANCE TO GAIN AN ADVANTAGE OVER IT.
IT WAS CLEAR THAT THE MONSTER WOULDN'T SHOW ITSELF BEFORE ITS COMPANION HAD OPENED HER EYES...
AFTER SO MANY YEARS OF LIVING LIKE AN ANIMAL...
...IT KNEW HOW TO MOVE ABOUT WITHOUT BEING SEEN OR HEARD.

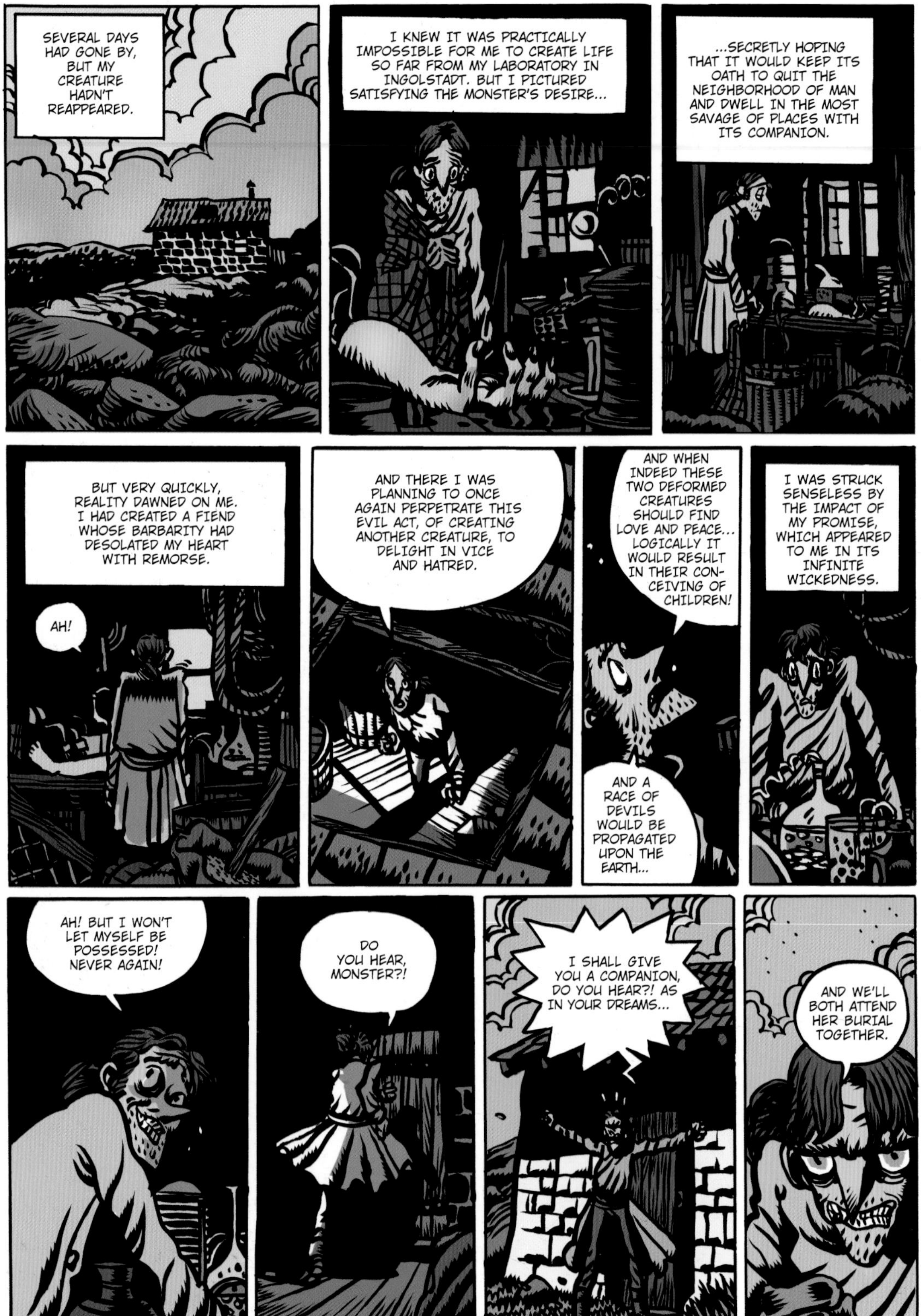
SEVERAL DAYS HAD GONE BY, BUT MY CREATURE HADN'T REAPPEARED.
I KNEW IT WAS PRACTICALLY IMPOSSIBLE FOR ME TO CREATE LIFE SO FAR FROM MY LABORATORY IN INGOLSTADT. BUT I PICTURED SATISFYING THE MONSTER'S DESIRE...
...SECRETLY HOPING THAT IT WOULD KEEP ITS OATH TO QUIT THE NEIGHBORHOOD OF MAN AND DWELL IN THE MOST SAVAGE OF PLACES WITH ITS COMPANION.
BUT VERY QUICKLY, REALITY DAWNED ON ME. I HAD CREATED A FIEND WHOSE BARBARITY HAD DESOLATED MY HEART WITH REMORSE.
AH!
AND THERE I WAS PLANNING TO ONCE AGAIN PERPETRATE THIS EVIL ACT, OF CREATING ANOTHER CREATURE, TO DELIGHT IN VICE AND HATRED.
AND WHEN INDEED THESE TWO DEFORMED CREATURES SHOULD FIND LOVE AND PEACE... LOGICALLY IT WOULD RESULT IN THEIR CONCEIVING OF CHILDREN!
AND A RACE OF DEVILS WOULD BE PROPAGATED UPON THE EARTH...
I WAS STRUCK SENSELESS BY THE IMPACT OF MY PROMISE, WHICH APPEARED TO ME IN ITS INFINITE WICKEDNESS.
AH! BUT I WON'T LET MYSELF BE POSSESSED! NEVER AGAIN!
DO YOU HEAR, MONSTER?!
I SHALL GIVE YOU A COMPANION, DO YOU HEAR?! AS IN YOUR DREAMS...
AND WE'LL BOTH ATTEND HER BURIAL TOGETHER.

THE NEXT DAY, I SET MY PLAN INTO MOTION...

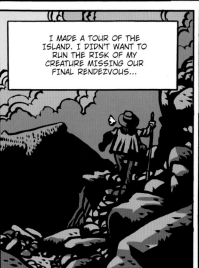

I MADE A TOUR OF THE ISLAND. I DIDN'T WANT TO RUN THE RISK OF MY CREATURE MISSING OUR FINAL RENDEZVOUS...

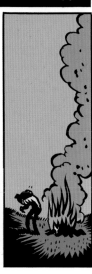

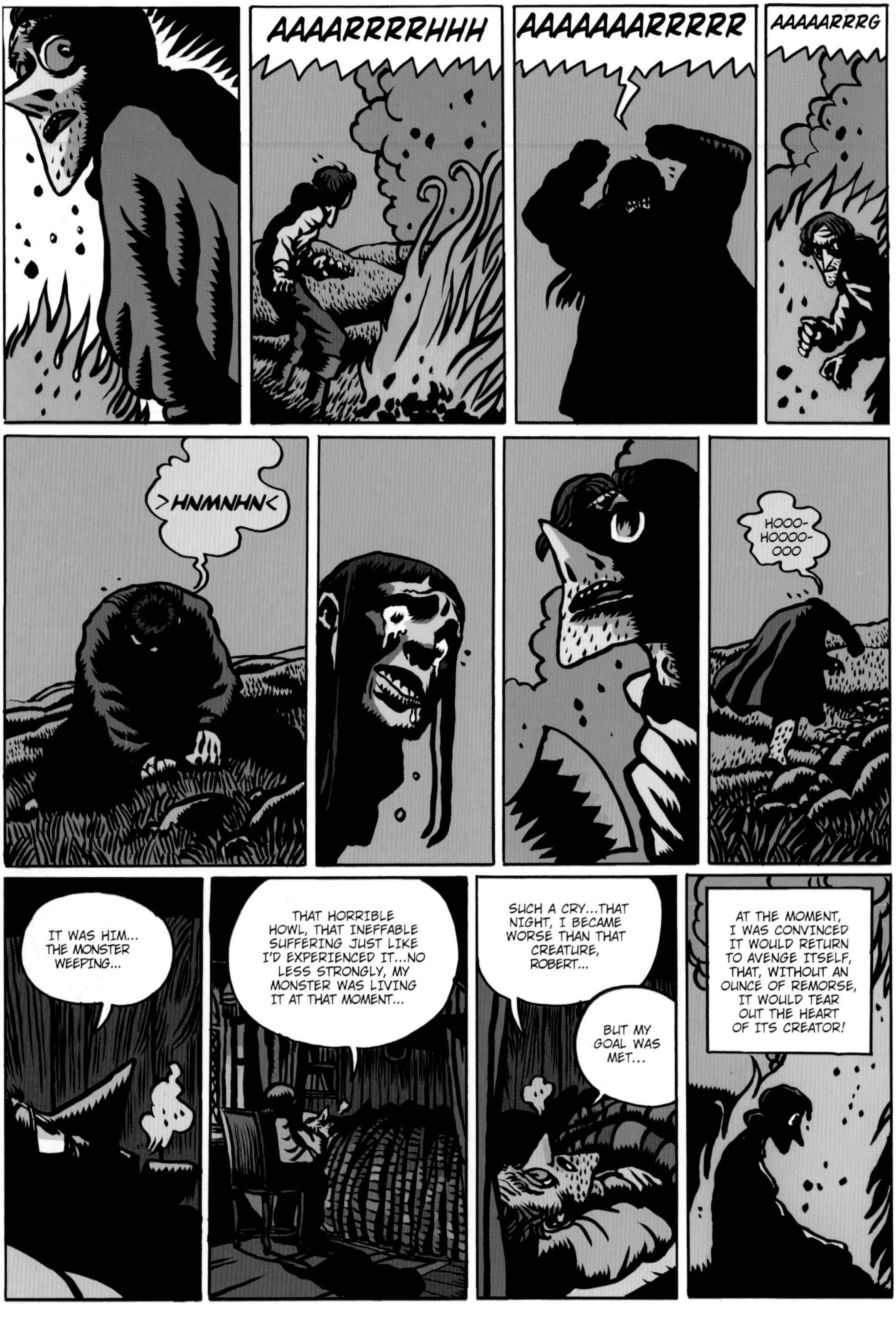
AAAARRRRHHH
AAAAAAARRRRR
AAAAARRRG
>HNMNHN<
HOOO-HOOOO-OOO
IT WAS HIM... THE MONSTER WEEPING...
THAT HORRIBLE HOWL, THAT INEFFABLE SUFFERING JUST LIKE I'D EXPERIENCED IT...NO LESS STRONGLY, MY MONSTER WAS LIVING IT AT THAT MOMENT...
SUCH A CRY...THAT NIGHT, I BECAME WORSE THAN THAT CREATURE, ROBERT...
BUT MY GOAL WAS MET...
AT THE MOMENT, I WAS CONVINCED IT WOULD RETURN TO AVENGE ITSELF, THAT, WITHOUT AN OUNCE OF REMORSE, IT WOULD TEAR OUT THE HEART OF ITS CREATOR!

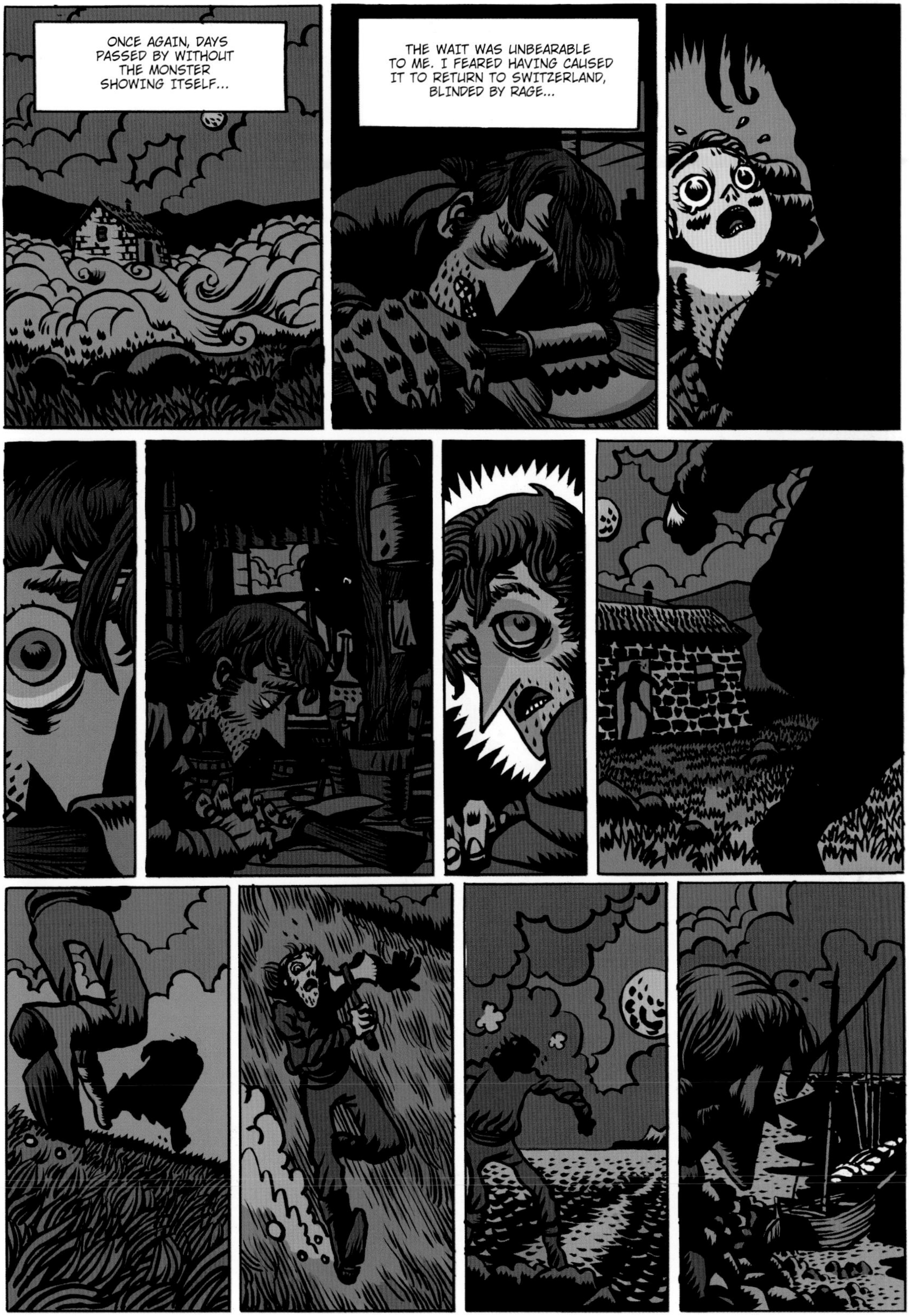
ONCE AGAIN, DAYS PASSED BY WITHOUT THE MONSTER SHOWING ITSELF...
THE WAIT WAS UNBEARABLE TO ME. I FEARED HAVING CAUSED IT TO RETURN TO SWITZERLAND, BLINDED BY RAGE...

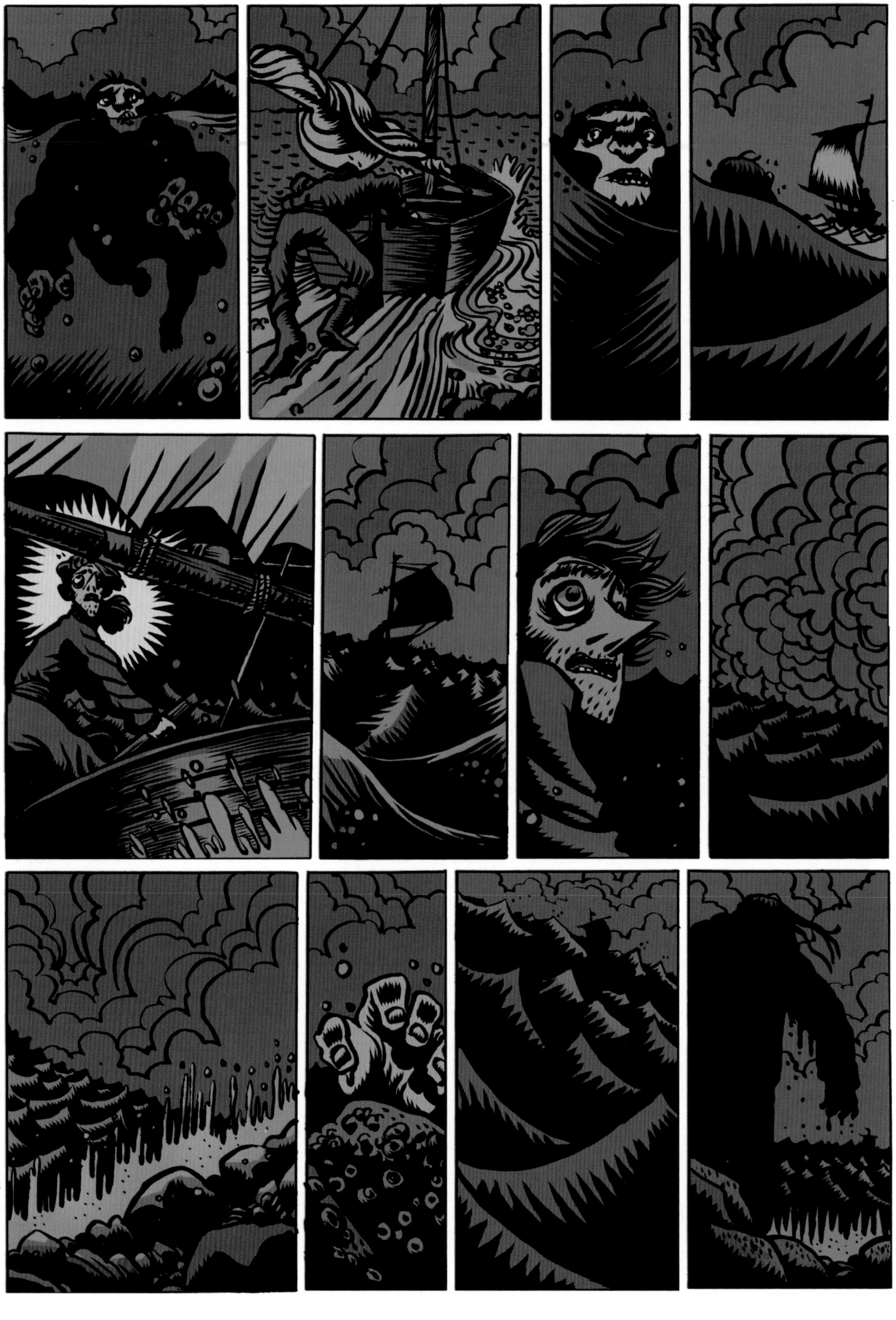

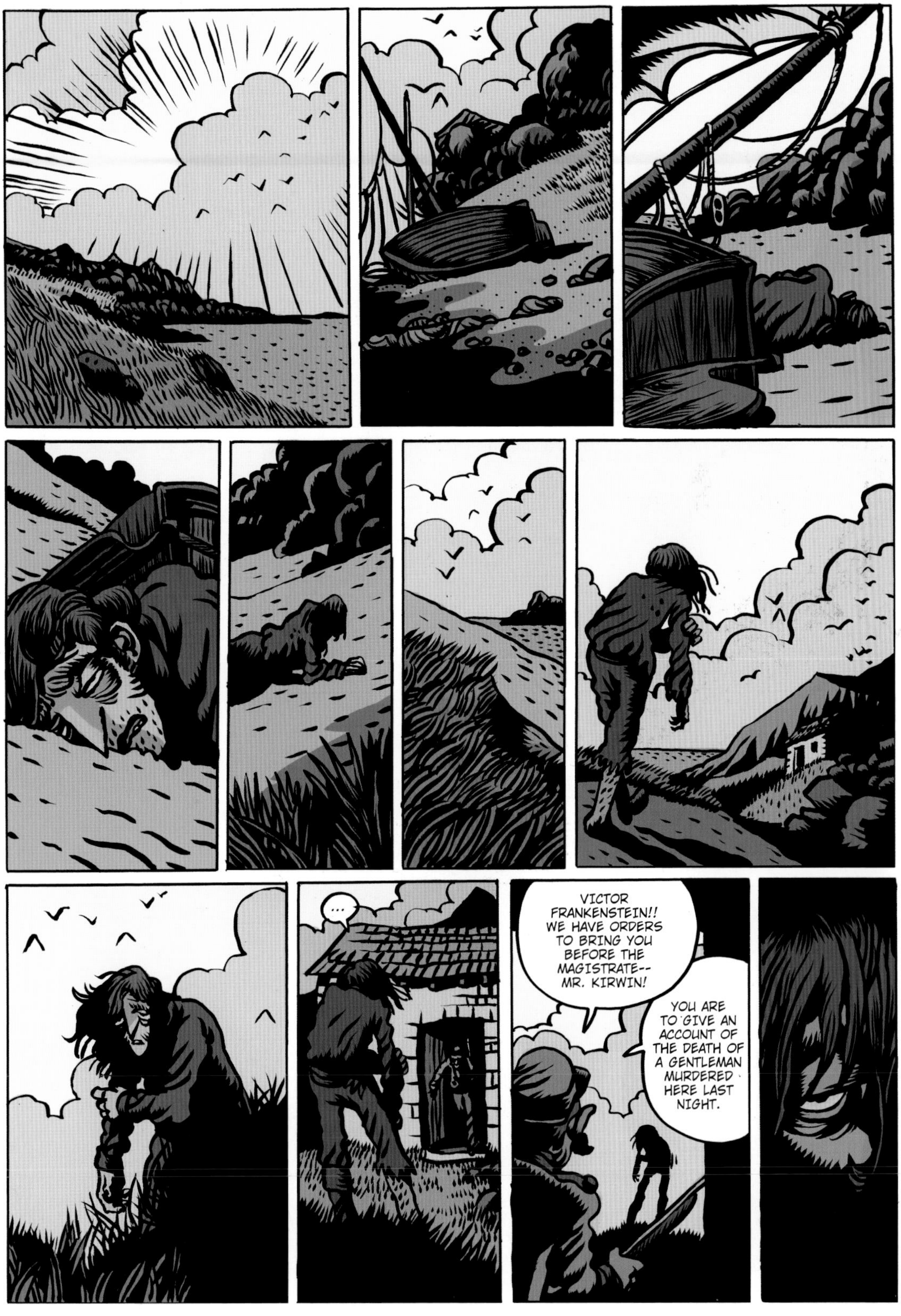
...
VICTOR FRANKENSTEIN!! WE HAVE ORDERS TO BRING YOU BEFORE THE MAGISTRATE-- MR. KIRWIN!
YOU ARE TO GIVE AN ACCOUNT OF THE DEATH OF A GENTLEMAN MURDERED HERE LAST NIGHT.

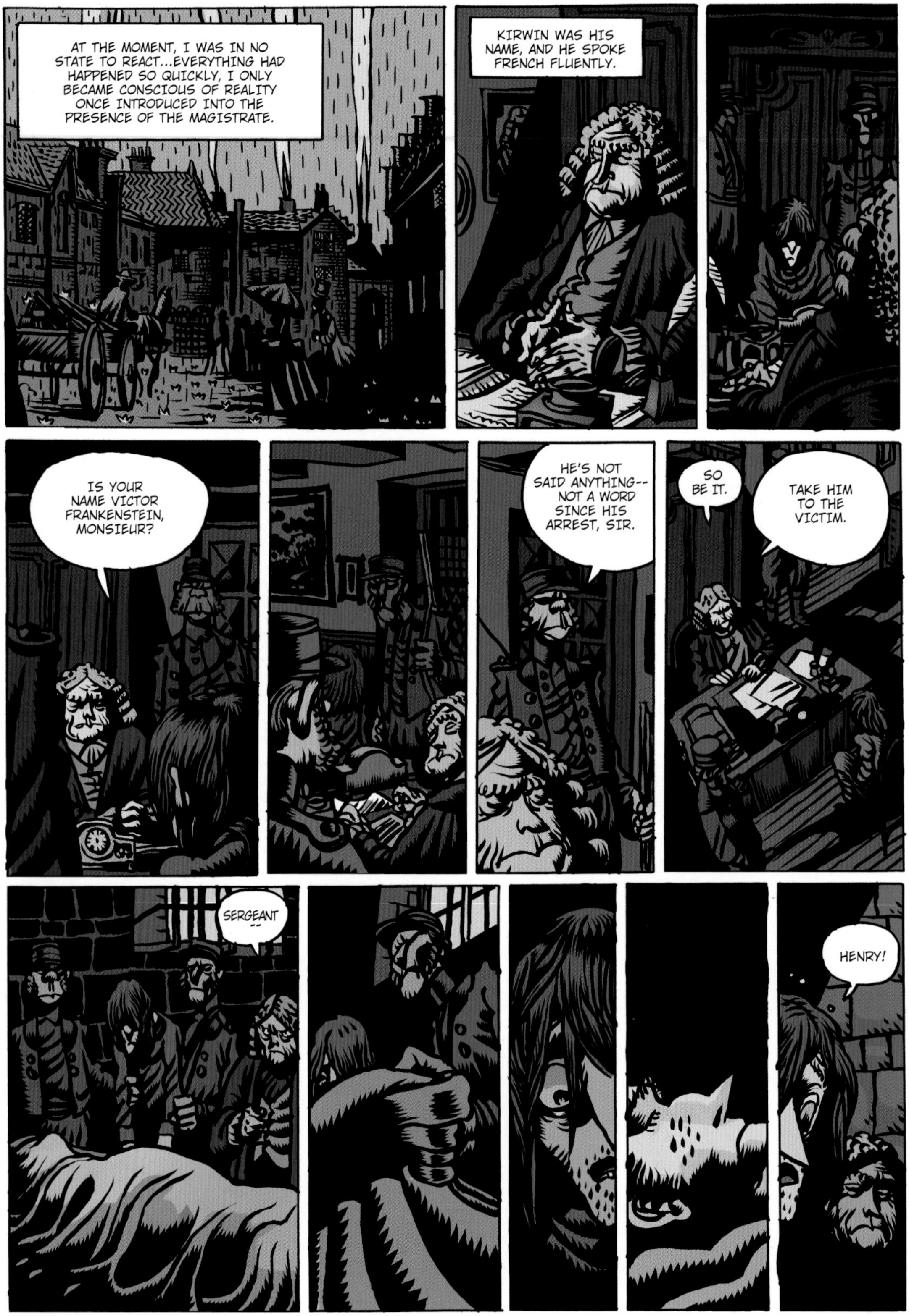
AT THE MOMENT, I WAS IN NO STATE TO REACT...EVERYTHING HAD HAPPENED SO QUICKLY, I ONLY BECAME CONSCIOUS OF REALITY ONCE INTRODUCED INTO THE PRESENCE OF THE MAGISTRATE.
KIRWIN WAS HIS NAME, AND HE SPOKE FRENCH FLUENTLY.
IS YOUR NAME VICTOR FRANKENSTEIN, MONSIEUR?
HE'S NOT SAID ANYTHING-- NOT A WORD SINCE HIS ARREST, SIR.
SO BE IT.
TAKE HIM TO THE VICTIM.
SERGEANT --
HENRY!

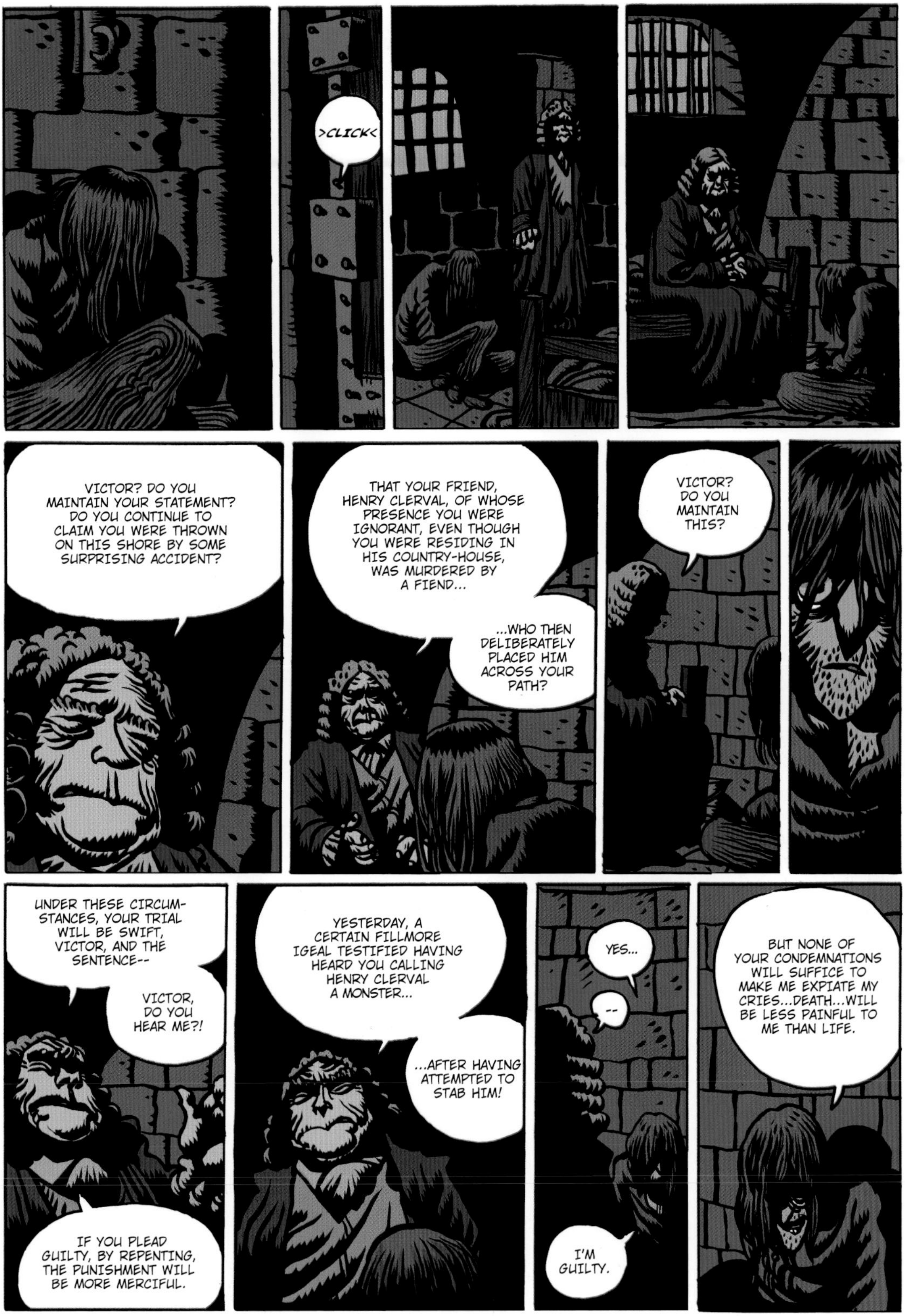
>CLICK<
VICTOR? DO YOU MAINTAIN YOUR STATEMENT? DO YOU CONTINUE TO CLAIM YOU WERE THROWN ON THIS SHORE BY SOME SURPRISING ACCIDENT?
THAT YOUR FRIEND, HENRY CLERVAL, OF WHOSE PRESENCE YOU WERE IGNORANT, EVEN THOUGH YOU WERE RESIDING IN HIS COUNTRY-HOUSE, WAS MURDERED BY A FIEND...
...WHO THEN DELIBERATELY PLACED HIM ACROSS YOUR PATH?
VICTOR? DO YOU MAINTAIN THIS?
UNDER THESE CIRCUM-STANCES, YOUR TRIAL WILL BE SWIFT, VICTOR, AND THE SENTENCE--
VICTOR, DO YOU HEAR ME?!
IF YOU PLEAD GUILTY, BY REPENTING, THE PUNISHMENT WILL BE MORE MERCIFUL.
YESTERDAY, A CERTAIN FILLMORE IGEAL TESTIFIED HAVING HEARD YOU CALLING HENRY CLERVAL A MONSTER...
...AFTER HAVING ATTEMPTED TO STAB HIM!
YES...
--
I'M GUILTY.
BUT NONE OF YOUR CONDEMNATIONS WILL SUFFICE TO MAKE ME EXPIATE MY CRIES...DEATH...WILL BE LESS PAINFUL TO ME THAN LIFE.

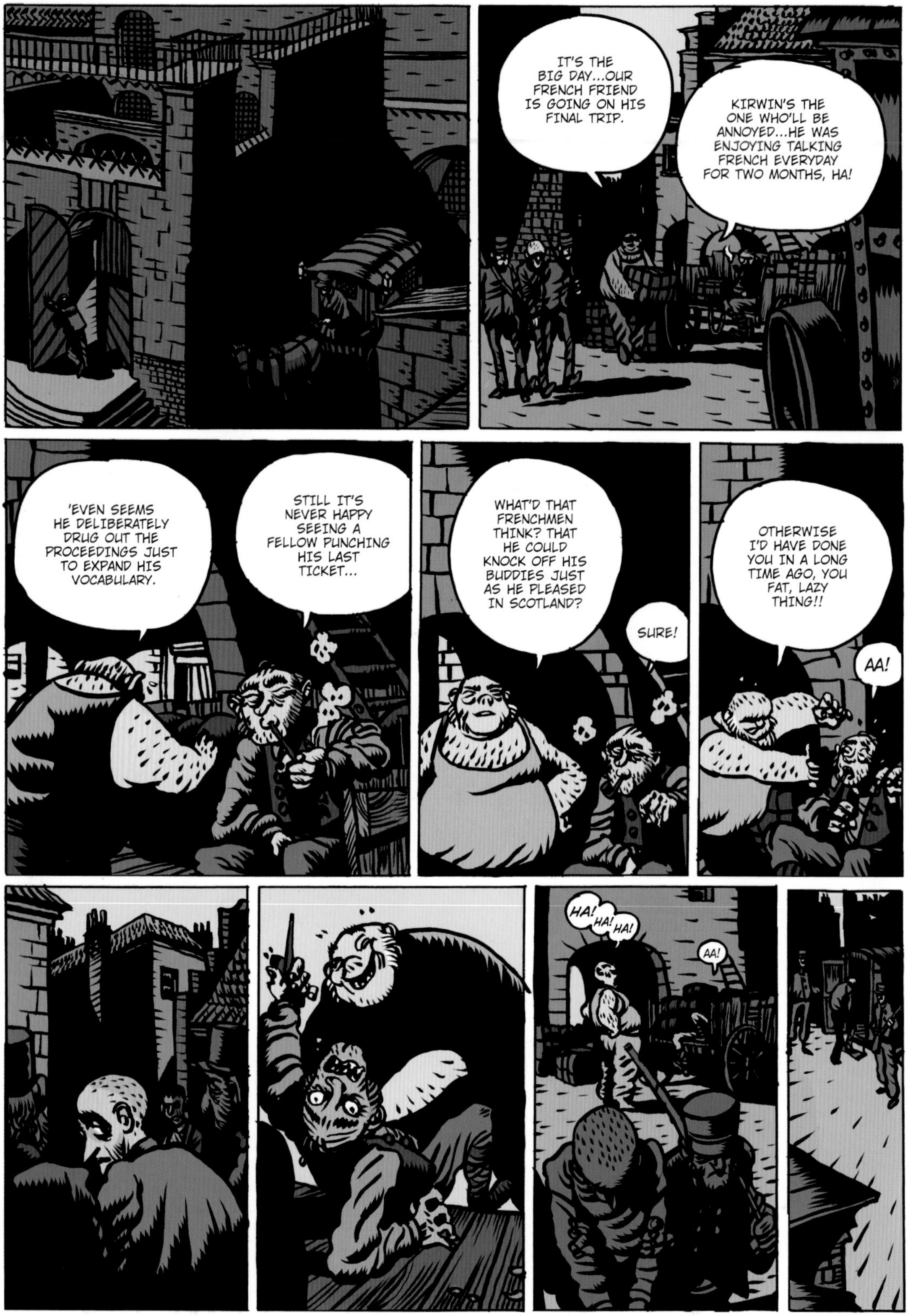

IT'S THE BIG DAY...OUR FRENCH FRIEND IS GOING ON HIS FINAL TRIP.
KIRWIN'S THE ONE WHO'LL BE ANNOYED...HE WAS ENJOYING TALKING FRENCH EVERYDAY FOR TWO MONTHS, HA!
'EVEN SEEMS HE DELIBERATELY DRUG OUT THE PROCEEDINGS JUST TO EXPAND HIS VOCABULARY.
STILL IT'S NEVER HAPPY SEEING A FELLOW PUNCHING HIS LAST TICKET...
WHAT'D THAT FRENCHMEN THINK? THAT HE COULD KNOCK OFF HIS BUDDIES JUST AS HE PLEASED IN SCOTLAND?
SURE!
OTHERWISE I'D HAVE DONE YOU IN A LONG TIME AGO, YOU FAT, LAZY THING!!
AA!
HA! HA! HA!
AA!

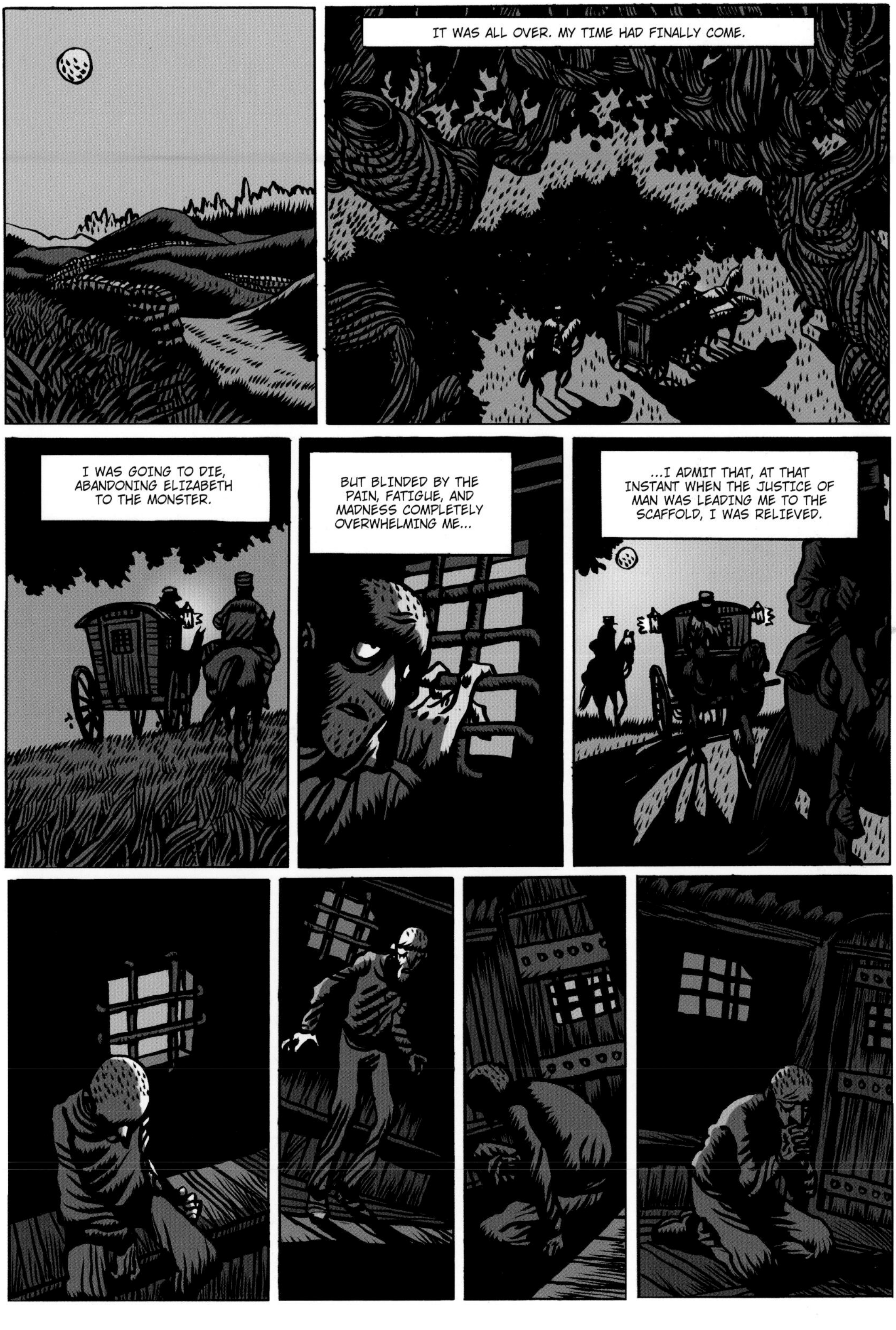
IT WAS ALL OVER. MY TIME HAD FINALLY COME.
I WAS GOING TO DIE, ABANDONING ELIZABETH TO THE MONSTER.
BUT BLINDED BY THE PAIN, FATIGUE, AND MADNESS COMPLETELY OVERWHELMING ME...
...I ADMIT THAT, AT THAT INSTANT WHEN THE JUSTICE OF MAN WAS LEADING ME TO THE SCAFFOLD, I WAS RELIEVED.

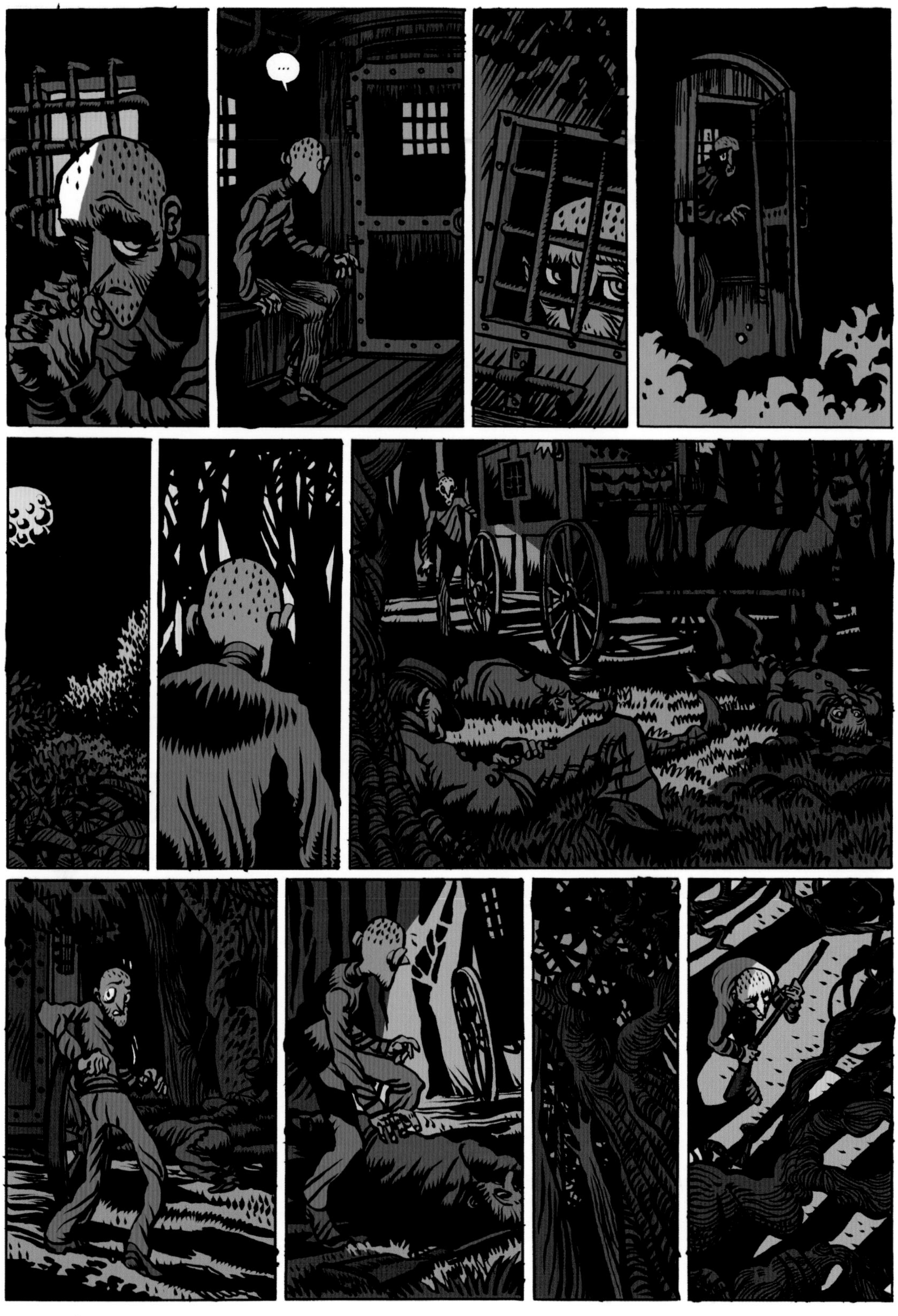
...

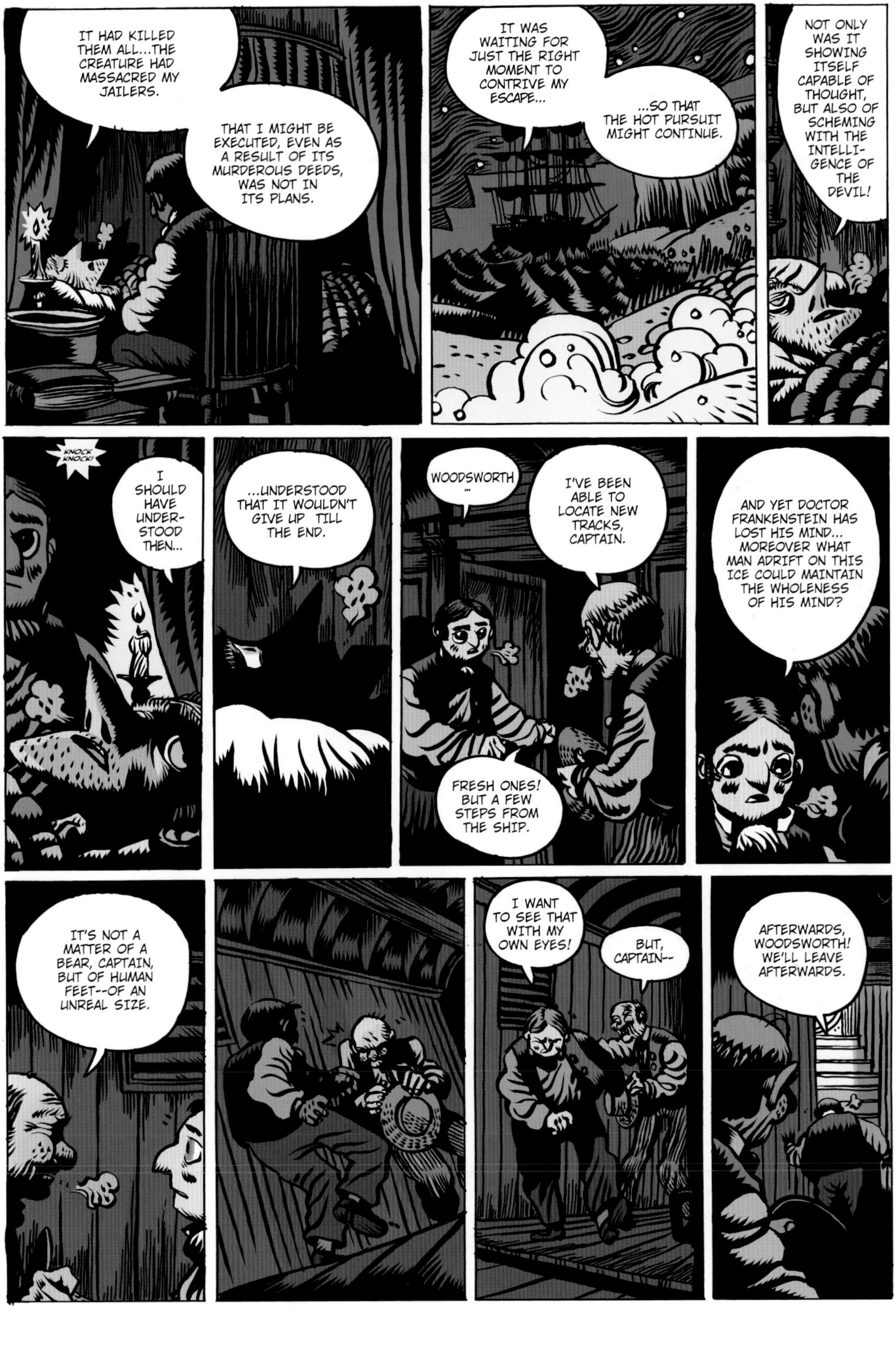
IT HAD KILLED THEM ALL...THE CREATURE HAD MASSACRED MY JAILERS.
THAT I MIGHT BE EXECUTED, EVEN AS A RESULT OF ITS MURDEROUS DEEDS, WAS NOT IN ITS PLANS.
IT WAS WAITING FOR JUST THE RIGHT MOMENT TO CONTRIVE MY ESCAPE...
...SO THAT THE HOT PURSUIT MIGHT CONTINUE.
NOT ONLY WAS IT SHOWING ITSELF CAPABLE OF THOUGHT, BUT ALSO OF SCHEMING WITH THE INTELLIGENCE OF THE DEVIL!
KNOCK KNOCK!
I SHOULD HAVE UNDERSTOOD THEN...
...UNDERSTOOD THAT IT WOULDN'T GIVE UP TILL THE END.
WOODSWORTH...
I'VE BEEN ABLE TO LOCATE NEW TRACKS, CAPTAIN.
FRESH ONES! BUT A FEW STEPS FROM THE SHIP.
AND YET DOCTOR FRANKENSTEIN HAS LOST HIS MIND... MOREOVER WHAT MAN ADRIFT ON THIS ICE COULD MAINTAIN THE WHOLENESS OF HIS MIND?
IT'S NOT A MATTER OF A BEAR, CAPTAIN, BUT OF HUMAN FEET--OF AN UNREAL SIZE.
I WANT TO SEE THAT WITH MY OWN EYES!
BUT, CAPTAIN--
AFTERWARDS, WOODSWORTH! WE'LL LEAVE AFTERWARDS.

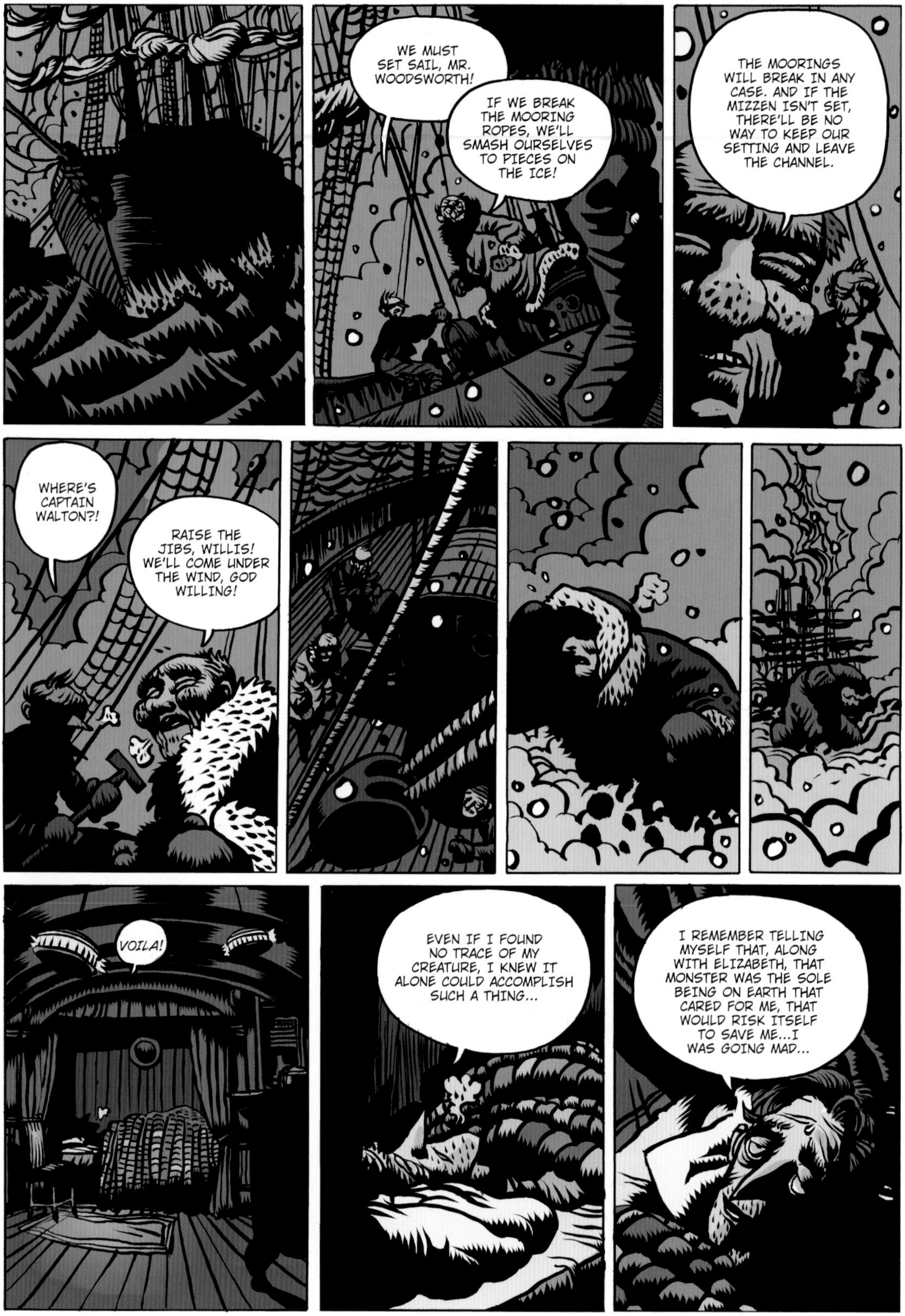

WE MUST SET SAIL, MR. WOODSWORTH!
IF WE BREAK THE MOORING ROPES, WE'LL SMASH OURSELVES TO PIECES ON THE ICE!
THE MOORINGS WILL BREAK IN ANY CASE. AND IF THE MIZZEN ISN'T SET, THERE'LL BE NO WAY TO KEEP OUR SETTING AND LEAVE THE CHANNEL.
WHERE'S CAPTAIN WALTON?!
RAISE THE JIBS, WILLIS! WE'LL COME UNDER THE WIND, GOD WILLING!
VOILA!
EVEN IF I FOUND NO TRACE OF MY CREATURE, I KNEW IT ALONE COULD ACCOMPLISH SUCH A THING...
I REMEMBER TELLING MYSELF THAT, ALONG WITH ELIZABETH, THAT MONSTER WAS THE SOLE BEING ON EARTH THAT CARED FOR ME, THAT WOULD RISK ITSELF TO SAVE ME...I WAS GOING MAD...

I WANDERED ABOUT FOR A LONG TIME, DAYS PERHAPS, EXHAUSTED, TRAVERSING THE MILES OF THIS COUNTRY WHERE I KNEW NOTHING AND NOBODY.

I KNEW I'D BE ABLE TO JOIN A CREW EASILY ENOUGH AS A HANDYMAN ON A SHIP BOUND FOR FRANCE...

IN THAT HOPE, I RETURNED TO THE CITY OF LONDON.

I SPENT SEVERAL MONTHS THERE, AT FIRST WITH THE FUNDS RESULTING FROM THE SALE OF MY HORSE...

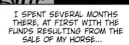

THEN, BY HELPING THE FISHERMEN ON THE DOCKS BY UNLOADING THEIR FISH FOR A FEW POUNDS.

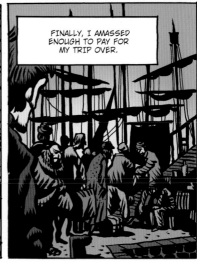

FINALLY, I AMASSED ENOUGH TO PAY FOR MY TRIP OVER.

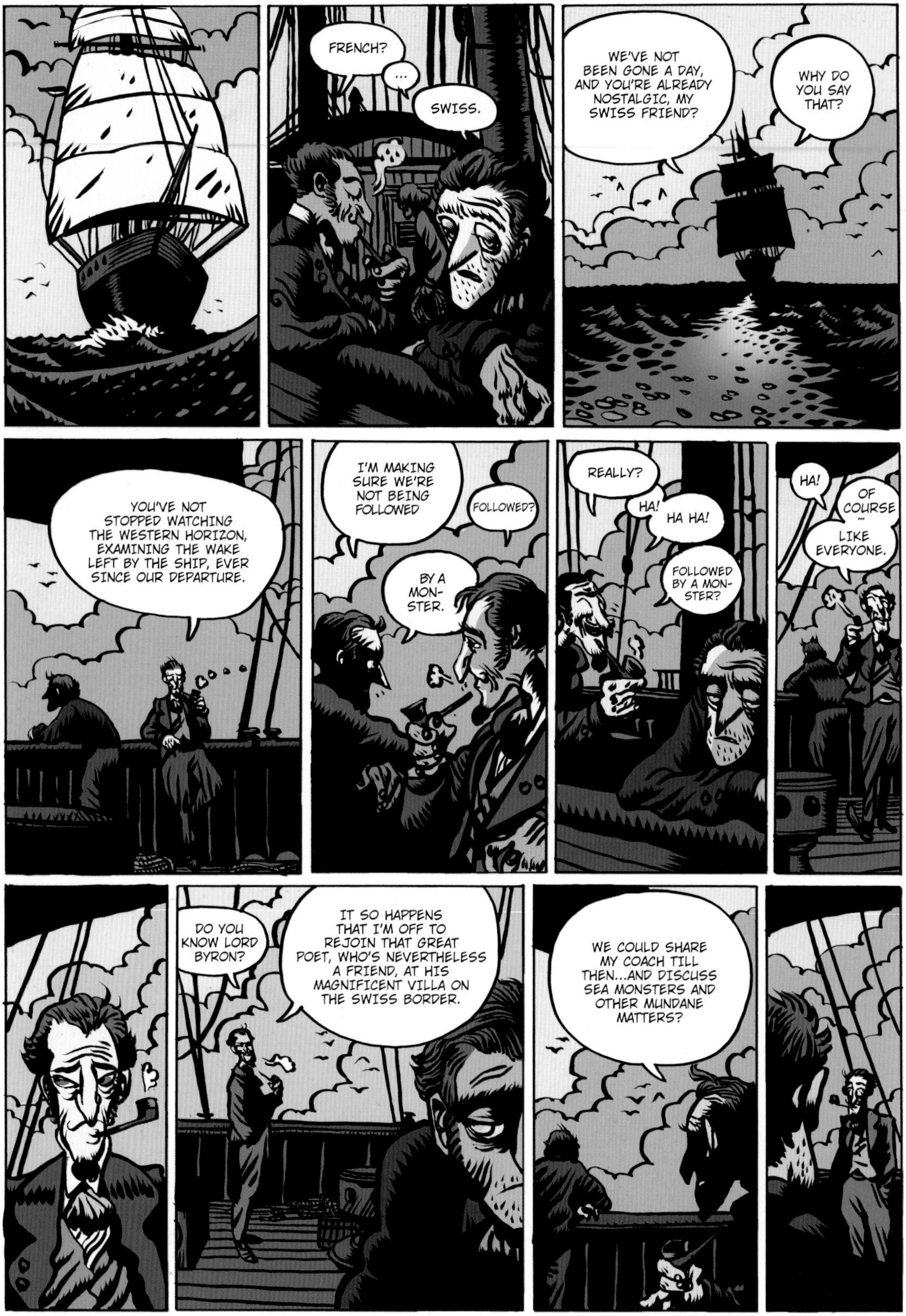
FRENCH?
...
SWISS.
WE'VE NOT BEEN GONE A DAY, AND YOU'RE ALREADY NOSTALGIC, MY SWISS FRIEND?
WHY DO YOU SAY THAT?
YOU'VE NOT STOPPED WATCHING THE WESTERN HORIZON, EXAMINING THE WAKE LEFT BY THE SHIP, EVER SINCE OUR DEPARTURE.
I'M MAKING SURE WE'RE NOT BEING FOLLOWED
FOLLOWED?
BY A MON-STER.
REALLY?
HA!
HA HA!
FOLLOWED BY A MON-STER?
HA!
OF COURSE ...
LIKE EVERYONE.
DO YOU KNOW LORD BYRON?
IT SO HAPPENS THAT I'M OFF TO REJOIN THAT GREAT POET, WHO'S NEVERTHELESS A FRIEND, AT HIS MAGNIFICENT VILLA ON THE SWISS BORDER.
WE COULD SHARE MY COACH TILL THEN...AND DISCUSS SEA MONSTERS AND OTHER MUNDANE MATTERS?

ABOUT TWO WEEKS LATER, I ARRIVED AT THE GATES OF BELRIVE...

MOTHER...

FATHER...

WHAT A HORRIBLE, WRETCHED SON I AM...

SHOULD I REJOICE THAT YOU NEVER KNEW?

THAT YOU NEVER REALLY KNEW YOUR OWN SON?

FRANKENSTEIN
caroline - ALYSS?
1772-1801
FRANKENST...
Victor - An...
17...

FATHER...HOW CAN I REJOIN THE COMPANY OF MEN NOW? WHEN I HAVE LOOSENED AMONG THEN AN ENEMY THAT TAKES PLEASURE IN SPILLING THEIR BLOOD AND DELIGHTS IN THEIR MOANS...

HOW?!

DO YOU THINK I'VE GONE MAD, MY DEAR PARENTS?

HEAVENS NO! I MURDERED THEM, WILLIAM, JUSTINE, HENRY --ALL DEAD BY MY HANDS!

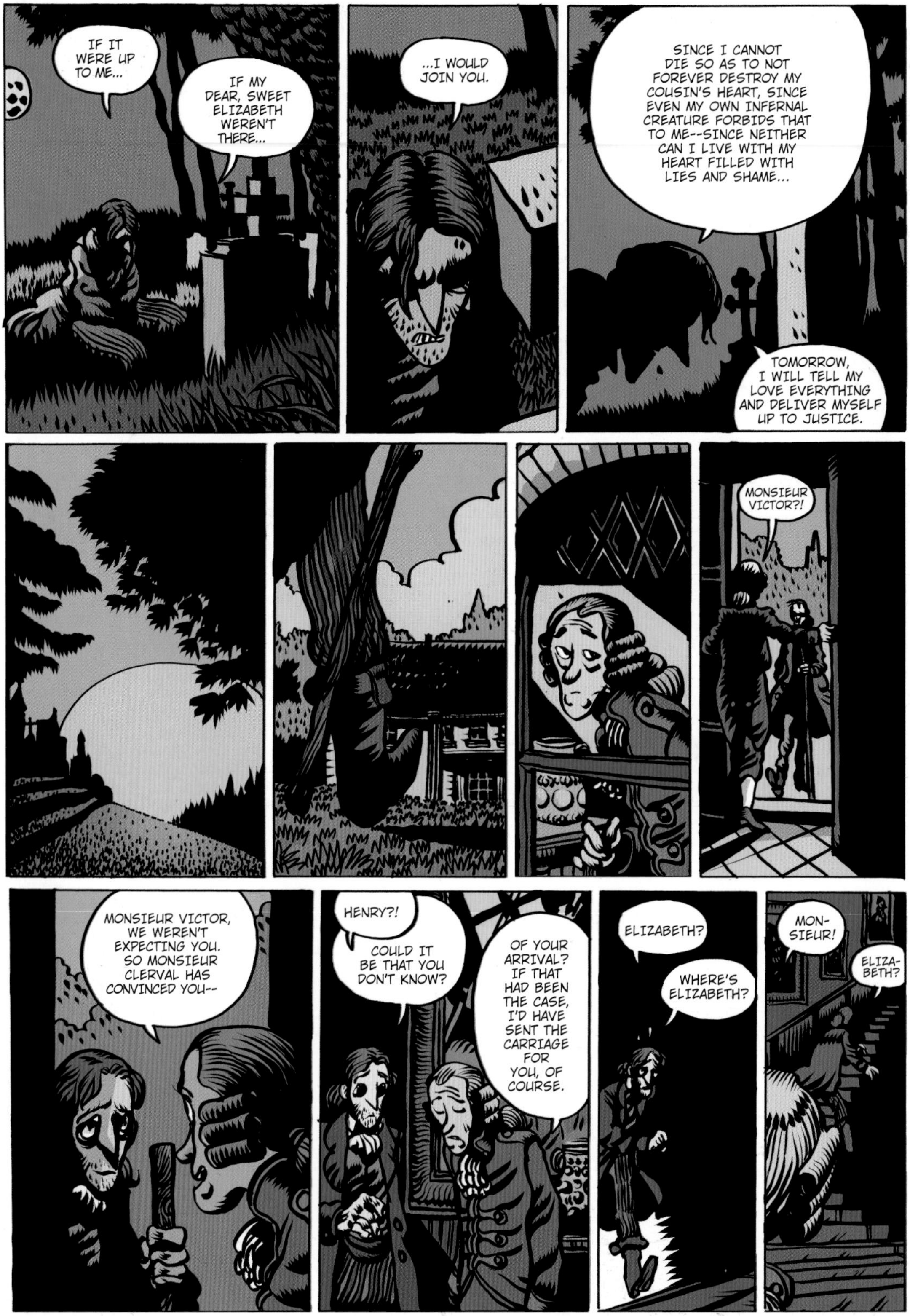
IF IT WERE UP TO ME...
IF MY DEAR, SWEET ELIZABETH WEREN'T THERE...
...I WOULD JOIN YOU.
SINCE I CANNOT DIE SO AS TO NOT FOREVER DESTROY MY COUSIN'S HEART, SINCE EVEN MY OWN INFERNAL CREATURE FORBIDS THAT TO ME--SINCE NEITHER CAN I LIVE WITH MY HEART FILLED WITH LIES AND SHAME...
TOMORROW, I WILL TELL MY LOVE EVERYTHING AND DELIVER MYSELF UP TO JUSTICE.
MONSIEUR VICTOR?!
MONSIEUR VICTOR, WE WEREN'T EXPECTING YOU. SO MONSIEUR CLERVAL HAS CONVINCED YOU--
HENRY?!
COULD IT BE THAT YOU DON'T KNOW?
OF YOUR ARRIVAL? IF THAT HAD BEEN THE CASE, I'D HAVE SENT THE CARRIAGE FOR YOU, OF COURSE.
ELIZABETH?
WHERE'S ELIZABETH?
MON-SIEUR!
ELIZA-BETH?

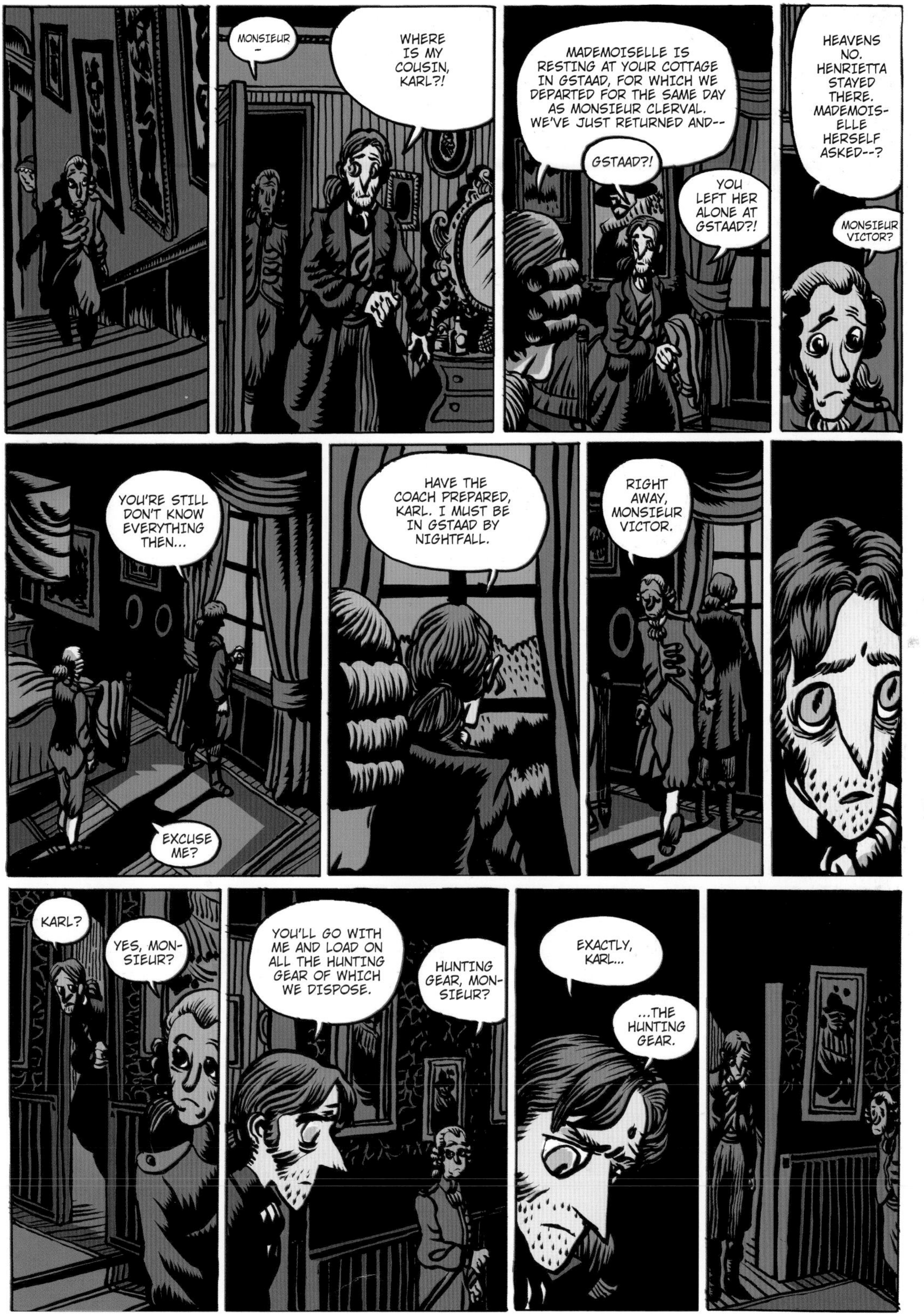
MONSIEUR-
WHERE IS MY COUSIN, KARL?!
MADEMOISELLE IS RESTING AT YOUR COTTAGE IN GSTAAD, FOR WHICH WE DEPARTED FOR THE SAME DAY AS MONSIEUR CLERVAL. WE'VE JUST RETURNED AND--
GSTAAD?!
YOU LEFT HER ALONE AT GSTAAD?!
HEAVENS NO. HENRIETTA STAYED THERE. MADEMOISELLE HERSELF ASKED--?
MONSIEUR VICTOR?
YOU'RE STILL DON'T KNOW EVERYTHING THEN...
EXCUSE ME?
HAVE THE COACH PREPARED, KARL. I MUST BE IN GSTAAD BY NIGHTFALL.
RIGHT AWAY, MONSIEUR VICTOR.
KARL?
YES, MONSIEUR?
YOU'LL GO WITH ME AND LOAD ON ALL THE HUNTING GEAR OF WHICH WE DISPOSE.
HUNTING GEAR, MONSIEUR?
EXACTLY, KARL...
...THE HUNTING GEAR.

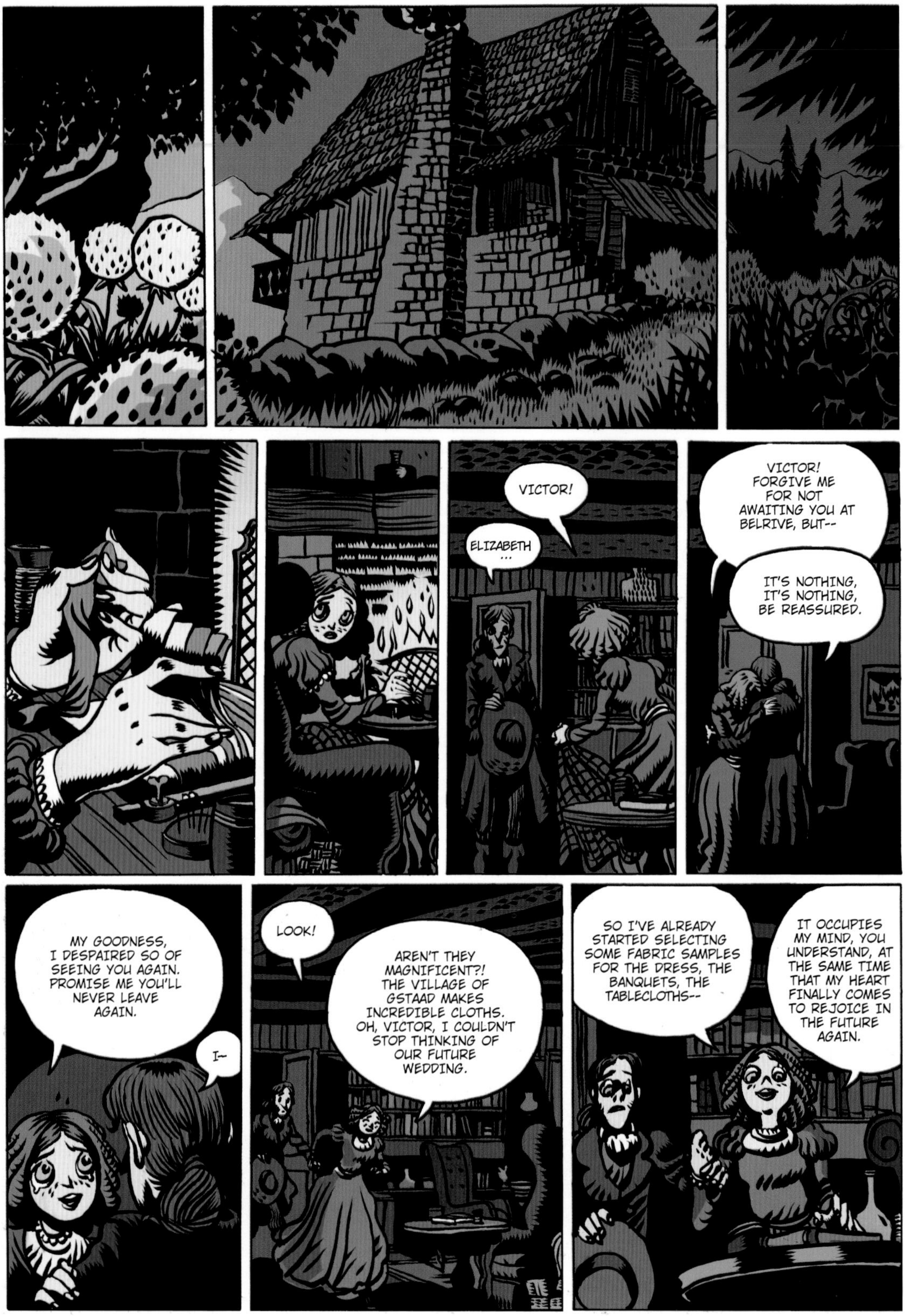
VICTOR!
ELIZABETH ...
VICTOR! FORGIVE ME FOR NOT AWAITING YOU AT BELRIVE, BUT--
IT'S NOTHING, IT'S NOTHING, BE REASSURED.
MY GOODNESS, I DESPAIRED SO OF SEEING YOU AGAIN. PROMISE ME YOU'LL NEVER LEAVE AGAIN.
I--
LOOK!
AREN'T THEY MAGNIFICENT?! THE VILLAGE OF GSTAAD MAKES INCREDIBLE CLOTHS. OH, VICTOR, I COULDN'T STOP THINKING OF OUR FUTURE WEDDING.
SO I'VE ALREADY STARTED SELECTING SOME FABRIC SAMPLES FOR THE DRESS, THE BANQUETS, THE TABLECLOTHS--
IT OCCUPIES MY MIND, YOU UNDERSTAND, AT THE SAME TIME THAT MY HEART FINALLY COMES TO REJOICE IN THE FUTURE AGAIN.

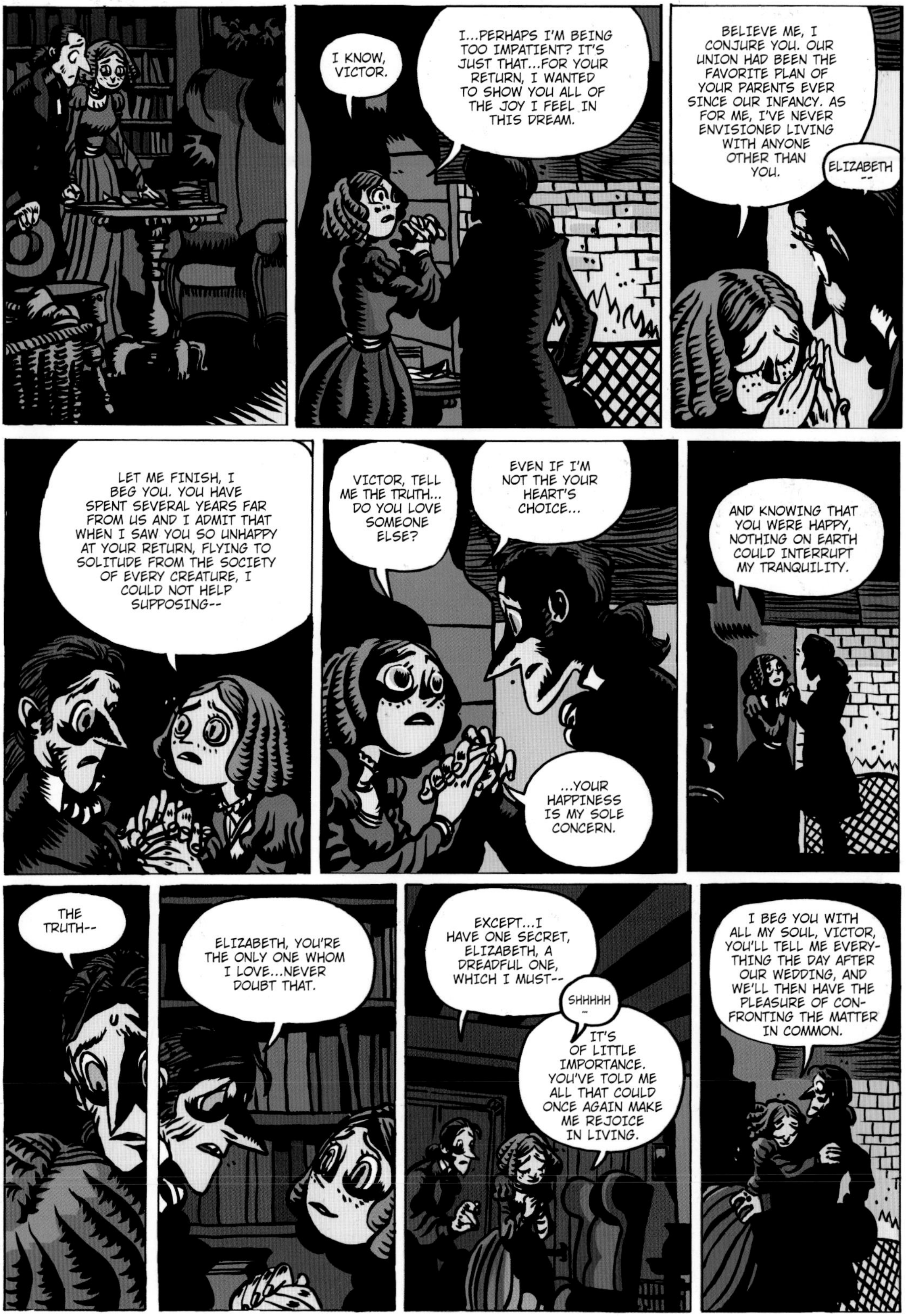
I KNOW, VICTOR.
I...PERHAPS I'M BEING TOO IMPATIENT? IT'S JUST THAT...FOR YOUR RETURN, I WANTED TO SHOW YOU ALL OF THE JOY I FEEL IN THIS DREAM.
BELIEVE ME, I CONJURE YOU. OUR UNION HAD BEEN THE FAVORITE PLAN OF YOUR PARENTS EVER SINCE OUR INFANCY. AS FOR ME, I'VE NEVER ENVISIONED LIVING WITH ANYONE OTHER THAN YOU.
ELIZABETH --
LET ME FINISH, I BEG YOU. YOU HAVE SPENT SEVERAL YEARS FAR FROM US AND I ADMIT THAT WHEN I SAW YOU SO UNHAPPY AT YOUR RETURN, FLYING TO SOLITUDE FROM THE SOCIETY OF EVERY CREATURE, I COULD NOT HELP SUPPOSING--
VICTOR, TELL ME THE TRUTH... DO YOU LOVE SOMEONE ELSE?
EVEN IF I'M NOT THE YOUR HEART'S CHOICE...
...YOUR HAPPINESS IS MY SOLE CONCERN.
AND KNOWING THAT YOU WERE HAPPY, NOTHING ON EARTH COULD INTERRUPT MY TRANQUILITY.
THE TRUTH--
ELIZABETH, YOU'RE THE ONLY ONE WHOM I LOVE...NEVER DOUBT THAT.
EXCEPT...I HAVE ONE SECRET, ELIZABETH, A DREADFUL ONE, WHICH I MUST--
SHHHHH...
IT'S OF LITTLE IMPORTANCE. YOU'VE TOLD ME ALL THAT COULD ONCE AGAIN MAKE ME REJOICE IN LIVING.
I BEG YOU WITH ALL MY SOUL, VICTOR, YOU'LL TELL ME EVERYTHING THE DAY AFTER OUR WEDDING, AND WE'LL THEN HAVE THE PLEASURE OF CONFRONTING THE MATTER IN COMMON.

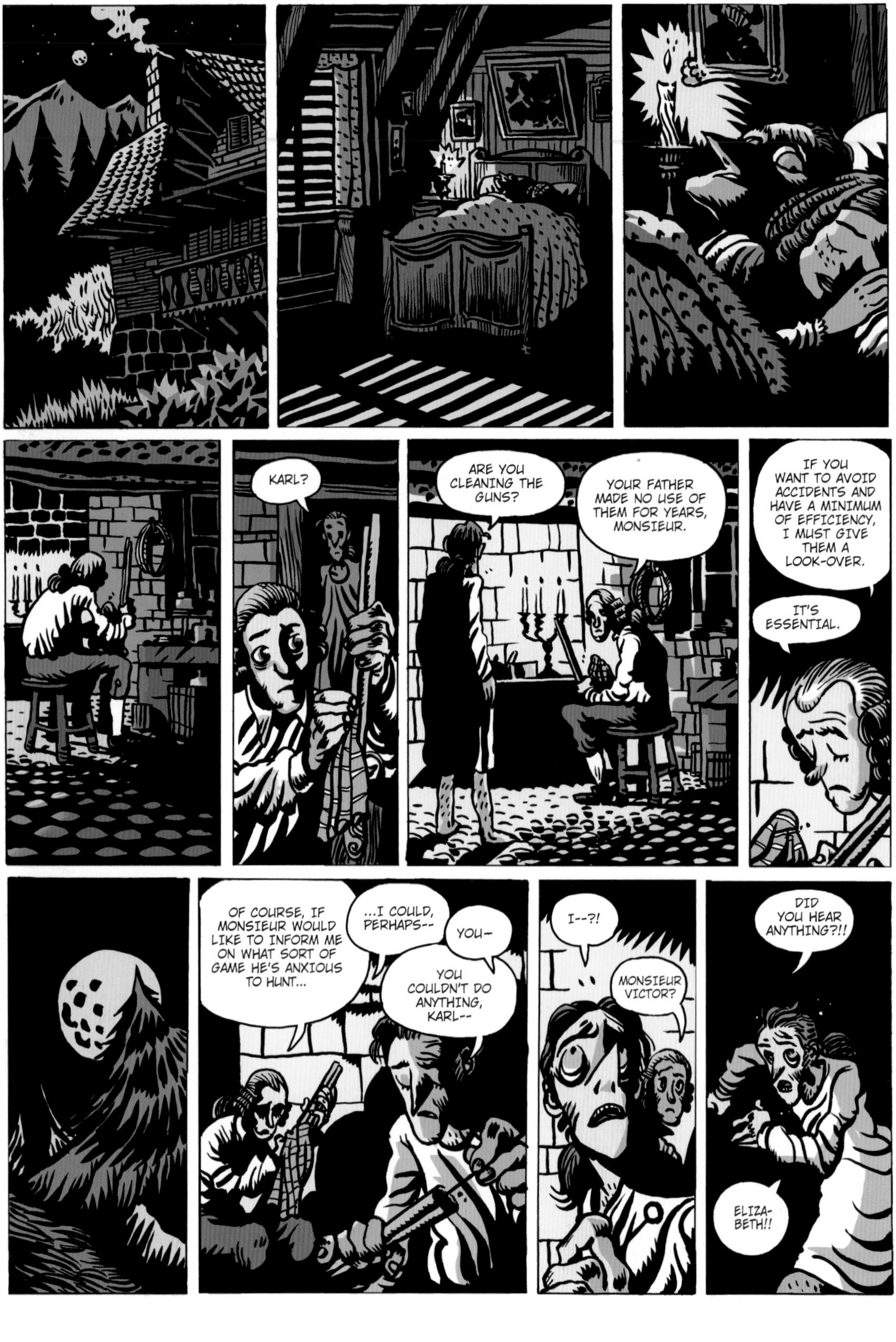
KARL?
ARE YOU CLEANING THE GUNS?
YOUR FATHER MADE NO USE OF THEM FOR YEARS, MONSIEUR.
IF YOU WANT TO AVOID ACCIDENTS AND HAVE A MINIMUM OF EFFICIENCY, I MUST GIVE THEM A LOOK-OVER.
IT'S ESSENTIAL.
OF COURSE, IF MONSIEUR WOULD LIKE TO INFORM ME ON WHAT SORT OF GAME HE'S ANXIOUS TO HUNT...
...I COULD, PERHAPS--
YOU--
YOU COULDN'T DO ANYTHING, KARL--
I--?!
MONSIEUR VICTOR?
DID YOU HEAR ANYTHING?!!
ELIZA-BETH!!

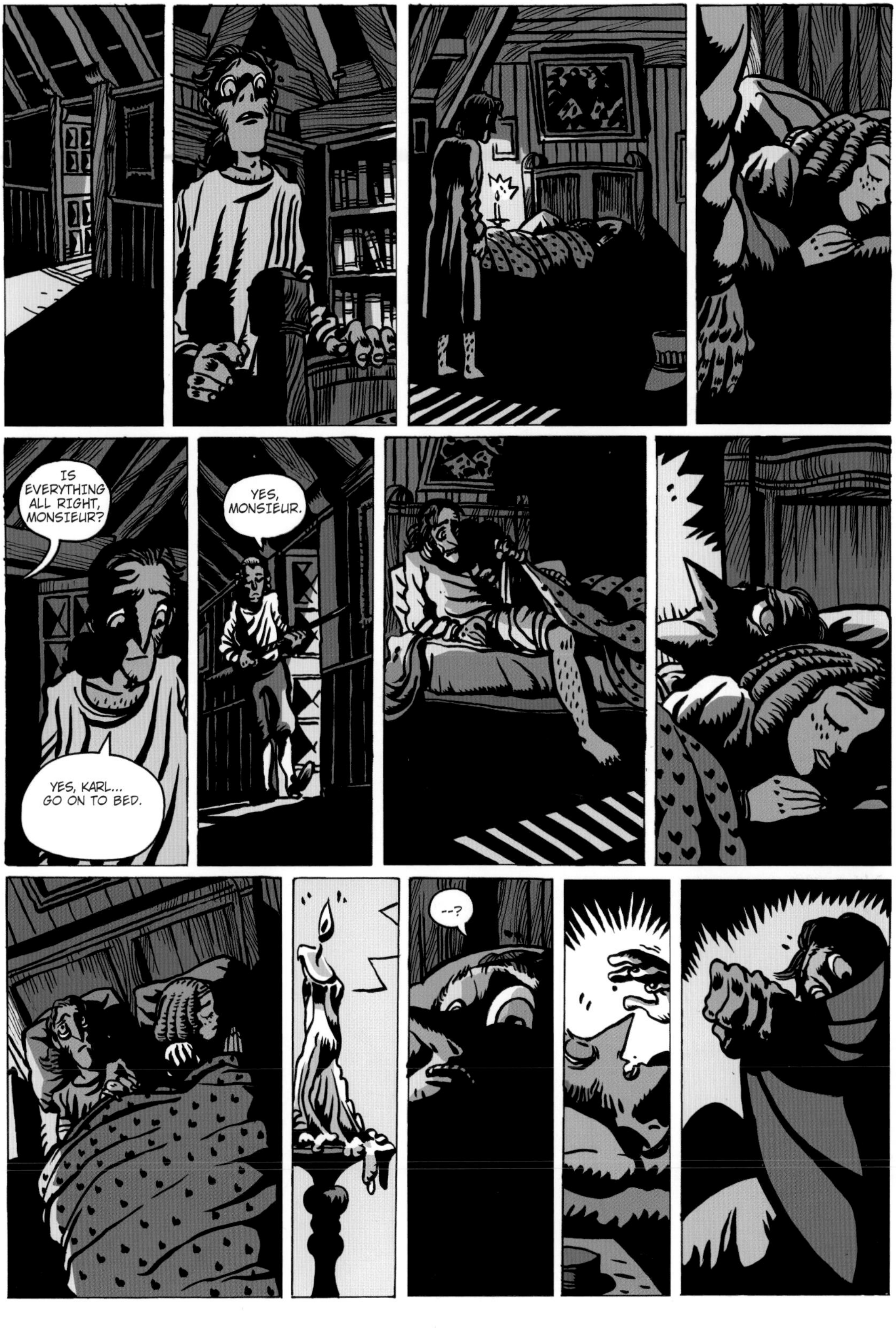
IS EVERYTHING ALL RIGHT, MONSIEUR?
YES, KARL... GO ON TO BED.
YES, MONSIEUR.
--?

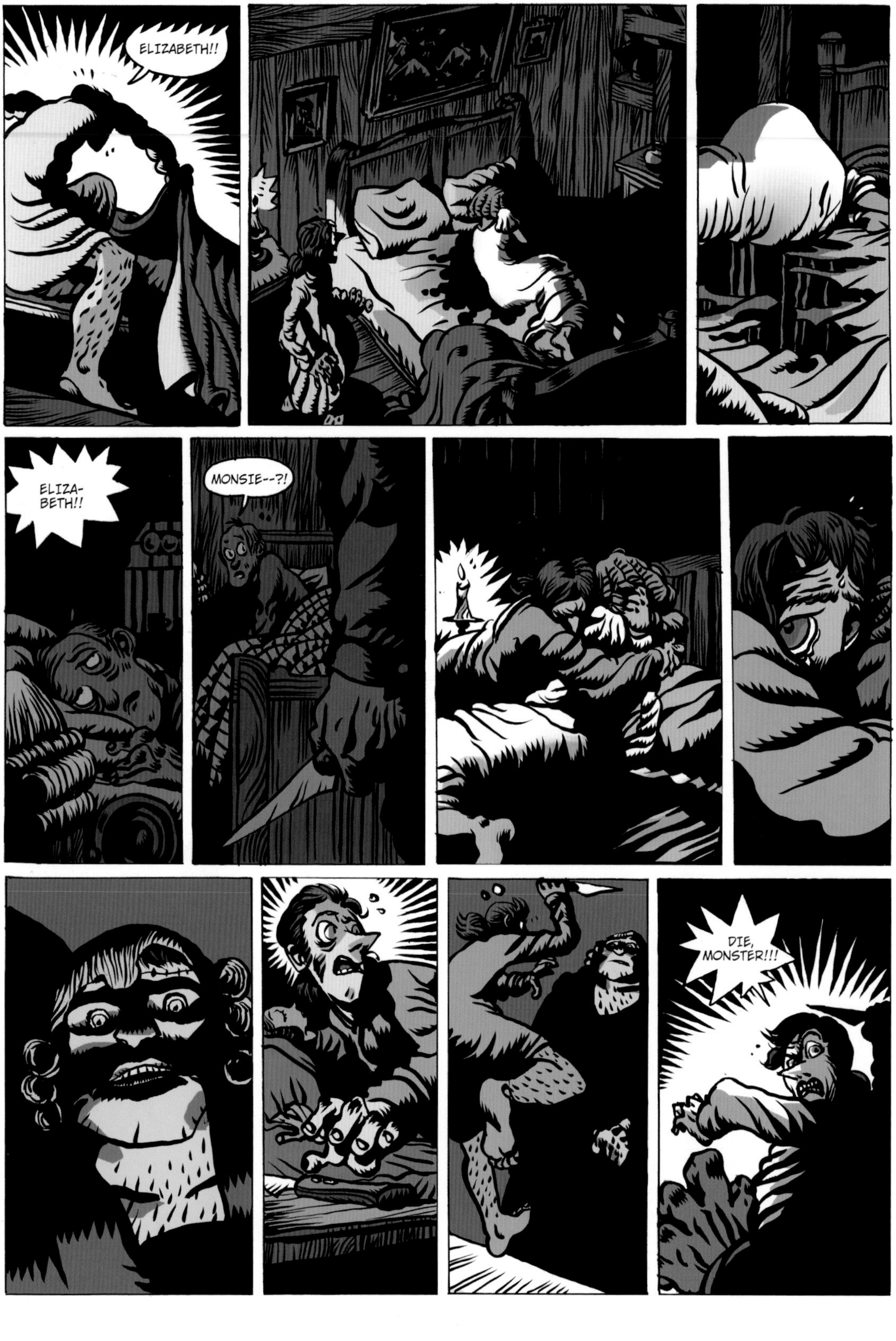
ELIZABETH!!
ELIZA-BETH!!
MONSIE--?!
DIE, MONSTER!!!

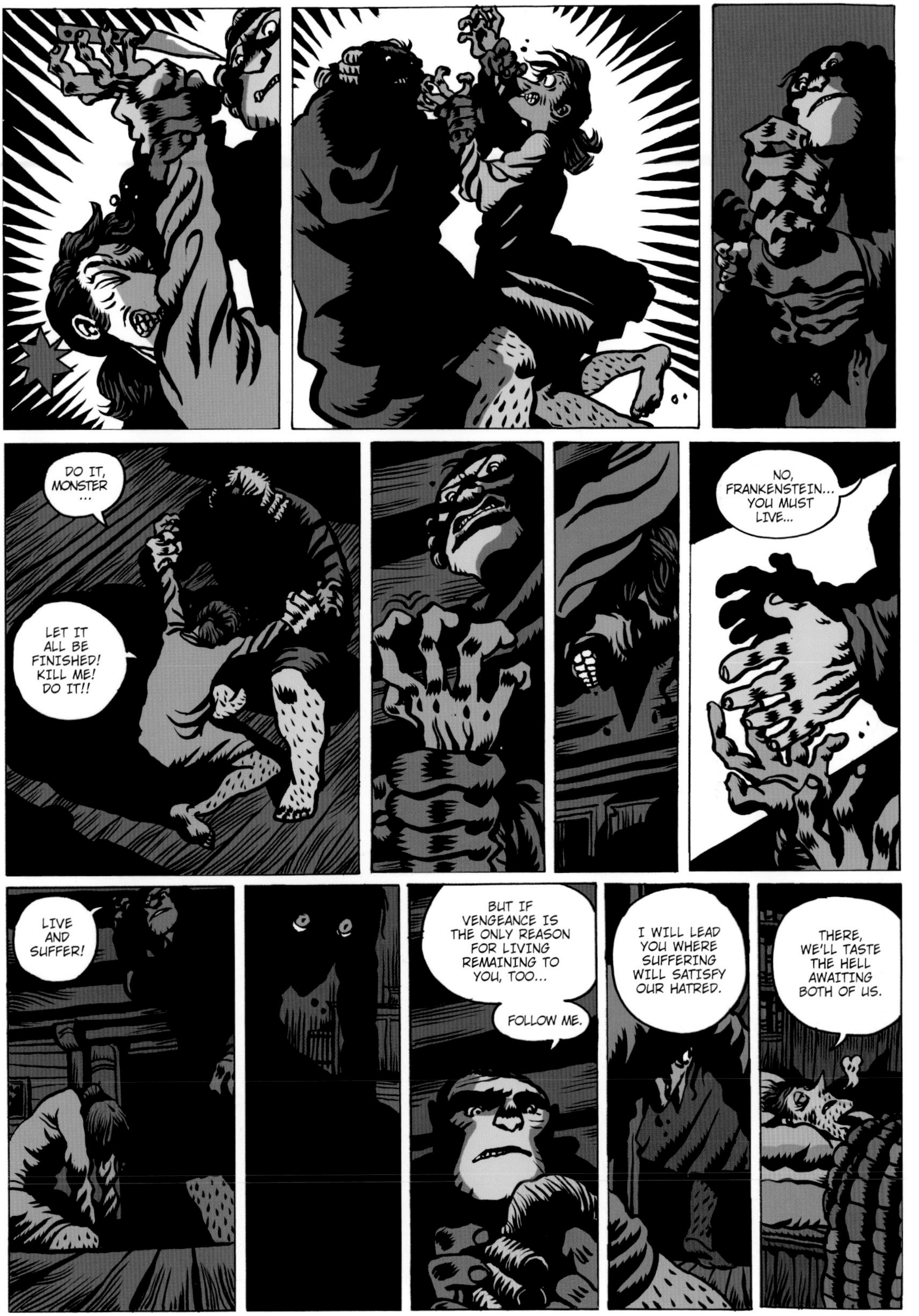
DO IT, MONSTER ...
LET IT ALL BE FINISHED! KILL ME! DO IT!!
NO, FRANKENSTEIN... YOU MUST LIVE...
LIVE AND SUFFER!
BUT IF VENGEANCE IS THE ONLY REASON FOR LIVING REMAINING TO YOU, TOO...
FOLLOW ME.
I WILL LEAD YOU WHERE SUFFERING WILL SATISFY OUR HATRED.
THERE, WE'LL TASTE THE HELL AWAITING BOTH OF US.

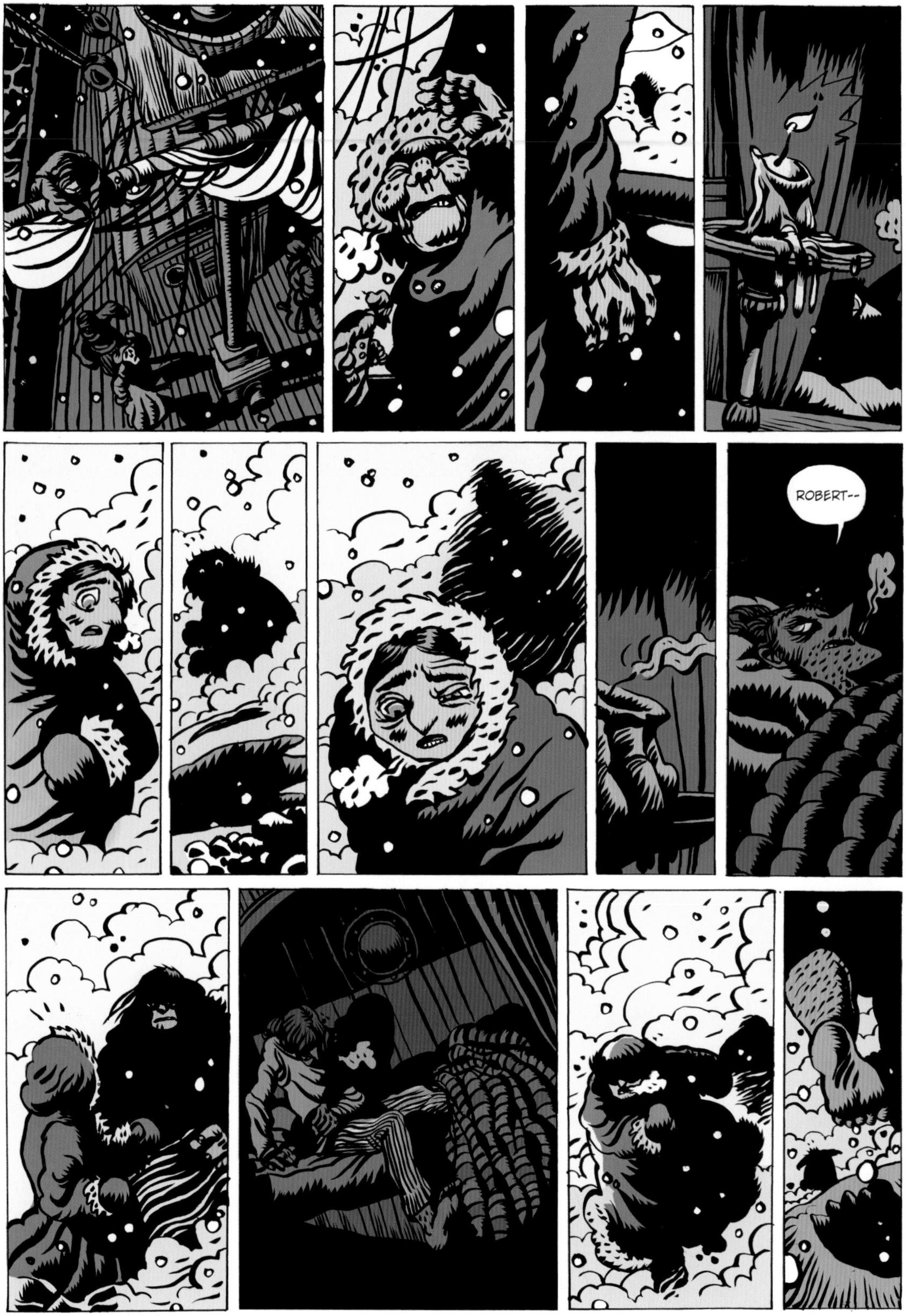
ROBERT--

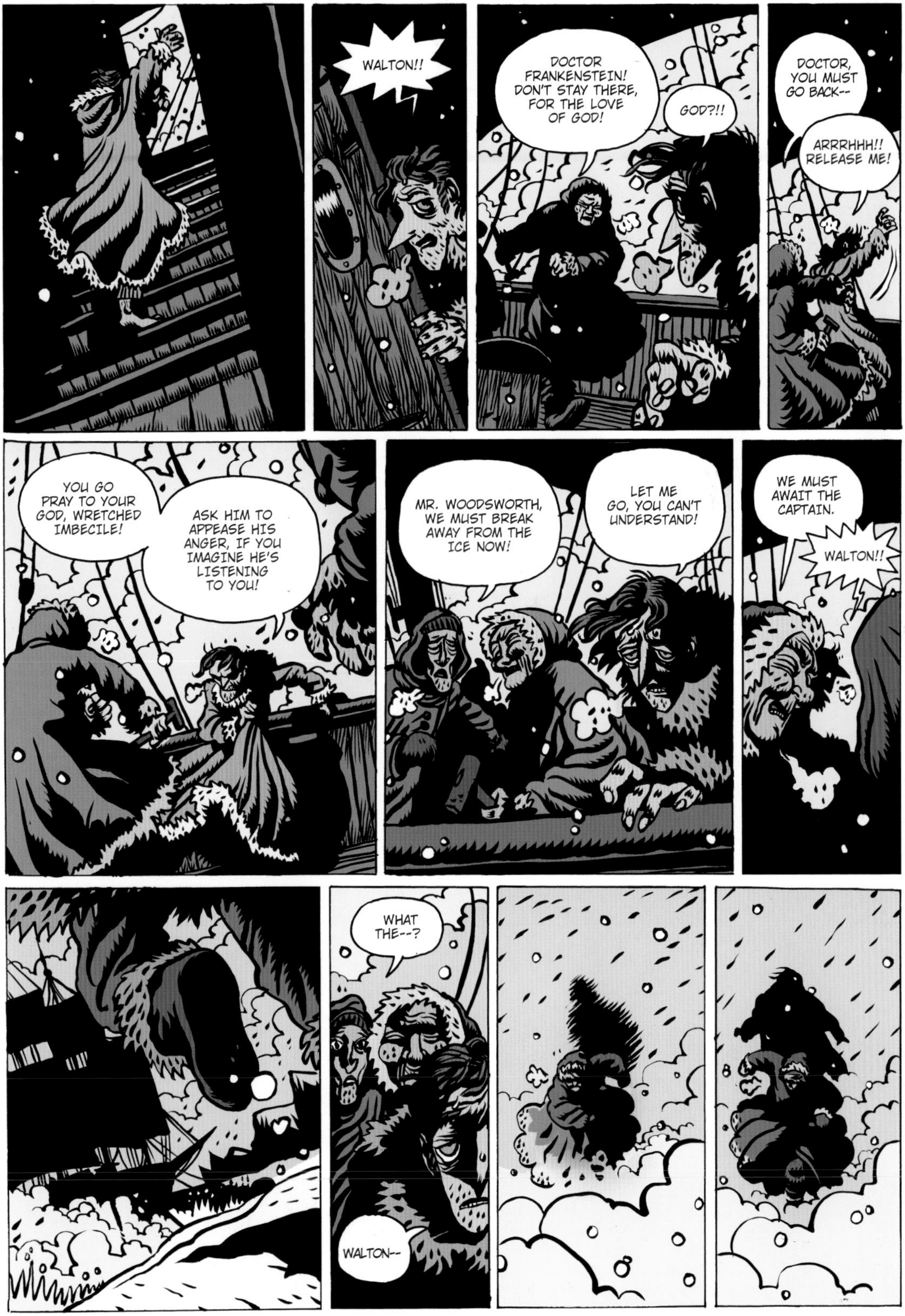
WALTON!!
DOCTOR FRANKENSTEIN! DON'T STAY THERE, FOR THE LOVE OF GOD!
GOD?!!
DOCTOR, YOU MUST GO BACK--
ARRRHHH!! RELEASE ME!
YOU GO PRAY TO YOUR GOD, WRETCHED IMBECILE!
ASK HIM TO APPEASE HIS ANGER, IF YOU IMAGINE HE'S LISTENING TO YOU!
MR. WOODSWORTH, WE MUST BREAK AWAY FROM THE ICE NOW!
LET ME GO, YOU CAN'T UNDERSTAND!
WE MUST AWAIT THE CAPTAIN.
WALTON!!
WHAT THE--?
WALTON--

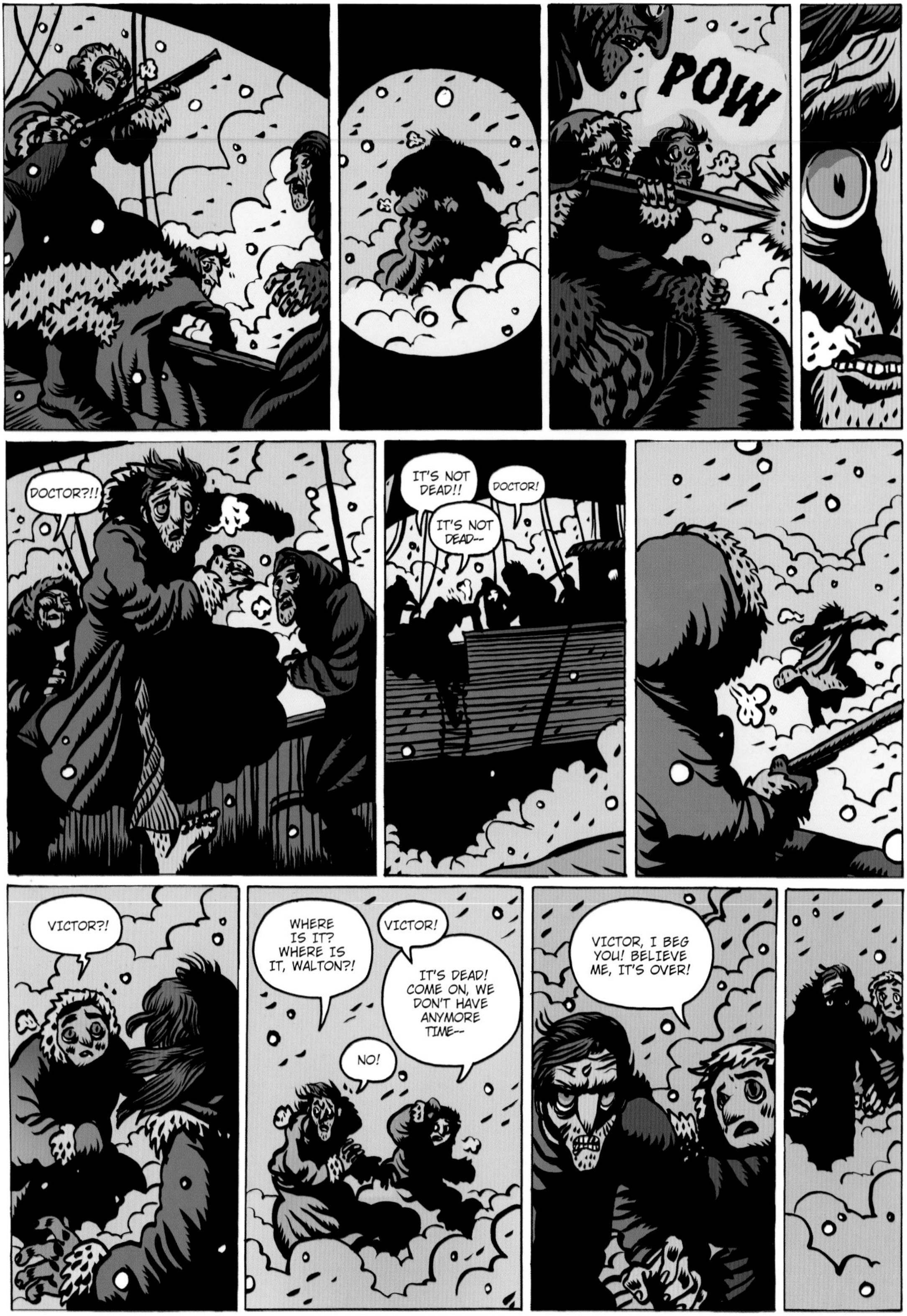
POW
DOCTOR?!!
IT'S NOT DEAD!!
DOCTOR!
IT'S NOT DEAD--
VICTOR?!
WHERE IS IT? WHERE IS IT, WALTON?!
VICTOR!
IT'S DEAD! COME ON, WE DON'T HAVE ANYMORE TIME--
NO!
VICTOR, I BEG YOU! BELIEVE ME, IT'S OVER!

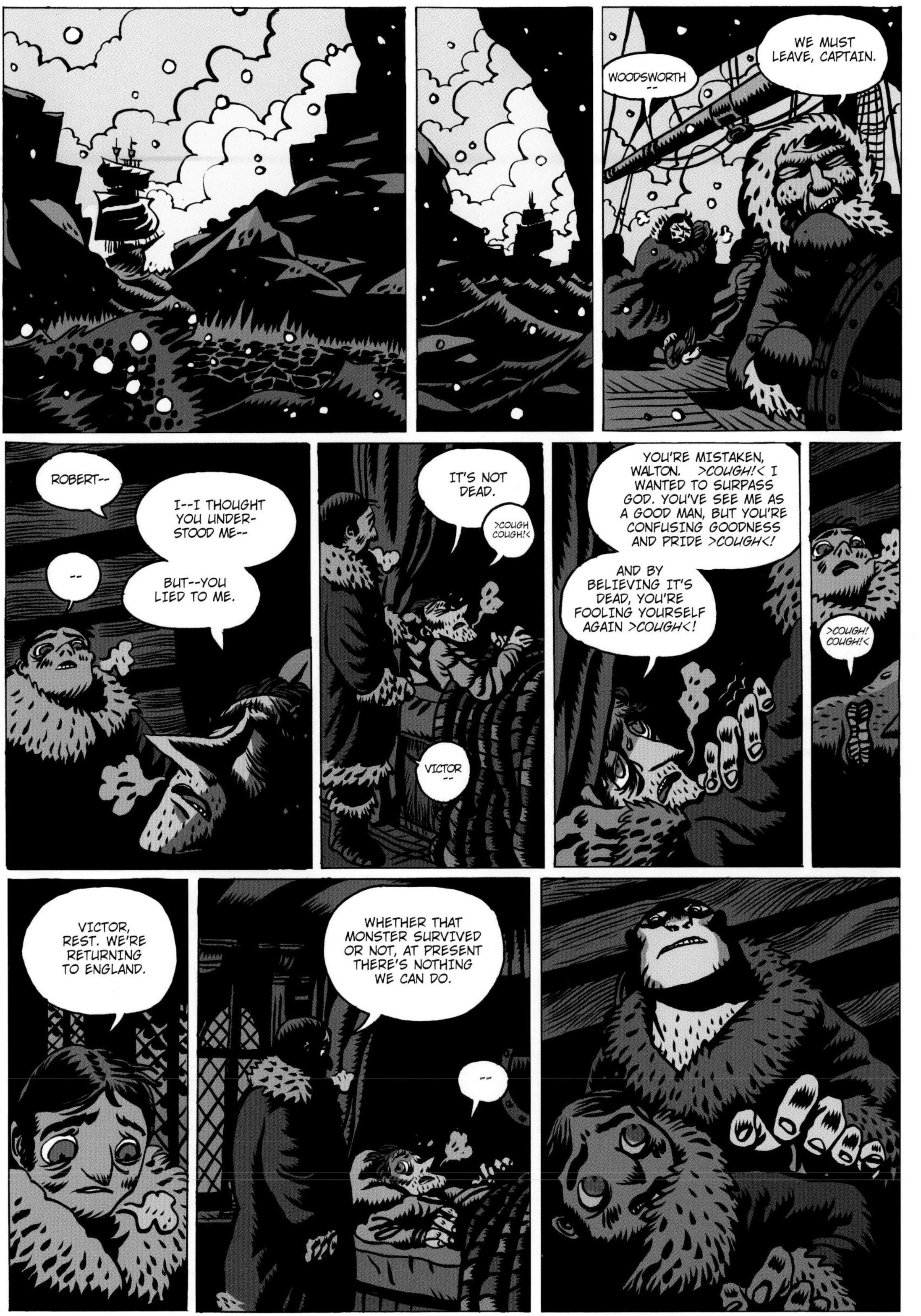
WOODSWORTH --
WE MUST LEAVE, CAPTAIN.
ROBERT--
I--I THOUGHT YOU UNDERSTOOD ME--
--
BUT--YOU LIED TO ME.
IT'S NOT DEAD.
>COUGH COUGH!<
VICTOR --
YOU'RE MISTAKEN, WALTON. >COUGH!< I WANTED TO SURPASS GOD. YOU'VE SEE ME AS A GOOD MAN, BUT YOU'RE CONFUSING GOODNESS AND PRIDE >COUGH<!
AND BY BELIEVING IT'S DEAD, YOU'RE FOOLING YOURSELF AGAIN >COUGH<!
>COUGH! COUGH!<
VICTOR, REST. WE'RE RETURNING TO ENGLAND.
WHETHER THAT MONSTER SURVIVED OR NOT, AT PRESENT THERE'S NOTHING WE CAN DO.
--

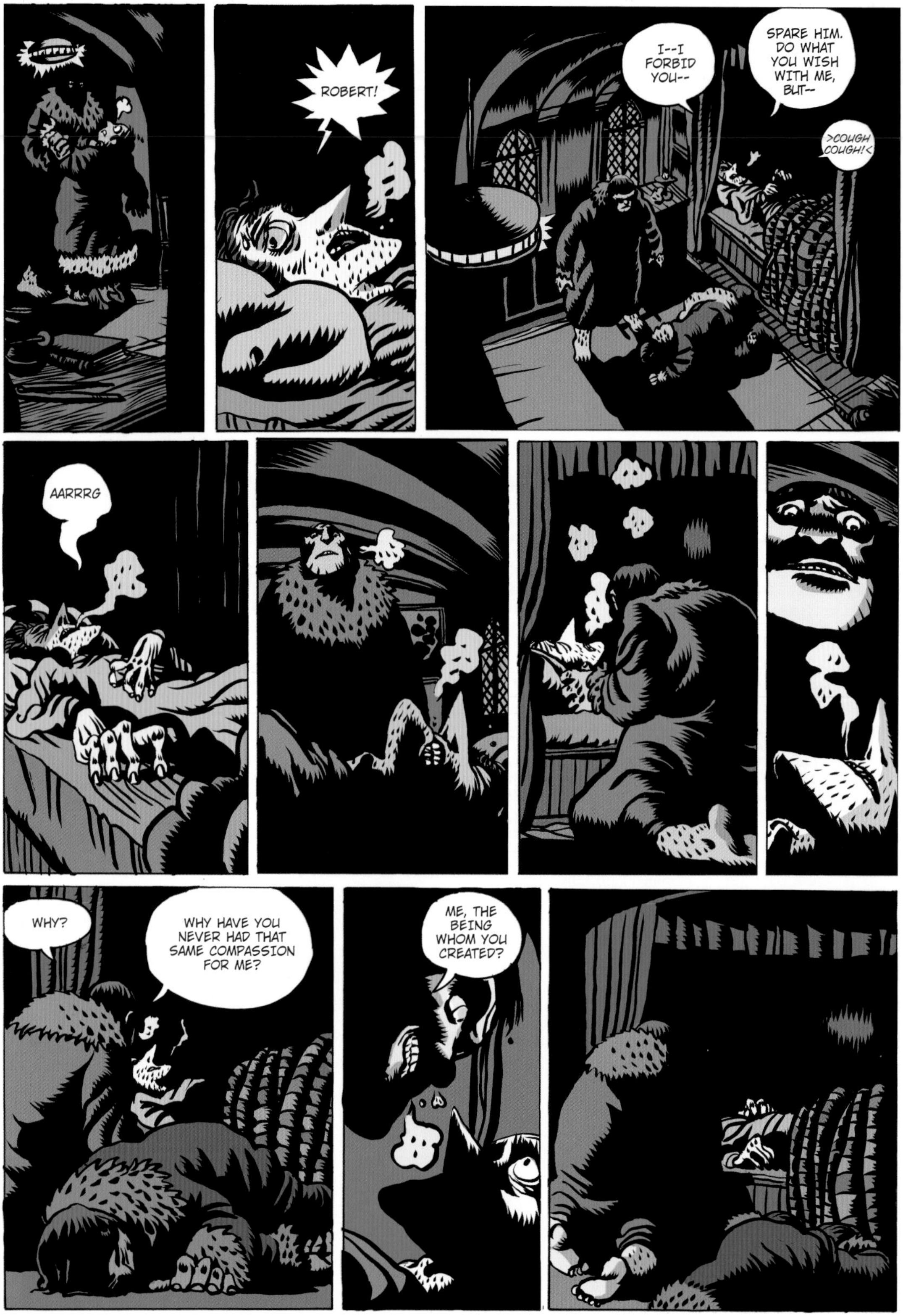
ROBERT!
I--I FORBID YOU--
SPARE HIM. DO WHAT YOU WISH WITH ME, BUT--
>COUGH COUGH!<
AARRRG
WHY?
WHY HAVE YOU NEVER HAD THAT SAME COMPASSION FOR ME?
ME, THE BEING WHOM YOU CREATED?

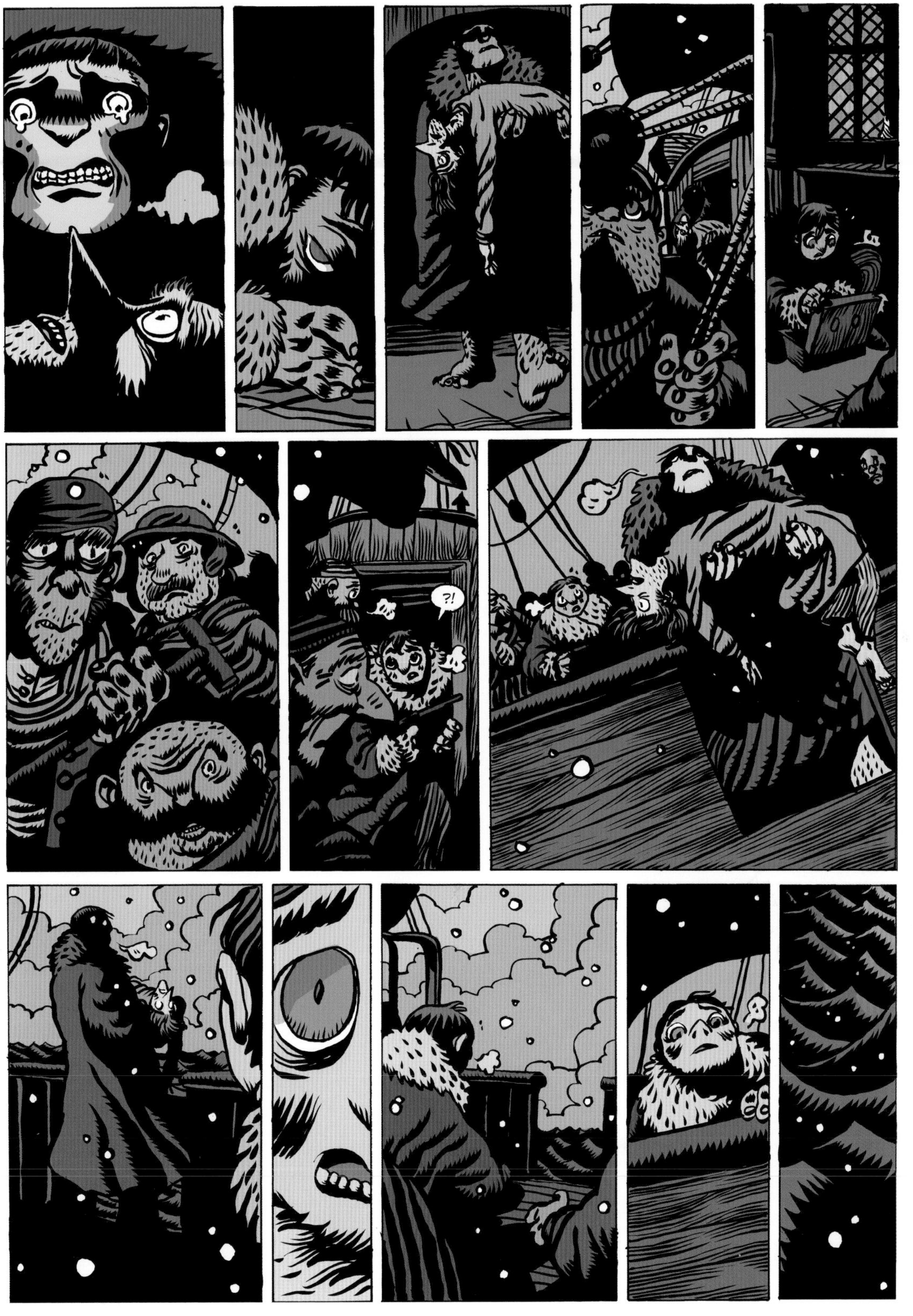
?!

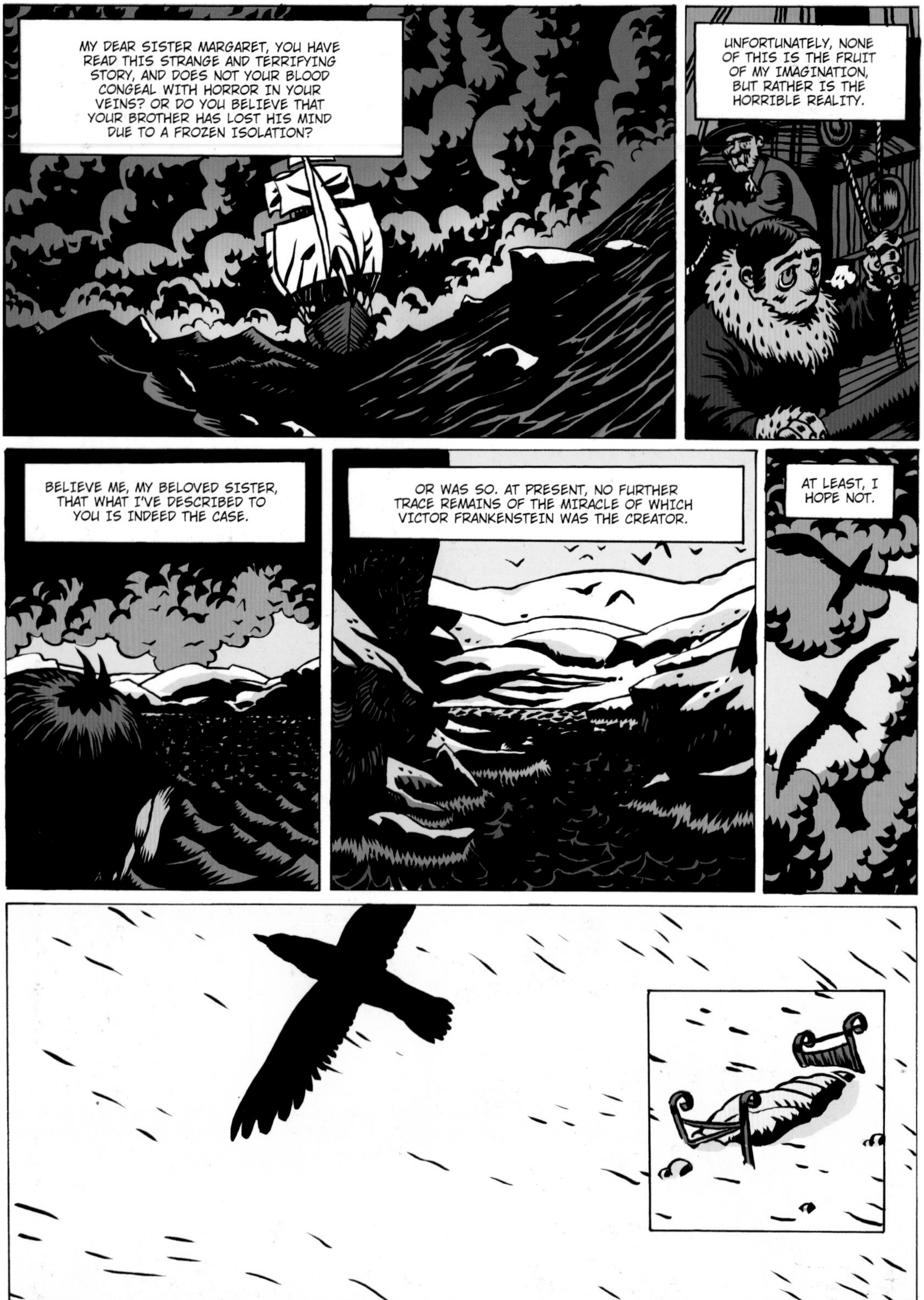
MY DEAR SISTER MARGARET, YOU HAVE READ THIS STRANGE AND TERRIFYING STORY, AND DOES NOT YOUR BLOOD CONGEAL WITH HORROR IN YOUR VEINS? OR DO YOU BELIEVE THAT YOUR BROTHER HAS LOST HIS MIND DUE TO A FROZEN ISOLATION?
UNFORTUNATELY, NONE OF THIS IS THE FRUIT OF MY IMAGINATION, BUT RATHER IS THE HORRIBLE REALITY.
BELIEVE ME, MY BELOVED SISTER, THAT WHAT I'VE DESCRIBED TO YOU IS INDEED THE CASE.
OR WAS SO. AT PRESENT, NO FURTHER TRACE REMAINS OF THE MIRACLE OF WHICH VICTOR FRANKENSTEIN WAS THE CREATOR.
AT LEAST, I HOPE NOT.

NOW THAT YOU HAVE READ THE CLASSICS Illustrated EDITION, DON'T MISS THE ADDED ENJOYMENT OF READING THE ORIGINAL, OBTAINABLE AT YOUR SCHOOL OR PUBLIC LIBRARY.

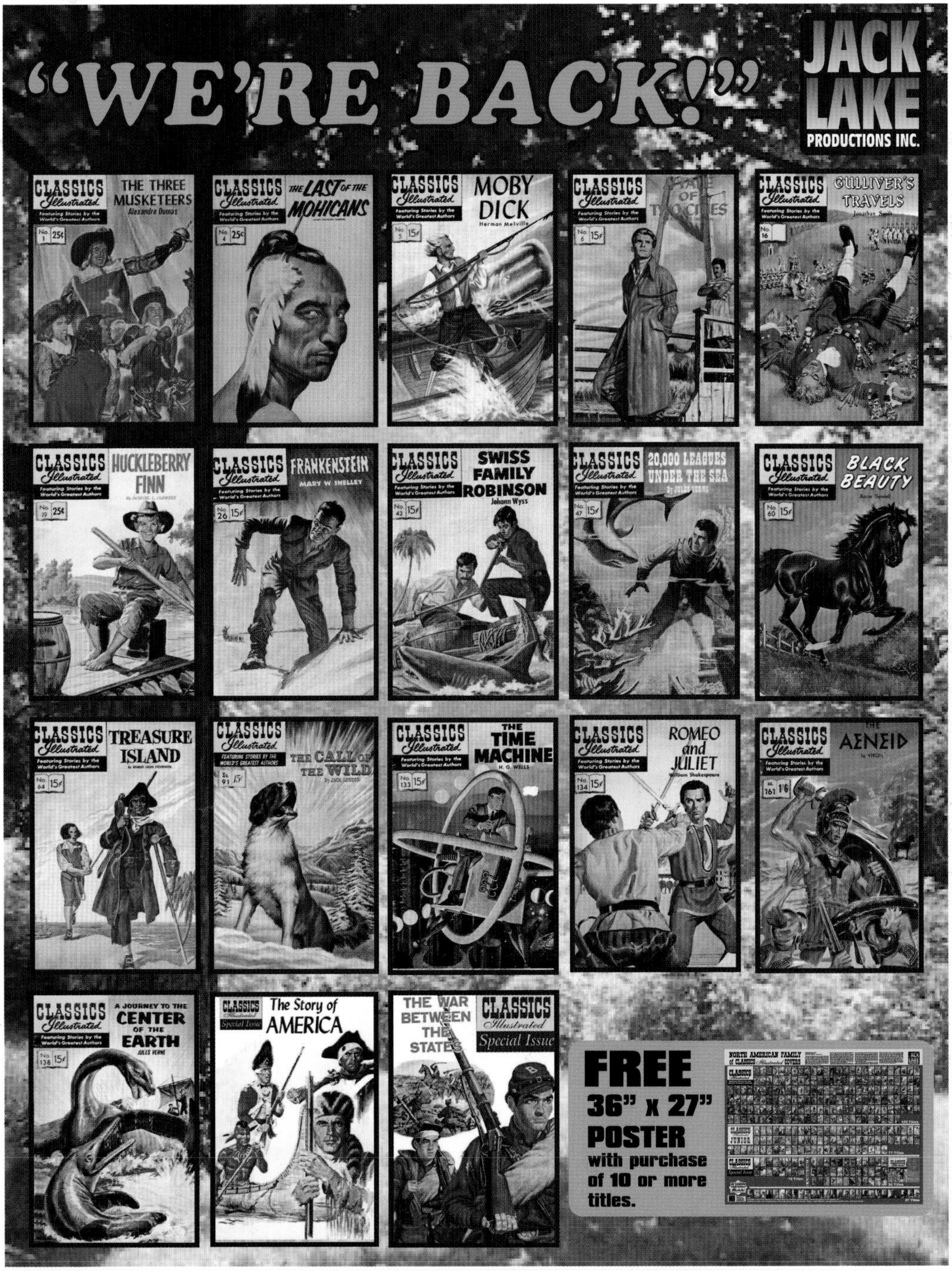
"WE'RE BACK!"
JACK LAKE
PRODUCTIONS INC.
CLASSICS Illustrated
THE THREE MUSKETEERS
Alexandre Dumas
THE LAST OF THE MOHICANS
MOBY DICK
Herman Melville
GULLIVER'S TRAVELS
HUCKLEBERRY FINN
FRANKENSTEIN
MARY W SHELLEY
SWISS FAMILY ROBINSON
Johann Wyss
20,000 LEAGUES UNDER THE SEA
BLACK BEAUTY
TREASURE ISLAND
THE CALL OF THE WILD
THE TIME MACHINE
H. G. WELLS
ROMEO and JULIET
William Shakespeare
THE AENEID
A JOURNEY TO THE CENTER OF THE EARTH
JULES VERNE
The Story of AMERICA
THE WAR BETWEEN THE STATES
Special Issue
FREE
36" x 27"
POSTER
with purchase of 10 or more titles.

MARY SHELLY

The daughter of Mary Wollstonecraft and William Godwin, two illustrious figures of the literary world, Mary Shelley loses her mother shortly after her birth. Neglected by her father, she grows up in London in a cultivated, anarchist milieu, benefiting from a solid cultural education. At the age of 16, she is carried off by the poet Percy Shelly, whom she marries several years later. Together, they travel through Italy and Switzerland, where they meet Lord Byron. On a bet at the age of 20, she writes Frankenstein or, The Modern Prometheus (1817). Plunged into mourning by the death of four of her children, then by the accidental death of her husband, from 1822 on, she undertakes the posthumous publication of the latter's works, while simultaneously penning the biographies of Italian writers.

In 1823, she publishes Valperga, which meets poor critical reception. Her second great novel, The Last Man, whose plot is set in 2073, appears in 1826. She spends the rest of her life between England, France, and Italy and publishes, among other things, two autobiographical works: Lodore (1835) and Falkner (1837).

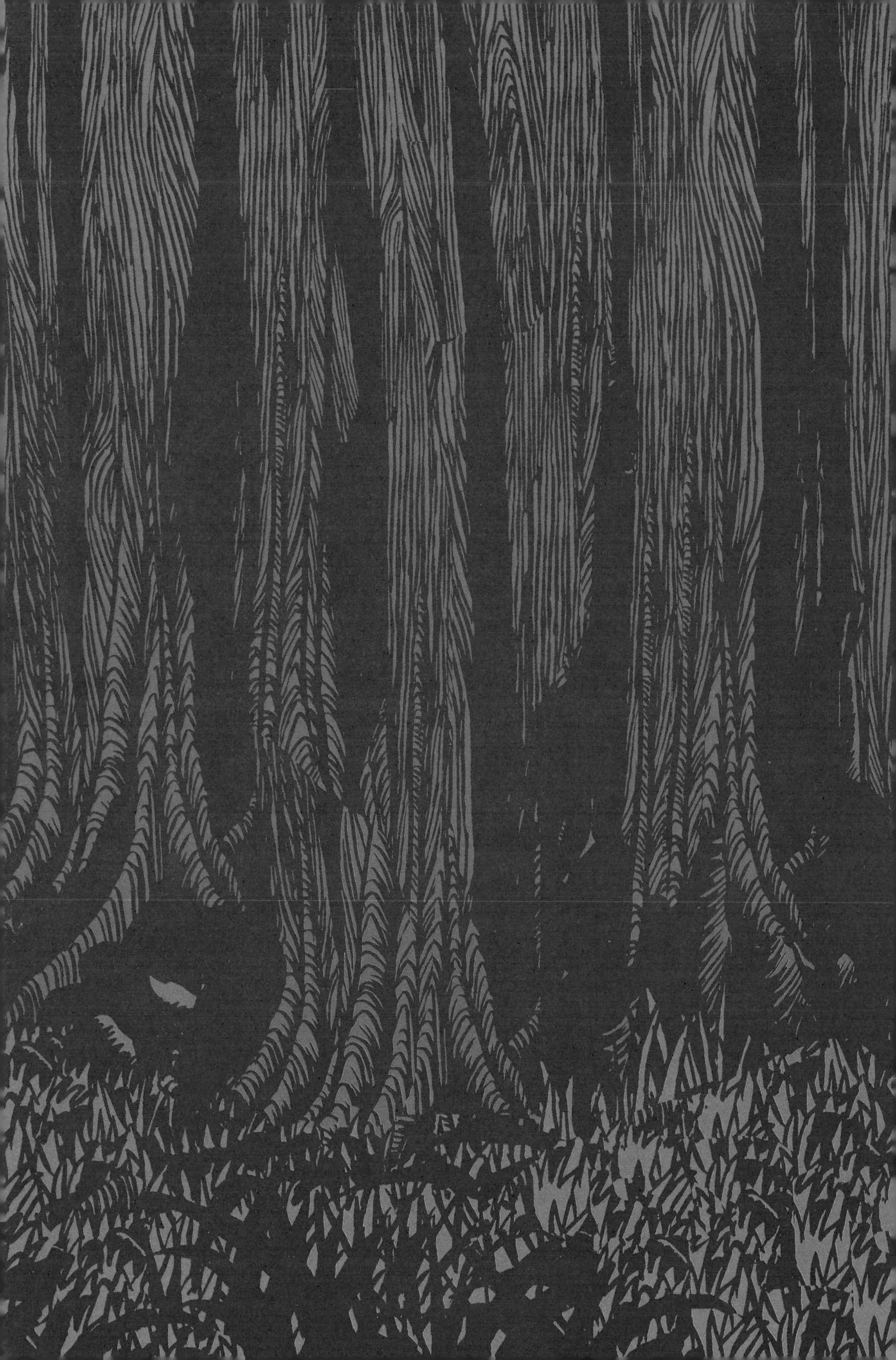